EVERY MOTHER'S SON

EVERY
MOTHER'S
SON

A NOVEL

C. DAVID STEPHENS

LLANO ESTACADO PUBLISHING

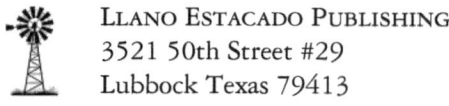 LLANO ESTACADO PUBLISHING
3521 50th Street #29
Lubbock Texas 79413

Cover design by Aero Gallerie

First printed November 2017 in the United States of America.

ISBN: 978-0-936158-02-0 paperback
ISBN: 978-0-936158-03-7 hardcover

10 9 8 7 6 5 4 3 2

For my mother,
Mary Garrison Stephens
1917–2012

And ye shall hear of wars and rumors of wars: see that ye be
not troubled: for all these things must come to pass,
but the end is not yet.

EVERY MOTHER'S SON

1

THE FLYING TIGER DC-8 Super 63 was eastbound in darkness over the Pacific with more than 250 souls on board. There was no first class, no coach, no economy—it was all the same—six across seating, three on each side of a very long aisle. The passengers were almost all young men in faded jungle fatigues. There were few women and even fewer people in civilian clothing. This was not a commercial flight. It was not even an ordinary charter flight. These were not tourists returning from vacation in Hawaii. This was a Freedom Bird.

Kevin Frazier's attention was diverted by an attractive young stewardess pushing a drink cart down the aisle. He checked his watch. He had no idea what time it was or what day it was for that matter. He had set his watch to twelve o'clock on leaving Viet Nam, allowing him to track elapsed time without regard to time zones. They had crossed the International Date Line, but he couldn't re-member if that added or subtracted a day. It didn't matter. He was on his way back to The World and surely there would be a clock, and calendar, when he got there.

Kevin smiled at the stewardess and handed her an empty milk carton. "How much longer?"

The stewardess checked her watch. "About an hour."

"Could I get some coffee?"

"Cream and sugar?"

"Just black."

Since he had started drinking coffee as a young boy Kevin had always added both cream and sugar, just like his dad. That was still the way he drank it, one cream and two packets of sugar, on the trip over last year when a stewardess poured his first cup shortly after takeoff. He still had half a cup when she returned a few minutes later and topped it off. Two packets of sugar made it too sweet so the next time he cut back on the sugar. After a few more cups he decided that measuring out the appropriate amount of cream and sugar was just too much trouble and started drinking his coffee black, which he had continued to do ever since.

It had been sixteen hours since Kevin stood in line at Bien Hoa Air Base, watching as a group of young soldiers in shiny new jungle fatigues filed past, their tour of duty just beginning.

"Come on, FNG," a soldier shouted. "Un-ass my Freedom Bird!"

"What a sorry looking bunch of cherries."

"Dead men walking."

"Suckers!"

"You should have taken a plane to Canada."

Kevin could muster no enthusiasm for joining in the taunts.

"Told you."

Kevin turned and recognized the speaker, a chatty soldier who had sat beside him on the ride to the terminal.

"Told me what?"

The soldier pointed at the plane parked on the tarmac in front of them. Painted in large letters on the fuselage was FLYING TIGER LINE.

"How did you know?" Kevin asked, now curious. He had assumed the soldier had just been running his mouth. There was no shortage of know-it-alls, or know-nothings, in the Army and it was hard to tell them apart.

"I'm a clerk. I work in transportation. I deal with this stuff all the time. It's right there on your boarding pass."

Kevin pulled out his boarding pass and looked.

The soldier pointed. "F2B4. The 'F' is for Flying Tiger Line."

"Huh?"

"Look on the back."

Kevin looked on the back of his boarding pass. There was a list of all airlines flying government contract charters and their code letters.

"Oh, okay. I came over on Capitol International." He looked again. "And went to Bangkok on Pan Am, and Sydney on World Airways. Neat."

"I came over on Continental," the clerk said. "I wish that's what we were going back on."

"What difference does it make? We're going home."

"Continental has better service and hotter stewardesses, the same ones that fly their regular routes."

"They do?"

"Definitely."

The clerk knew his business. Charters operated by the regularly scheduled airlines used the same crews and aircraft as their regular flights. Bids for the long charter flights across the Pacific, with a very polite load of passengers and no demanding businessmen or screaming babies, would normally have been snapped up by older stewardesses with seniority. Flying young men to their potential death could be quite stressful, however, so many of the more senior stewardesses bid on other trips, leaving the Viet Nam charters to the newer, and younger, employees. As a result, many of the stewardesses were the same age as their passengers.

"Is Flying Tiger any good?" Kevin asked.

"Sure. Ever see that John Wayne movie, *Flying Tigers*?"

"Yeah."

"Same guys."

The Flying Tiger Line was formed shortly after the end of World War II by pilots and ground crew of the original Flying Tigers, the fabled First American Volunteer Group who flew fighters over China and Burma in the early days of the war. The Flying Tiger Line was one of the first commercial air freight lines in the United States, taking advantage of the vast numbers of surplus aircraft and pilots with experience gained in flying aircraft of all types during the war. The line expanded rapidly into the passenger charter business and won government contracts to fly military personnel overseas.

Kevin glanced into the cockpit as they boarded. The silver-haired pilots were about the right age to have flown fighters during the war.

Freedom Birds always landed a few hours from Viet Nam in both directions not only to refuel but also to change crews and take on provisions. This allowed aircraft to load and take off as quickly as possible. A big fat Freedom Bird was a tempting target for Viet Cong rockets and mortars, so limiting their time on the ground was of utmost importance.

As soon as the wheels left the runway the pilots, real Flying Tigers or not, punched it and the airplane assumed an attitude as near vertical as a fully loaded DC-8 could possibly achieve, which only further embellished the legend of the Flying Tigers. They had no intention of remaining in range of small-arms fire or rocket-propelled grenades any longer than necessary.

When the shouting and cheering died down after takeoff the passengers began eating and drinking everything that was available, which the smiling stewardesses in short skirts were happy to provide. The first carts down the aisle were heavily stocked with small cartons of milk, which everyone seemed to want. The stewardesses didn't even bother to ask, they just passed out two cartons to everyone onboard. If anyone didn't want it, someone else in the row would be more than happy to take it off their hands.

Milk served to the military in Viet Nam was reconstituted. It looked like milk, smelled like milk, and tasted like milk, but it didn't *feel* like milk. The stewardesses knew this and knew that the first thing everyone wanted to drink on every Freedom Bird was milk. It wasn't really everyone's first choice, but this was a Military Airlift Command charter—no alcohol was allowed to be served.

WHEN HE WAS DRAFTED Kevin had taken the bus to Amarillo, where the Armed Forces Examining and Entrance Station was located and spent the night in the Herring Hotel. Once the crown jewel of Amarillo's hotels, the Herring hosted many lavish parties and events, as well as being the gathering place for Panhandle cattlemen. In its heyday it was a favorite of travelers arriving at the Santa Fe depot just blocks away but was now quiet and smelled musty, its life extended by the dozens of rooms rented every night by the United States Government for the daily stream of enlistees, draftees, and men reporting for physicals.

Kevin's first airplane ride, and each one since, had been compliments of the US Army. He flew from Amarillo to Dallas on a Continental Airlines DC-9, with a stopover in Lubbock. From Dallas Love Field he flew on a Trans-Texas Airways DC-3. As the vintage propeller plane swooped down through the trees for a night landing at Polk Army Airfield in Louisiana, he came to understand why the airline was derisively referred to as Tree-Top Airways.

Kevin had registered for the draft on his eighteenth birthday. The draft influenced every decision including work, school, and marriage. Some fled to Canada, some enlisted hoping to get a better deal, but Kevin drifted, working part time at the grocery store, hanging out with friends. At his mother's insistence he enrolled at Texas Tech after graduating from high school, but his heart wasn't in it. He found the professors and classes less than stimulating and saw no reason to suffer through four more years of mind-numbing boredom. The draft board wasted no time in reclassifying him 1-A and shortly thereafter a letter arrived in the mail: "Greetings."

Enlisting in the Army meant three years but being drafted was only two. By enlisting, if you could pass the tests and had a clean record, you had a reasonable chance of training in a field somewhat less dangerous than the infantry. Draftees had nothing but chance. Lawyers found themselves assigned as clerks, truck drivers as cooks, teachers as artillerymen, but most draftees went into the infantry, and Kevin was no exception. The year of his life that he saved by not enlisting suddenly seemed not so important when during the last week of basic training he received orders for Advanced Infantry Training at Tigerland. Located at Fort Polk, Louisiana, Tigerland prepared infantrymen for only one assignment: Viet Nam.

On arrival in Viet Nam Kevin was assigned to the First Cavalry Division (Airmobile). The division had been operating in the northern part of the country since its arrival in 1965 and had fought in some of the bloodiest battles of the war, the Ia Drang Valley, the A Shau Valley, street fighting in the Battle of Hue, and the relief of the besieged Marines at Khe Sanh. There was furious activity when Kevin arrived—the entire division was preparing to move. No one knew exactly where, but the rumor mill was working overtime, and everyone agreed it was not going to be Hawaii. Moving an Army division, even an airmobile one, was no easy task and Kevin's first few days in-country more resembled manual labor than combat.

Rumors ran rampant as the division loaded onto Navy transports, and Kevin soon found himself at the division's new forward base, Camp Gorvad, near Phuoc Vinh, north of Saigon. It wasn't long before he was in the bush, interdicting NVA supply lines, and business was booming.

KEVIN SIPPED HIS black coffee and flipped through a folder of papers, running the math one more time. He was returning to the United States from a combat zone with just under five months remaining on his two-year commitment, which meant he would be eligible for early release from active duty on arrival. For the Army it simply was not worth it to reassign a soldier to a new post for just a few months. The Army also had an ulterior motive. Soldiers were allowed to extend their tours in Viet Nam by just enough days to fall within the five-month cutoff. Soldiers with a year in-country were far more valuable to the Army than one fresh off the plane. Every 365 days served by any number of soldiers on extension eliminated the need for one replacement who had to be drafted and trained at considerable expense, not only monetary but social and political as well. Kevin had taken advantage of this policy and extended his tour by a few weeks—no easy decision for an infantryman—but he had made it out alive and would be a civilian within a matter of hours.

Satisfied that his count of days was accurate he opened a paperboard folder and stared at a picture of Amy Evans.

"She's cute."

Kevin looked up to see a stewardess pushing a drink cart.

"Yes, she is," he said, smiling.

He handed over an empty coffee cup.

"I'll bet she'll be glad to see you."

"I certainly hope so."

As the stewardess pushed the cart forward Kevin stepped into the aisle to stretch his legs. He looked forward and aft, judging distance from the two doors—not that it mattered—the buses wouldn't leave Travis until everyone was off the plane.

There were a considerable number of black soldiers onboard, something Kevin had grown accustomed to since his first day in the Army. It wasn't difficult to understand why—young black men were being drafted in disproportionate numbers.

On Kevin's first day of basic training at Fort Polk a drill sergeant stood in front of the company and said, "There ain't no black people in the Army." Kevin, and most of the others, thought this an odd statement. The drill sergeant himself was black, as were dozens of the troops assembled in front of him. "There ain't no white people in the Army." After a few nervous laughs he said, "There's only *green* people in the Army." He then said, "It don't rain in the Army." The troops thought he was off his rocker as the rain drizzled through every opening in their ponchos and trickled down their necks. "It rains *on* the Army," the drill sergeant bellowed, whereupon the company set off on a five-mile run in the rain.

Kevin was reminded of that speech on a miserable day during monsoon season, pinned down by enemy fire in dense jungle when, in a blaze of gunfire, a black soldier with four bandoliers of ammunition dashed through the bush and rolled up beside him. "Bet you were never so glad to see a Negro with a gun," the soldier said as he reloaded. Kevin laughed so hard it must have scared off the enemy, or maybe it was Kevin and his new best friend raking the jungle with automatic weapons fire.

The steady hum of the jet engines suddenly softened, and an eerie silence fell over the interior of the airplane. Kevin had flown enough to know what that meant—the pilots had throttled back the engines for descent. He looked out the window and saw the lights of the Golden Gate Bridge in the distance.

The screeching of tires and roar of thrust reversers was almost drowned out by the cheers of passengers as the Freedom Bird landed in darkness at Travis Air Force Base. There was no rush for the door. Everyone on board was accustomed to waiting.

For some it had been an uneventful tour. For others it had been a year-long nightmare. For all of them it was over. Some would have thirty days leave before going to their next post, but many, like Kevin, were going home for good, their military career over. The feeling of relief was palpable.

As the DC-8 taxied to a stop, service vehicles swarmed around. Jetways were a luxury reserved for civilian airports. Although this was a civilian aircraft it was a military charter arriving at an Air Force base, so a mobile stairway attached to a pickup was driven into place. Duffel bags, B-4 bags, AWOL bags, and other baggage was loaded onto flatbed trailers.

Most of the stewardesses gathered at one of the doors to say good-bye, shake hands, and occasionally hug one of the soldiers. The head stewardess stood at the top of the staircase, greeting each soldier as he deplaned. She wore an oversized khaki shirt over her uniform, completely covered with pins and patches from various units in Viet Nam, including the big yellow and black patch of the First Cavalry Division. Kevin shook hands with her, walked briskly down the stairs, and joined the others boarding buses.

The first stop after arrival at Oakland Army Base was the mess hall, open twenty-four hours a day where soldiers returning from Viet Nam were served steak, as much as they wanted, cooked to order and washed down by coffee and fresh milk. While they ate, a team of women, working efficiently from the orders and records enclosed in stacks of personnel folders, quickly attached all the appropriate stripes, patches, pins, ribbons, and medals to new class A uniforms.

Showers beckoned, with limitless hot water, and the soldiers quickly stripped off. Most tossed their jungle fatigues and boots into waiting hampers, but a few kept at least their boots. Their new uniforms were ready by the time they finished showering. Kevin checked his uniform out of habit. It had sergeant stripes, two overseas hashes, and a large assortment of ribbons and medals, including a Bronze Star with a "V" device, Purple Heart, Viet Nam Service Medal, and Air Medal. Above the right breast pocket were the First Cavalry Division's Presidential Unit Citations. He smiled at seeing the big yellow and black patch on the left shoulder. The ladies hadn't missed anything. Had he been staying in the Army, the division's patch would have been on the right shoulder, signifying that he had served in combat with the division. If his next unit was known that unit's patch would have been on the left shoulder, but separation orders were in Kevin's personnel folder. Today was his last day on active duty, and this was his last official uniform, so the First Cavalry Division patch remained on the left shoulder.

While other soldiers stopped at the bank of pay phones to place long-distance calls to mothers, wives, and girlfriends, Kevin stepped out into the early morning darkness and found a long line of taxis waiting. Word spread quickly when a Freedom Bird arrived at Travis and the taxi drivers knew there would be plenty of passengers waiting at Oakland Army Base. Most of them would be headed across the bay to San Francisco International Airport, a very good fare. Three other soldiers shared a taxi with Kevin, bound for SFO.

As soon as the taxi pulled through the main gate it was surrounded by long-haired protesters, carrying signs, yelling, displaying obscene gestures, and spitting.

"Welcome home boys," one of the soldiers in the taxi said.

"Some parade," another said.

As the taxi crossed the Bay Bridge, Kevin looked out at the glittering lights of San Francisco. He had briefly considered staying over a day or two but dismissed the idea. He would have spent most of it sleeping anyway and he wanted to get home.

"What airline?" the taxi driver asked as they approached the airport.

"Pan Am," one of the passengers said.

Everyone in the taxi had an airline ticket that said Pan Am right on it, but Kevin was unable to persuade the others that didn't mean they were flying Pan Am, which had no domestic routes. Kevin lost the argument; the taxi stopped at the international terminal and the other soldiers jumped out. The taxi driver demanded a separate fare to drive him over to the domestic terminal, so Kevin got out and walked, lugging his bags. When he turned to look a few minutes later the other soldiers were following.

The clerk had been right again. It didn't make sense for every airline to operate a ticket office on every military base, so only one airline, frequently Pan Am, operated the Joint Airline Military Ticket Office, printing tickets on Pan Am stock for any flight on any airline.

2

BOBBY DALTON STOPPED his 1966 GTO at the stop sign on the corner of the town square. The car rumbled, the mufflers as loud as the law would allow, just the way Bobby liked it. His hair, having been burr cut twelve weeks ago, was short and unruly. He wore Levi's and a black letter jacket with a gold "P" on the chest, "15" on one sleeve, and a state football championship patch on the other.

Preston, Texas, population 3,438, was just a small frontier settlement in the early days of the twentieth century, when cattle, exponentially outnumbering people, grazed on an endless sea of buffalo grass. There was a general store, a blacksmith, a wagon yard, and not much else.

The railroad changed everything. In 1914, through subsidiary companies, the Atchison, Topeka and Santa Fe Railway laid track northwest from Lubbock to Farwell, connecting with the Santa Fe line between Clovis and Amarillo, completing the Coleman Cutoff, linking the Port of Galveston to the west coast, "Santa Fe all the way." The Santa Fe built sidings and a simple wooden depot, identical to dozens of others across the Llano Estacado. The rest was up to the newly formed town of Preston.

With beef prices down, the vast cattle ranches in the Texas Panhandle began selling off sections of land to farmers. Preston, suddenly connected to the rest of the country by its new railroad, became a shipping center for their crops.

Like most other towns, large and small, served by the Santa Fe, the streets of downtown Preston were paved with red brick. While it was possible to haul by wagon enough lumber to build a house or store, bricks were another matter entirely. The arrival of the railroad, which was the town's very reason for being, made it possible to haul in brick by the trainload.

The courthouse was the first brick building, followed by the bank, a hotel, and various commercial buildings. As the town and county prospered a new brick depot was built, capped by red Spanish tile. There were also several brick homes along Second Street, never known locally as anything other than Silk Stocking Street, a broad, tree-lined boulevard where the county judge, bankers, doctors, lawyers, and other well-to-do residents lived in large two-story homes, many of them brick.

The VFW Hall, where veterans of foreign wars met for supper every Monday night, was a block off the square. Veterans of two world wars and Korea were being supplemented by the current crop of young veterans returning home from Mr. Johnston's war.

Bobby started to go straight, but he noticed the lights were on at the *Preston Post.* He turned, pulled in, and parked next to a pickup being loaded with bundles of newspapers by teenager Teddy Parker.

With daily papers from both Lubbock and Clovis coming in on the bus the *Post* published twice weekly, providing local news. Since the Kennedy assassination, most Preston residents now got their news from television anyway, pointing their rooftop antennas toward Lubbock where there were two stations.

Tuesday's edition caught everyone up on who was visiting at each church on Sunday morning, who had accepted the Lord Jesus Christ as their savior, and most importantly, the in-depth coverage of the Friday night games.

The Friday paper had more pages, serving the same purpose as the Sunday paper in larger cities. Bob's Food Store always had the back page. The Friday paper also had the movie times for the Llano Theater on the square and the XIT Drive-In south of the highway. Classifieds, obituaries, the school cafeteria menu, and various other announcements ran both days.

After exchanging greetings, nothing more than a nod of the head, Teddy followed Bobby into the newspaper office.

The ceiling, twelve feet high, was patterned tin, and light fixtures hung from long rods, illuminating the floor below in large circles. The front half of the building had hardwood floors that might once have been varnished but were now worn and dull. A wooden counter loosely defined the public area, containing a couple of wooden chairs and a small table with today's paper. Those too poor, or too cheap, to buy a copy could sit in the office and read the paper for free. On the counter were several job printing orders waiting to be picked up.

A pungent odor hit Bobby as he walked around the counter. Teddy's older brother had once tried to explain the chemistry of offset printing, but all Bobby knew was that it would clear your sinuses. He inhaled deeply and waved at Teddy's father as he washed up the offset press.

Teddy's mother sat at the Graphotype, a machine that could best be described as an armored typewriter with a large electric motor and flywheel. It didn't sit on a desk like a typewriter—it had its own iron legs, which were bolted to the floor to keep it from walking around as it operated. It sounded like a gunshot when the operator pressed a key on the keyboard. This one punched little metal plates used to address newspapers, but Bobby had seen an identical machine recently at the reception station at Fort Polk, used to produce the dog tags that hung on a chain around his neck.

The floor in the back of the building was reinforced concrete to support the weight of the enormous Linotype machine and its accompanying apparatus, including heavy metal cabinets, steel tables, and a pile of lead ingots. For decades, while their mothers shopped on the town square, children would dart into the newspaper office and peer over the counter to watch the Linotype machine in operation, fascinated with all its belts and gears, whirring, spinning, and clicking. They weren't allowed to go anywhere near the beast, as it produced type by pouring molten lead into brass matrices.

The Linotype sat silent and cold this morning, now used only occasionally for job work, replaced by much smaller and faster typesetting machines for the newspaper. Teddy's grandfather had retired when his son purchased these abominations. The old man still came in a day or two a week to fire up the Linotype or Ludlow, or patiently sit at his bench, selecting individual letters from one of the many wooden cases stacked in racks against the wall, carefully lining them up in a composing stick. His son had reluctantly agreed to hold onto all the Industrial Revolution equipment until the old man was dead and buried. Like the tens of thousands of steam locomotives retired from the country's railroads, the old typesetting equipment would eventually be sold for scrap and melted down. At least the big iron would die with dignity—the wooden type cases would end up adorning suburban walls, infested with bric-a-brac.

Even in retirement Old Man Parker continued to write editorials, much to the chagrin of his son, who couldn't afford to offend any advertisers. Fortunately, most of the advertisers agreed with his father's politics. For several months every other year, for as long as the paper had been published, a single line ran above the masthead: "Hold onto your wallets—the Legislature's in session."

Teddy's sister, Becky, was busy wrapping papers. "Do you want your daddy's paper?" she asked.

Becky was a junior in high school and she had a crush on Bobby when she was a freshman. He had that effect on girls. He picked up a newspaper from her stack and left a nickel on the table.

"Nah, I'm on my way to Spalding's," Bobby said. "I don't know how long it'll be before I get to the store, and I don't want Daddy to miss his paper."

"Here," Teddy said, handing Bobby a bundle of newspapers. "You can carry these out to the Hi-Way and save me a trip."

"Then I'm keeping my nickel," Bobby said, picking up the coin.

Teddy laughed. Bobby was entitled to a free paper anyway. The *Post* provided complimentary subscriptions to all the local boys in the military. Bobby was home on leave and his subscription would be reactivated as soon as they received his new address.

Bobby tossed his purloined paper and the bundle into the front seat of the GTO and circled the square. The streets around the square were wide, with a row of angled parking spaces down the middle, so drivers could pull in from either direction. Too many unfortunately didn't bother to back out when they left but pulled out straight ahead and drove on the wrong side of the street until the corner, resulting in lots of horn-honking and yelling, but only an occasional collision.

There was only one car parked at the courthouse, a pink and white 1958 Nash Rambler. It belonged to the night dispatcher at the sheriff's office. She was about five-foot-two, but if you included her hair, a shade of pink like her car, closer to five-eight. She wasn't alone in the otherwise dark building, however. There was also the night jailer, who lived near enough to the courthouse that he walked to work when the weather allowed, as it did today, a chilly but dry and calm November morning. There were almost certainly a couple of overnight guests bedded down in the county jail, but they hardly required convenient parking.

Bobby waved at people on the sidewalk as he drove past the Preston Café next to the Western Auto. The café didn't open for another quarter hour, but the door was unlocked, and the locals were already streaming in. They would go behind the counter and pour themselves a cup of coffee while the waitress wrapped silverware and slipped the daily specials into the menus.

Preston was a three-stoplight town. All of them were on Main Street, which ran along the western side of the square. The two lights downtown were, to most observers, upside down—green was on top and red on the bottom. They had been hanging there that way, strung between telephone poles, since the 1930s, a time when there wasn't much standardization of traffic signals. The housings were also painted silver rather than the more familiar yellow. Nobody seemed to care—red still meant stop, no matter which end it was on, and people still ran the red light.

Bobby looked up at the stoplight. It flashed red in both directions and would continue to do so until it resumed its regular cycle at six a.m., more or less—city employees weren't very conscientious about keeping the timer adjusted properly.

Out of habit, Bobby looked over at Bob's Food Store, which was catty-corner to the courthouse, across Main Street. There were four grocery stores in town, but Bob's was by far the largest and nicest. It was well-stocked, with wide aisles, plenty of light, and, most importantly, it was surrounded by a large gravel parking lot, a distinct advantage over the main competitor on the square where parking was often at a premium. The butcher at Bob's Food Store was something of a curmudgeon, but he was an artist with a knife and had never been accused of keeping his thumb on the scale while he weighed a customer's purchase. He also did custom butchering for those who kept a few cows or hogs on the homestead. The night lights were on in the store and there was no sign of a break-in. All was well.

The plate glass windows of Bob's Food Store, along with nearly every other place of business on the square and along the highway, were painted with slogans and encouragement to the local high school football team, the Preston Panthers, along with the denigration of the opposing team, and various incitements to murder and mayhem. This time tomorrow, a teenager with a long-handled brush, a squeegee, and a pail of water would be busy washing away the water-based paint, providing a clean canvas for the local signwriter on Sunday, his day off from the lumberyard. He earned a tidy sum of cash during football season, and he had a vested interest in tonight's game—if the Panthers lost, he would have to wait until next September for another part-time payday.

Bobby hung a left on Main Street, which was also a state highway. Land in west Texas was surveyed into sections, one mile square, six hundred forty acres per section. County roads tended to run due north–south and east–west, with a road every mile, along section lines, some paved, but mostly dirt. State highways would often replace a county road, which was the case with the one running through Preston. Like most other towns and cities on the mostly featureless High Plains, Preston was laid out "square to the world" along the state highway.

Bobby made a rolling stop at the next flashing red light and continued south to the town's third stoplight, this one painted yellow and conventionally oriented, also flashing red, at the intersection with US Highway 84. Railroad tracks ran parallel to the highway just before the intersection. Bobby stopped before the tracks. It had been drilled into him, and every other teenager in Preston, and it was right there on the sign: DO NOT STOP ON TRACKS. Most of the locals were aware of the danger, but not those passing through. Too many times to count the crossing arm had come down on a vehicle stopped on the tracks. The locals could tell by the train's extended whistle that there was a problem, and always waited for the sound of a crash. Those happened infrequently, most notably back in '62 when an eastbound freight smashed into a truckload of hogs. Fortunately, the engineer, aware of the dangerous intersection, had managed to slow down considerably before impact. The fool driving the truck was unharmed, but a few hogs were killed or wounded. Dozens more made a run for it, chased by young boys, including Bobby, all over Preston.

The meat market at Bob's Food Store, along with the others in town, butchered a lot of hogs over the next few days. The insurance company paid for the load of hogs, and the truck, so no one felt even a twinge of guilt, but they got really tired of pork chops and ham.

Bobby looked right, and then left, where he saw the headlights of an oncoming train, but there was no whistle, and the crossing arms did not come down. He paused for a moment—the train was clearly moving slowly—and then he continued across the tracks, briefly stopping again in the space between the tracks and the highway.

The highway intersection was not at all square. Railroads didn't care about being square to the world—they wanted the shortest route between two points, in this case Lubbock and Farwell, which was nearly always a straight line. As in most other cases where railroad tracks ran parallel to the highway, the railroad tracks were there first. South of the railroad, and highway, Preston resumed being square to the world.

For many years, in deference to its larger volume of traffic, the light would flash yellow at night on US Highway 84 and red for the state highway. After several collisions, including more than one fatality, the lights were changed to flash red both ways. This worked out well for Joe Spalding—since drivers were forced to stop it made it easier for them to pull in and buy something.

Joe Spalding's Texaco filling station occupied the northeast corner of the intersection, allowing easy access from either highway. It was an art deco structure, with sweeping awnings over the pumps and yards of neon tubing on the roof. It had been built by Texaco in the early 1930s, and Joe's father had managed to hang onto it during the Depression, when nobody had any money, and the war, when gasoline was rationed. He made up for the loss of business by expanding into delivery of diesel, propane, and butane to surrounding farms, which remained a significant portion of Joe's business.

On the eastern end of the building was the Hi-Way Café, operated by Joe Spalding's wife. Sandwiched between the two was a small office, serving as the TNM&O bus station. It was rarely occupied these days—like the railroads, bus companies had been losing passengers to automobiles and airlines and there were fewer buses stopping daily at Preston. Joe Spalding was the local agent and tickets could be purchased in the office of the filling station.

Package express was still a significant source of revenue for TNM&O however, and there were nearly always packages being picked up or dropped off, including prescriptions for the local pharmacists. Bundles of newspapers from both Lubbock and Clovis arrived daily. Some went into the racks inside the café, alongside the *Preston Post,* some to the newsstand in the drugstore, and still others to the post office for delivery to those who could afford a daily out-of-town paper.

Gasoline was twenty-eight cents a gallon in Texas, but more than *forty cents* in New Mexico, a price no self-respecting Texan would willingly pay. There were filling stations in Farwell, just before crossing the state line, but Joe Spalding had continued his father's tradition of clean restrooms, easy access, and friendly, around-the-clock service, so the Texaco did a brisk business. New Mexicans headed to Lubbock also knew to wait until Preston to fill up, and then again on the return trip, even if it was only a few gallons.

Bobby parked at the café and carried the newspapers inside. There was a foyer between two sets of doors which helped keep the west Texas wind from sucking out all the heat in the winter, although holding back the dust was a never-ending battle. A pay phone hung on the wall above a gumball machine and three newspaper racks. Bobby loaded the newspapers into the appropriate rack. It was an open rack, entirely dependent on the honor system to deposit the required coins, but in those days, honor was a given.

Booths lined the walls of the café and there was a large, U-shaped dining counter, with tables between the counter and booths. A large opening in the wall between the kitchen and dining room allowed waitresses to pick up an order, turn around and serve it with a minimum of steps. The configuration also allowed the cook a full view of not only the counter, but the front door. Crime was not a significant problem in Preston, but the café on the highway might seem an inviting target for some ne'er-do-well passing through. All the locals knew there was a pump-action shotgun on the wall in the kitchen, just out of sight of diners. Chips in the tile and plaster near the front door indicated the shotgun had been used at least once. The glass in the door had to be replaced, along with the blood lost by the would-be armed robber as he attempted to flee.

On the wall near the cash register were black-and-white, eight-by-ten photographs of various celebrities, quite common in Los Angeles, but a bit out of place in west Texas. Owing to the location halfway between Lubbock and Clovis they were mostly musicians, including Buddy Holley, Waylon Jennings, Roy Orbison, Johnny Cash, and many others, all signed. A photograph of Elvis Presley had long been the subject of debate. He had performed in Lubbock more than once, but no one could remember ever seeing him in the Hi-Way Café. Mildred, Joe Spalding's wife, was known to be an Elvis fan, so most put it down to that. When asked about the origin of the photo, she had always just smiled and said nothing. Along with her husband, Mildred had seen Elvis perform at the Cotton Club in Lubbock in 1955, before he hit it big, and she had driven one of the cars in a convoy of women and teenage girls to his performance at Fair Park Coliseum in 1956, where he had signed not just photographs and records, but various body parts of willing young women. Elvis also had the respect of the local men—when called he served, unlike some celebrities, especially these days, when burning draft cards had become a cause célèbre.

It was busy in the café, mostly truckers, along with a few travelers off the highway, and some locals. It was open all night, while the café on the square didn't open until six, and each had their regulars. Bobby took a seat on a stool and placed his folded newspaper on the counter.

Hank Harding drove his police car slowly past a line of trucks parked along the south side of the highway across from the café, his spotlight illuminating the license plates. The police car made a U-turn and Hank examined the trucks parked on the north side before pulling into the café and parking beside Bobby's car. As he stepped out of the police car, he looked in the direction of the train. It was stopped at a marker which indicated the point at which it would trigger the crossing arms on the state highway. Although a train could legally block a roadway for longer than anyone felt reasonable, it was considered good policy to not do so when it could be avoided. The train crew dismounted and headed toward the café.

Hank's official title was chief of police, but the department was just Hank and one other officer, along with the night watchman, whose salary was paid by the savings in fire insurance for local businesses. The Preston Police Department shared a dispatcher with the sheriff's office, and the police station was nothing more than a desk in city hall.

Hank tapped the hood of Bobby's car as he walked past. He was quite familiar with the GTO and what it could do. What was under the hood of his police car, on the other hand, was the subject of continuous speculation from the local teenagers. What was known was that it could catch just about any car in town. Even if someone did manage to outrun him, as Hank often said, "you can't outrun the radio." The sheriff's office and highway patrol were more than willing to join in a chase. Unlike in the movies, crossing the state line offered no sanctuary—the Texas lawmen would continue in hot pursuit, now joined by their counterparts in New Mexico, who expected, and readily received, reciprocity for eastbound evaders.

A foot chase offered the scofflaw a better chance, as Hank walked with a noticeable limp, the result of severe wounds suffered just weeks before the war ended, after a violent tour of Pacific islands with his fellow Marines. He was awarded the Silver Star for action on Okinawa, and then spent months in various military hospitals before stepping off the Santa Fe at Preston in 1946. Whether it was respect for his war injury, fear of being shot in the back with the government-issue Colt 1911 he carried, or the certainty that he not only knew who you were but also knew your daddy, few local boys ever fled on foot. There was also speculation over the number of Japanese soldiers Hank had killed. Like most of the other veterans in Preston, he rarely spoke of the war, at least not outside the local VFW Hall.

Hank held the café door open for the train crew. The line through Preston merged onto the Belen Cutoff forty miles away just before the New Mexico border, so it was not unusual for westbound trains to stop and wait for position on the busier line, and right next to the Hi-Way Café was as good a place as any.

Hank stepped up to the counter and sat down beside Bobby as a waitress put a cup in front of him and poured coffee.

"Anything in the paper?" Hank asked.

"Don't know," Bobby said. "Haven't looked."

"You're up early."

"Joe lets me use the lift if I get here before it gets busy."

"How much longer you got at home?"

"Ten days."

Hank leaned back as the waitress put bacon and eggs on the counter in front of him.

"You heard from your partner in crime?"

"Kevin?"

"He's due in, isn't he?"

"Maybe today, probably tomorrow. His mama said he would either call the house or the store when he hits the states and let her know what flight he'll be on."

"I guess times are changing. In my day we took the train after getting off the boat. Gave you time to ease back in. Nowadays you can go from the battlefield to your own bed at home in a matter of hours."

Hank ate a few bites, shook his head and smiled. "Kevin really creamed that boy, didn't he?"

"What boy?"

"Down in Sweetwater, back in sixty-six."

"Oh yeah, that boy." Bobby smiled and nodded.

"Miss Clara said Terrell is doing okay."

"I haven't heard from him in a while."

"I really thought he would get a football scholarship to Prairie View," Hank said. "It didn't work out though, did it?"

"No, it didn't."

Sports had been severely limited at the colored school in Preston, but Terrell Washington went out for football his freshman year at Preston High, the first year the schools had been integrated. After the initial shock of one black player on an otherwise all-white team, Terrell proved himself under fire and along with his mother changed a lot of attitudes in Preston.

"His mama said he has a few months left to do," Hank said.

"Sounds about right."

They sipped coffee in silence for a moment.

"Boy howdy, that was some game, wasn't it?" Hank said.

"Yes, it was."

THE LOCAL COTTON HARVEST ran late in 1966, as the Preston Panthers slogged their way through the playoffs. There was some degree of truth in the running joke that world cotton markets were affected. The stands at the stadium were filled every afternoon with cotton farmers, along with ranchers, merchants, and just about anyone else, nearly all male, who could take off work to watch football practice.

Teams shared game films, but coaches sometimes slipped in new plays during practice before a big game, so any stranger showing up to watch practice was immediately challenged.

The Panthers had easily won the bi-district and regional games, but the quarter- and semi-finals were brutal. By the time they had advanced to the state championship game the entire squad was badly battered and bruised.

Preston's opponent in the state championship game was a team from central Texas, near Temple. Rather than risking losing the coin toss and facing a very long trip home, both teams had agreed to meet in the middle at a neutral site. There was no need to look at a map— they would meet at the Mustang Bowl in Sweetwater, one of the finest high school stadiums in the state, constructed in 1939 by the Civilian Conservation Corps.

Impromptu meetings quickly sprang up at the Hi-Way Café, the drugstore, the Preston Café, and anywhere else people gathered, finally converging on the VFW Hall, where a plan was agreed upon. Left to their own devices most would have just driven to Sweetwater, but they agreed that since so many people were going it would be better to charter buses. TNM&O, headquartered in Lubbock and locally known for their charter service, could have provided as many buses as needed on short notice.

Someone suggested the train, but the *California Special,* an odd name for a train that operated between Houston and Clovis, only ran once daily in each direction and did not offer a convenient schedule. A dozen or more charter buses would have been required for the hundreds of locals planning to make the trip, but one train could carry that many and more, with passengers able to stroll up and down the entire length of the train, visiting with everyone else on the trip. The station agent at the depot in Preston went to work on the telephone and Teletype, and the Santa Fe quickly agreed to run two special trains, one from each town in the state championship game, meeting in Sweetwater.

The pep rally in the gym on Friday was standing room only, and even more people assembled for the bonfire that lit up the night sky. The rules allowed it, money was no object, and the coach wanted to arrive in town the night before the game, so the football team boarded a yellow school bus at the bonfire and set out for Sweetwater.

On Saturday morning the high school band and cheerleaders, followed by a gathering throng of townspeople, marched all the way from the high school, with a detour around the town square, to the depot, where the Santa Fe *Panther Special,* consisting of ten chair cars, a baggage car and a dining car, led by three diesel-electric locomotives, wearing the legendary red and yellow Santa Fe Warbonnet livery, stood waiting.

Sweetwater was a railroad town with service from three major railroads. The Santa Fe tracks conveniently ran just two blocks from Mustang Stadium, so the two special trains parked nose to nose, eliminating the need to bus hundreds of football fans between the depot and stadium. When a team scored, the locomotive from their train would blow the whistle. There was a lot of whistling that Saturday afternoon in Sweetwater as the teams traded touchdowns.

The Panthers were down by four points with just seconds left on the clock when their starting quarterback was injured. Although in range, a field goal would have been useless. Bobby, the sophomore backup, came in and called a pass play that sent all eligible receivers into the end zone. Kevin Frazier, the left halfback, put a hit on a pass rusher that was still spoken of with reverence in Preston, allowing Bobby enough time to select his best target and throw a bullet that hit Terrell Washington right in the shoulder pads so hard that the entire stadium, holding their collective breaths, heard the slap of leather. Terrell caught the pass for the winning touchdown and the crowd went wild. Well, half the crowd went wild; the other half stood in stunned silence.

The Preston school bus returned home empty. Jubilant fans waited on the train, replaying the game, while the team showered and then piled onboard, where they were served steak in the dining car as soon as the train rolled out of Sweetwater. The rest of the passengers ate box suppers at their seats, but nobody complained.

Girls and boys were not allowed to sit together after dark on school trips, but that rule seemed to have fallen by the wayside on this one, which wasn't officially a school trip anyway. The lights were on and there was a steady stream of traffic up and down the aisles, so the kids couldn't have gotten away with much. The principal, teachers, and chaperones were more concerned about teenagers getting their hands on one of the many flasks of liquor that were surely onboard.

Freshman cheerleader Amy Evans, sore from all the jumping and hoarse from all the cheering, snuggled with her boyfriend as the train rolled through the night. She cringed as her daddy stood in the aisle and leaned over, certain he was about to tell her to change seats.

"Good game, son, good game," Howard Evans said, shaking hands with Amy's boyfriend.

"Thank you, sir."

Howard looked at Amy and smiled. She put her head back on her boyfriend's shoulder.

Bobby started as quarterback his junior year, but the team had lost too many seniors, including Terrell and Kevin, and their glory days were behind them.

BOBBY AND HANK sipped their coffee and reminisced. They both looked up at the sound of a train whistle. The train crew had refilled their thermoses and gone.

The train whistle blew again, answered by the clanging of bells as the crossing arms on the state highway came down. Bobby and Hank watched as the train passed the café. It was a Santa Fe intermodal freight, mostly trailers on flatcars, although a few carried new Bell AH-1 Cobra helicopters, bound for west coast ports for transshipment to Viet Nam.

3

THROUGH HALF-OPEN EYES, Amy Evans could see light under the door to her bedroom. She glanced at the clock radio on the nightstand, rubbing her eyes, trying to determine the time. It was a lost cause, but the alarm had not yet gone off, so she pulled up the covers and closed her eyes. There was a soft knock on the door.

"I'm up," Amy lied.

The door opened and the light from the hallway flooded in. Howard, wearing pajamas and a robe, leaned through the door.

"You said you wanted to get up early."

"I have a lot to do today," Amy said, looking at the clock, the hands now barely visible. "What time is it?"

"Almost six."

Amy pulled back the covers and swung her bare legs out of bed. Her long hair was pulled back in a ponytail.

"It's cold."

Howard saw no reason to pay good money to heat an entire house at night when everyone was in bed under fluffy quilts, stocks of which were frequently replenished by Amy's grandmother, who sewed them by hand. Amy could hear the gas furnace crackling in the hallway, which her daddy always turned up when he got up in the morning, usually early enough to take the chill off before she arose.

"Well, if you wore pajamas you wouldn't be so cold," Howard said.

"Pajamas are for little girls," Amy said as she rolled out of bed and planted her feet on the floor. She had slept in panties and a T-shirt since she was eleven, and her T-shirt collection had continued to expand thanks to gifts from her boyfriend.

"I wear pajamas."

"And old men," Amy teased, rubbing her face.

Her T-shirt had been purchased in one of the shabby shops along the main drag in Leesville, Louisiana, that catered to the never-ending stream of young soldiers passing through Fort Polk. There was a peace symbol on the front. She never knew if it was supposed to be a political statement and she never asked. She liked it and her daddy didn't, so it served its purpose.

"What?" Amy asked, her T-shirt finally providing some degree of modesty as it draped over her hips when she stood.

"Nice shirt," Howard said as he backed into the hallway.

Amy picked up a framed eight-by-ten black-and-white photograph of her boyfriend in an Army uniform. It was identical to thousands of others produced each week in basic training posts across the country and mailed home to mothers, wives, and girlfriends. She put her fingers on her lips, pressed them on the face of the soldier in the photograph, and returned the frame to the nightstand.

THE COLD WAR was already underway, and millions of Americans were in uniform as Howard's high school graduation approached in 1950. With large occupying forces in Germany and Japan, as well as other military commitments around the world and at home, the draft loomed large for all young men as their eighteenth birthday approached. Howard was no exception. He had no desire to go to college—he had been cutting hair all through high school and expected to continue, eventually taking over the shop when his father retired. Rather than wait to be drafted Howard did what many other young men did at the time—he joined the National Guard and set off for basic training shortly after graduation. He would be away only a few weeks and then back home at his job at the barbershop. After that, one weekend a month and two weeks in the summer for a few years seemed like a lot better deal than two, three, or four years in uniform posted who-knows-where.

After training Howard returned home on the train and immediately went to work at his father's barbershop on the town square, where the Russians and their new A-bomb were discussed endlessly.

"We should have wiped out the Russkies as soon as we finished with the Krauts."

"It's all Truman's fault."

"Too bad General Eisenhower ain't still in charge."

"There ain't nothing to worry about. The Russians have to get their A-bomb past our Air Force before they can drop it on us."

That was no small feat as the US Air Force, recently split off from the Army, was a formidable force with thousands of bombers and fighters arrayed across the United States and around the world.

Howard wasn't too worried. Russia was a long way off. Soldiers wouldn't matter much anyway in an atomic war. Entire cities would be vaporized. He had money in his pocket from cutting hair all week, along with a little extra from the Guard, and he headed out to Lubbock on Saturday nights to cruise the Hi-D-Ho picking up girls. Life was good.

HOWARD HEADED DOWN the hallway toward the kitchen, oak floorboards creaking, as Amy slipped into the bathroom. Like most houses of its vintage, it had only one bathroom, which had become a growing problem with three children at home, all girls. Howard and his wife had rented a small house for a few years while saving up to buy a home of their own. They had their eye on one of the new ones being built on the edge of town, but those were tract homes, rather boring, and as Howard's father insisted, built like crap and overpriced so that the banker could get even richer.

Howard's father, a World War I veteran, often held forth on subjects such as politics and economics while cutting hair. Social Security was a scam, he declared. Those thieves in Washington had set the retirement age at sixty-five at a time when life expectancy was sixty-two for women and fifty-eight for men. The banker tried to explain to him that those figures were *average* and included infant mortality, which was quite high around the turn of the century, not to mention wars, and accidents on the job, and having survived not only a world war and the Spanish flu, along with various other scourges, he could expect to collect his benefits for several years after turning sixty-five.

Never one to be proven wrong, Howard's father dropped dead of a heart attack at sixty-four while cutting hair in the barbershop, no doubt cursing the government. After her husband's affairs were settled Howard's mother decided to sell the house and move in with her eldest daughter, whose husband managed the cotton warehouses that spanned several blocks along the railroad tracks. Having prospered in business he and his wife lived in a large brick home on Silk Stocking Street. Howard bought his mother's house, insisting on paying fair market value. The banker set up the mortgage and Howard's payments would provide his mother with a supplement to her Social Security check, which she drew off her late husband.

Vivian, Howard's wife, loved the old prairie-style house with large windows, an enormous porch, hardwood floors, and high ceilings. It was a three-bedroom, which meant the two youngest girls would have to share a room, and Howard and Vivian began making plans to add a master bedroom and, even more importantly, a second bath-room. There was a lot of deferred maintenance, which kept Howard busy on his day off for quite some time, and the new addition was still nothing more than a foundation. Now that Amy was a senior in high school and would soon be going away to college, or more likely getting married, the new addition was less important.

The Evans house was located three blocks from the town square, allowing the young family to get by with just one car. Vivian would drive the girls to school, where she taught fourth grade, and Howard would walk to work at the barbershop. He had since bought a used pickup to haul construction material, but he continued to walk to work most days.

Howard considered himself lucky that Amy had not pressed him to buy her a car. Going steady since freshman year had obviated the need for a car, but even with her boyfriend away in the Army she always seemed to have a ride.

Nearly all the boys and many of the girls at Preston High, espe-cially the upperclassmen, had cars. Fourteen was the minimum age to get a driver's license in Texas if you took driver's education in school, which nearly everybody did. It was blatant age discrimination to the students, but common sense to the school board to divide the freshman class equally, with the older students taking driver's educa-tion in the fall semester and the younger ones in the spring. As a result, nearly everyone was fifteen or close to it when they received their unrestricted license. It didn't really matter—many teenagers were driving long before they had a license. Few were allowed to drive to Lubbock without a license, and certainly not allowed to cross the state line, but around town the law looked the other way, at least until there was a wreck or some other problem, especially alcohol. The highway patrol, on the other hand, would not hesitate to issue a ticket for driving without a license. Even the highway patrol allowed some latitude during the cotton harvest, when it was not unusual to see a twelve-year-old girl driving a pickup pulling a trailer load of cotton while her brothers, no matter what their age, were in the fields driving cotton strippers.

Howard's eldest daughter seemed to be quite mature and level-headed. He set a curfew, but had always been willing to be flexible, for example, if she wanted to see a late movie in Lubbock. Oddly enough, she had never pushed it. The only time she ever came home late from a date was when her boyfriend had a flat tire taking her home. While he changed the tire, she ran to the nearest house to call her daddy. It was a considerable distance as they had been parked in the country, making out. She got home four minutes after midnight and her boyfriend spent another four minutes apologizing to Howard, who gritted his teeth and twisted his face to conceal the grin as he noticed the lipstick on the boy's face. It would only be a matter of hours before a farmer would open the door of the barbershop and ask, "Did your girl make it home all right last night?"

Emily, the middle child, fourteen going on twenty-one, was another matter. When she was born, Amy had insisted on sending back the insolent interloper who seemed to scream at the top of her lungs for hours on end for no apparent reason. Eventually, after much hair pulling, the sisters came to a truce. With both now in high school, and having boys, clothes, rock and roll, dances, and other teenage activities in common, they managed to get along most of the time. Howard feared that Emily was going to be a lot more trouble than her elder sister. Emily had an eye for the boys.

So far, the youngest, Lily, eleven, appeared to be following in Amy's footsteps, quiet and polite, but as Howard well knew, puberty could change all that.

AMY CLOSED THE bathroom door, stripped off her clothes, what little there were, pulled up her hair, and stepped into the ancient claw-foot tub. Amy preferred a shower when she was in a hurry, as she was this morning. Her daddy had rigged up a shower head and an oval-shaped rod that hung from the ceiling, with two curtains that surrounded the tub.

Her mind wandered, as it often did, while she stood in the shower. She had a busy day ahead. She had to finish painting signs and decorating the gym for the pep rally after school. Kevin was due in today or tomorrow. She would try to find out at lunch, using the pay phone outside the school. Lots of kids left school for lunch, either across the street to the school store, or to the Panther, a drive-in hamburger joint on the highway. As long as you were back by the time the bell rang nobody cared.

Amy, lost in her thoughts, didn't realize she was not alone in the bathroom. Lily, wearing a white, ankle-length nightgown, stood in front of the lavatory, brushing her teeth. Emily, who was cold-natured, wore long-legged flannel pajamas, the bottoms of which were currently down around her ankles as she sat on the toilet. She turned and flushed. As cold water surged into the toilet tank, the water in the shower suddenly became very hot.

Amy shrieked, turned off the water, and ripped back the shower curtain. Lily continued to brush her teeth while watching the unfolding drama.

Emily stood and pulled up her pajama bottoms while enduring her sister's savage stare. "What?" Emily asked.

Amy started to scream "Daddy!" but thought better of it. She stepped out of the tub, wrapped herself in a towel, and stomped across the hall into her bedroom, leaving the bathroom door open, but being sure to close her own. The whole point of getting up early was to avoid the traffic jam in the bathroom. Now she was going to be late.

With three girls getting ready for school, the hallway at the Evans house was crowded. Howard, now dressed for work, headed from his bedroom to the kitchen, colliding with Amy, in her underwear, as she darted out of the bathroom. He grimaced. "Honey, can't you at least put on some clothes?"

"I had to brush my teeth and didn't want to splatter on my sweater," Amy said, shrugging.

Emily, also in her underwear, squeezed past Howard and into the bathroom.

"I give up," Howard said, shaking his head as he walked away.

Amy leaned out her door and called after him. "At least we're wearing underwear."

Vivian stepped out of the kitchen and looked down the hall.

"What was that all about?"

"Girls," Howard said, turning into the kitchen, where Lily, fully dressed, sat at the table. He leaned over and kissed her on the head. "Thank you, princess."

"For what?"

"Wearing clothes."

Shortly later, Amy, now wearing a cheerleader skirt and sweater, swooped into the kitchen and grabbed a piece of toast off the table as the rest of the family ate breakfast.

"I may not be home after school," Amy said.

"Why not?" Howard asked.

"If Kevin gets in today, we're going to the airport to meet him."

"You are not cutting class."

"Don't worry. I'm not cutting class."

"Can I go?" Emily asked.

"No," Amy quickly answered.

"Why not?"

"We're going to the dentist in Lubbock," Vivian said.

"Do I have to?" Emily whined.

"You wouldn't if you took better care of your teeth," Howard said, turning to Lily, who flashed her pearly whites.

"I'll miss the pep rally," Emily said.

Vivian ignored her, turning to Amy. "You have to pick up Lily at piano," Vivian said.

"Why can't she walk?" Amy asked. "I did when I was her age. It's not that far."

"Someday you'll have children," Vivian said, "and then you'll understand."

Amy's body language clearly indicated she was not pleased, but resistance was futile. "Fine. I'll pick her up from piano and bring her home before we go to the airport."

"I don't want her home alone," Vivian said.

"Then I'll drop her off at the barbershop," Amy said, flustered.

Lily looked at her daddy and smiled. She knew she wouldn't be held captive until he got off work or her mother returned from Lubbock. There was plenty for a kid to do around the square, and often other kids to do it with.

"What time is he coming in?" Howard asked.

"I don't know," Amy said. "Bobby checked the airline schedules and said there's a flight at five-thirty."

"So you're going to drive a hundred miles round-trip to see if he's on the plane?" Howard asked.

"No," Amy said, drawing out the word. "He's supposed to call his mom when he gets in and let her know what flight he's on."

"Don't you have a game tonight?" Howard asked.

"I'll be back in time," Amy said as she turned to walk away.

"Hold on, young lady," Vivian said. "Let's review."

Amy turned back and crossed her arms on her chest, one of those looks on her face.

"Emily and I will drop Lily off at piano right after school. You will pick her up from piano and take her to the barbershop. You'll let your daddy know if you are going to the airport or not, and if so, what time you expect to be back."

"Okay, fine," Amy said. "If we're running late, I'll just take Lily with me to the airport."

"Cool," Lily said.

"Why does she get to go to the airport?" Emily asked.

"Do not make me call long-distance from Lubbock to see where Lily is," Vivian said firmly.

Amy was agitated. "Kevin may not even make it in today. It might be tomorrow, or Sunday."

"But you'll pick up Lily anyway," Vivian said.

"Yes," Amy said. "I'll pick up Lily. She'll be with me. I'll take her to the game if I have to." She headed toward the door.

"I need to change clothes for the game," Lily said.

"Then I'll drop you off at the barbershop and Daddy can take you to the game," Amy called out as she opened the front door.

"If you'd buy me a car there wouldn't be any problem," Emily said.

"How's that?" Howard asked.

"I could drive myself to Lubbock."

"That'll be the day."

"What will you do if the dentist dopes you up and you can't drive home?" Vivian asked.

"Call Granny," Emily said matter-of-factly.

Amy dashed out the front door of her house and into a Corvair Monza, driven by Sandra Brewster, also a cheerleader. More than once the boys had picked up the front end of the Monza with Sandra and Amy still inside, squealing. It must have taken the entire football team, along with a couple of lookouts, but Sandra once found her car parked on the sidewalk in front of the high school.

"Oh!" Amy said, flustered.

"What's wrong?" Sandra asked.

"Remind me to pick up Lily from piano after the pep rally."

"I thought you were going to the airport."

"I won't know until later. I need to call the store, or we need to run by there at lunch."

Sandra honked and waved at her father as she drove past the dry goods store, which her parents owned. Preston was far enough from

Lubbock to support an assortment of local merchants, while small towns closer in had already been losing business as residents drove to Lubbock to shop. Sales at the dry goods store were down, but not nearly as much as the furniture store, which some days didn't make a single sale. People were willing to drive a hundred miles for a new sofa or refrigerator, but they still picked up underwear and bedding in Preston.

The dry goods store hardly carried the latest in fashion, but Sandra accompanied her parents to market in Dallas, offering a teenager's advice on styles, as well as getting a sneak peek at upcoming trends. They traveled to market by car, a long, boring trip for Sandra. Her father preferred Chryslers, but the only dealership in Preston was Chevrolet, so that's what he bought, and the dealer's wife reciprocated by shopping in his store instead of driving to Lubbock. The current Brewster family car was a 1968 Chevrolet Caprice custom sedan.

Sandra read all the fashion magazines, mailed to the store so they would be tax deductible, and Sandra and Amy would pore over them for hours. They had to buy fan magazines with their own allowance, but always shared their copies, and were careful to never buy duplicates. Amy supplemented her allowance with occasional babysitting, but since she had been going steady since freshman year, she had no entertainment or dining-out expenses.

The cheerleaders wore their uniforms to school on Friday during football season. When Amy was a freshman their cheerleader skirts were still just above the knee, following the same rules as all other skirts and dresses in high school. The miniskirt craze, already well underway in London, spread rapidly, and teenage girls were aware of fashion trends. High school hemlines headed higher in defiance of dated dress codes, which were grudgingly relaxed, but only slightly.

Pants were forbidden for girls in all grades. No one would even dream of wearing shorts other than in PE class. Levi's, not just blue jeans, were the uniform of the day for boys in or out of school. Girls often changed as soon as they got home, and Levi's were common, although they didn't fit girls very well. When the knees wore out girls would cut off the legs and hem them up as shorts. Since they were never worn to school there was wide latitude in the length of cutoffs, from just above the knee to barely covering anything, depending on the occasion, and the girl.

At the start of Amy's sophomore year, the cheerleaders successfully lobbied the school board to be allowed to wear skirts several inches above the knee. Aware that the but-everybody-else-is-doing-it line rarely worked, the cheerleaders instead took the position that it was a matter of school pride—the Panther cheerleaders couldn't look like schoolmarms while the other teams' cheerleaders wore the latest fashion. The school board insisted that a lady would never expose her underwear in public, and the Preston cheerleaders were expected to present themselves as ladies. The cheerleaders were prepared, countering that the twirlers wore skirts that were mid-thigh. Were they not ladies?

The head cheerleader held up for the board's examination a pair of briefs, to be worn over the underwear and under the skirt. The briefs were gold, the skirts black, their school colors. They explained that the briefs were the exact same garments the twirlers wore under their skirts, which everyone present had seen many times. After much grumbling, the school board reluctantly agreed.

New cheerleader uniforms were quickly ordered from Dallas and even members of the school board had to admit the Preston cheerleaders looked good and had more spring in their jumps and bigger smiles on their faces when wearing the new uniforms. Unfortunately, however, the short skirts had not caused the football team to perform any better.

The cheerleaders were even allowed to continue the practice of wearing their uniforms to school on game day, which took some getting used to, and special exemptions from the dress code, as the skirts were considerably shorter than otherwise allowed, but despite the Baptist preacher's dire warnings, no cheerleaders became pregnant, no boys were whipped into a frenzy, order was maintained, and grades did not plummet.

The cheerleaders always called in reinforcements on Friday to help decorate the gym for the pep rally, and there was never a shortage of girl volunteers, or boys to climb the ladders and hang the banners. Where there were girls there were boys, so there were several teenagers at work in the gym before school.

Amy and Sandra, along with other cheerleaders, were sprawled out on the gym floor painting signs on butcher paper. They didn't have to worry about getting their uniforms dirty. The gym floor was always kept spotlessly clean by Benjamin Washington, the quiet and unassuming school janitor, who nearly always kept his head down, even when not sweeping. While the other girls painted signs for the pep rally, Amy painted one that said WELCOME HOME KEVIN, along with a crude approximation of the yellow and black First Cavalry Division patch.

4

THE HEADSIGN ON THE TNM&O bus said ALBUQUERQUE as it cruised along US Highway 84, headed northwest, slicing through vast fields of cotton. Kevin looked through the window at a big machine stripping the fluffy white fiber from the plants. He was momentarily startled as an eastbound Santa Fe freight train crossed his view and whizzed past. He turned to watch it as far as he could, and then sat back and smiled.

For generations Preston men had gone to war and returned home on the Santa Fe. Too many of them had returned in the baggage car. Kevin remembered a statistic from American History class—during World War II the population of the United States was 130 million, and 13 million of them were in uniform. Taking away those too young or too old, along with most of the women, meant a staggering percentage of men, and a considerable number of women, served in uniform during the war. Preston was no exception, and Kevin could count off a great many men in their forties and fifties, along with his own late father, who were World War II or Korea veterans. Add in World War I, and now Viet Nam, and the VFW chapter in Preston had a long membership roster. He himself would soon be on it. He certainly met the only membership requirement—he was a veteran of a foreign war. He wasn't exactly ready to settle into middle age and start sharing war stories on Monday night, but he had earned a place at the hall, and he loved Miss Clara's cooking.

As a boy, when Kevin had listened to the veterans talk, they nearly always mentioned the trains. With gasoline rationed during World War II, passenger rail traffic, which had been in decline during the Depression, suddenly exploded, and on top of that there were millions of soldiers, sailors, and Marines crisscrossing the country by train. For mass movements there were troop trains, some of which came through Preston, but rarely stopped, with many more passing through Clovis on the way from Chicago to the west coast. There was a seemingly endless stream of long freight trains laden with tanks, trucks, jeeps, artillery, ammunition, and other war materiel.

With long lines across the southwest, where water was scarce and coal had to be hauled in for their steam locomotives, the Santa Fe had begun switching over to the new diesel-electric locomotives during the Depression when other railroads were loath to invest in new equipment. When war broke out every steam locomotive in the country that could raise a head of steam was pressed into service. The production and sale of diesel engines was strictly controlled by the War Production Board, so most of them went into trucks, tanks, landing craft, submarines and other military equipment, with far fewer allocated to the railroads. The sleek Santa Fe diesel locomotives became a familiar sight in Preston during the war, awe-inspiring for many young boys, who would race to the depot when they heard the whistle where they would sit on the platform and watch the train rumble by.

When the war ended, the work of the railroads, unlike most other war industries, was far from over. While there had been a steady stream of troop trains during the war, there were suddenly millions of GIs disembarking at ports on three coasts, from passenger liners, troop ships, merchant vessels, battleships, and aircraft carriers, where they slept on cots and hammocks, and then piled onto thousands of troop trains carrying them home. The government's interest in getting them home as quickly as possible wasn't entirely altruistic— after four long years of war the Treasury was depleted and getting millions of GIs off the payroll was a top priority. For months following the war's end the people of Preston turned up at the Santa Fe depot to welcome their boys home, cheering and waving flags. Girls blew kisses and planted more than a few directly on the faces of returning servicemen.

Even though many were still serving in the occupation forces, Preston held a celebration on Armistice Day in 1945. The festivities were more somber, but just as well-attended, the following Memorial Day, and all stops were pulled out for the Fourth of July, when the parade stretched seemingly for miles, including high school bands from every town in the county, scores of horses, bicycles, colorful floats, and anything else that could be marshaled for the event. Veterans rode on flatbed trailers pulled by John Deere tractors.

Kevin's expectations were somewhat more limited.

The bus slowed coming into Preston, following a cotton trailer pulled by a pickup. Kevin looked out the window at a big sign on the side of the road: WELCOME TO PRESTON, TEXAS / STATE FOOTBALL CHAMPIONS 1966.

As the bus approached its stop Kevin looked out at the Santa Fe depot and wondered what they would do with it. The last passenger train had left Preston more than a year ago, after the Post Office Department cancelled all railway mail contracts, switched all first-class mail to the airlines, and everything else to trucking companies. "A pack of politicians pocketed a pile of payola for that sweet little deal," Old Man Parker opined in an editorial. It sounded like a good deal to most Americans, who had been paying extra for airmail, but few had considered the unintended consequences. With passenger rail traffic in steep decline since the end of the war, carrying the mail was the only thing that kept many passenger trains profitable, and most railroads immediately began canceling passenger service. The government squawked, but the railroads were quick to point out that it was the government's own doing. The Santa Fe held on longer than many, and insisted on top-notch service until the bitter end, but while Kevin was at Fort Polk, he read in the *Preston Post* that Santa Fe's *California Special* would make its last run on July 18, 1968.

Kevin had left Fort Polk with orders to report to Oakland Army Base after thirty days leave and a bit of travel time. He took a Trans Texas Airways DC-3 from Fort Polk to Dallas and a Continental DC-9 into Lubbock. He had expected to fly from Lubbock to San Francisco, but while home on leave he discovered the *San Francisco Chief* was still operating through Clovis, just fifty miles away. He decided to take the train to Oakland in lieu of flying. It would only cost him one day at home, but his mother would be working anyway, so really just a few hours. He could forego one more day with his friends, most of whom were either away from home or still in high school, in order to see the country, at government expense, on the long trip across the southwest.

More than once, Kevin had sat in the Dalton parlor with his best friend Bobby, listening to Bobby's grandmother talk about the glory days of passenger trains. After her husband's death, Grandmother would put aside a little money each month from her retirement check and take Bobby on a grand adventure every summer by train. They had been up and down the west coast, to the Grand Canyon, Galveston, and Chicago, often on the Santa Fe. Bobby also took another vacation every summer by car, with his parents, while Grandmother stayed home. She didn't care for long car trips, nor for sleeping in a camper or tent, or cooking on a Coleman stove. She declared she had done her share of roughing it on the frontier.

It was an easy decision to make, and Kevin went to the depot where, after commiserating with the station agent over the loss of passenger rail service to Preston, and possibly his job, purchased a ticket to Oakland. His travel pay would cover the cost of the ticket, but he would have to sleep in his seat. Bobby drove him to Clovis where he boarded the *San Francisco Chief*, bound for Oakland. The conductor smiled and escorted him to a private room—he had been upgraded compliments of the station agent in Preston. Like his father before him, Kevin Frazier left for war aboard the Santa Fe.

THE BUS PULLED OVER and stopped between the Hi-Way Café and the Texaco. Kevin was the only passenger leaving the bus. The driver opened the cargo bay and quickly pulled out Kevin's bags as well as a few packages and a bundle of evening papers from Lubbock.

Kevin pushed his bags up beside the building, waved at Joe Spalding as he approached the bus, and then stepped into the café. He smiled as he listened to Ernest Tubb singing "Waltz Across Texas" on the radio, which was always tuned to a country music station. He took off his hat and hung it on the rack by the door. As Natalie, the young waitress, turned away from a booth, he slipped his hand around her waist and danced her across the floor.

He glanced down at the large bump in her belly.

"Six months," Natalie said.

"Couldn't be mine then," Kevin joked as he released her and took a seat on a stool at the counter.

"Jerk. You know exactly whose it is." She extended her left hand, displaying a plain gold wedding ring. "We got married before he left so I could get an allotment."

"Did he get drafted?"

"He was about to, so he joined the Air Force."

"Ugh, Air Force."

"What's wrong with the Air Force?"

"That's four years. I wouldn't join a church for four years."

Natalie didn't get it.

"Plus, the uniforms are ugly," he said. "They look like that bus driver that just dropped me off."

"I'll probably have the baby at the air base either at Clovis or Lubbock," she said. "I haven't decided."

"Lubbock."

"Does Reese have a better hospital?"

"I have no idea, but the baby will be a native Texan."

She laughed. "Good point."

"Where's he stationed?"

"San Antonio for now. He doesn't know where they'll send him when he finishes training. Hopefully it will be in the states so I can go with him. They won't let low-ranking enlisted men take their families overseas."

Kevin nodded.

"You want something to eat?" she asked.

"Cheeseburger and fries," he said.

"You want onions on that?"

"Is there any other way? And milk."

"Milk? You sure you don't want a Dr Pepper?"

"Milk."

He chugged the glass of milk as soon as Natalie set it on the counter. "Bring me another one," he said.

"There's no free refills on milk."

"I don't care. Bring me another one."

She picked up the empty glass and returned with it full.

When his food arrived Kevin removed the toothpick that held the paper in place, carefully folded back the paper, and stared at the cheeseburger.

"What's wrong?" Natalie asked.

"Nothing. Not a damn thing."

He picked up the cheeseburger and took a huge bite.

"Don't they feed you in the Army?"

"Not like this. I haven't had a decent cheeseburger since I left Texas." He took another bite.

"You want another glass of milk?"

He nodded as he slopped ketchup on his fries.

When he finished his cheeseburger and fries, he slung his duffel bag over his shoulder, picked up his AWOL bag and headed out. The music from the café faded, soon replaced by music from the same station as he rounded the corner of the Texaco. Joe Spalding loved country music. Kevin didn't particularly care for it—he was into rock and roll—but as a Texan in the Army he was frequently obliged to defend country music against the Yankees and Californians.

"Welcome home, son," Joe said as he shook hands with Kevin and slapped him on the shoulder. "You coming to supper at the VFW Monday night?"

"Is Miss Clara still cooking?" Kevin asked.

"She is."

"Then I'll be there."

Kevin walked away from the station and headed toward town, suddenly jumping when he heard a siren blast. He turned toward the sound and watched as Hank made a U-turn and pulled up in front of him, cutting him off.

Hank stepped out of the police car, looked over the roof and said, "We don't allow no hitchhiking around here, boy."

"Hey, Chief," Kevin said.

"You headed to the store?"

"Yeah."

"Get in. I'll carry you up there."

Kevin opened the back door, dumped in his bags, and sat in the front seat.

"You come in on the bus?" Hank asked.

"Yeah."

"Your mama said you were going to call her to pick you up at the airport."

"I thought I'd surprise her." Kevin checked his watch.

"You could've come on the train, at least part of the way. The *San*

Francisco Chief is still running through Clovis. Not sure how much longer though."

"I thought about it, but I was in a hurry to get home. I have people to see and things to do."

Hank laughed heartily. "I'll bet you do, son. I'll bet you do."

Both traffic lights on the town square were red as the police car approached, so Hank turned on his flashing red lights and siren, quickly looked both ways, and plowed right through.

"This is your parade," Hank said.

Kevin laughed. "Thanks. That's more than most of us get. Hell, hippies spit on the taxi outside Oakland Army Base."

Hank whipped his head around, fire in his eyes. "Anybody pulls that shit around here, you let me know. I'll run their sorry commie asses out of town."

"I'll keep that in mind," Kevin said as the police car pulled into the parking lot at Bob's Food Store.

Patty Dalton peered through the glass doors, looking to see what the siren was all about. She turned and yelled "Irene!" as Kevin stepped out of the police car. Before he could open the back door to retrieve his bags Kevin was besieged, first by Patty, who quickly stepped back in favor of Irene, clinging to her son while sobbing and praising God.

Kevin picked up his AWOL bag, while Hank carried his duffel bag and followed him and the women into the store. Shoppers abandoned their carts and congregated around the checkout stands, welcoming Kevin home. Hank slipped out the door with a smile on his face.

There was commerce to attend to, and Irene quickly returned to her cash register and continued checking out her customer. Kevin picked up a paper bag, whipped it open, and began sacking groceries for his mother.

"Irene, why don't you take the rest of the day off," Patty said as she returned to her own register.

"It's Friday," Irene said. "We're busy."

"We'll be okay when Robert gets back."

"Kevin's home. That's all that matters."

"Where is Big Bob, down the street drinking coffee?" Kevin asked.

"Pep rally," Patty said.

Irene suddenly stopped and turned to her son. "I didn't expect you till tomorrow. Why didn't you call?"

"I decided to surprise you."

"Did you eat?"

"At the Hi-Way when I got off the bus," Kevin said. "Couldn't you smell the onions?"

"Yes. I could."

Robert Dalton pushed open both doors and walked in. He was a big man, rather imposing, wearing a white short-sleeved shirt with "BOB" embroidered above the left pocket. A white grocery apron was rolled up around his waist. There was an anchor tattoo on his left bicep. He had been a Navy corpsman on a jeep carrier in the Pacific in World War II. Kevin had once made the mistake of saying, "At least you were on a ship instead of in the middle of all the fighting." Robert quickly set him straight. Kevin had seen enough war movies as a boy to know that the Army called out for a "medic" while the Marines shouted "corpsman," but he never knew that the Marines relied on the Navy for medical personnel. Although assigned to an aircraft carrier, Robert had gone ashore with the Marines on islands across the Pacific. He and Hank Harding, who had grown up together, had a lot to talk about on Monday evenings at the VFW. Having recently been intimately involved with Army medics, Kevin now had even more respect for Robert Dalton.

"Welcome home, son," Robert said as he slapped Kevin on the back. He turned and walked toward his wife's checkout counter, calling over his shoulder. "When are you coming back to work?"

"I just got in," Kevin said. "I won't even be a civilian until midnight."

Robert began sacking groceries for his wife.

"He's not coming back to work," Irene said. "He's going to college on the GI Bill."

Kevin, along with everyone else in the store, turned toward the sound of a blood-curdling scream as Amy and Bobby pushed through the door. Kevin braced himself, but still staggered backward as Amy launched herself into the air, threw her arms around his neck, clamped her legs around his waist, and began showering him with kisses. She tucked her face into his neck and hugged him tightly. He looked up to see Bobby leaning on the soft drink cooler, grinning broadly. Amy finally released her death grip and slid down and backed away slightly so that she could study his face for a moment before kissing him squarely on the lips.

Kevin managed to disengage with Amy, or at least their mouths, long enough to say to Bobby, "What are you doing home, Section Eight?"

Bobby laughed. "Leave."

Amy turned to face Bobby, but with her head firmly planted on Kevin's shoulder, his arm holding her tightly. The boys reached around Amy to shake hands, and then Bobby took over sacking groceries for Kevin, whose hands were otherwise occupied.

Amy looked up at Kevin. "We were going to meet you at the airport. I made a sign and everything."

"I decided to surprise my mom."

"Are you going to the game?"

"I'm going to bed if I can get a ride home. I'm beat."

"You can take the pickup," Irene said as she took a check from her customer.

"How will you get home?" Kevin asked.

"You can come back and pick me up."

"I'll be asleep."

"But everybody wants to see you," Amy said.

"They'll have to wait," Kevin said. "I've been up for two days, maybe more."

"We can give you a ride," Bobby said.

Bobby and Kevin divided the sacks of groceries and headed for the door with Amy close behind.

"You didn't sleep on the plane?" Amy asked as she squeezed in between the boys.

"Have you ever tried to sleep on a plane?" Kevin replied.

"I've never been on a plane."

As they approached a car in the parking lot Amy stepped forward and opened the back door. Bobby put his sacks in first.

"You finish AIT?" Kevin asked.

"Yeah," Bobby said as he backed out of the car.

"You have orders?" Kevin asked as he handed his sacks to Bobby.

Amy's smile disappeared.

"Yeah," Bobby said. He slammed the car door and faced Kevin. "Viet Nam."

Amy buried her face in Bobby's chest, and he hugged her.

"Shit, man," Kevin said.

5

BUCKET SEATS HAD definite advantages, especially in a car with a stick shift, but your girlfriend couldn't sit close beside you, which was the standard configuration for teenagers in west Texas at the time. For a couple going steady there was never any decision to be made—the boy opened the driver's side door, the girl got in and slid over just enough to allow room for him. If they weren't going steady, then much more thought went into the process. Sit too close and a girl might get a reputation as easy—too far away and she might be considered a cold fish or playing hard-to-get. If the boy opened the door and expected her to get in on the driver's side, he might be considered pushy. If he opened the passenger door, she might think he wasn't really interested. The permutations were endless, and much agonizing went into both the decision and the response. Sadie Hawkins dates added a whole other dimension.

Bobby's GTO had bench seats, and Amy sat between him and Kevin. The car kicked up gravel as it slid off the parking lot and onto the brick-paved highway, burning rubber.

"You're going the wrong way," Kevin said.

"I thought I'd make a round first," Bobby said. "Maybe hit the Panther."

Bobby stopped at the red light on the corner of the town square, his foot on the clutch, gunning the engine, something that always annoyed Amy.

"What are they building at the courthouse?" Kevin asked.

There was a cement mixer parked on the corner and workmen poured concrete into wooden forms.

"A war memorial," Amy said.

"Oh, yeah," Kevin said. "I saw something about it in the paper."

"They were talking about it when I left for basic," Bobby said.

"Who's doing it, the VFW?" Kevin asked.

"Sort of," Amy said.

"How do you sort of build a memorial?"

"They started out to build one just for the guys who got killed, but the town thought it should be for all the veterans who served."

"Works for me. I'm a veteran."

"Me too," Bobby said, "or will be."

"Daddy said you shouldn't build a monument to yourself, so there weren't many donations from veterans," Amy said. "The town started having fund raisers, bake sales and stuff. The cheerleaders had a car wash, but apparently it costs a lot, and it was going to take a long time to raise the money, so the banker just wrote a check."

Bobby laughed.

"What's so funny?" Amy asked.

"He was probably feeling guilty," Bobby said.

"About what?" Amy asked.

"He went in for his physical the same time my dad and several other guys did. He failed the physical and spent the war at Baylor studying business and learning how to rob people legally."

"What was wrong with him?" Amy asked.

"Yellow fever," Kevin said.

Bobby laughed.

"Yellow fever?" Amy said.

Kevin started to explain, but decided to drop it, and Amy didn't pursue it. The light changed and Bobby peeled out, looking over his shoulder at the work in progress.

"Hey, I just realized something," Bobby said. "We're going to have our names carved in stone at the courthouse."

"There it is," Kevin said.

A pickup, driven by Doug Carlton, with Sandra planted firmly at his side, pulled up alongside the GTO and honked. Kevin rolled down the window.

"Hey, Kev," Doug said.

"Hey."

"I thought you were coming in tomorrow," Sandra said.

"He came in early and surprised his mom," Amy said.

"You going to the game?" Doug asked.

"I'm going to bed," Kevin said.

"It could be our last game," Sandra said.

"Don't jinx it," Doug said. "We're going to win district."

Doug waved and turned while Bobby continued straight on Main Street. A Corvette, driven by Logan Wallace, pulled up alongside. Logan's father, the banker, bought a new Corvette every year for his only son and paid the exorbitant liability insurance for a seventeen-year-old driving a highway-patrol magnet. Everyone thought a new Corvette every year was extravagant, but the banker was nothing if not frugal. It was cheaper to buy a new one than to keep replacing engines and transmissions blown out by street racing. The Chevrolet dealer, who depended on the bank to finance his inventory, clinched his teeth, smiled, and gave the banker bluebook for the trade-in. He knew he couldn't possibly sell it off his own lot in Preston and didn't want to sully his reputation with other dealers, so he sent it to the auto auction in Lubbock—as is, where is, buyer beware, and Logan screeched off the lot in his new Corvette.

"When did you get in, Kevin?" Logan asked.

"Last week," Kevin said.

Amy looked at him curiously.

"I'm just wearing the uniform to impress girls," Kevin said.

"Is it working?" Logan asked.

Kevin put his arm around Amy and pulled her close. "Seems to be."

"When are you leaving, Bob?" Logan asked.

"Monday week," Bobby said.

"See you later, Amy," Logan said.

"Asshole," Bobby said, suddenly making a U-turn.

"What was that about?" Kevin asked.

"He's been after me ever since Bobby left for basic," Amy said.

"Well, he does have a nicer car," Kevin said.

"Up yours," Bobby said.

"Does Sandra still have her Monza?" Kevin asked.

"Yes," Amy said.

Bobby laughed. "Fun times." He stopped at the light on the square where the memorial was going up.

"We should put the Monza in that concrete before it dries," Kevin said.

"I'm in," Bobby said. "I'll call some guys."

"You boys are awful," Amy said as Bobby turned onto the town square.

"I thought we were going to the Panther," Kevin said as Bobby circled the courthouse.

"That's where Logan was headed," Bobby said. "I don't need any more of his shit today."

"And we have to pick up Lily," Amy said, "from piano."

"Is she any better at it than you were?" Kevin asked.

"Thanks a lot."

"Hey, not everybody has a gift for music," Kevin said. "I sure don't, although I wouldn't mind being a rock star. Those guys get laid a lot."

"Oh yeah," Bobby said.

Amy shook her head and tried to ignore them.

ROBERT DALTON'S GROCERY business had prospered, and the Dalton house, a large old Victorian, reflected his status. The banker's house, even grander, was a block down the street.

In the evenings, when the weather was agreeable, Bobby's grandmother could often be seen in a rocking chair on the wraparound porch.

A detached garage, or carriage house, as Grandmother called it, sat behind the house on a long driveway. All the houses on Silk Stocking Street sat several feet above the street, making them appear even more imposing. There were two steps from the street to the sidewalk, and three more up to the yard.

As the kids climbed even more steps onto the porch, they could hear piano music. Bobby opened the door and they stepped in. The living room was spotless, the furniture mostly antiques that had been in the family for decades, although Patty had purchased several pieces herself. The walls were papered, and the ceilings were high. There was a large rug in the center of the room over a hardwood floor. A baby grand piano held a commanding position in the room. The dining room, with a large dining table, china cabinet, and sideboard, was separated from the living room by a cased opening.

Bobby's grandmother was impeccably dressed, as always, looking very much the schoolmarm she had been until her retirement some years back. Her hair was silver, not white, her head held high, keeping time to the music as she sat, perfectly erect, on the piano bench beside Lily, who struggled at the keys, leaning forward to read the sheet music in front of her.

Detecting movement out of the corner of her eye, Lily turned her head ever so slightly toward the door. Without a word, Grandmother's hand quickly found the top of Lily's head and screwed it around, facing the music.

Bobby smiled. The piece was from his grandmother's youth. He often teased her about being born in the nineteenth century.

The kids sat on the sofa and waited. Amy could sense Kevin staring at her. She turned and smiled.

"What?" Amy said softly.

"I missed you," Kevin whispered.

"I missed you too."

"Didn't anybody miss me?" Bobby said, too loudly.

Grandmother's hand shot up over her head and she snapped her fingers. The three miscreants giggled and then shushed.

When the piece ended the only sound for a moment was the ticking of a grandfather clock in the hallway. Lily sat silently until Grandmother nodded her head, and then she slipped off the bench and raced toward Kevin, who stood to catch her. She wrapped her arms around his waist and planted her face in his chest.

Kevin pulled away from her. "Let me look at you, Squirt. Wow. You must be driving the fifth-grade boys crazy."

"I'm in the *sixth* grade," Lily corrected.

"Then you must be going out with junior-high boys," Kevin teased.

"I don't go out with boys," Lily said. "Boys are icky."

Kevin continued to hold onto Lily while hugging Grandmother and inhaling the distinctive aroma of Estée Lauder.

"I'm so glad you're home safe, Kevin," Grandmother said. "Do you have to go back?"

"No, ma'am. I'm done playing soldier," Kevin said. "I'm letting Bobby take over for me."

"He will be the sixth man I've sent off to war," Grandmother said. "I think I've done my share."

"More than your share," Kevin said. He squeezed Lily's shoulder. "What was that you were playing?"

"Um." Lily raised her head and looked up, trying to remember.

"The answer is not on the ceiling," Grandmother said, pointing toward the piano. Lily dashed over and looked at the sheet music.

"'Solace,' composed by Scott Joplin," Lily said, returning to Kevin's side.

"Well, I loved it," Kevin said. "It was better than Beethoven."

"It was *different* from Beethoven," Grandmother said. "It was what I listened to when I was a girl Amy's age."

"They had radio in the olden days?" Bobby teased.

"We had pianos and sheet music," Grandmother said. "We made our own entertainment, in parlors like this." She swept her hand across the room. "We courted. We didn't go out, at least not without a chaperone."

Amy smiled, and hugged Bobby. "Your grandson is a perfect gentleman. You raised him right."

Grandmother laughed. "You kids had better get out of here. I'm sure Kevin wants to get to bed."

"How could you tell?" Kevin said.

Grandmother smiled. "And Amy has a game tonight, so off you go." She followed the kids onto the porch.

"Shotgun!" Lily shouted as she raced down the sidewalk while Kevin hugged Grandmother again.

BOBBY TURNED OFF the state highway onto a more-or-less paved farm-to-market road five miles north of Preston. A mile later he turned onto the dirt driveway at the Frazier farm and pulled up beside the house, which was very much the worse for wear. There were two large pecan trees in the front yard and two more between the house and barn.

Lily rode shotgun, albeit in Kevin's lap. The doors opened and the kids piled out.

"You sure you don't want to come to the game?" Bobby asked over the top of the car.

"I'm sure," Kevin said as he hugged Lily and kissed her on the head.

Bobby opened the trunk and retrieved Kevin's bags. Kevin released Lily and then turned to Amy, who put her arms around his neck, hugged him and then kissed him on the lips, and not just a friendly peck.

"What the hell?" Bobby said as he deposited Kevin's bags on the ground.

"Butch is stealing your girl, Sundance," Amy said.

Bobby laughed.

"Huh?" Kevin asked.

"Butch Cassidy and the Sundance Kid," Amy said.

"Don't you get movies over there?" Bobby asked.

"Yeah, but not very often in the bush."

"I'm so glad you're home," Amy said.

"I'm glad to be home."

Bobby and Kevin shook hands and then Bobby headed around the car. Kevin held the door open for Amy and kissed her as she slid in.

"Enough kissing," Bobby said. "Get your own girl."

Kevin hugged Lily and kissed her on the cheek. "Can I have this one?"

"Okay, sure," Lily said with a twinkle in her eye, and then added seriously, "I'll have to ask my daddy."

Lily got in the car and Kevin closed the door.

Kevin waved as Bobby backed up and pulled onto the road. The girls waved back. Kevin watched as the taillights disappeared into the dust, and then turned and looked at the house. The screen door needed work, as did the rest of the house. His mother was barely getting by on her salary from the grocery store, and there was no money left over to hire someone to do repairs. The roof needed shingles. Some of the trim needed replacing. Everything needed painting. He turned and looked at the barn, barely standing upright. Fortunately, it had not collapsed on his car, sitting on blocks inside.

The windmill had not run for years. They hadn't really needed it as the electric pump on the well had furnished all the water they needed for the house. He mentally added the windmill to his list. Hopefully it wouldn't need much in the way of parts, just elbow grease and actual grease, and it could be put back in service to provide water for the garden while saving a few dollars on the light bill. The fence around the garden, intended to keep out the critters, had fallen down, and the chicken coop, now vacant, needed new wire.

He opened the door, dragged his bags into the large kitchen, once the center of activity for the farm family, and switched on the light. The linoleum, which he had helped his father lay just a few years ago, was already worn and needed replacing. Violent spasms of coughing had plagued his father for months, but when he coughed up blood onto the new linoleum, Irene insisted he see a doctor.

The sink was empty, the countertops uncluttered. Kevin had never known his mother to go to bed or leave the house without first doing the dishes. He opened the refrigerator and held the door open while he chugged milk from the carton.

He stepped into the hallway and looked around. The living room was to the right, barely illuminated by the light spilling out of the kitchen. It wasn't used much anymore. His mother worked at the store twelve hours a day, sometimes fourteen on Saturday, with a half day off during the week.

His father had lived six months after being diagnosed with lung cancer, refusing to give up his cigarettes until the end. Irene had thrown out the last half pack when he died and tried her best to air out the house, but it still smelled like cigarette smoke seven years later.

Kevin's father died with too little insurance and too much debt, after the cancer had drained not only his life, but the family bank account. The banker held off for as long as he could, but Irene met with him two days after her husband was buried in the cemetery just outside town, with full military honors. Kevin was thirteen, and although he tried to be strong for his mother, he cried like a little girl in front of the whole town.

Irene had hoped to rent out the section of land to another farmer and use the rent payments to keep up on the bank loans, with enough left over to live on, but the banker warned her that bad weather or low cotton prices for just one season would put the farm into foreclosure, and if the irrigation wells ran dry it would be all over. It had long been thought that the Ogallala Aquifer held a limitless supply of cold, clear, fresh water in the sands beneath the Llano Estacado, but experts had begun to sound the alarm—the aquifer was being drained faster than it was being replenished. Irrigated cotton produced far more revenue, and profit, than dryland, and without water, farmland was worth far less.

They finally worked out a deal where Irene sold the farm but kept the house and five acres. Irene was now successfully raising a bumper crop of weeds on the five-acre plot. She had kept a small Ford tractor and a few implements, which Kevin had used to grow hay, bringing in a few dollars. With Kevin in the Army and the tractor broken down, she couldn't even manage that. There were times she wished she had sold it all and moved into town, but the old house and dilapidated outbuildings weren't worth enough to buy anything decent in town. At least she wasn't paying rent.

When he turned fourteen Kevin had started working part time at Bob's Food Store, sacking groceries, working produce, sweeping, mopping, unloading trucks, stocking shelves, sorting Coke bottles, and anything else that needed to be done, for the princely sum of seventy-five cents an hour. He and his co-worker Bobby had been almost inseparable ever since, until Uncle Sam sent his greetings.

Kevin dragged his bags down the hall into his bedroom and switched on the light. It was exactly like he had left it, other than the bed being made up for winter, with two quilts. The wallpaper was brittle and peeling. His mother had made some repairs with Scotch tape. He tossed his hat onto the bed, pulled off his jacket, and dumped it onto a chair. He pulled off the black necktie and tossed it at the jacket, followed by the rest of his clothes, leaving him in brand new white boxers, issued by the Army just hours ago, still creased from when he had unfolded them. They were also huge, billowing out from the waist like old-timey bloomers.

He pulled a Nikon F camera from his AWOL bag and placed it carefully on the dresser, along with a few more items. He lifted one end of his duffel bag and started to dial the combination lock but yawned instead and dropped the bag back onto the floor. He rubbed his arms—it was cold in the house. He was in a fog from all the time zone changes, the long trip, the taxi, the airplanes, the bus, his friends, his mother. He thought about Amy leaping onto him at the store, throwing her arms around his neck, showering him with kisses. He took a breath, trying to recall her scent, but Grandmother's Estée Lauder overpowered it.

The time, or day, for that matter, continued to elude him, although people kept asking him if he was going to the game, so it must be Friday. It was dark outside—Daylight Saving Time, or Government Time, as Old Man Parker called it in an editorial when the bureaucratic boondoggle was first visited upon taxpayers, had thankfully ended for the year. Kevin pulled back the curtain and looked out. There was a soft glow from the lights of Preston. He could make out the flashing red light at the top of the grain elevator. The brightest lights on the horizon were from the high school stadium. He released the curtain and turned away from the window. It was completely quiet in the house. There was no drone of irrigation wells, the growing season over for the year, the cotton fields around his house already stripped bare. Even the refrigerator and water heater were silent.

He looked at the bed, and then at the door. He was exhausted, but still wired from caffeine, and events of the day. Maybe a shower would relax him. The shower won out. He went back to the duffel bag, dialed the combination, opened the bag, and dug out his shaving kit. It was cold in the house, especially wearing nothing but boxer shorts, so he knelt and turned up the wall furnace in the hallway on the way to the bathroom.

The water heater began to pop and crackle as soon as he turned on the shower and continued in a valiant effort to supply enough hot water as it flowed over him, filling the bathroom with steam. He looked down and could still see traces of red mud, although he had showered at least three times since leaving the bush. A smile crossed his face. The last time he had been really clean was six months ago at a bathhouse in Bangkok, really clean, compliments of a very attentive staff.

The water heater finally lost the battle and Kevin stepped out of the shower when the water was barely lukewarm. He wiped the fog from the mirror, which proved to be futile, and two more swipes did little but clump up the moisture into rivulets. He decided against shaving and just brushed his teeth.

He walked naked into the kitchen, opened the refrigerator and finished off the milk, tossing the empty carton into the trash can. Awakened from its slumber, the hum of the refrigerator now joined the popping of the water heater and quiet roar of the wall furnace to create a veritable cacophony as he walked down the hallway and into his room.

The Motorola clock radio on the dresser was the size of a bread-box, with an AM dial in the center, flanked by a large clock face and the grill on the monaural speaker. The second hand was not moving, and the clock face was not illuminated. He traced the power cord behind the dresser and plugged it in. The clock face lit up, revealing the exact time his mother had unplugged it many months ago. He checked his watch and started to set the time, but realized he wasn't even sure if his watch was correct, so he switched on the radio instead.

There was a small radio station in Preston, with a transmitter atop the grain elevator, but no one in town under twenty would ever admit to listening to it unless they were unable to attend the Friday night football game, which was broadcast live. Preston was near enough to Lubbock to pick up a variety of stations, but most of them were country or old-people music. KSEL was a local favorite with teenagers, especially for afternoon cruising, but when the sun went down radios were tuned to 1520 on the AM dial. Hundreds of miles away in Oklahoma City, KOMA was one of the so-called "flamethrower" stations, licensed to broadcast fifty-thousand watts at night on a clear channel, bouncing their "skywave" off the ionosphere. For teenagers on farms and ranches and in small towns across the American west, KOMA was their lifeline to rock and roll. It wasn't all rock though. There were slow songs and love songs in the mix, ideally suited for impromptu dance parties wherever teenagers gathered, inside or out, as long as there was a radio. The dial was still set to 1520 when Kevin switched on the radio. The disc jockey in Oklahoma had already made the perfect selection for Kevin's mood, as he retrieved a large manila envelope from the AWOL bag and dug into it. He pulled out a paperboard folder and sat on the bed. He opened the folder, wondered why they always had fuzzy edges, looked at a photograph of Amy, and smiled as he listened to Roy Orbison sing "In Dreams."

6

ONE OF THE ADVANTAGES of a girl sitting in the middle of the front seat, as closely as possible to her boyfriend or date, was a matter of public safety. The driver did not have to lean halfway across the seat and risk losing control of his vehicle while responding to the infamous KOMA Kissing Tone. In further deference to safety, the entire spot was thirty seconds long and most of it was the buildup, allowing drivers time to slow down, check their surroundings, or preferably pull over, before hearing the signal to kiss your sweetheart. For teenagers going steady, response to the KOMA Kissing Tone was almost pro forma. For those on a first date, much like the decision on which door to open and where to sit, it was either an awkward moment or a golden opportunity. Ideally, those in such a situation would be parked at the Panther, and not in motion, allowing more time for critical thinking and the formulation of an appropriate response. Headed home after the game, and a few other activities, Bobby and Amy dutifully kissed on cue.

The Panther anchored one end of the drag, the preferred route for cruising for local teenagers, with the high school parking lot at the other end. There were stopovers along the way, such as the depot, with an empty parking lot since the *California Special* had rolled through Preston for the last time, as well as the abandoned icehouse.

There was an established protocol at these stopover points—light PDA was allowed, but for heavy duty smooching, or petting, participants were obliged to find a more secluded spot. Anything more required even greater discretion—tongues wagged, and it would be only a matter of hours before everyone in high school knew your business, whether true or not.

The lights at the stadium stayed on long enough for everyone to get to their vehicles and leave the area and were then turned off the last time for the 1969 season. The Panthers had failed in their district bid. There would be no playoffs this year. The man who moonlighted painting store windows during football season would have to rely on his regular job at the lumberyard until next fall.

Following their team's loss, cruising tonight was a mostly solemn affair, mixed with gallows humor. The Friday night football game was a major social event, not only for teenagers, but adults as well. The game would be replayed Monday morning at the drugstore, the cafés, and the barbershop, but there would be no football in Preston until next August when two-a-days started. The Monday-morning quarterbacks were already handicapping the next season, most of them having attended the junior-high games, scouting eighth graders.

Doug's pickup was parked next to Bobby's GTO at the old icehouse. The building, with its thick, insulated walls, had never been repurposed and still stood, surrounded by fat elm trees that shaded the roof from the sun, important for an icehouse.

The trunk of the GTO stood open while Bobby smashed a bag of ice onto the pavement. Amy and Sandra pulled paper cups from a grocery sack. A police car pulled up and Hank cranked down the window. Doug reached into the trunk of the GTO, pulled out a six-pack of Coca-Cola, and held it up. Hank chuckled.

"Good game, Doug," Hank said. "We'll get 'em next year."

"You maybe, not me."

"There's some good prospects coming up from junior high," Hank said.

"They can have it. I'm done with football."

Bobby ripped open the bag of ice and the girls filled cups.

"You want a Coke, Chief?" Amy asked, holding up a cup of ice.

"No, thanks. I'm on duty," Hank said with a sly grin on his face.

Amy held her breath. He clearly knew what they were doing.

"You don't think you'll get a scholarship?" Hank asked.

"I doubt it," Doug said. "The college scouts will have forgotten all about me by the time the playoffs are done."

"Well, you kids be careful," Hank said before driving away.

"That was close," Sandra said.

"Why?" Bobby asked. "He can't search the trunk without a warrant."

"Yeah, like that's going to stop him," Doug said.

A charge of minor in possession didn't have to stand up in court. There was no need for a trial—all Hank had to do was call your daddy, or see him at the café, the barbershop, or the VFW, and your ass was grass.

Bobby unscrewed the lid from a bottle of rum and started pouring the liquor into two paper cups held by Sandra. He looked at Amy, who also held two cups. She pulled back one cup, shook her head and said, "My daddy always waits up for me, and he always kisses me goodnight," Amy said.

"So?" Doug said.

"He would be able to smell the booze," Bobby said.

"He could probably smell you through the door," Doug said.

"Or on me," Amy said, "so no more making out when you've been drinking."

"Come on, hon," Bobby pleaded. "Don't cut me off right before I go to Viet Nam."

Doug laughed. Amy held Bobby's cup while Doug poured rum.

"Do you have a church key?" Sandra asked, holding a bottle of Coca-Cola.

Doug dug in his pocket and retrieved the required instrument.

Drinks prepared, the kids climbed onto the wooden dock where blocks of ice were once transferred into waiting vehicles, and hung their legs over the edge, easier for the boys than the girls, who both wore short cheerleader skirts and had to beware of splinters.

Like the nearby depot, the icehouse was once vital to the community. Every morning blocks of ice would be loaded onto wagons, and later trucks, for delivery to every house in and around Preston. A card was placed in the customer's window, rotated to signal how much ice was needed that day, and the iceman would use large metal tongs to carry blocks of the required size to the porch.

The icehouse hung on for several years after nearly every home in Preston had replaced their ice boxes with electric, or gas, refrigerators. People still bought blocks of ice to make homemade ice cream, to ice down drinks for large gatherings, and nearly everyone preferred the chips of hard, clear ice in their iced tea and other drinks to the soft, cloudy stuff from their refrigerators. Many teenagers, especially the boys, could remember going to the icehouse with their daddies to pick up blocks of ice, which would be wrestled into a porcelain dishpan on Granny's screen porch, where she would attack it with an ice pick. The kids would hold up their hands to fend off the flying ice chips, and then chase the slippery slivers as they slid across the floor. They would then line up, holding their glasses of ice, and Granny would dispense Coca-Cola or Dr Pepper from a six-ounce bottle, with two kids often sharing one bottle. Their noses would tickle from the bubbles. Years later they could still feel the burn. Most everyone agreed that the beginning of the end of the golden age of soda pop was the introduction of king size bottles. Nothing was ever the same after that.

Amy sipped her Coke, the bubbles tickling her nose.

Doug reached into the Coca-Cola six-pack, pulled out a bottle, turned it upside down, and said, "Plainview." He handed the six-pack to Bobby, who studied it for a moment, flipped it around and chose a bottle.

"Alpine," Bobby said.

"Shit!" Doug said. "How do you do that?"

"Do what?" Sandra asked.

"We're playing Faraway," Doug said, turning his bottle upside down and pointing. "They stamp where the bottle is from on the bottom."

Both Sandra and Amy leaned in and looked.

"I never noticed that," Amy said.

"And Bobby always wins," Doug said.

Bobby smiled and took a swig of rum and Coke.

"Come on, Bob," Doug said. "Tell me how you do it."

"Sack-boy secret," Bobby said. "I'll take it to my grave."

They sat and sipped in silence for a bit and Bobby never revealed the secret.

"What are you going to do if you don't get a football scholarship?" Amy asked.

"I don't know," Doug said. "Join the Marines, I guess."

"You're not joining the Marines," Sandra said.

"I'm not going to hang around here, waiting to get drafted," Doug said. "What a crock."

"Crock of what?" Bobby asked.

"You can't drink, legally, or vote, until you're twenty-one, but they can draft you and send you to Viet Nam when you're eighteen."

"There it is," Bobby said.

"Isn't there something in the Constitution about involuntary servitude?" Doug asked.

"I don't think that counts," Sandra said.

"Well, it should," Doug said.

"It's just a couple of weeks until the draft lottery," Bobby said. "Maybe your number won't even come up."

"That's just for guys born up to nineteen-fifty," Doug said. "Who knows what they'll do next year? I might as well get it over with. You did."

"You could join the National Guard," Sandra said.

"Or the reserves," Bobby said. "They have an engineering outfit in Lubbock. You could learn to drive a bulldozer and get a good job with the highway department."

"I don't know," Doug said. "We'll see. I just want to get out of this shit-hole town."

"Why?" Amy asked. "I like it here."

"It's a good place to be from," Sandra said, "but there's a great big world out there."

"You can't even buy booze here, except from the bootleggers south of the highway," Doug said.

"The war can't last forever," Bobby said. "They're already reducing troop strength. The Ninth Infantry just came home."

The Ninth Infantry Division hadn't actually come home. The only soldiers in the division who came home were those already nearing the end of their tour. The rest were disbursed to other units around the country and the Army slowed the stream of replacements for a few weeks. The effect was the same—the number of troops in Viet Nam had been reduced by the size of a division but casing the Ninth Infantry Division's colors on television played a lot better to the public.

"Enough war talk," Sandra said, turning to Amy. "We need to go to Lubbock and start scouting bands for the New Year's dance."

"I guess I'll skip that one," Bobby said.

Amy's eyes cut quickly to Bobby.

"But you should go, hon," Bobby said.

"She'll go with us," Sandra said.

"Just don't dance with Logan," Bobby said.

Amy had already struggled through an entire summer with her boyfriend in the Army. Now she faced the rest of senior year without him, although there weren't really that many school events, such as senior prom. Dancing on school property or at any school-sponsored event was strictly prohibited in deference to local churches. Homecoming was a major event, with a homecoming queen, a parade, a barbecue on the town square, but no dance. There were instead parties in private homes all over town, or sometimes at the VFW Hall, but with strict rules. Bobby's attendance at homecoming this year had been in question. Had he drawn an assignment anywhere but Viet Nam he could have been dispatched immediately following training, with little or no leave. Everyone sent to Viet Nam, however, was entitled to thirty days leave. Bobby was home in time to escort Amy, the homecoming queen, onto the field at halftime. She insisted he wear his Army uniform.

There was a senior banquet in lieu of prom. A hall in Lubbock would be rented and the seniors, along with their dates, the school superintendent, principal, and high school teachers, would eat dinner, pass out awards, and listen to speeches. All school-district employees would then excuse themselves, chaperones would magically appear, the tables would be pushed back, the band would set up, and the dance would begin, all paid for, including a portion of the hall rental, by the parents, not the school district.

Amy sat on the dock of the icehouse and watched as couples drove by and waved. It saddened her to think that she would have no date for the New Year's dance, senior banquet or anything else for the coming year, but she knew in her heart that millions of other young women and girls had been in the same position for as long as men had gone off to war.

IRENE COULD HEAR Kevin snoring as soon as she stepped through the back door. She put a grocery sack on the table, removed a few items and put them in the refrigerator. She noticed there was no milk, and then looked into the trash can where she saw the empty carton. Odd, she thought, as her son had not been much of a milk drinker since he was a child.

She turned down the wall furnace in the hallway, trying to remember when the last delivery of propane had been. With winter coming, and her son at home, she would be using more propane. She would send him out tomorrow to check the gauge on the big silver tank.

Kevin's door was open, and Irene peeked in to check on him. He was sprawled out, face down, one arm hanging over the side of the bed. She pulled up the quilts around his shoulders and tried to cover his dangling arm.

She retrieved a wooden hanger from the closet, carefully folded his uniform pants, placed both the pants and jacket on the hanger and hung it in the closet, where it would no doubt remain for at least a few years, just like millions of others, including her late husband's. The black Army tie went on his father's tie rack, along with many others in various widths and patterns as styles had changed over the years. His father's clothes didn't fit him, but Kevin wore his ties on the few occasions he wore a suit, which, if his mother had anything to say about it, would be every day once he graduated from college and got a good job.

She picked up his shirt, carried it into the bathroom, and dropped it into the hamper on top of his boxers and T-shirt.

BOBBY'S GTO WAS parked in the driveway, the position carefully chosen after years of trial and error. It afforded the worst possible view from the living room windows. The car's windows were fogged from the heavy breathing. Amy had no problem with the heavy-duty kissing, including lots of tongue, but she pushed away Bobby's roaming hands, which continued to land where they had no business landing, grabbing what was not theirs to grab. Whether out of desperation, the realization that his days left in Preston were numbered, or the rum, Bobby was even more aggressive than usual.

One hand slid under her sweater and quickly found its target. It certainly wasn't the hand's first such foray onto her breasts, and she was resigned to allowing a certain latitude tonight, especially as long as her sturdy bra prevented any actual skin-to-skin contact. Her bra had not always successfully held the line, however, and only Amy's iron resolve had prevented any further escalation, no small feat after three years of going steady, and that was the problem. A runner had to get to second base before he could get to third. Amy had to make it clear that just because, in a moment of weakness, she had allowed him to hit a double in the past was no guarantee she wouldn't strike him out the next time at bat.

Location was an additional consideration, as was the clock, and Bobby well knew it. Amy had the home-field advantage, and it was bottom of the ninth. He had gotten even further when they were parked out in the country, but never in front of her house, with her daddy sitting in his favorite chair, re-reading the newspaper, waiting for the witching hour.

The porch light flashed off and on.

"I have to go in," Amy said, pushing away Bobby's hand.

"Just a few more minutes," Bobby said. He was on a roll.

"Now!"

Amy pushed him away, checked her makeup in the mirror, and ran her fingers through her hair. She retrieved a breath mint from the glove box, popped it in her mouth, and crushed it between her teeth. She hadn't been drinking, but Bobby certainly had, and bodily fluids had been exchanged. There was no scientific evidence, to her knowledge, that breath mints would mask the aroma of alcohol, but it was worth a shot. Besides, it tasted good and made her breath feel fresh.

7

WHOOSH. BOBBY RIPPED OFF a piece of masking tape. Amy, holding Kevin's welcome-home banner against the wall, as high as she could reach, alarmed by the sound of the tape, looked over her shoulder at Kevin, face down on the bed, dead to the world. She turned to Bobby and put a finger to her lips. Bobby used the strip of masking tape to fasten the corner of the banner to the wall. He removed the next piece more quietly, as Amy spread out the paper along the wall.

Their work done, Amy padded quietly around the bed and leaned over, carefully examining Kevin. He was still asleep, facing away from her. Bobby held out his hands, palms upward. Once more Amy put a finger to her lips. Bobby, resigned to letting it play out, whatever it was, stood quietly and watched. Amy carefully slipped under the covers without waking Kevin. She brushed her fingers across his hair. No response. Again. Nothing. Her fingers traced across his ear, and then onto his cheek. He swatted at the disturbance, but she was able to pull her hand away in time. She paused for a moment as he dozed off. She brushed her fingers across his bare shoulder. He finally awoke and saw Bobby leaning against the door frame. He rubbed his eyes.

"Hey, man," Kevin said.

"How long have you been asleep?"

"What time is it?"

"Around nine."

"What day is it?"

Bobby laughed. "Saturday."

"Did we win?"

"Nope. Season's over."

Kevin looked at the banner on the wall. "Is that the sign Amy made?"

"Yeah."

"Where is she?"

"In bed," Bobby said with a slight grin.

Kevin rolled over on his side. Amy backed away, still undetected, and covered her mouth to keep from laughing.

"You get this over there?" Bobby picked up the Nikon camera from the dresser.

"Yeah, mail order from the PX," Kevin said, rolling back toward Bobby and tucking the pillow under his chest.

"Nice."

"I like it. Beats what I had." He again swatted at whatever pest was upon him.

Bobby removed the lens cap, held the camera up to his eye, and focused on Kevin. "Wow, cool. I'll have to get one of these."

"Look at the catalog and ask around first. You can order pretty much anything you want from the PX and save a lot of money."

Feeling something on his waist, and convinced it was more than a bug, Kevin looked over his shoulder. Amy ducked. Bobby continued to play along. Kevin searched under the covers with his hand and found something soft. Startled, he quickly rolled over, face to face with a now laughing Amy, and put his arm around her.

Amy shrieked and leapt out of bed, covering her face. "He's naked!"

Bobby laughed.

"That's how we sleep in the jungle," Kevin said, nonchalantly.

Amy dashed around the bed, hands still covering her face, bumping into things, tripping over Kevin's duffel bag, finally taking cover behind Bobby.

Kevin swung his legs over the side of the bed and planted his feet, dragging the sheet over his lap. Amy peeked out from behind Bobby as Kevin started to stand.

"Don't get up!" Amy pleaded, again covering her face.

"I need a shower." He was a bit unsteady on his feet after sleeping the clock around.

"I'll make you some breakfast," Amy said, turning to go while holding her hand up to the side of her face like a horse's blinder. She scurried down the hallway.

"Can she cook?" Kevin asked.

"Not that I know of."

"I can hear you!" Amy called out from the kitchen. "Kevin, what do you want for breakfast?"

Bobby stepped aside and Kevin leaned through the door into the hallway. "Three eggs, over medium, and bacon, really crisp, and sausage. I'm starved." He stepped into the hallway, headed for the bathroom.

"And coffee," Bobby said, and then lowered his voice. "I guess biscuits and gravy is asking too much."

"What did you say?" Amy said, stepping into the hallway from the kitchen. Seeing Kevin completely naked, she screamed, covered her face, and darted back into the kitchen.

The boys laughed.

"Toast," Bobby said. "He said he wants toast."

Amy removed her hands from her face, which was quite red. She took a deep breath and then a mischievous smile began to grow on her face.

Amy cooked while Kevin showered. Now fully dressed, or at least Levi's and T-shirt, he stepped into the kitchen and sat at the table with Bobby, who sipped coffee.

"Sorry about that," Kevin said.

"What?" Amy asked.

"I thought you were in the kitchen. I didn't mean to flash you."

"That's okay," Amy said, turning toward him, her face again flushing. "I'll get over it."

"When I first got to Viet Nam, at the replacement center, I walked out of the shower naked and there was a Vietnamese woman sweeping the floor."

"Did she look?" Amy asked.

"She didn't not look. There were naked guys everywhere, and she didn't seem to care. It was downhill from there, or uphill, depending on how you look at it."

Bobby choked on his coffee.

"They had a massage parlor at the PX in Tay Ninh," Kevin said, "with cute Vietnamese girls."

"A massage parlor?" Amy asked.

"Yeah."

"Did you get a massage?"

"Of course."

"From a girl?"

"Yep."

"Were you naked?"

Kevin nodded his head.

"That would be weird," Amy said.

"It would be weird if they were guys," Kevin said.

"Were the girls naked?" Bobby asked.

Kevin smiled and sipped his coffee.

"Where did you say that was?" Bobby asked.

"Tay Ninh," Kevin said. "Probably a lot more places."

"Don't even think it," Amy said, pointing her finger at Bobby.

Bobby held up his hands. "I'll be good, hon. I promise."

Amy picked up the percolator from the stove and poured a cup of coffee for Kevin.

"I hope this is okay," Amy said. "My mom's percolator is electric."

"It's a little strong," Bobby said.

"Why didn't you say something?"

"If you made it, babe, I'll drink it," Bobby said, and then took another sip.

"I like it strong," Kevin said.

Amy put a carton of milk on the table. Bobby pushed a bowl of sugar toward him. Kevin shook his head.

"And black," Kevin said.

"When did you start drinking your coffee black?" Bobby asked.

"Last year, somewhere over the Pacific."

Kevin took a sip of coffee. "Um, good. In Viet Nam they drink their coffee so strong you can stand a spoon up in it."

Amy reached for the milk carton and Kevin put his hand on her wrist. "Leave it," he said.

"I thought you wanted it black," Amy said.

"I do, but I need a glass, if you don't mind."

Amy opened a cabinet and reached for a glass.

"She's going to make somebody a good little wife," Kevin said.

Amy slammed the cabinet door. "Get your own glass."

"Sorry," Kevin said, pushing back his chair.

"I'm kidding," Amy said, putting a glass on the table and filling it with milk, which Kevin promptly downed.

"I thought I finished off the milk last night."

"We went by the store and your mom said to bring some," Amy said.

Kevin poured another glass and chugged it.

"What's with the milk?" Bobby asked.

"You'll find out," Kevin said, without elaborating.

"What about Kathy?" Amy asked, turning back to the stove.

"What about her?" Kevin asked.

"We're trying to find you a date for tonight," Bobby said. "It's Saturday and I'm guessing it's been a while since you had a date."

Kevin nodded.

"She's at Tech," Amy said. "I can get her number."

"That's over," Kevin said. "Never was, really."

"We'll find somebody," Bobby said.

"Everybody your age is either married or gone off to college," Amy said, "and everybody my age is seriously involved."

"Or knocked up," Kevin said.

Amy turned and looked at him, puzzled.

"I had a cheeseburger at the Hi-Way when I got in," Kevin said.

"Oh, yeah," Amy said. "At least they got married before she started showing."

"Has anybody streaked at the high school yet?" Kevin asked.

"Not yet, thank goodness," Amy said as she put his plate on the table. "What brought that up?"

"Naked guy in the hall—" Kevin said, pointing over his shoulder.

"Ah, that," Amy said, grinning.

He looked at the plate of food in front of him. "Looks good."

"Like you said, I'm going to make somebody a good little wife." Amy returned to the stove for the percolator.

Kevin dug in.

"Sandra said there were naked hippies everywhere at Woodstock," Amy said, pouring coffee. "I could never do that."

"Was she there?" Kevin asked.

"No, but she knows some models in Dallas who were," Amy said as she sat down.

"Were they naked?" Bobby asked.

"Ooh, naked models," Kevin said.

"Do boys always think about naked girls?" Amy asked.

"Pretty much," Bobby said as Kevin nodded, his mouth full of food.

"Speaking of naked girls," Kevin said, swallowing. "I like the new cheerleader uniforms."

"Thanks," Amy said. "I guess."

"Do they let you wear them to school?" Kevin asked.

"Yeah," Amy said, "after the battle."

"What battle?" Kevin asked.

"We had to go in front of the school board," Amy said.

"And lift their skirts," Bobby said.

"Did not!" Amy said emphatically.

"Things have certainly changed since I was in high school," Kevin said. "It was really hard to get a good look up a girl's skirt in the old days." He leaned over and looked at Amy's legs. She immediately tugged at her skirt.

Bobby laughed.

"High school boys these days have no idea how good they have it," Kevin said.

"You can say that again," Bobby said.

Amy shook her head. "Boys."

BOBBY'S GTO COVERED the five miles into town in substantially less than five minutes. Amy didn't like going so fast, but the boys certainly did, so she didn't complain. She sat in the middle between them, her knees pointed slightly toward Kevin to keep them clear of the stick shift. Her skirt, already short, was hiked up considerably and she caught Kevin looking at her legs.

"Sorry," Kevin said.

"For what?" Bobby asked.

"He was checking out my legs," Amy said.

"I know you're horny, man, and I'm working on it, but hands off my girl," Bobby said.

"It's okay to look, though," Amy said. "I guess you haven't seen a lot of girls in short skirts lately."

"Donut Dollies," Kevin said, "but they wore really ugly dresses, and they weren't all that short."

Amy laughed. "Donut Dollies?"

"Red Cross girls. They were stationed on the base camps, and you could go to the rec center and play ping pong or whatever, or just sit and talk, probably whine about your girlfriend back home cheating on you."

"Did you whine about your girlfriend?" Amy asked.

"I didn't have a girlfriend to whine about. And I was never on a base camp for very long, so I didn't go to the rec center. Sometimes the Donut Dollies would fly into a firebase and stay a couple of hours."

"Did they bring donuts?" Amy asked.

Kevin nodded.

"Were they hot?" Bobby asked.

"The donuts?" Kevin asked.

"The Dollies."

"Like anywhere else," Kevin said. "Some were, some weren't. I guess they all looked better since there weren't that many round-eyed girls around, except for the Army nurses, and they were all officers so they couldn't fraternize with lowly enlisted men."

"Did they put out?" Bobby asked, drawing a look from Amy.

"Not that I know of," Kevin said. "I damn sure never got any, but there were plenty of rumors, just like high school."

"Just like high school," Amy said, nodding knowingly.

"Are girls allowed to wear short skirts to school these days, other than cheerleaders?" Kevin asked, taking advantage of the opportunity to have another look at Amy's legs.

"I wear this to school," Amy said.

"Skirts were really short in Sydney," Kevin said.

"Sydney?" Amy asked.

"Australia."

"When did you go to Australia?"

"A few weeks ago. I guess I never mentioned it."

"No, you didn't."

"I thought you went to Bangkok on R&R," Bobby said.

"I did. Everybody gets an R&R, but you can also get a week's leave if your CO allows it. We were on palace guard, so he let me go. I didn't even know where I was going until I got to the R&R Center. The clerk said since I'd been in-country long enough I could go to Sydney. And boy, am I glad I did. Wow. They've got some really hot chicks there, or Sheilas, as the Aussies call them."

"What's palace guard?" Amy asked.

"They keep an infantry battalion at division headquarters at all times in case there's a ground attack and Charlie breaks through the wire."

"Screw that," Bobby said. "What about the Sheilas?"

"They wore skirts so short you could see their—" Kevin smiled at Amy.

"Their what?" Amy teased.

"Everything," Kevin said. "I went to a movie downtown and when I came out there were girls in miniskirts everywhere. I'm talking short. Barely-covering-their-ass short."

"What movie did you see?" Amy asked.

"*Battle of Britain*," Kevin said. "Then I just wandered around for hours, looking at legs. Damn, I love Australia."

"Sounds like heaven," Bobby said.

"The movie?" Amy asked.

"The girls in short skirts," Bobby said.

"That was nothing compared to *Hair*," Kevin said.

"Do Australian girls all have long hair?" Amy asked. "They do in the fashion magazines from London, and really short skirts."

Kevin grinned. "They do, but I mean the musical. I saw *Hair* live on stage."

"You did?" Amy said. "Was it any good?"

"Did they get naked?" Bobby asked.

"Oh yes, they got naked," Kevin said, grinning as he turned to Amy. "And it was very good."

Amy shook her head as Bobby pulled in and parked at Bob's Food Store. The store was bustling with activity as Amy and the boys swooped through the door. Both Patty and Irene were busy checking out groceries while teenage boys filled grocery sacks.

"Help me shop," Amy said to Kevin. "I have my mom's grocery list."

"I'll work the phone," Bobby said, making a beeline for the telephone at his mother's checkout stand. "There has to be a desperate chick out there somewhere."

"You can sack groceries," Patty said. "It's Saturday."

"In a minute, Mom," Bobby said. "This is important."

Bobby plopped onto a stool by the phone, picked up the receiver, and put his finger in the rotary dial.

Kevin pushed Amy's cart through the store as she checked off her grocery list. He looked around and took a deep breath.

"What are you doing?" Amy asked, puzzled.

"The colors, the smells."

"What smell?" Amy asked, looking around.

"Produce, meat market. In Viet Nam everything was all green and brown and smelled like wet canvas and diesel fuel."

Amy put a head of lettuce in the cart, looked up and smiled.

"And shit," he said.

Amy wrinkled her nose.

Kevin took a can of hairspray from Amy's cart, sprayed a little into the air and sniffed.

"What are you doing?" she asked.

"One of the Donut Dollies used this same hairspray."

"You remember her hairspray?"

"Sure. It smelled good." He sprayed some at Amy. "See?"

"I know exactly how it smells," she said, backing away.

Kevin replaced the cap and dropped the can into the cart.

"How are you holding up?"

"What do you mean?"

"With Bobby leaving in a few days."

"Oh, that. It's hard, but I'm doing okay, I guess. It was really hard when he left for basic. We hadn't gone more than a day or two without seeing each other for nearly three years, well, except for when he went on vacation, or I did."

Kevin nodded.

"And when he was in basic, he couldn't even call very often," she said. "All we could do was write."

"Did you write to him every day?"

"Of course. How often did I write to you in Viet Nam?"

"Not every day."

"But a lot though, right?"

"Yes, a lot, especially the last few months, and you have no idea how much it meant to me."

"I got really lonely during the summer, so I wrote to you and Bobby both. And that jerk Logan kept hitting on me, like I was going to just dump Bobby while he was away from home, *serving his country.*"

"Guys like him are called Jody."

"Jody?"

Kevin nodded. "Jody is the civilian puke who tries to get your girl while you're in the Army. I have no idea why they call him Jody, but it's been that way since forever. Ask your daddy."

"Jody," Amy said, making a mental note.

"What did you do all summer?"

"I did some babysitting, worked part-time at the five-and-dime. Caught up on my reading."

"No, I mean for fun."

"I went riding around and to the movies with Sandra and Doug.

We hung out at the Panther and the icehouse. I'm sure Doug didn't like having a third wheel along, but he never said anything."

"Don't worry about Doug. I'm sure he got plenty of action after they dropped you off."

"I'm sure he did," Amy said, grinning. "What about you? What are you going to do?"

"Double date with you and Bobby, apparently."

"With your life, now that you're back home and out of the Army. You don't have to go back, do you?"

"As of midnight, I am a PFC," he said.

"I thought you were a sergeant."

"A proud . . . civilian."

She laughed.

"I guess I'll go back to school at Tech," he said, "but I want to take some time off first. My mom wants me to start the spring semester, but that's coming up real soon. I'll probably work at the store, maybe drive a tractor next summer and start school in the fall. It's easier to schedule classes that way."

"Oh, yeah, I guess that makes sense."

"That's what I'm telling my mom anyway, when she squawks about it."

"We could be freshmen together."

"Are you going to Tech?"

"Probably. I could live with my grandparents and save a lot of money."

"I could be your bodyguard, to help you fight off the boys."

"Sometimes I wish Bobby had gone to college instead of enlisting, but he would have probably gotten kicked out."

"The boy does like to party."

"Tell me about it."

"How's he treating you?"

"What do you mean?" Amy asked, surprised.

"He's my best friend and all, but he's used to getting his way.

Don't let him take you for granted. You deserve to be treated with respect."

"Yes, I do. He can be a jerk sometimes, but I love him. Maybe three years in the Army will be good for him, and me. We can both grow up a little."

"Good, but if he gives you any crap, you let me know, and I'll kick his ass."

"You and my daddy both."

"I'm going to kick Jody's ass anyway," Kevin said as he wheeled the cart up to Patty's register.

"Who's Jody?" Patty asked.

"Just some guy I know," Kevin said, brushing against Amy as he squeezed past, inhaling the scent of her hairspray. He picked up a grocery sack and popped it open. He sacked as Patty rang up Amy's groceries.

Bobby hung up the phone. "No luck."

"Bobby, are you going to help us or not?" Patty asked.

"Where's Dad?" Bobby asked, dialing the phone.

"Where do you think? At the drugstore, drinking coffee and replaying the game."

Patty finished checking and asked, "Do you want me to put this on your daddy's account?"

"Yes, ma'am."

Bobby slammed down the phone and reached for a sack of groceries. "I have a delivery."

Kevin picked up the rest of the sacks, and Amy followed the boys out the door.

"What about Nikki?" Bobby asked, looking over his shoulder at Amy.

"What's a Nikki?" Kevin asked.

"She's a cheerleader," Amy said.

"Pretty cute," Bobby said, "and built like a brick shithouse."

"Do I know her?" Kevin asked.

"Not really," Amy said. "She's, um, new."

The boys loaded Amy's groceries into the back seat of the GTO.

"I'm going to stay and help Mom," Bobby said. "Kevin can take you home. I'll call you later." He kissed Amy.

"Are you going to call Nikki, or do you want me to?" Amy asked.

"You'd better do it. You know her better than I do."

"Okay," Amy said.

Bobby sprinted toward the store.

"I guess it's you and me, kid," Kevin said as he stepped around her.

"Where are you going?"

"I'm going to open the door for you."

She laughed. "I'm used to getting in on this side." He held the door open for her, and then got in behind her as she slid over to the passenger side.

"This feels weird," he said as he started the car and backed out. "I haven't driven a car for over a year." It came back quickly as he pulled out of the parking lot onto Main Street. As he waited at the stoplight, he looked over at her. She was crying.

"What's wrong?" He was alarmed.

She wiped a tear. "What do you think?"

He extended his hand, and she took it, held it for a moment, and then slid over next to him as the light changed. He turned left, shifted gears, then put his arm around her as they passed by the dry goods store. Sandra, on the sidewalk in front of her parents' store, started to wave, but saw Kevin pull Amy close and kiss her on the head. She watched as they drove by.

EMILY AND LILY started digging through the grocery sacks before Kevin and Amy had even put them down on the kitchen counter.

Vivian hugged Kevin. "I'm so glad you're home safe," she said. That appeared to be the standard greeting for a returning warrior.

"I'm glad to be home," Kevin said. He had already run out of responses.

Emily left Lily to ransack the groceries long enough to hug Kevin. "Hi, Kevin."

"Look at you. All grown up. I may have to throw Lily over for you."

Lily laughed. "You can have her."

Amy followed Kevin to the front door and hugged him. "I'll see you tonight."

"I don't have a date yet."

"Don't worry about it. We'll go out anyway."

"Are you sure? Wouldn't you rather be alone with Bobby?"

"That's okay."

"I know he'd rather be alone with you."

8

AFTER SHOWERING ONCE MORE and then shaving, Kevin opened the medicine cabinet and found the bottle of English Leather right where he had left it last year. He smiled and splashed it on liberally, feeling the burn. The aroma was almost overpowering, especially compared to the plain alcohol he had been using for the past year. Grunts in the bush in Viet Nam were cautioned against the use of strongly scented aftershave, which was rumored to give away your position to the enemy. A more likely reason was that it attracted mosquitoes, which were not only annoying, but potentially deadly.

For the second time in one day Kevin was faced with a decision over what to wear, something that had not been an issue for quite some time. It was to be a casual date, so his wardrobe wasn't difficult—it was the same thing he had worn in high school, Levi's and a shirt, along with cowboy boots. He reached for his letter jacket but chose instead his Army field jacket.

He hadn't had any input into planning. Amy simply said he had a date with her cheerleader friend and that they would be going riding around, which was fine with him. It would allow him to reconnect with old friends while cruising, parked at the Panther, or sitting on the dock at the icehouse.

He felt like he was back in high school as he waited nervously for Bobby to pick him up, trying to remember what it was like to go out with a girl. As he filled his pockets with keys, wallet, and accoutrements he heard Bobby's GTO approaching. As he stepped through the back door, he was surprised to see not just Bobby, but Amy and a cute young girl pile out of the car. He had expected Bobby to pick him up first and then they would pick up the girls, but he wasn't complaining. Nikki was as advertised, cute and built. She was also very enthusiastic, rushing into Kevin's arms and hugging him tightly.

"Hi, I'm Nikki."

"Kevin."

Nikki didn't let go, so Kevin put his arms around her back and squeezed, causing her to move even closer, if that was possible. He looked over her head at Amy who smiled, clearly pleased with her matchmaking. The double date was off to a good start.

"You drive," Bobby said as he opened the passenger door and followed Amy into the back seat.

Nikki released her death grip on Kevin and sat in the passenger seat. Kevin closed the door and by the time he made it around the car and opened the driver's door Nikki was almost behind the wheel. The date was getting even better.

As Kevin sat down, he noticed that Nikki's skirt, already short, barely covered anything and she made no effort to adjust it. She was also short, allowing her to point her knees toward him rather than away to avoid the stick shift. He started the car and as he reached out to shift gears, she pressed even closer, making it impossible to shift without his arm bumping into her left breast. The date was now in uncharted territory.

No one seemed to be mourning the loss of the district title as teenagers cruised on Saturday night. There were so many kids cruising, not only from Preston but nearby small towns, that it was at times bumper to bumper along the drag. Kevin's first stop was the Panther, which was crowded with teenagers and cars, rock and roll blasting from the radios. Kevin glanced in the rearview mirror as they ate their cheeseburgers and fries. Although Amy had slid over enough to allow room for her and Bobby to eat, Nikki hadn't budged, reminding him of eating on the DC-8 with his elbows pressed against his sides. His current seatmate was much smaller than the hulking soldier he sat beside across the Pacific. She was also significantly sexier, and she kept looking up at him with those big eyes.

"It's nice having a chauffeur," Bobby said from the back seat as they cruised after leaving the Panther. He had a beer in one hand and the other was planted firmly on Amy's thigh. She quickly determined his reason for letting Kevin drive was to free up his hands for more important pursuits.

"Where would you like to go, sir?" Kevin asked.

"To the icehouse, James," Bobby said, affecting some sort of accent, trying to sound sophisticated.

"We'd better hit the filling station first," Kevin said, looking at the dashboard. "It's nearly on empty."

Kevin started to turn into a nearby station on Main Street.

"Go out to the Texaco. It's a penny cheaper and Joe lets me use his lift."

Nikki whipped her head around and looked at Amy, who shrugged. Kevin made a course correction and headed for the highway.

Like many of the other teenagers on the drag tonight, they were listening to KOMA on the radio when the familiar jingle began playing. Nikki looked expectantly at Kevin, who smiled and turned his attention back to the road until the Kissing Tone played. Amy looked up from kissing Bobby to see Nikki grab Kevin and really plant one on him. The GTO, like several other cars on the drag, swerved until Kevin managed to extricate himself from Nikki's lip-lock and regain control.

The kids sang along with the music on the radio as Kevin pulled into the Texaco. The music died when Kevin turned off the ignition, replaced by the country music from the radio in the station, growing louder when Kevin rolled down the window.

Nikki, suddenly feeling the urge to tie her shoe, slid across the seat to the passenger side and bent over, head down, hair covering her face.

Joe Spalding stepped up to the driver's side window and said, "Fill 'er up?"

Bobby leaned forward from the back seat and handed Joe two dollar bills. "Two dollars' worth, ethyl."

As Joe began pumping gas, Kevin poked his head out the window. "How's Sharon?"

"She's at school down in Abilene, going to make a teacher," Joe said. "She'll be home for Christmas. You should give her a call."

"I will."

Kevin looked over at Nikki, still tying her shoe, and then leaned out the window. "Don't you have another girl at home?"

"Yes, we do," Joe said as he approached the window. "Nicole. She's the baby."

"What is she now, a junior?"

"She's a freshman."

"At Tech?"

"At the high school."

"Do the kids call her Nikki?"

"Yes, I believe they do."

Kevin and Joe both looked at Nikki, head down, still tying her shoe.

"Do you want me to carry her home or leave her here?" Kevin asked.

"Just leave her here," Joe said. "The Albuquerque bus is due in, and the restrooms need cleaning."

"Daddy!" Nikki said as she sat up.

"I thought you said you were going riding around with the cheerleaders," Joe said.

"Amy's a cheerleader," Nikki said.

"Sorry," Kevin said. "I didn't know. She looks a lot older."

"That she does," Joe said, shaking his head.

Nikki slid over and kissed Kevin on the cheek. "I had a nice time," she said. She slid back across the seat, opened the door, got out and stomped away.

"They grow up fast these days," Kevin said.

"Yes, they certainly do," Joe said.

"Well, again, I'm sorry," Kevin said, looking over his shoulder. "I was misled by my friends."

Bobby laughed. Amy covered her face.

"Truth be told I'd rather she was out with you than some of these high school horndogs, but she lied to me, so she'll be grounded for a couple of weeks." Joe slapped Kevin on the shoulder. "Glad you made it home safe, son." He leaned in the window. "Bobby, you take care over there."

"Yes sir," Bobby said, trying to hide his beer.

"Wipeout" played appropriately on the car radio as Kevin pulled out of the Texaco, with Amy and Bobby now relocated to the front seat.

"A freshman?" Kevin said, incredulously.

Amy shrugged.

"Beggars can't be choosers," Bobby said.

"She's jailbait," Kevin said.

"It's not like you stuck your tongue down her throat or felt her up or anything."

"You didn't, did you?" Amy said.

"No way. She jumped me."

"She's boy crazy."

"She's the same age as Emily."

"She's boy crazy too."

"You have to admit she's pretty cute, and has a hell of a rack," Bobby said.

"And nice legs," Kevin added. "That skirt was nearly up to her waist."

"Like the girls in Australia?" Amy teased.

"Girls didn't look like that when I was a freshman," Bobby said.

"Thanks a lot," Amy said.

"You were in eighth grade when I was a freshman," Bobby said.

"And he already had his eye on you," Kevin said.

"He did?" Amy said, and then turned to Bobby. "You did?"

"Yep," Bobby said. "I like 'em young."

"Then we should have swapped tonight," Kevin said, looking at Amy. "I prefer a more mature woman."

"You should definitely call Sharon when she gets home," Amy said. "She's really nice."

"And boring," Bobby said, taking a sip of beer. "She's going to be a schoolteacher."

"My mom's a schoolteacher," Amy said. "So was your grandmother."

Bobby shrugged.

"Hide the beer, man," Kevin said, looking up at the rearview mirror. "Chief Harding is right behind us."

Bobby turned his head, caught a glimpse of the police car, and then kissed Amy on the cheek. Kevin pulled into Bob's Food Store. Hank waved as he passed by and continued his rounds.

"Why are you stopping at the store?" Bobby asked.

"I'll help out and then ride home with my mom. Y'all can go park and make out," Kevin said.

"You sure?" Bobby asked. "I have more beer in the trunk."

Amy looked at Kevin but didn't speak.

"Or you could stay here and sack groceries and I'll go park and make out with Amy," Kevin said as he put his arm around her, pulled her close, and kissed her on the cheek. She played along, scooting over close to Kevin, looking down her nose at Bobby.

"In your dreams," Bobby said as he finished off his beer, handed the bottle to Amy, and opened the door. "Beer's getting warm. I need some more ice." He climbed out of the car and headed toward the large ice box on the sidewalk outside the store.

"How romantic," Amy said, looking at the bottle.

"How many beers has he had?" Kevin asked.

"Too many."

"Do you want me to take you home?"

"No, that's okay. I'm used to it."

"Well, good night," Kevin said as he kissed Amy on the cheek. "I had a nice time."

"So did Nikki," Amy called out as Kevin stepped out of the car.

As THE SANTA FE converted to intermodal freight, thousands of old boxcars were sold off, the undercarriages for scrap, while many of the cars themselves found their way into farmers' fields across the plains. They made usable, although small, barns for livestock or farm equipment. The steel boxcars were cheap, prefabricated, conveniently sized, had large doors, and would still be standing long after wooden barns had succumbed to the west Texas wind and sun.

The boxcars also made an ideal place for teenagers to park, providing some degree of cover from passersby on the dirt road. The teenagers knew which farmers were likely to look the other way, and which ones would call the sheriff if they happened to spot a car on their way home from town. The cotton harvest was still underway, and strippers ran into the night, so Bobby had to carefully select a parking spot in a field that had already been stripped.

One such rusty boxcar, still bearing the name "Santa Fe" on the side, was located about two miles north of the Preston city limits, where Chief Harding had no authority, and well off the highway. A light fixture attached to the top of the boxcar created a pool of light around Bobby's GTO. This was important on a moonless night— teenage boys wanted to not only cop a feel but a look if they were lucky enough to dislodge enough clothing to bare some skin.

Bobby was well underway on his mission, as music played on the car radio. Amy's blouse was unbuttoned, her skirt hiked up, and Bobby seemed to have three hands. As quickly as she would push one hand away two others would spring into action, all the while kissing her face, her mouth, the bare skin above her bra. She could smell the beer and knew it was getting all over her. Hopefully he hadn't spilled any on her clothes. She would make him stop at the Hi-Way Café on the way home so she could run in and wash up, but she knew she couldn't wash out the smell of beer from her blouse.

He managed to get his fingers under her bra and pushed it upward. She quickly grabbed it with both hands and wiggled it back into place before too much had been exposed. With her hands occupied he moved south, territory previously covered, but this time he shoved his hand forcefully between her thighs.

"Stop it!" She grabbed his hand and tried to pull it away, but he persisted. She shoved him hard and pushed away, sliding across the seat to the passenger side, her feet tangled up with the cooler and empty beer bottles on the floor. She kicked at the bottles, and then stared straight ahead, trying to ignore him. She flinched as he leaned over and reached out his hand toward her legs. She tugged at her skirt, prepared to fight him off again, but the cooler was his intended target. He retrieved a bottle of beer and settled back in the driver's seat. She watched cautiously as he opened the beer and took a long swallow.

"Come on, Amy. We've been going steady for three years. You know I love you."

She glared at him but said nothing.

"I only have a few days left."

"Not like this. It's supposed to be special, not in your car parked out in the country beside some old train."

"We could go to a motel."

"A motel? You're drunk and we're fighting."

"We'll go wherever you want."

She turned away. "I want to go home."

He took another swig of beer.

"I'm just not ready," she said.

"I could be dead before you're ready."

She whipped her head around, clinched her teeth and stared. If looks could kill he would be dead right now.

He chugged the rest of the beer and tossed the empty bottle into the pile at her feet. He knew better than to toss it out the window. Farmers might look the other way when teenagers parked and made out on their property, but they weren't about to clean up their trash, especially beer bottles and used condoms.

Bobby started the car and backed away from the boxcar, ignoring the tears streaming down Amy's face. The GTO kicked up a cloud of dust as it fishtailed onto the dirt road and pointed toward town.

Hank, his police car hidden among the farm equipment at a dealership on the north end of town, heard the GTO before he saw it. He started his car and waited as the GTO blew past. He immediately gave chase.

Amy turned to see the red lights flashing behind them. "It's Chief Harding," she said.

"So what." Bobby ignored the pursuing police car and continued on Main Street, although he did slow down a bit.

"Bobby, pull over!"

Bob's Food Store had been closed for more than two hours, which was fortuitous as Bobby's GTO sat in the parking lot, just ahead of the police car, red lights still flashing. Amy sat in the passenger seat, both embarrassed and angry. Bobby stood beside the GTO, leaning defiantly against the front fender as passing teenagers shouted taunts.

Hank shined his flashlight into the car. "Have you been drinking?"

"No sir!" Amy responded quickly. "I don't drink."

"Then you drive."

"Yes sir."

"She can't drive a stick," Bobby said.

"And you can't drive shit tonight," Hank said. "I guess we could leave it here and your daddy can drop you off on the way to church in the morning."

That solution was obviously not acceptable to Bobby. Amy slid over under the wheel and awaited instructions.

"I'll follow you to Bobby's house and then carry you home."

"Yes sir," Amy said, her mind racing through all possible permutations of how this could end badly.

Bobby turned and walked around the front of the GTO.

"Where are you going?" Hank asked.

"To get in the car."

"I don't think so. You ride with me."

AMY STOOD ON THE front porch, trying to smooth out the wrinkles in her clothing. She turned and waved at Hank, hoping he would drive away, but he was apparently intent on waiting until she was safely inside the house. At least he hadn't walked her to the door and knocked. She stepped through the door and quickly closed it behind her. Howard looked up from the newspaper and checked his watch.

"You're home early," Howard said.

"Bobby wasn't feeling well," Amy said, without actually lying.

She stopped at her daddy's chair, kissed him briefly on the cheek, and headed down the hall, hoping to get into her bedroom with no further interaction.

"Hold on," Howard said as he stood up.

Amy froze, just short of her bedroom door, closed her eyes, held her breath and waited for it.

"I can smell the beer."

Her planned trip to the Hi-Way Café to clean up had been ruined by Bobby's run-in with the law.

"I haven't been drinking. I promise."

"I can smell it all over you."

"It was Bobby."

"Bobby was all over you?"

"He had a couple of beers. We kissed, but that's all."

"A couple?"

"A few."

"Was he drunk?"

"I guess."

Howard took a deep breath and paused. "Honey, I know you've been going steady for a long time, and I know you're under a lot of pressure with Bobby going to Viet Nam and all but be careful."

"I am."

"I know what boys want."

"I'm okay, Daddy. I can handle it."

He leaned over and kissed her on the cheek. "Good night, honey."

"Good night, Daddy."

She opened her bedroom door.

"Amy."

She stopped and turned.

"Yes sir?"

"Your blouse is buttoned wrong."

She looked down while running her fingers over the buttons on her blouse, and then closed her eyes and wanted to die.

9

THE WEATHER AND west Texas are often at odds. Preston was on the edge of the state's most productive cotton growing region, with Lubbock at ground zero. In the fall, when the cotton matured, the bolls opened and the fluffy white fiber emerged, at the mercy of the weather, especially rain, which would reduce the value of the cotton. Getting the mature cotton out of the field and into the gin as quickly as possible was a priority. Cotton strippers ran into the night, floodlights mounted on top, several feet above the ground, lighting the way. The lights also accentuated the clouds of dust kicked up by the ungainly machine, making it look like something out of a science-fiction movie, lumbering through the night, seemingly on a collision course with unsuspecting travelers on the highway.

Cotton gins operated around the clock during the season and burned the residue from ginning cotton. The acrid smoke, mixed with the dust and particulate matter scooped up by the strippers along with the cotton, drifted for miles across the South Plains.

Kevin coughed and sneezed—the warm, moist air of Southeast Asia suddenly seeming not so bad after all. A blue norther had blown in late Saturday night, dropping temperatures by thirty degrees, and the wind continued to howl much of the day on Sunday. Fortunately for the cotton farmers, or depending on one's religious persuasion, by the grace of God, the norther had been dry, and the cotton harvest continued unabated, except for church on Sunday morning.

Kevin's mother was still driving her late husband's pickup, which was hardly new when he died. Kevin had encouraged her to drive his two-door 1962 Chevrolet Impala while he was away, but she declared it too sporty for an old lady, so Bobby had helped him put it up on blocks before he left.

The Impala was Kevin's pride and joy, and completely unaffordable on his sack-boy salary, especially part-time, but the job at Bob's was steady and year-round. He had three years' experience driving a tractor when his father died so he hired out every summer on his days off from the store. After a bit of a breather, if football season could be considered a breather, he worked the rest of the cotton harvest while still sacking groceries. The Impala was his reward for all that hard work, and he had paid cash for it.

He wanted a '57, arguably the most beautiful Chevy ever built, but he hadn't saved up enough money to buy a car until the spring of 1965, when the fifty-sevens were going on nine years old. Like every other teenage boy in west Texas, he was intimately familiar with every post-war model built by Chevrolet. The 1962 models were, in his opinion, the last of the great Chevys. He would not have been embarrassed to be seen driving a '63 or '64, but it was all downhill from there.

The Super Sport 409 was his first choice, but there were none available in Preston, and he was leery of buying one out of town without knowing how hard it had been run, and 409s, by their very nature, had often been run hard. He settled on a 327 with three-on-the-tree and bench seats, and with a history known to the local Chevrolet dealer. It would be cheaper to run and easier to maintain—he could do most of the work himself in the barn.

Bobby had promised to help him with his car, but had not shown up on Sunday, so Kevin had spent much of the day working inside the house, where there were plenty of repairs to be done.

As was often the case after a blue norther, Monday dawned cold and crisp with clear blue skies. The smoke from the cotton gins had been visited upon neighbors to the south, but soon returned, mixed with the sour scent of crude oil, now fanned by gentle southerly breezes.

Kevin drove his mother to work so he would have the pickup to run into town and pick up parts and supplies to get his car running. Bobby showed up not long after Kevin had returned from town. The boys had made good progress—the Impala now sat on tires, not cinder blocks, but had yet to start. The hood was open, and Kevin leaned in, tools in hand.

"She can barely drive a stick," Bobby said as he stepped out of the driver's seat. "My car was going like this." He made a lurching motion with his body.

"You're lucky he didn't throw your sorry ass in jail."

"What's he gonna do, send me to Viet Nam?"

"Even if he locked you up, and your daddy bailed you out, you'd still have to appear in court. You think the Army is going to let you hang around your hometown while you hire a lawyer and see the judge?"

Bobby shrugged.

"You fail to show up at Oakland and miss that flight to Viet Nam and your ass is in a world of hurt," Kevin said. "You're not just AWOL—you're a deserter in time of war."

"That's what Chief Harding said."

"What about Amy?"

"What about her?"

"You get drunk, roll your goat and kill your fool self, that's one thing, but Amy never signed up for any of that shit."

"I drive careful when I'm drunk. You know that."

"The chief stop you for driving too careful?"

"So I was driving a little fast. Amy's fine. She'll get over it."

"How did she get home?"

"Chief Harding took her."

"Does her daddy know?"

"I guess I'll find out, if she ever speaks to me again."

"You haven't talked to her?"

"She hung up on me when I called."

"You didn't see her in church?"

"I didn't go to church. I was kind of hung over. Did you see her?"

"I slept in. Still trying to get back on Texas time." Kevin stepped back from under the hood. "Try it again."

Bobby tried it again, but it didn't start. Kevin went back to work.

"She was already pissed off when I got pulled over," Bobby said, stepping out of the car. "That's why I was driving so fast."

"So it's Amy's fault?"

"That's not what I said."

"Well, if it wasn't the driving drunk, then what got her so hot?"

"That's the problem. I was all hot and bothered, and she wasn't."

"Ah, now I get it. You used the old I'm-going-off-to-war line, trying to get laid."

"It was worth a shot."

"How romantic."

"How long is a guy supposed to wait?" Bobby pleaded.

"You mean you two never—"

"Well, I have, of course, but we never—she never."

"Amy Evans is a virgin?"

Bobby nodded. "She damn sure better be."

"You went steady for three years and never did it?"

"Not even close," Bobby said, and then grinned. "Well, close, but no cigar."

"Wow," Kevin said, smiling and shaking his head.

"A guy can try, can't he? It's kind of our job. Besides, everybody else is doing it, Age of Aquarius, free love, and all that shit."

"That's for hippies."

"At least hippies get laid."

"It's a big step for a girl, especially a nice girl like Amy."

"But if she loves me then she should want to do it, right?"

"If you love her, you shouldn't push her to do something she doesn't want to do, at least not right now. Give her time."

"I don't have time. I leave for Viet Nam a week from today." He paused for a moment as Kevin worked on the car. "I'm not a coward. I'll go. But I hear about guys getting their balls blown off by booby traps."

"What booby traps? You're a supply clerk. That is what you went to AIT for isn't it?"

Bobby nodded. "Mortars and rockets then."

"Okay, now that could be a problem. That shit falls on everybody."

"I love Amy and she loves me, or I hope she still does. But what if I come back with no dick?"

"I don't know what to tell you. I was a grunt, and I came back with mine."

"Yeah, and you're not even using it."

Kevin laughed. "I need to get some wheels under me so I can chase tail."

"I set you up with some tail and you didn't even nail it."

"Yeah, good thing too, or Joe Spalding and Chief Harding would both be up my ass." Kevin stepped back. "Now try it."

Bobby tried it again and it started.

"The way I see it, you have two choices, provided she hasn't already dumped you," Kevin said. "One, get down on your knees, beg her to take you back, stop trying to force her to put out, go to Viet Nam and spend three hundred sixty-five nights dreaming about what it's going to be like when you get home and she's decided that she's ready. She'll be out of high school then, probably living in Lubbock, going to Tech."

"What's number two?"

"Keep trying to shove your hand down her panties and see where that gets you."

"I haven't had much luck with that one."

"Look on the bright side."

"What bright side?"

"If Amy won't put out for you then Logan doesn't stand a snowball's chance in hell while you're gone."

"Good point," Bobby said, nodding. "But keep an eye on him for me anyway."

10

AS THE POPULATION of Preston swelled in the years after its found-
ing, no sooner was a schoolhouse built than it had to be expanded
or replaced. Locals still argued over the identity of the arsonist, but
prevailing opinion was that forty years on he was a well-respected
businessman, and a long-time member of the volunteer fire department. Others insisted that there were more than one, a gang of rowdy
high school students, liquored up after a visit to the bootlegger south
of the tracks. It was an act of youthful indiscretion they would take
to their graves. The coffee drinkers would nod knowingly—who
amongst them had not done things during their teenage years they
would sooner forget? Regardless of who was responsible, the result
of the school burning to the ground in 1927 was the two-story,
red-brick structure that still stood grandly at the north end of Silk
Stocking Street.

The building had served as both junior high and high school until
the late fifties when the first wave of baby boomers along with con-
solidation of some of the rural schools in the county necessitated a
new building for the junior high on the adjacent block. After troopers

from the 101st Airborne escorted black students into Little Rock Central High School, the Preston school board reluctantly accepted that desegregation was inevitable and there would soon be even more students to house. The new junior high had lower ceilings and concrete floors covered with tile, but still no air conditioning. It was, for reasons no one could remember, or admit to, constructed of blond brick, an affliction common to many other schools and public buildings across west Texas in the post-war years. The new junior-high building was, in a word, ugly. Even in a light sandstorm it blended into the sky. In the winter, when the grass was dormant and the few trees leafless—it had occurred to no one to plant evergreens—an artist would have required only a small palette to commit the drab scene to canvas. As far as anyone knew, no artist had ever done so.

The high school, on the other hand, was a thing of beauty, reminiscent of ivy league universities, without the ivy, which didn't exactly thrive in the semi-arid climate of the Llano Estacado. Hedges ran under the windows on the front of the building and prairie oaks dotted the lawn. Like most high school football fields, the one in Preston ran due north–south, so a line of cedars provided some measure of protection from blue northers.

Although the building was only two stories tall, the ceilings were twelve feet high, and the high school towered over its pipsqueak neighbor. There were large transom windows above every interior door that, combined with the huge double-hung windows on the outer wall that ran the length of every classroom, provided adequate ventilation, until the west Texas wind came up suddenly and students rushed to close the windows. A shellacked hardwood pole with a brass tip leaned in the corner beside the door. Its purpose was to open and close the transom window over the door, but there was never really a need to close them, summer or winter, so the poles were used more often, when no teacher was present, to poke at one's fellow students, despite the constant admonition, "you could put out somebody's eye with that thing." No one ever understood how using the pole to lift a girl's skirt could possibly lead to poking out an eye, unless the girl grabbed the pole and poked back, which had happened more than once over the years.

Kevin's Impala, now oiled, lubed, gassed, vacuumed, washed, waxed, plated, and inspected, with tires mounted and inflated, pulled in and parked directly in front of the high school. The boys leaned on the hood of the Impala and looked up at the second floor of the school, waxing nostalgic. Bobby wore one of his letter jackets and Kevin his Army field jacket. His new Nikon camera hung by a strap around his neck.

"Good times, good times," Bobby said, smiling.

"Sometimes," Kevin said. His own memories of Preston High were somewhat less fond. As a member of the football team and a hero of the state-championship game in Sweetwater he was afforded a certain respect and status, but the principal social divider in high school was money. Like many other farmers, his father's financial fortunes had risen and fallen with cotton prices, often at the mercy of the weather, but overall, Kevin and his family enjoyed a modestly comfortable life. With his father and the farm now gone, and his mother working as a cashier at Bob's Food Store, Kevin's social status at school had been negatively impacted. Unlike Bobby and many others, Kevin's limited financial means reduced the dating pool—most of the more desirable girls expected their dates to spend lavishly on them, including frequent trips to Lubbock for dinner and a movie. Oddly enough, as far as Kevin knew, Amy was not one of those girls. Although she had gone steady with Bobby since she was fourteen and was arguably the most beautiful and desirable girl at Preston High, it did not seem to be Bobby's money or social position that attracted her. She was just as happy cruising the drag, sitting on the dock at the icehouse, or eating burgers at the Panther as she was going out to eat in a fancy restaurant or to the Caravan of Stars when it played at the Municipal Coliseum in Lubbock. Kevin liked that about her.

Bobby would have been satisfied to be a high school senior forever, but Kevin was happy to be out in the real world, even if that had meant being drafted and sent to Viet Nam. At least that was now done, and he could get on with being an adult, and hopefully finding a woman instead of a teenage girl to date.

Sandra, sitting near the windows in English class, looked out and saw Kevin, leaning against the Impala, laughing at Bobby, who was on his knees on the sidewalk, his hands clasped under his chin. She tapped Amy on the shoulder.

Amy first checked the teacher, Maggie Mills, who was writing on the chalk board, and then looked out the window at Bobby. Unmoved by his pleadings, Amy shook her head and turned away. She didn't know how long she could stay away, but he deserved the cold shoulder for at least a while longer. As a practical matter she wanted to wait and see if Chief Harding had ratted her out to her daddy. If so, then she could claim to have already dumped Bobby rather than waiting for Daddy to order her to put an end to it. The advantage, for the moment, was hers.

Maggie was Amy's favorite teacher, perhaps because she was not that much older than Amy. She was the youngest teacher at Preston High since its earliest days when it was not unusual for the school-teacher to be very young, with little or no college. Like many other recent college graduates with a teaching certificate, Maggie had accepted an offer to teach in a small town, far from the big city lights. Most of them expected to teach only a year or two in Hicksville before moving on to a bigger school with better pay and more opportunity for advancement, as well as somewhat closer to civilization. Others only expected to teach until finding a husband, and a small town, where everybody knew everybody, was as good a place as any.

Kevin turned to look as an Army sedan pulled in and parked next to the Impala.

"The MPs are here for you," Kevin said as Bobby stood and wiped the dust off the knees of his Levi's.

"Those aren't MPs."

Two soldiers, wearing class A uniforms, stepped out of the Army car.

"Afternoon," a well-decorated staff sergeant said.

"He's right over there," Kevin said, pointing at Bobby. "You can go ahead and take him."

"Ha-ha," Bobby said.

The sergeant looked confused, but he was trained to avoid unnecessary engagement with civilians if there was any possibility of hostility toward the Army. Such was rarely the case in small towns in west Texas, but the one who spoke was wearing an Army field jacket with the First Cavalry Division patch on the left shoulder and might have been a draftee opposed to the war. The sergeant just smiled and continued smartly up the sidewalk with his associate.

The bell rang and Bobby and Kevin watched as students rushed out of classrooms and soon began swarming through the front doors of the school. Kevin waved at Amy and Sandra.

"What are those Army guys doing here?" Amy asked.

"Recruiters," Sandra said. "Doug and some of the other guys are meeting with them."

"Is Doug going to join the Army?"

"Who knows?"

Kevin hoisted his camera to eye level as the girls approached. Bobby held out his arms, but Amy ignored him. The girls stopped, smiled, and posed for Kevin, who snapped a picture.

"Babe," Bobby said, once again holding out his arms.

"I'm still mad at you," Amy said, turning to Kevin. "Hi, Kevin." She hugged him. "Did he tell you what happened?"

"Oh yes," Kevin said. "I told him he was an idiot."

"Thanks for coming to pick me up," Amy said, continuing to ignore Bobby, "but I'll ride home with Sandra." She hugged Kevin and kissed him on the cheek. "Bye."

"Bye, Kevin," Sandra said, also ignoring Bobby.

Bobby followed the girls as they walked away.

"I'm sorry, hon. I was drunk. It won't happen again."

Amy stopped, turned back and looked at him, but was determined to remain strong. She turned and walked away, Bobby right behind.

"I promise," he said.

Sandra could see Amy was weakening. "Don't do it," she said.

Amy slowed down.

"I don't want to lose you," he said.

Amy stopped walking.

"I can't lose you," he said. "I love you."

Amy's resolve weakened.

"More than anything," he said. "More than life itself."

Amy relented. Sandra was indignant. Her best friend had barely put up a fight. She turned and walked away. Amy was on her own.

Kevin snapped a picture of Amy as she walked toward Bobby, and then several of her and Bobby, hugging and kissing. After a short session of smooching, they headed for the Impala, holding hands.

Kevin drove, Amy in the middle, although closer to Bobby. She was holding hands with Bobby and smiling, so apparently all was forgiven, at least for the moment. Her daddy, however, was still an unknown quantity. After stopping off at the Panther, where Kevin shook a lot of hands and hugged a lot of girls, they made a couple of rounds, waving at other teenagers doing the same, before turning onto the town square. Kevin slowed and all eyes turned as they drove past the barbershop, as if a glimpse of Howard cutting hair would somehow give them a clue as to his disposition.

"He didn't say anything?" Bobby asked, craning to watch Howard.

"Not really," Amy said. "But he could smell the beer."

"Busted," Kevin said.

"Didn't you eat any mints?" Bobby asked.

"I grabbed a handful when I drove your car home," Amy said, "but that doesn't really work anyway. Then there was my blouse."

"Your blouse?"

"Did you puke on her blouse?" Kevin asked, laughing.

"No. I didn't, did I?"

"Spill your beer on her?" Kevin continued his line of questioning.

"I don't know, maybe," Bobby said defensively.

"It was buttoned kind of whompyjawed," Amy said.

Laughing, Kevin pulled into a parking space near the drugstore. "Whompyjawed?"

Amy pulled one collar of her blouse up and the other down.

"Ah," Kevin said. "I see."

"We didn't do anything!" Amy said.

"You can say that again," Bobby said.

Kevin smiled, imagining Amy with her blouse unbuttoned, wondering what else might have been undone. "Did your daddy see your blouse that way?"

Amy nodded.

"Bob, you probably want to put off getting a haircut for a few days," Kevin said. "And lay off the booze."

Kevin and Bobby walked down the aisle of the drugstore while Amy debated over the proper shade of lipstick.

"Need some help with film?" Kevin asked.

Cliff Billingsley, twenty-five, a tall, athletically built, neatly dressed black man with a well-groomed mustache, looked up from the Kodak display, holding two boxes of film.

"Do you work here?" Cliff asked.

"No, but I know a little something about thirty-five-millimeter film."

Cliff noticed the patch on the sleeve of Kevin's Army field jacket. "First Cav?"

Kevin nodded. "Second of the Twelfth."

"When were you over there?"

"Last week," Kevin said as Amy stepped up and stood between the boys, holding the selected lipstick.

"Hi, Mr. Billingsley," Amy said with a small wave of her hand.

"Hello, Miss Evans," Cliff said, and then turned to Kevin. "Hundred and First."

"The wannabe air cav," Kevin said.

"There it is," Cliff said, smiling.

"Grunt?" Kevin asked.

Cliff nodded. "Platoon leader. Company commander for the last three months."

"OCS?"

"ROTC. Prairie View A&M."

"Better than a ninety-day wonder," Kevin said. "I went through a couple of those."

Cliff laughed. "So did I." He held up the two boxes of film. "Plus-X or Tri-X?"

"Depends on what you're shooting," Kevin said. "Plus-X is good for bright sun or even open shade if you hold the camera still. Tri-X is a lot faster, so you can shoot in low light or fast action, like stopping chopper blades. I used to use it a lot for sports when I shot for the newspaper."

"So, Plus-X," Cliff said, moving to put back the Tri-X.

"Unless you want grain," Kevin said.

"What's that and why would I want it?"

Kevin held up his hands, framing Amy's face. "Let's say I was shooting this lovely face in the studio."

Amy self-consciously lowered her head.

"I would use Plus-X," Kevin continued. "I'd have plenty of light, probably a strobe, and Plus-X gives me the f-stop I want."

"Okay," Cliff said, unconvinced.

"You want her portrait to be sharp, with fine grain, like in a yearbook photo, or something to send to her boyfriend in Viet Nam," Kevin said.

"Your boyfriend is in Viet Nam?"

"I'm right here," Bobby said.

"He leaves Monday," Amy said.

Kevin ignored the interruption. "But if I were shooting say, a figure study." His eyes settled on Amy.

"What's a figure study?" Amy asked.

"Nudes," Maggie said, suddenly appearing beside Cliff.

Amy shrieked, covered her reddening face and ducked her head. Bobby doubled over, laughing.

Maggie wore skin-tight blue jeans, not Levi's, and a T-shirt under a leather jacket. The jacket, even open as it was, interfered with the boys' view of her chest, but it was clear she wasn't wearing a bra, an unusual sight in Preston.

"Hi, Miss Mills," Amy said.

"Hi, Amy."

"Yes, nudes," Kevin said. "If I was shooting nudes, I might want some grain, for artistic purposes."

"Naked pictures," Bobby said, straightening up, looking at Amy's chest. "I can dig it."

"You wish," Amy said, trying to regain her composure.

"Definitely," Bobby said.

"Let's go, Cliff," Maggie said. "We're going to be late, and I'll have to stop at a pharmacy when we get there."

Cliff put the boxes of film back on the display.

"I'll see you tomorrow, Amy," Maggie said, walking briskly away with Cliff close behind as both boys watched.

"Why didn't you introduce us?" Bobby asked.

"She kind of caught me off guard," Amy said.

"Who is she?" Kevin asked as he picked up two boxes of Tri-X.

"My English teacher."

"That's your English teacher?" Kevin said, flabbergasted.

"She's new."

"What happened to Mrs. Westmoreland? She's been teaching English at Preston High since the old one burned down."

"She retired."

"I thought she'd die at her desk quoting Shakespeare."

"Nobody would notice until the janitor came in to sweep up," Bobby said.

At the cash register, Amy paid for her lipstick and Kevin his film.

"She looks really young," Kevin said as they walked through the door and onto the sidewalk.

"Who?" Amy asked.

"Your hot young English teacher," Kevin said.

"She just graduated from college. It's her first year teaching."

"She looks like she's still in high school."

"The senior boys hit on her all the time. It's ridiculous."

"She wasn't wearing a bra," Bobby said.

"I noticed that," Kevin said. "And that ass. How do you get into a pair of pants like that?"

"First you buy her a drink."

"Ha-ha," Amy said. She had heard the tired old joke before.

"You should fix Kevin up," Bobby said. "We could double date."

"I am *not* double dating with my English teacher."

"You might get lucky," Bobby said to Kevin. "It's obvious she puts out."

"How is it obvious?" Amy asked.

"You could practically see her nipples through that shirt," Bobby said.

"And everybody knows hippie chicks put out," Kevin said.

"Y'all are awful," Amy said. "I'm walking home."

The boys watched as Amy walked away. After a few yards it was apparent she was not going to change her mind, so the boys hopped in the Impala and gave chase. Kevin had to make a U-turn, and Amy had walked half a block before they caught up to her.

"Hey, hot stuff, want a ride?" Bobby asked, leaning out the open window.

Kevin stopped the car. Amy stared at Bobby for a moment. He got out and held the door open and she got in the back seat.

He started to follow, but she pulled the seat back, blocking him, so he sat in the front and Kevin drove on to her house, just a few blocks away.

KEVIN STOOD IN THE open doorway of the bathroom, focusing his camera on Amy as she leaned over the lavatory, trying out her new lipstick.

"Those aren't going to come out," Amy said, checking her lips.

"Why not?" Kevin asked.

Amy pointed at the light bulb directly above the mirror. "The light is supposed to be behind the photographer."

Kevin smiled. "Lens flare. It's all the rage in Europe."

He stepped into the bathroom and focused on a close-up.

"You should take a picture of me," Emily said.

"Oh, shit!" Kevin said, turning toward the sound as Emily, in the bathtub, pulled back the shower curtain.

Amy laughed. Kevin was relieved to see that Emily was wearing Levi's and a T-shirt.

"Why are you taking a bath with your clothes on?" Kevin asked, raising his camera.

"I'm shrinking my new Levi's."

She mugged for the camera as Kevin snapped pictures.

"Why?"

"So they'll fit."

"Why don't you just buy them the right size?"

"So they'll fit her bottom," Amy said.

"Do you do that?" Kevin asked.

"Everybody does that."

"I don't do that."

"You're a boy," Emily said.

Everyone in the bathroom turned toward the sound of screaming. Bobby carried Lily, kicking and screaming, over his shoulder.

"You have to practice," Bobby said.

Kevin raised his camera and followed them down the hallway, finally grabbing a shot or two in the living room before Bobby deposited Lily beside the piano. She sat on the piano stool and Bobby took a seat beside her. The Evans piano was an old upright, not nearly as nice as the Dalton's, but it worked, and it was in tune.

Bobby rifled through sheet music as Lily fidgeted.

"Let's play something good," Bobby said.

He picked a song and showed it to Lily. "Pachelbel?" she asked, grimacing.

"Do you know it?"

"Not very well. I play it sometimes with your grandmother. She sent home the sheet music so I could practice."

Amy and Kevin stood and listened as Lily and Bobby began to play a duet. Kevin quietly slipped away and pulled back the curtains behind the piano, flooding the pianists with a soft light. He stalked around, bending, leaning, kneeling to get his shots. Satisfied with what he had, he stepped back and turned to Amy, on the sofa, tears streaming down her face. He sat down and put his arm around her.

"What's wrong?" Kevin whispered.

"He can be such a jerk, and then he does something like this," Amy said, wiping tears.

Kevin kissed her on the cheek, she put her head on his shoulder, and they listened as Lily and Bobby played "Canon in D Major."

11

THE REST OF THE week was rather idyllic as Amy and the boys were almost inseparable, except for school, where Bobby and Kevin waited every day to pick her up. She never knew which car they would be driving, nor did she care. They would cruise the drag, drink Dr Pepper in the drugstore, at the Panther, or the Hi-Way Café, sit on the dock at the icehouse and talk. Kevin shot roll after roll of film, some of Amy and Bobby together, some, using a timer and tripod, of all three of them, but many were of just Amy.

It was mid-November, when nights were cool, sometimes freezing, but winter had not fully set in, and days were often sunny. It was cool but calm today, perfect weather for working outside. It was also the kind of day that made it difficult to pay attention in class. Amy glanced out the window as Irene's pickup rattled to a stop in front of the high school. Kevin and Bobby stepped out and waved. Amy smiled. Both boys wore Levi's and white T-shirts, rather dirty. They both crossed their arms, muscles rippling, as they leaned against the hood of the pickup. Amy wanted to laugh at their pose, wondering if it was intentional, or just boys being boys. Whatever it was it looked to her very much like a movie poster—*Hud* came immediately to mind. She had seen it at the drive-in years ago with her family. Her daddy loved it. So did her mother, who was a big Paul Newman fan.

"We're working on Kevin's roof," Bobby said as Amy approached after the bell rang. "We'll drop you off and then go finish."

They kissed and he took her books.

"You aren't dropping me off anywhere," Amy said. "I'm going with you."

"We'll be working, hon," Bobby said as he opened the door to the pickup.

"So? I can do homework and listen to the radio until you finish."

Kevin shrugged. Amy slid into the middle of the seat. Bobby climbed in beside her and put her books under his feet on the floorboard.

AMY WENT INSIDE Kevin's house while the boys unloaded shingles from the pickup and wrestled them up a ladder to the roof. She dumped her books on Kevin's bed and turned on the radio. She raised the window and said, "Can you hear it?"

"Turn it up," Kevin said.

"Why didn't we think of that?" Bobby asked.

Kevin laughed. "That's why we have Amy," he said as he climbed down the ladder, which was directly in front of the open window. He was startled to see Amy take off her blouse and toss it onto his bed. He knew he shouldn't be looking but continued to watch as she unzipped her skirt and stepped out of it. Chivalry, or fear that she would turn around and catch him peeking, won out and he quietly dismounted the ladder and turned away. He grabbed a box of roofing nails from the pickup and pondered his next move. He had to climb back up the ladder, which would require enormous discipline to not take another look. Even worse, he might get caught.

"Catch!" Kevin shouted as he approached the ladder. He launched the box of nails toward Bobby on the roof, who somehow managed to catch it without spilling the nails. Having given fair warning to Amy, Kevin climbed back up the ladder without incident. He said nothing to Bobby about what he had seen and hoped Amy hadn't caught him.

The boys hammered away for a few minutes while listening to the radio and then Bobby glanced toward the ladder.

"What the hell?" Bobby said.

Amy, wearing one of Kevin's flannel shirts and a pair of his Levi's, the cuffs rolled up, climbed the ladder with one hand, holding the Levi's at the waist with the other. Kevin, who was closer to the ladder, reached out and took her hand, steadying her as she stepped onto the roof.

"I wasn't going to sit in the house while y'all talked about me."

A black cotton web belt with a brass buckle was threaded through the loops of the Levi's.

"I couldn't figure out how to work the buckle."

"It's an Army belt," Kevin said. He sat back onto the roof and pulled her toward him. He tugged at the belt, just above eye level, only inches away.

"Hey, I'm in the Army," Bobby said as Kevin buckled the belt, with several inches sticking out beyond the buckle.

"That's okay," she said. "Kevin fixed it."

"Be careful," Kevin said, releasing his grip on the belt. "It will hurt like hell if you fall off the roof."

As the boys hammered away, Amy sat down, pulled her knees up under her chin, and gazed out.

"You can see the elevator from here."

"You can see even more from the windmill," Kevin said.

"I don't think I want to climb up there. It looks kind of rickety."

Kevin laughed. "That's next on the list."

"You can't climb the water tower anymore," Amy said.

"You can't?" Kevin said.

"They were afraid somebody would fall and break their neck, so they put a stop to it."

"Kids today," Bobby said. "Pussies."

"Did you climb it?" Kevin asked Amy.

"Of course. It was kind of scary."

Climbing the water tower had been a freshman rite of passage for decades until the city built a cage around the ladder and padlocked it for fear of liability.

AMY AND BOBBY had already seen it in Lubbock, but *Butch Cassidy and the Sundance Kid* opened Friday at the Llano Theater on the square in Preston, working its way through the small-town circuit.

"Now I get it," Kevin said as they walked out of the theater.

"Take her," Bobby said.

"Okay," Kevin said, putting his arm around Amy.

"Did you like it?" Amy asked.

"Yeah. It was really good. I have a lot of catching up to do on movies."

They cruised for a while until Kevin suggested they take him home. He didn't mind hanging out with the lovebirds after school or even into the night, but he always tried to allow them some alone time. Although Kevin was unaware, Amy had lately dreaded being alone with Bobby, fearing a repeat of his previous ungentlemanly behavior.

There was no time to park in the country and make out after they dropped off Kevin, so Bobby took Amy home. The kissing became hot and heavy in front of Amy's house, but Bobby kept his hands somewhat in check. She would have allowed a bit more tonight, but she didn't want to release the beast. She could live with deep French kissing and no hands.

Bobby had not had a drink since Saturday night, at least not around her, but Amy held out little hope it was permanent. It was nice to just kiss and make out and not have him groping roughly at every private part. It was also a relief to not have to worry about being stopped again for drunk driving, or worse, crashing the GTO.

His hand rested on her knee, where it often did, even when driving. She was used to it, and it was entirely non-threatening. He cautiously moved his hand slightly higher on her leg, whether out of habit or testing her current limits. She didn't respond. His hand moved higher still onto her thigh, and still nothing. He did note that her other leg wasn't clamping down like a vise grip as it always had in the past. He tilted his head, covering the movement with a strange kissing maneuver, and glanced down to reconnoiter the area of operations. Her legs were spread, only slightly, but even that was most unusual. He summoned his courage and slipped his hand even further, pushing her skirt up until he could see her white panties out of the corner of his eye.

He had not even unbuttoned her blouse, much less copped a feel of her breasts, and he wasn't sure why he had dared venture so far up her thigh, and even less sure why she hadn't repelled his probe, as she always had before. He left his hand in place for a moment, considering his options. He broke off kissing briefly to gaze into her eyes. She smiled, put her fingers on his cheek, leaned forward and kissed him. His heart was pounding. So was hers. Something else was throbbing and he was certain she could hear it, feel it, or at least sense it. He saw the porch light flashing.

"Why aren't you pushing my hand away?" he asked.

She smiled. "I'm ready."

"Ready for what?" he asked cautiously.

She put her hand on his but didn't push it away from her thigh. He looked down at their hands. Never had his hand spent so much time pressed against her thigh, so far up, so close. She moved his hand, but not away. If he wiggled his fingers, they would touch what she had guarded tenaciously for years. This had to be a trap. The porch light flashed again. He tore his gaze, but not his hand, away from her thigh, and looked her in the eye. "Are you sure?"

"I'm sure."

"Right here? In front of your house?"

"No, silly. Tomorrow night. I want it to be special."

"It will be special."

"Do you love me?"

"You know I do."

"Say it."

"I love you."

"And I love you, but if I don't go in right now, I'll be grounded tomorrow night and you'll have to deal with that on your own."

She glanced down. She squeezed his hand and then placed her hand on his leg. Even through his Levi's he felt her fingers gently caressing his inner thigh, although they didn't quite reach what he had hoped was their intended target. His heart pounded as she pulled her hand away.

He flung open the door and turned to take her hand, but to save precious seconds she had already opened the other door and was sprinting toward the house. He caught up to her on the porch, opened the screen door and they clinched, bumping up against the door. She didn't care if her daddy heard it. At least he would know they were on the porch.

It may have been short, but the goodnight kiss was not sweet— it exploded with anticipatory passion. Bobby was so thrilled he didn't even grope her bottom, as he often did, but was surprised when she briefly grabbed his and pulled his hips close to her own. She finally broke away to go in, almost hitting him in the face with the screen door. He stood there long after the door closed, wondering if it had been real. Did she really say what he thought she said? Tomorrow would tell.

12

PLANNING FOR THE assignation took a serendipitous turn when Kevin agreed to fill in for one of the sack boys at the store Saturday. Although he had been very good about making himself scarce every evening, tonight was special, and Amy and Bobby needed as much alone time as possible.

While Amy and Sandra were busy doing girl things, Bobby insisted Kevin accompany him to the barbershop. Things had been going so well that Bobby assumed, or at least hoped, Howard was not going to slit his throat in the barber chair. Nevertheless, he wanted backup and Kevin was his man. Bobby had been dying to tell him what had happened last night, and what would happen tonight, but was overcome by a sudden, and unexpected wave of maturity. Or maybe he didn't want to jinx it. Either way, he held his tongue.

Bobby sat in the barber chair while Howard cut his hair. He was not bleeding profusely from the neck, although a straight razor sat menacingly on the counter within easy reach, so that was a good sign. Kevin sat in the row of chairs along the wall, along with several other men. Some read the newspaper, others talked, mostly politics, since football season was over, and nobody much cared about basketball.

"I seen 'em together, in that hippie's little Volkswagen bug, headed out the highway towards Lubbock," one of the men said. "No telling where they was going."

"The school board done lost their minds," another said. "That little girl don't look much older than sixteen."

"She looks like Marilyn Monroe, sashaying around town without no brassiere."

"How's she gonna handle those big-ole high school boys if they get out of line?"

"She graduated from college, so she has to be at least twenty-two," Bobby said.

"Don't matter. She's still a damned hippie."

"I heard she was at that Woodstock outfit."

"Nekkid, prob'ly."

Kevin smiled and lifted his eyebrows at Bobby as the gossip continued.

"Damned hippies."

"They didn't have no choice but to hire that Billingsley feller."

"He's a Viet Nam veteran," Kevin interjected. "Hundred and First Airborne."

"A lieutenant," Bobby added.

There was a "harrumph" or two.

"Well, it ain't right, I tell you. That little white girl traipsing off at night with a colored man."

"No telling what they was up to."

After Howard finished cutting his hair, Bobby stepped out of the chair and reached for his wallet.

"This one's on me," Howard said.

"Thanks," Bobby said.

"Be careful over there, son, and come home safe."

"Yes sir."

"Kevin, you're next," Howard said, whipping the cape to shake out the hair trimmings.

"Not me," Kevin said. "I'm going to let my hair grow down my back like a hippie." He looked around for the reaction. Several of the men laughed. "Besides, I need to get back to work."

"Are you working at the store?" Howard asked.

"I'm filling in for Eddie this afternoon. He has a hot date tonight."

"What about you, Bobby?" Howard asked. "Do you have a hot date tonight?"

"Uh," Bobby stammered, unsure how to answer. "We'll probably go to Lubbock for a nice dinner, and maybe a movie."

ALTHOUGH SHE HAD seen "art" films with Bobby at the Fine Arts Drive-In in Lubbock, and some fleeting, almost always female nudity, in mainstream movies at respectable theaters, Amy knew full well she was in uncharted territory. No male had seen her naked since she was a small child, not even her daddy, although she was sure Bobby must have caught an occasional glimpse when he had managed to work her bra loose, but it was always dark and her clothes were never actually off, just in disarray, so maybe not. With the recent exception of Kevin, and that was really nothing more than a fleeting glance before she covered her eyes, she had never seen a man naked. She was at once terrified and excited. She was about to become a woman. From what little she had gleaned from the movies, magazines, and girlfriends, especially Sandra, the act itself would be quite physical.

She was quite proud of the fact that it was planned, or at least scheduled, rather than just finally giving in during a random make-out session while parked beside a boxcar. This way she could enjoy the full effect of anticipation, and certainly had, for the past eighteen hours. She had agonized over what to wear—she didn't really have any sexy underwear, but at least she wasn't wearing granny panties. She had selected a bra with the least padding and the most lace, not that it mattered—there was no need to be seductive. She had offered herself up and he had accepted. Dress or blouse and skirt? She decided on a simple skirt and white blouse. She was not yet sure how things would proceed, foreplay-wise, whether they would be sitting or standing or lying down, and at what point in the procedure clothing would be removed, or who would do the removing. Dresses zipped up the back, depriving the male participant the opportunity to savor the undressing. A blouse could be unbuttoned slowly, hopefully not ripped off in the heat of passion, exposing her heaving breasts, covered at first by her lacy bra, and then bare. Nude. Naked. She shivered at the thought.

She already felt naked, emotionally anyway, as she stopped off at the barbershop to kiss her daddy. It wasn't something she normally did before a date when her daddy was at work, but this date was special, and she felt somehow compelled to share the moment with him, hoping he didn't sense something was afoot. Bobby thought it was not at all a good idea, but he was not about to do anything to cause Amy to change her mind, so he checked his tie in the rearview mirror, popped a mint into his mouth, went into the barbershop and shook hands with Howard, absolutely convinced that he knew what they were up to.

"Have you been drinking?" Howard asked.

"No sir!" Bobby replied.

"Do you have any alcohol in your car?"

"No sir! Tonight's all about Amy. Whatever she wants." He hoped that wasn't the wrong thing to say. "And she doesn't want me drinking."

"Good. You kids have a nice time."

Amy kissed him again and she and Bobby turned to go.

"And be careful," Howard said firmly.

Both Amy and Bobby, holding hands on the way out the door, closed their eyes and gritted their teeth. He knew. Daddies always knew.

Amy sat in the GTO at the Texaco as Joe Spalding filled the tank. She turned her head and shoulders, watching Bobby as he went around the front of the car and into the restroom. She waited nervously, hoping Joe wouldn't try to engage her in conversation. It was just two teenagers going on a date—he couldn't possibly know where they were really going.

Bobby put coins in the slot of the condom vending machine, shoved it in, and his prize dropped into the hopper. There was a standby condom in his wallet, but it seemed reasonable that there was some unspecified use-by date, especially when the thing had rubbed around in his hip pocket for months. He wanted a new one for tonight. He reached for the doorknob, thought better of it, dug in his pocket, produced the requisite coins, and purchased another. It wasn't like this was a maybe-maybe-not kind of thing, overcoming her defenses at the last minute before getting lucky and then rushing her home in time for curfew. This was a sure thing and they had at least two hours, so he wanted to be prepared.

Amy watched as Bobby went into the office to pay for the gas, and then her eyes followed him all the way back to the car.

"Did you get it?" Amy asked as Bobby plopped into the driver's seat and closed the door.

He nodded, not daring to tell her he got two.

Bobby pulled out of the Texaco onto the highway, gunning the engine so people would notice as he headed east.

"Are we going to Lubbock first?" Amy asked.

"No, but it has to look like we are. We can't just blast down Main Street and hope nobody notices."

Bobby turned off the highway shortly later and headed north on a dirt road.

"Are you okay?" Bobby asked as he wended his way around Preston.

Amy nodded and smiled, not wanting to admit that she was filled with apprehension. Her mouth was dry, and she tingled all over. She had made her decision and the time had come, or was fast approaching as the GTO raced along, headed west, kicking up a cloud of dust.

"HELLO!" Bobby called out as he stepped through the back door of the Frazier house, with Amy close behind, holding his hand. "Anyone home?" He flipped the light switch. "The coast is clear."

"It's cold," Amy said, rubbing her arms.

"They've been at the store all day. No reason to heat an empty house."

"Are you sure this is okay? It feels weird."

"You didn't want to do it in the car. We can't go to my house because my grandmother is there, and you didn't want to go to a motel."

"Did you tell Kevin?"

"You said you didn't want anybody to know, right?"

She nodded.

"Did you tell Sandra?"

She shook her head.

"Good," he said.

"What if they come home early?"

"It's Saturday," he said as they walked down the hallway, still holding hands. "They won't be home for at least two hours, probably longer."

Bobby flipped on the light as they stepped into Kevin's bedroom. Amy looked around the room. The duffel bag was still on the floor. Kevin hadn't finished unpacking.

Amy had always assumed her first time would be in the back seat of a car, like Sandra and a few others who had talked about it. It was almost always on the spur of the moment, in the heat of passion, rough, crude, over quickly, and anything but satisfying for the girl. Some clothing nearly always remained on. No one ever bothered to undress completely. Owing to the unplanned nature of the act, the blouse was usually unbuttoned but not removed, the bra unhooked or dislodged, often just pushed up around the neck. With that part of the task successfully accomplished, the boy would lift her skirt and tug at her panties until they came off. It was short work after that, and not at all romantic or even erotic.

By agreeing in advance to do it at an appointed time, and with the advantage of having a private place, and a bed, Amy's imagination had run wild. Bobby would slowly undress her like in the movies, and then take off his own clothes, while she stood there naked and watched.

She slipped out of Bobby's letter jacket, walked around to the other side of the bed and dropped the jacket onto a chair, unsure what to do next. As she turned, Bobby was already ripping off his shirt. So much for slowly undressing her.

Bobby had not bothered to turn up the furnace, so Amy decided that undressing herself and getting under the covers quickly would be the best course of action. Bobby stared as she unbuttoned her blouse. His pants came off concurrently with her skirt, but his eyes never left her. She dropped the blouse and skirt onto the chair and tried to cover herself with her hands for a moment. Bobby, and many other boys, had seen her in a swimsuit, even a bikini, so she wasn't really exposing anything that hadn't been seen before, and in public, but she felt exposed. She glanced down. The lacy bra was nearly see-through, her panties were hip huggers—both articles carefully selected for tonight. She finally lowered her hands, straightened up and looked him in the eye. His eyes were up and down her body trying to take it all in at once.

Whether from the cold or her current state of undress she had goose bumps, so she quickly turned and sat on the bed, unhooking her bra. She could feel him watching. She made a point of leaning to the side to drop her bra on the chair instead of tossing it, giving him a brief glimpse of her breast, which he much appreciated.

Barely lifting her hips off the bed, she slipped off her panties and tossed them onto the chair, providing even more skin on display, which Bobby happily took in. She lay back, stretched out on the bed, and pulled up the covers, all in one fluid motion, allowing him little more than a glimpse.

"Are you shy?" he asked.

"Yes, and cold."

"I'll warm you up."

She watched with interest, eyes widening, as he peeled off his Jockey shorts and then quickly slipped under the covers. They lay quietly for a moment, staring at the ceiling, both wondering what to do next.

"Are you going to turn out the light?" she asked.

"In a minute," he said. "I want to look first."

She instinctively covered her breasts with her hands as he pulled the covers down to her waist. She took a deep breath, smiled weakly, and pulled her hands away. She watched him looking.

"I've dreamed about this for a long time," he said.

"Me too," she said, suddenly and strangely at ease being naked with a boy.

"You have, really?"

"Well, maybe not as much as you have. I mean you're a boy and all, so you probably did a lot more than dream about it."

He grinned and nodded.

Her initial embarrassment had turned to anticipation and excitement that almost matched his. Well, almost. She wished he had lowered the sheet a bit more, and briefly thought of doing it herself, in order to have a better look. She continued to breathe rapidly, her chest rising and falling with each breath as he watched.

"I'm really nervous," she said.

"You aren't backing out, are you?"

"No, I'm not backing out."

Emboldened by success so far, Bobby pulled the covers back even more, below her waist. She flinched, her hands instinctively reaching out to cover herself, but then relaxed, hands returning to her sides.

After years of pushing his hands away from their intended target there it was, right in front of him, free for the taking, and all he did was look.

"Are you through looking?" she asked after a moment.

"Not really. I've waited a long time for this."

"Me too, but I'm really cold."

"Oh, yeah, sorry," he said, quickly pulling the covers up over her and rolling over to face her. She did the same, and hands suddenly found something to touch.

"Okay, this is weird," she said.

"What?" he asked, concerned.

"I've been in this exact same bed with two different naked boys in just one week."

"I hope you don't scream and run away this time."

"Then you'd better behave."

She kissed him and her hand did something it had never done before—it roamed across a boy's naked body.

"Are you ready," he asked.

"I'm ready."

"Are you sure?"

"I've never been more sure of anything," she said as she rolled over on her back, pushing away the covers.

Taking that as in invitation, he started to climb on. She held up her hands and stopped him.

"Wait," she said.

"What's wrong?" he asked, suddenly alarmed.

"There's no hurry." She put her hand on his cheek and kissed him, slowly, deeply, and then took his hand and placed it on her breast. "Take your time. Do it right. This has to last a long time."

13

WHEN AMY AWOKE Sunday morning, she could hear activity in the hallway, water running in the bathroom, pots and pans clanging in the kitchen. She glanced at the alarm clock, easy to see as sunshine peeked through the curtains. A sly smile crossed her face. She knew she needed to get out of bed, shower, and get ready for Sunday school, but she didn't want to wash away Bobby's scent, which was all over her. She wondered what he was thinking at this moment. Was her scent also on him? Probably so, she decided, hoping it would bring back memories of last night—not that he needed anything to jog his memory—it would certainly be on his mind for some time to come, as it would hers.

From reading what little was available in the library, movies, and first-hand accounts, true or not, of those who claimed to have done it, she assumed it would be rather dreadful, painful, and over quickly. She had anticipated lying submissively on her back and waiting for him to do it to her. Then he would be happy, and she would no longer be a virgin.

It had been nothing of the sort. Nature had taken its course and she quickly found herself an equal participant, which Bobby found somewhat surprising, though pleasantly so. Years of anticipation, on both their parts, had exploded simultaneously. It was exhilarating and she thought for a moment she would pass out. Bobby's face was red and sweat poured off them both although it was quite cold in the house. When he finally rolled off, she could see her chest glistening as it heaved.

She smiled; the entire experience replayed on her face. She caressed the pillow as if it were Bobby. She badly wanted to see him, to hold him, kiss him, talk with him. The telephone wouldn't be nearly private enough. Bobby hadn't been to Sunday school in years so her best opportunity was at church and surely he would be in attendance today. She could no longer hear water running, so she rolled out of bed and dashed across the hall into the bathroom. Emily was still in there, primping in front of the mirror. For a moment Amy wanted to tell her, confide in her, offer advice from her experience and newfound expertise, but the urge quickly passed. Emily ignored her presence, clearly not sensing the enormous change in her sister's life. A zit on her forehead was far more important.

The shower washed away Bobby's scent, but not the memories, now indelibly imprinted in Amy's consciousness. She looked down, searching for bruises, which she expected after all the bumping and grinding. The act itself had been far more physical than she had imagined, but there was no visible evidence. She stepped out of the shower and wrapped herself in a towel.

"Did you and Bobby break up?" Emily asked.

"Why in the world would you ask that?"

"You got home early last night and didn't make out in the car for a half hour like you usually do."

"You were spying on me?"

"I noticed."

Amy smirked. "Well, we definitely didn't break up."

Emily shrugged.

"Someday you'll have a boyfriend," Amy said.

"How do you know I don't have one already?" Emily said, peeling off her pajamas.

"I haven't seen one around here, or at school."

Emily stepped into the shower. "Maybe we sneak around, and nobody knows." She closed the shower curtain and turned on the water.

Amy shook her head and then stared into the mirror, searching for a sign, something that might give away her new status, if not as a woman, at least as a non-virgin. She looked the same. She smiled. Maybe no one else would know, other than Bobby, but she knew. The smile turned to a frown. Today was Bobby's last full day at home. She would not see him again for a year.

It had been difficult facing her daddy after her special date. She had often made out, French kissed, had even been pawed and groped by Bobby in the driveway just before kissing her daddy goodnight, but last night was decidedly different. Bobby's hands, and mouth, had been all over her naked body. He had been inside her. She had no desire to sit and chat with her daddy after all that, so she had kissed him quickly and said goodnight, but she now had to face him again at breakfast. She ran through her cover story one more time.

"What movie did you see?" Emily asked at breakfast, wasting no time trying to trap her sister.

"*Paint Your Wagon*," Amy answered immediately.

"I've been wanting to see that," Howard said. "Was it any good?"

"It was okay, kind of long, and there was a lot of singing."

"Who was in it?"

"Lee Marvin and Rowdy Yates."

Howard chuckled.

"At the drive-in?" Emily asked, looking up from her pancakes.

"Yes, at the XIT."

"I thought you went to Lubbock."

"We did, for dinner, and then we came back and saw a movie."

"Where did you eat?" Emily grinned; certain she had her now.

"At the Brookshire Inn."

"Where's that?"

"On Broadway. It's new." Amy turned to Howard. "You should take Mom there. It's really nice."

"What did you have?" Emily pressed on.

"Steak. It's a steakhouse."

Emily was good, but Amy had three years' experience on her. Sandra had been to the Brookshire Inn with her parents, so she filled Amy in on the details, including the menu. Amy and Bobby had seen the movie, or at least part of it, after their tryst. Like most teenagers on a date, Bobby parked in the very back row, and they made out while occasionally glancing up at the movie for later reference.

SUNDAY SCHOOL LESSONS were always tailored for the group in question. Amy was in the teenage class, both boys and girls, and she felt a tingling in the back of her neck when the lesson for the day was announced. Although it was couched in terms designed to avoid even the utterance of the word "sex," the lesson was about abstinence. Surely the Sunday school teacher had prepared the lesson in advance and could not possibly know what Amy had done last night. None of the other teenagers in class looked at her accusingly, so she just listened quietly as the teacher laid out all the reasons she should have waited.

There was an unwritten seating protocol at the First Baptist Church in Preston. Teenagers sat with their parents for the Sunday morning service but flocked to the "courting corner" at the back of the sanctuary for evening services. A Methodist or two was often spotted in the courting corner—a herald bearing the location of the after-church party, where there would be dancing, which was a sin for Baptists.

The Evans and Dalton families had sat together in church since Amy and Bobby started going steady. Amy craned her neck to see if they had arrived. She was certain they had, as Grandmother had already taken her seat at the organ, but Bobby was nowhere to be seen. He was in the foyer, shaking hands and receiving best wishes from other churchgoers. Amy grinned when she saw him, almost sprinting down the aisle ahead of his parents. He wanted badly to kiss her when he took his seat, and she wanted badly to be kissed, but it seemed somehow inappropriate in a place of worship. There was also much to say, but again, this was hardly the place, especially as Grandmother began playing the organ and the service got underway and Bobby slipped in and sat beside her.

Bobby and Amy sat quietly, holding hands, exchanging knowing looks, occasionally glancing around at the congregants, convinced that everyone present knew what they had done last night. Lightning had not yet smashed through the stained-glass window and struck her down, so maybe not.

Amy didn't really feel any different and was determined to not feel guilty—she had done nothing wrong. She did feel a twinge of guilt, not for what they had done, but for the deception, if not outright lies involved. She quickly dismissed those thoughts. It's not like she could have said, "Daddy, Bobby and I are going to have sex tonight. Don't wait up." She could have said it, but the outcome would not have been to her liking.

The benediction was barely over before Amy and Bobby raced down the aisle, hand in hand, for a few brief minutes of privacy while everyone milled around after services were over, "visiting," as they say in west Texas.

"Are you okay?" Bobby asked as they arrived at her family's car.

"I'm fine," she said.

"Do you feel any different?"

"No. Should I?"

He shrugged. "I don't know."

"I don't feel guilty, if that's what you mean."

"Good."

"But I am kind of sore," she said, ducking her head and covering her face.

"Sorry. I guess I got carried away."

A line had been crossed, and they both knew it. Things would never be the same. They hadn't just had sex spontaneously in the back seat, pulling away only enough clothing to provide access, but had made love, in bed, completely naked. He had taken his time. He had done it right.

"And I don't feel like I got pressured into doing something I shouldn't do," she added.

"I know I pushed you, a lot, for a long time, and I'm sorry."

"That's okay. It worked out fine."

"It did?"

"It did."

"Did you like it?"

"I liked it. I didn't think I would, not the first time anyway, but I did."

"Do you want to do it again?"

"Um, we're at church."

"Tonight."

"I thought it was family day with your parents and grandmother."

"They go to bed after the ten o'clock news. That would give us an hour and a half before your curfew."

She laughed. "Slam, bam, thank you ma'am. No, thanks. I'd rather just remember last night. I don't think it could get any better, definitely not a quickie in the back seat of your car."

"I guess you're right," he said, smiling and looking at her chest, which she immediately covered with both hands while turning her head to see if anyone was watching.

"Don't look!" she said, feigning embarrassment.

He smiled and continued to look. "I'm just reminiscing."

"Me too," she said, glancing down below his waist.

"Do you think anybody suspects anything?"

"Emily tried to trip me up at breakfast, but I remembered enough about the movie that I think Daddy bought it."

"I don't remember anything about the movie. All I remember is your boobs."

"Stop it!" she said, covering her face.

It had been a most unusual evening. While a couple would normally have dinner, see a movie, and then have sex, the order had been reversed last night to take advantage of the availability of Kevin's room. Sex first, then hot dogs and Cokes at the drive-in while watching the movie, along with hot and heavy making out, or "after" play, as Amy had dubbed it. After years of pushing away his hands in the GTO she allowed them free rein and even felt a twinge of guilt at how much she enjoyed it.

"I thought about calling this morning," he said, "but you only have one phone, and it would be hard to have a private conversation with everybody getting ready for church."

She nodded. "That's what I figured."

"Here they come," he said before quickly kissing her. It was more than brief, but not enough to offend churchgoers, all of whom knew he was leaving tomorrow morning for Viet Nam, having been announced, and prayed over, at the service just concluded. She turned to look. Both their families were approaching.

"I wish we could spend the day together," he said, "and the night."

"It's okay. I understand." She grinned and kissed him briefly on the lips. "Last night should hold you for a while."

He chuckled. They kissed again and then clung to each other as the families, and a throng of others, arrived.

Howard shook hands with Bobby. Vivian and the girls hugged Bobby and then stepped aside as churchgoers lined up to wish him well and tell him they would be praying for him. Amy stood beside him, arm in arm. Howard made no attempt to pry her away, although her mother and sisters were already in the car.

BOBBY ARRIVED AT ten-thirty-five, duly noted by Emily, who was still up. Howard turned off the television, picked up a book, and moved toward the hallway, suggesting they could use the living room to talk. It was all pro forma—he knew the last thing the two wanted was to sit in the living room while Emily was on patrol.

"I thought we'd grab a Coke at the Panther and make one last round, see a few friends," Bobby quickly said, with Amy nodding affirmatively.

"Don't be too late." Howard sat in his chair and opened his book. If there was ever a time he was prepared to waive Amy's curfew, this was it.

Less than an hour later, however, the headlights from Bobby's GTO lit up the drapes.

Bobby tried to kiss away Amy's tears but was unsuccessful. The kissing was deep, wet, passionate, and then turned soft, somber, melancholy, as the minutes ticked away.

At straight-up twelve the door opened, and Amy stepped in, head down, in tears. She walked over to her daddy's chair and kissed him. "Good night, Daddy."

He reached for her hand and pulled her back as she started down the hallway. "Are you okay, honey?"

"No, not right now, but I will be," she said, wiping tears.

She turned and sat in his lap, hugging him tightly. "I love you, Daddy."

"I love you more."

14

CLOTHING AND VARIOUS other items were spread out on the bed in Bobby's room, some spilling from an open duffel bag. Kevin sorted, folded, and inspected while Bobby piled on more. A pair of black, spit-shined Army low-quarter shoes sat on the floor.

"How was the big date Saturday night?" Kevin asked.

Bobby hesitated, wondering if Kevin suspected something. "It was great," Bobby said, fighting off the urge to spill the beans, describing the experience, and Amy's naked body, in intricate detail.

"Is she okay?"

"Yeah, I guess. It's been pretty hard on her for the last few days. Have you talked to her?" Surely Amy hadn't blurted out anything to Kevin, but he was taking no chances.

"Not since Friday. Is she going to the airport with us?"

"She wants to but doesn't think her daddy will let her."

"Are you sure your folks don't want to go? We can cover the store."

"No. We said our goodbyes this morning before they went to work."

"What about your grandmother?"

"Her too, but I'll hug her again before we leave."

Kevin looked up to see Bobby zipping a pair of khaki pants.

"What are you doing?"

"Zipping up my pants."

"It's winter. Why are you wearing khakis?"

"It's not winter over there, is it? Do they even have winter?"

"Not really. It can get a bit chilly at night in the central highlands during monsoon season. Wear your class A uniform from here to Oakland."

Kevin went to the closet and returned carrying two green uniforms on a hanger. He handed one to Bobby. "Wear this one."

"It's not that cold in California."

"That one's heavy wool. The Army is phasing them out. I'm surprised they even issued you one. You'll only wear it as far as Oakland. Then you'll turn it in. They'll put it in your records, and when you get back, they'll issue you another one of these." He held up the other uniform. "The new ones are lighter weight."

Kevin put the uniform back in the closet.

"I might need a heavy one when I get back. What if they send me to Alaska?"

"Not likely."

"What about Germany?"

"They aren't sending you to Germany."

"How do you know?"

"It's another overseas tour. There's no way you get two of those back-to-back except in wartime."

"It is wartime."

"World wartime. You'll probably end up at some shithole like Polk to do the rest of your time."

"Ugh. I hope I never see that dump again."

"I hear Fort Ord is nice. Maybe they'll send you there. There was a guy in my platoon at Tigerland who went through basic at Ford Ord. He said it was paradise compared to Polk, but all the Californians complained about how much it sucked."

"Where is Fort Ord?"

"On Monterey Bay, south of San Francisco."

"What about southern California?" Bobby asked as he changed uniforms. "I'll bet Amy would like that. She could come visit and see some movie stars."

"Not much Army in southern California. Plenty of Marines and Navy, though, down in San Diego."

Bobby shrugged.

"Don't worry about it," Kevin said. "You'll have what, eighteen months left when you get back?"

"I guess."

"It'll be over in no time."

"Yeah, while Amy's getting hit on by college boys."

"Occupational hazard. If she loves you, she'll wait for you."

Bobby nodded.

"Or do you plan on getting hitched before your hitch is up?" Kevin asked.

"We never really talked about getting married. It's just always kind of been expected, I guess, like everybody else going steady in high school. It's just what you do."

"Pack one pair of khakis," Kevin said, as he folded the khaki pants. "You might need them for R&R."

"Do you have to wear a uniform on R&R?"

"Depends on where you go. You might wear a uniform on the plane, but not while you're there. Some places you wear civilian clothes on the plane, depending on treaties or whatnot."

"Do I wear khakis on the trip over?"

"No. Jungle fatigues. They'll issue those at Oakland."

"I thought you couldn't wear fatigues on a plane."

"You can on that one. It's a military charter."

Kevin continued folding and packing as Bobby dressed. Bobby picked up his watch from the dresser and slipped it on his wrist.

"Put that away someplace dry, like an ammo box, as soon as you get there, and buy a cheap watch with a plastic band at the PX. That expansion band will tear up your arm in the heat and humidity."

Bobby looked at his watch and then reached for his wallet.

"Same with your wallet," Kevin said. "Get a plastic one with the clear pouches that seal. You don't want your pictures of Amy getting wet."

"Does it rain that much?"

"You have no idea. It can rain more in eight hours than it does here all year. You're pretty much wet the entire monsoon season, even if you're inside. Whatever you do, don't put two pictures of Amy face to face. They'll stick together and get ruined if you try to pull them apart."

"Did you get the pictures back?"

"Not yet, but I'll send them as soon as I do."

"Much obliged."

"I'll shoot some more along and send them to you."

"Great."

Kevin picked up a box of envelopes. "Leave these here."

"My grandmother gave me those."

"Then you'll have to take them. The flaps will get damp and seal the envelopes while they're still in the box. Use them up as soon as you can, and then get some self-stick ones at the PX." He tossed the box of envelopes on the bed and held up a pad of writing paper. "This is okay. You'll need this, and you'll use it up fast, so get more at the PX when you get there, or even at Oakland. The PX tends to run out of stuff, so get these whenever you see them, same with envelopes."

Bobby rifled through his wallet, tossing a couple of items. "What about my driver's license?"

"Take that with you. If you have to drive a jeep or a three-quarter-ton, which you probably will, show it to them and they'll issue you a government license."

Kevin picked up Bobby's keys from the dresser. "You definitely won't need these, so there's no reason to lug them around for a year."

"Will you take care of her while I'm gone?"

"Your car?"

"My girl."

"Of course I will."

"No, I mean take her out if she wants to go to a movie or something. She likes movies. And there's all the dances, and parties and stuff. It's her senior year, and she can't always tag along with Doug and Sandra."

"Sure, no problem. I like the kid too, you know."

"And if anything happens to me—you know what I mean."

"Stop talking shit."

"Promise me you'll be there for her."

"I'll be there. And I'll be at the airport a year from now, with Amy, when you drag your horny ass off that airplane."

They hugged.

Bobby picked up two sealed envelopes from the dresser and handed them to Kevin, who fanned them out and looked. One said "Amy" and the other said "Mom."

"You know what to do with them," Bobby said.

Kevin nodded and slipped the envelopes in his hip pocket.

"WHY CAN'T I GO to the airport?" Amy asked at breakfast.

"You've been with Bobby every day for a month," Howard said. "You aren't missing school to spend two more hours with him."

That was not what Amy wanted to hear. Emily and Lily both looked up, waiting for the fireworks, but none were launched. The doorbell rang instead. Amy sprinted to the door, where Bobby waited on the porch.

Amy could have defied her daddy and gone to the airport anyway, but that wasn't her—she was a good girl. Kevin drove the GTO, eyes on the road, avoiding looking at Amy, clinging to Bobby, fighting tears, as the minutes ticked away.

Saying goodbye five months ago when Bobby left for basic was just a warm-up. Amy had lived in fear this day was coming and now here it was. She knew that millions of women had been in this same place before, wives, girlfriends, mothers, sisters, daughters, and millions more would no doubt follow. Amy thought about her own parents, and Bobby's, and Kevin's, and Sandra's, and all the other men from Preston who had gone off to war, and the women they left behind. She was now one of those women. Suddenly high school and cheerleading and dating and going steady and making out seemed insignificant. This was serious. This was real life.

At the high school, Kevin leaned against Bobby's car, taking photographs as Amy clung to Bobby while friends said goodbye.

Doug shook hands with Bobby. "Keep your head down, man."

Sandra hugged Bobby, as much as possible with Amy still attached. "Bye, Bobby. Take care of yourself." She kissed him on the cheek.

The bell rang, cutting through Amy like a knife. Now in tears, she clung even more tightly to her man, not just another man going off to war, but *her* man. It had now come down not to weeks, or days, or even minutes, but seconds. Just hours ago, she was in a state of bliss, wondering why she had put it off for so long, looking forward to the next time, one year from today. But now there were only heartbeats left.

Doug took Sandra's hand and they walked toward the school, turning to look back and wave, but Bobby's face was buried in Amy's hair. He had held it in as long as possible, but he was now crying, tears running off his face as Amy bawled.

The bell rang again. Bobby and Amy kissed one last time, and then she ran away, determined not to look back. Bobby didn't want to look either, bowing his head and wiping tears.

"Shit, man," Bobby said, trying to compose himself. "I didn't think it would be *that* hard."

"Just keep thinking about the day you come home, and how happy she will be."

"It's a good thing you're the only one going to the airport with me."

"Why's that?"

"I couldn't handle Amy and my mom all at the same time."

"There it is."

"I'll drive. One last run in the goat, for old times' sake."

15

WIPING TEARS, AMY yanked open the heavy steel door and rushed into the high school. Stragglers scattered as she scurried past Principal Klein. She would normally have said "good morning," not because she cared if he had a good morning, but because she was a good person. She had bigger things on her mind this morning, so she ignored him.

"You're late, Miss Evans."

Principal Klein was a dour man. He was never known to smile, or to wear a suit or tie other than black. But for his disagreeable demeanor he might have been mistaken for an undertaker. He was also a small man with a receding hair line and a pot belly who tried to make up for his physical shortcomings by exercising his authority, real or imagined, on defenseless high school students.

Amy stopped, wiped tears, and stared him down, actually down—she was fully two inches taller than the little weasel. She was in no mood for a confrontation and knew from experience that no explanation, or even apology, would matter anyway, so she simply turned and walked away. He could give her detention if it made him feel like more of a man. At least girls didn't get licks. She had nowhere to go after school anyway. Her life was over.

The hallway was deserted as Amy swapped books from her locker. She slammed the door shut, the sharp sound reverberating off all the hard surfaces, tile floor, tile walls, tin ceiling, steel lockers. It was again unlike her, but today was a day like no other. She composed herself and headed for first period.

KEVIN KNEW HE WAS in for a wild ride, but he also knew exactly how Bobby felt, and he wasn't about to deny his best buddy a high-speed run to the Lubbock airport. Bobby turned up the radio and it blasted rock and roll as the GTO flew along the highway.

"Fuzz!" Kevin called out.

Bobby lifted his foot off the accelerator but didn't hit the brake. By the time they met the highway patrol car the GTO was just under seventy. Bobby smiled and waved and then punched it again, barely slowing down before careening onto a farm-to-market road at Shallowater. It allowed him to avoid the traffic, and police in Lubbock, but made the trip even more perilous. With the cotton harvest well underway they passed slow-moving farm equipment and cotton trailers on a two-lane blacktop.

Bobby had allowed plenty of time to get to the airport and then got there even earlier by driving like a bat out of hell. The wait was uncomfortable, but not nearly as much as it would have been with Amy there. All his most difficult goodbyes were behind him. The boys made small talk. Bobby asked more questions about what it would be like, and Kevin provided additional tips. Finally, a Continental Airlines DC-9, "The Proud Bird with the Golden Tail," taxied up to the terminal. The time had come.

Bobby posed at the fence with the DC-9 in the background as Kevin snapped a picture. They shook hands, hugged, and then Bobby sprinted across the tarmac to the waiting plane where a cute young stewardess, wearing a short skirt, stood waiting.

Kevin smiled, remembering his conversation with the clerk as they waited to board the Freedom Bird just a few weeks ago. Continental Airlines definitely had hotter stewardesses.

FOR THE REST of the day Amy went to class, walked the hallway, took books from her locker and put them back, just a normal school day, but there was nothing normal about it. While her friends chatted about the upcoming basketball season, boys, movies, clothes, and all the other gossip, Amy was in a daze. It was like a cherry bomb had gone off near her head—she could see people's mouths moving, somewhat blurry, but couldn't hear them speak, just a ringing in her ears. She had no idea what Cliff Billingsley was saying in history class as he slapped the map with a pointer. It was a map of Viet Nam, which just made Amy feel even worse.

Sandra suggested the Panther for lunch, but Amy just shrugged. She had spent many hours there, with Bobby's arm around her shoulder, or his hand on her leg. The cafeteria would be less painful, and maybe Miss Clara would have words of encouragement.

"How are you holding up?" Doug asked as Amy poked at her food in the cafeteria.

"Okay, I guess," Amy said, wondering why people kept asking her that.

"Hi, Amy," Logan said. "Did Bob leave yet?"

"Get lost, jerk," Sandra said.

The jerk took the hint and got lost, quickly spotting a cute freshman to pester.

Amy managed a small smile. "Thanks."

"If he gives you any trouble, I'll beat him up," Doug said.

"You and Kevin both."

The only good thing that happened that blue Monday was that

no note was delivered to class informing Amy that she had detention after school. Maybe the tiny tyrant had a heart after all. Or maybe he just forgot or became preoccupied with a more serious offender.

THE RETURN TRIP to Preston took Kevin somewhat longer. He drove into Lubbock to stock up on film for his camera. He had promised Bobby he would take more pictures of Amy, and he was nothing if not a man of his word. There was a larger selection, deeper stocks, and prices were cheaper at Gibson's Discount Center than at the drugstore in Preston, so he swung by and did some shopping.

After swapping cars at the Dalton House, Kevin drove home and dug through the duffel bag in his bedroom. He had been with Amy and Bobby nearly every day since he returned home, and unpacking hadn't been a priority. He had clothes in the closet and underwear and socks in the dresser drawers. There was nothing in the duffel bag necessary to his daily life, but it was underfoot and needed to be dealt with.

He pulled out a bundle of letters, tied with string, then another and another, stacking them in the crook of his arm. He opened dresser drawers until he found an empty one and offloaded the bundles. He plopped his Army personnel file on the dresser, and on top of that several green plastic folders and small boxes. He pulled two posters from a paperboard tube and spread them out on the bed, with a couple of pillows pressed into service to help take out the curl. He checked his watch. He started out the door, but stopped, picked up the folder with Amy's photograph, flipped it open and propped it up on the dresser.

AMY, CONVOYED BY Sandra and Doug, transited the corridor in front of the principal's office unmolested. Doug slammed the bar on the steel door with a bang, pushed it open, and Amy escaped without detention.

"What are you doing here?" Amy asked, surprised to see Kevin leaning against the hood of the Impala parked in front of the school.

"I got used to picking you up from school with Bobby."

"You don't have to keep doing it. I can get a ride."

"I just thought—"

"She can ride with me," Sandra said.

"Okay," Kevin said, sliding off the hood. He stepped around to the driver's side.

"Wait," Amy said, and then turned to Sandra. "I'll ride with Kevin, if that's okay."

"Fine with me."

"Bye," Amy said as Doug and Sandra walked away. She headed toward the passenger side of the car and Kevin bolted in her direction. She laughed. "You don't have to open the door for me."

By then Kevin was right behind her, reaching for the door as she stepped aside.

"But as long as you're here," she said, smiling.

Kevin opened the door and she sat down. She waited until he was in the driver's seat.

"I had a really hard day at school and coming out and not seeing Bobby, or you, would have made it even worse." She leaned over and kissed him on the cheek. "Thank you."

"You're welcome." He started the car. "Do you want to go straight home? I have a couple of errands to run."

"Do you think Bobby will call?"

"Probably not until tonight. He'll be really busy, standing in line from the time he gets there and then standing in line at the pay phones."

"Then I'm all yours."

KEVIN'S IMPALA WAS parked under the awning at the Panther, along with a few other cars, mostly occupied by teenagers. Amy took a sip from a paper cup and then looked around.

"It feels weird sitting over here."

"Over where?"

"I've been sitting over there for three years," she said, pointing at the middle of the seat.

"Oh, yeah, and getting your knees bruised by the stick shift."

"Yeah, and that."

"Bobby had to special order his GTO to get bench seats."

"He did?"

"It's hard to cop a feel in bucket seats," he said, extending his hand toward Amy's leg but stopping short of touching it.

"I'll let you give me a ride home, but don't be trying to cop a feel," she teased.

"Yes, ma'am."

"Where do you think he is right now?"

"Hard to say. He didn't have to report in until six, which would be eight our time, so he may be hanging out on the beach, picking up California girls."

"Uh-uh. It would be okay if he wanted to do some sightseeing, maybe at Fisherman's Wharf, or ride the cable cars, but no California girls. This Texas girl is the only one for him."

"Well, let's see," Kevin said, checking his watch. "His plane didn't leave Lubbock until about ten-thirty. He had to change planes in El Paso, stopover in Phoenix, change airlines in Los Angeles." He checked his watch. "He's probably just now getting into San Francisco."

"Then what?"

"If he checks in early, they will probably start processing him and maybe get on an earlier flight, which means he might be home a day early next year."

"Good. That's what he should do."

"It's not really up to him. They may just send him to the transient barracks and wait until tomorrow."

"What happens tomorrow?"

"He'll turn in some stuff like his winter uniform, the one he was

wearing this morning. They'll issue jungle fatigues and green underwear, which he'll hardly ever wear."

"Why not?"

"Moisture. The humidity over there is awful. They tell you when
you get there to not wear underwear. Guys do wear boxers like Ber-
muda shorts around the company area when they're off duty, or going
to the showers."

"Going to the showers?"

"Unless you're on a big base like Long Binh you have to take a
walk outside to get to the showers."

"Like an outhouse?"

"Yeah. They have those to, but they're separate from the showers."

"What's Long Binh?"

"It's a huge logistics base north of Saigon. There's probably fifty
thousand guys there. They have actual barracks, not tents or hooches,
and cafeterias, hamburger joints, a bowling alley, swimming pool, a
movie theater. I heard they even have a golf course."

"That doesn't sound too bad."

"It's good duty, if you can get it, but it's all luck of the draw. He
won't know where he's going until he gets over there."

Amy nodded, concerned.

"Look, Amy, he's in supply, not the infantry. Worst case he'll
probably end up on a big base camp, maybe not Long Binh, but not
out in the boonies. It'll be tough, but it's not like in the movies."

"It's not?"

"No. In the movies they're shooting and bombing and blowing
up stuff all the time. If war was really like that there wouldn't be
many wars. Nobody would show up or if they did, they wouldn't last
long. The movies cut out the boring parts. War is mostly the boring
parts, except when the shit hits the fan."

"Now you're scaring me."

"Bobby's a supply clerk. There's a reason they don't make war
movies about supply clerks."

"But you were in the infantry, right?"

"Cavalry, actually, but yeah, I was a grunt."

"And you made it back safe."

"Yeah. I did." He saw no reason to mention the wounds, the fear, the moments of stark terror.

"So, when he gets his jungle fatigues and stuff, then what? Go to the airport?"

"He'll take a bus to Travis Air Force Base and fly out of there."

"On an Air Force plane, like paratroopers?"

Kevin laughed. "You've seen too many war movies. He'll go on a regular airliner, chartered from Pan Am or Continental or somebody. I came back on Flying Tiger."

"Do they have stewardesses?"

"Oh, yeah," Kevin said, grinning. "In short skirts. When they bend over you can see their panties. And they bend over a lot."

"He'd better keep his eyes off some girl's panties."

"That's hard to do. They wear really short skirts," he said wistfully. "Sometimes guys in the window seat would ask a stewardess for help with his seat belt, or working the seatback, or whatever, to get her to bend over. Then the guy on the aisle would get an eyeful, and the guys across the aisle would get a good look." He grinned. "Really good."

"Guys are awful."

"Hey, we were horny. We just looked. We didn't touch. And I'm quite sure the stewardesses knew exactly what was going on."

"I guess it's okay for you to look. You're single."

He looked at her legs.

"At the stewardesses," she said with a grin, tugging at her skirt. "How long is the flight?"

"About eighteen hours, depending on the route and how many stops. They change crews at the stopover, so Bobby will get a new crop of stewardesses to ogle."

Amy rolled her eyes.

"Hopefully they'll be cute young ones," he said. "We had a few on the way over that must have been forty."

He leaned forward and started the car.

"You didn't really have any errands to run, did you?"

He shrugged. "I didn't want you to be alone today after school. We've had kind of a routine for the last week or so."

She smiled. "Thanks."

"But I do need to pick up a couple of things at the five-and-dime."

"Oh, good, me too."

As KEVIN SEARCHED through rows of merchandise, separated by glass dividers, he felt something on his arm. It was Amy. He looked up and smiled. He liked that she always stood close, even touching. She held up a small box of envelopes.

"I'm going to need a lot of these."

Kevin nodded.

"What are you looking for?" she asked.

"Thumbtacks." He held up a package.

"Thumbtacks?"

"To hang my figure studies on the wall."

"Do you really have naked pictures?"

"I was hoping you'd pose for me."

She squealed and raised her hands to cover her face, dropping the box of envelopes, spilling the contents. He knelt and gathered the envelopes, glancing up at her legs, only inches away, while she regained her composure.

"So that's a no on the nudes?"

"What do you think?"

He shrugged. She held open the box and he stuffed it with envelopes.

"I missed you," she said. "I'm glad you're back. You could always make me laugh."

———

AMY PAUSED FOR a moment in the living room, watching Lily play the piano. Like the children of so many other middle-class couples in the postwar years the Evans kids had taken piano after school. Emily hated it, preferring to climb trees and ride bikes with the boys, until puberty hit and then she suddenly wanted to do other things with boys. Amy dutifully sat through her lessons and learned something about music, at least enough to appreciate it, but in Grandmother's words, would be most likely to find fulfillment in other artistic endeavors, perhaps sketching. Lily, however, took to piano like a duck to water, not exactly a prodigy, but she improved almost daily and really seemed to enjoy it. Howard loved listening to her play.

"I'm home," Amy called out. She could hear her mother in the kitchen. Her mother may have answered, but the only sound Amy heard was the telephone ringing. She dumped her books onto the sofa and raced down the hallway.

Amy and Emily, in a rare moment of agreement, had lobbied for a second phone. They wanted two more, one for each of their rooms. They both knew this was like asking for a car, so they settled on one additional phone, preferably a private line, but an extension would be better than nothing. Since Amy was the eldest and had a steady boyfriend, said phone would be located in her room. Amy thought Emily had surrendered far too easily on this point, but she was thinking ahead. Amy was a senior and would soon vacate her room to get married or go off to college, and Emily would take it over, along with the new phone. Howard listened patiently, complimented the girls on their thoughtful, reasoned arguments, and' promptly rejected them all.

With longer legs, and unencumbered by a bedroom door, Amy beat Emily to the phone by a fraction of a second and snatched the receiver.

"Hello," Amy said expectantly, turning away from Emily, hugging the wall for privacy. Her face fell and she handed the receiver to Emily. "It's for you."

———

THE TELEPHONE HAD not rung again while Amy struggled through homework and false starts at a letter to Bobby. At dinner she sat with her chair pulled away from the table at an angle in order to save herself a valuable second or two when the call came.

"What do you think of the new teacher?" Howard asked.

"Which one?" Amy said.

"Miss Mills."

"I like her."

"So do the boys," Emily added.

"The boys?" Vivian asked.

"She's hot," Emily said.

"And young," Howard said.

"How old is she?" Vivian asked.

"Twenty-one," Amy said. "She skipped a grade in elementary school."

"How do you know this?"

"We talk. She's really nice."

"Is there anything going on that I should know about, or the school board?" Howard asked.

"Like what?" Amy said.

"With the boys."

"Oh, that. The senior boys hit on her all the time, but she just laughs and blows them off. She's not stupid."

"What about Mr. Billingsley?"

"The boys don't hit on him. I'm pretty sure he'd hit back, hard."

Emily snickered. Amy glanced at Lily. Her little joke obviously went over Lily's head.

"He was in Viet Nam," Amy said. "Kevin said he was a grunt."

"What's a grunt?" Lily asked.

"He was in the infantry, like Daddy and Kevin."

"Mr. Billingsley and Miss Mills," Howard said.

"Oh, you mean are they going out?" Amy said.

Emily snickered again.

"Yes," Howard said.

"I don't know," Amy said, making eye contact with her daddy. "It's really none of my business, is it?"

THE EVANS HOUSE was dark, the silence suddenly shattered by the phone ringing. Amy flew out of bed and answered it. Emily didn't bother—who would be calling her this time of night?

Howard, rightfully concerned, stepped into the hallway as Amy cradled the phone. He cringed—she was wearing panties and a cropped T-shirt with PHS FOOTBALL stenciled on the chest, leaving little to the imagination.

"Who is it?" Howard asked.

"It's Bobby."

"It's after midnight."

"Bobby says 'hi,' and it's only ten out there."

"Well, don't stay up talking too long." He knew that Bobby could only have so many quarters in his pocket, so the long-distance call would be self-limiting. "And put on some pajamas."

He turned away and cringed when he heard Amy say, "Panties and your football T-shirt," in answer to Bobby's obvious question.

Howard shook his head and went back to bed.

16

KEVIN STARTED WORKING a regular part-time schedule at the grocery store after Bobby left, and was at work on Tuesday, double-stamp day, so Amy rode home with Sandra, and stopped off at the store. The girls quickly cornered Kevin.

"Did Bobby call?" Amy asked.

"Yes," Kevin said.

"When?"

"Couple of hours ago. He was about to get on the bus to Travis."

"Do you think he'll call me from there?"

"I doubt it. The bus pulls right up on the tarmac and then it's load and go. He's probably already in the air."

"He promised me he'd call before he left."

"He did," Kevin said quietly. "He said he called the school first, but Colonel Klink refused to get you out of class."

Disappointment turned to rage. Amy started shaking.

"That asshole," Sandra said, saving Amy from having to speak words she rarely used.

"How could he be so mean?" Amy asked, but already knew the answer.

Students called him Colonel Klink behind his back. While millions served overseas, including many of the students' own fathers, Principal Klein had spent the entire war guarding German prisoners at Roswell, perfect training for a high school principal.

"Sorry," Kevin said. "He tried."

"I need to go lie down."

Kevin watched as the girls left the store, and then turned to see Maggie pushing her grocery cart up to the cash register. Her jacket was draped over the handle of the cart, which was just fine with Kevin because her blouse was almost see-through, if you looked hard enough. It was just a plain white blouse, but he had stared through plenty of those back in the day. Having come directly from school, she was wearing a bra, unlike their previous encounter.

Kevin sacked her groceries as his mother checked. Fortunately, Maggie had two sacks of groceries. He would have gladly carried one small bag, but that might look awkward, except for little old ladies, which she wasn't.

"Miss Mills, right?" Kevin asked as he followed her to her car.

"Maggie. Do I know you?"

"We met last week at the drugstore."

"At the drugstore?"

"You were there with—"

"The black guy?"

"The lieutenant. Cliff. I couldn't think of his name."

"You were with Amy Evans."

"Yes."

"I thought you went to Viet Nam."

"That's Bobby. I'm the other one."

"Amy keeps a boy on standby? I'm impressed."

Kevin smiled. "We're just friends. Bobby's her boyfriend."

"Ah, yes. You're the nude photographer."

"I usually wear clothes when I'm taking photographs."

"Funny."

He put the groceries in her car, a Volkswagen.

"Does this thing get good gas mileage?"

"I have no idea. My daddy pays the credit card bill."

He smiled and waited for her to get into the car, but she didn't.

"What do young people do for fun in this town, go down to the crick and howl at the moon?"

"There ain't no crick. In these here parts kids mostly just cruise the drag, sit on the dock at the icehouse, grab a burger at the Panther. Not sure what the old folks do."

"The Panther is the hamburger joint on the highway, right?"

"Yeah. The burgers are better across the street at the Hi-Way Café but most of the kids hang out at the Panther. Then there's the picture show on the square, or the drive-in south of the highway."

"Yeah, I saw that. Funny name for a drive-in, XIT."

"It's named after the XIT Ranch. You never heard of it?"

"Can't say that I have. I'm a Dallas girl, Highland Park, actually."

"It used to be the biggest ranch in the world. Covered all or some of ten counties in Texas, including the one you're standing in."

"Oh, okay. I get it, XIT, ten in Texas. They should have named it TIT."

"Probably couldn't put that on a sign. And they don't really show any TIT at the XIT. You have to go to Lubbock if you want to see art films."

"Sounds like a blast. Maybe we should hang out sometime."

"You want to hang out with me?"

"There don't seem to be many men my age around here, single or otherwise."

"From what I hear you could have your pick of the senior class."

She laughed and shook her head.

"It's a small town," he said.

"I'm into men, not boys."

He held the door while she got in her car, his gaze immediately shifting to her legs. "Aren't you going out with the lieutenant?"

"Cliff? No way."

"Not your type?"

"He's engaged. His fiancée is a senior at Texas Southern."

"While the cat's away."

"Huh?"

"Word is you two leave town together a lot."

She laughed. "We both take a night class at Tech, so we carpool."

"Ah," Kevin said, nodding his head.

"Don't nark on us. The locals think we're dating."

"I've heard the gossip."

"I'm not dating anyone, actually."

"Maybe I'll see you down at the crick."

"Maybe," she said, closing the door.

There was a spring in Kevin's step as he returned to the store.

As the Continental Airlines Boeing 707 taxied across the tarmac at Bien Hoa Air Base all heads were turned, all eyes staring out the windows. For almost all it was their first time in a war zone, and it was already a bit surreal. Brightly painted commercial airliners shared the runway with fighter jets, modern C-7, C-123, C-130 transports along with C-47s left over from World War II, and all manner of other aircraft, including helicopters. Fighter jets roared off the runway, the noise deafening, even inside a sealed airliner. While airlines were under increasing pressure from cities to abate the noise of their jet engines, warplanes were exempt, especially in a war zone.

Three things hit Bobby simultaneously as he stepped off the airliner onto the boarding stairs: the sunshine, heat, and humidity, all quite the opposite of the chilly climate-controlled cabin he had enjoyed for the past sixteen hours.

Bobby had been following in Kevin's footsteps for years and he now wished he had asked more questions. It did not really matter of course, there was a well-oiled procedure in place and all he had to do was stand in line and wait. One bit of advice from Kevin quickly paid off. Finding your own duffel bag in a pile of 250 identical bags stacked like cordwood was a lot easier if you painted your initials and/or a brightly colored blob on the bottom. Unfortunately, that advice had been shared widely and there was a lot of paint on the pile.

Dragging his duffel bag, Bobby stood in line and waited. He glanced up at a large clock on the wall. Another tip from Kevin: the time difference between Viet Nam and Preston was 13 hours, so just swap AM and PM and you're close, depending on Daylight Saving Time. It was nighttime in Preston and Amy was in bed. He smiled, wishing he had a picture of her that way.

AMY SAT ACROSS from Sandra and Doug in a booth at the Hi-Way Café, sipping drinks. She looked up and saw Kevin coming through the door. She scooted over and he plopped down beside her.

"Well?" Amy asked excitedly.

"Well what?" Kevin teased.

"Where are they?"

Kevin dug into the large pockets of his Army field jacket and produced several envelopes of pictures. Amy, Sandra and Doug all grabbed an envelope and dug in.

"These are good," Amy said.

"Let me see," Sandra said, picking up Amy's discards.

"Try to keep them in the right envelope," Kevin said.

Doug grabbed one of Amy's photos.

"Never mind," Kevin said. He had already marked the roll and frame numbers on the back of all the prints. It was impossible to keep prints in order once anyone other than the photographer touched them.

"Where did you learn to take pictures like this?" Sandra asked.

"He was on the yearbook staff, when we were freshmen, remember?" Amy said.

"Oh, yeah," Sandra said. "He took a lot of pictures of the cheer-leaders."

"You ladies were a lot cuter than the football players," Kevin said.

"And had better legs," Doug added.

"I read a lot of photography magazines and books while I was in the Army," Kevin said. "I didn't get to practice much on cute girls, though."

"I like this one of me and Bobby," Amy said.

"There sure are a lot of just you," Sandra said.

Kevin froze.

"Wasn't that the point?" Doug asked.

"What point?" Sandra said.

"Guys want to put pictures of their girlfriends on their lockers," Doug said and then turned to Kevin. "Do they have lockers over there?"

Kevin relaxed. "More or less. Made from ammo boxes. The remfs probably have the real thing, and beds."

"What's a remf?" Amy asked.

"R-E-M-F," Kevin said. "Rear echelon . . . people."

Doug laughed.

"Is Bobby a remf?" Amy asked.

"Yeah," Kevin said, "probably, depending on where he gets assigned."

Doug picked up a photo of Amy from the expanding pile. "Wow. You look hot."

Sandra elbowed him. Amy smiled.

"Well, she does," Doug said.

Kevin looked at the photo and nodded. "Definitely hot."

Amy lowered her head, embarrassed.

Doug checked his watch. "Come on, babe. We'd better go if we want to make the movie on time." He stood.

"Amy, are you coming?" Sandra asked as she slid over.

"No, I think I'll stay here and go through the rest of the pictures. Kevin can give me a ride home." Amy turned to Kevin. "If that's okay."

"Of course it's okay," Kevin said.

Sandra hesitated, and then followed Doug. She looked back as Doug held the door for her. Kevin did not bother to move to the other side of the booth, remaining shoulder to shoulder with Amy. He waited patiently, occasionally commenting, as Amy carefully studied every picture, some multiple times, and made little piles of her favorites. He wished he had moved across the booth so he could see her face better without turning his head, looking like he was staring, but he could feel her warmth against him. If he moved now, it would look weird. Besides, it was easier for them both to look at the same picture this way. She would hold one up between them, tilt her head, look up at him and smile. Sometimes she would nudge him playfully. A traveler stopping in off the highway might easily have mistaken them for a young couple in love.

She gasped. "Wow! That's me?"

"That's you. Pretty good huh?"

"I look like a pinup girl."

"That's the idea. We should shoot some more, make them look like a real pinup girl."

She threw back her shoulders, stuck out her chest, lowered her chin, and looked at him. "Like this?"

"Like that, but with some cleavage."

She glanced around, saw no one looking, and pulled her blouse open slightly, not really exposing much, but the effect was the same. He smiled and nodded as she quickly closed her blouse and covered it with her hand.

17

AS BOBBY HAD DOZED across the Pacific, Teletype machines in Viet Nam were clattering, pumping out names and numbers of all aboard. By the time he arrived in-country he had already been matched with a vacant slot for a 92Y, unit supply specialist, in the 229th Assault Helicopter Battalion, First Cavalry Division (Airmobile). It was a short bus ride to the First Cavalry Division's rear base camp at Bien Hoa. There he would spend a few days at the First Team Academy, or FTA, pun probably intended, where everyone assigned to the division, regardless of rank or job description, confirmed their familiarity with the M-16, rappelled off a tower, warned to not walk into helicopter rotors, and were flooded with information about their new division. One of their first duties at FTA was to fill in the blanks on a standard press release which would be sent to their hometown newspaper. Everyone was provided with their new mailing address and instructed to write home immediately, today, right now.

———

AMY WROTE TO Bobby every day, but kept the letters in her school notebook, waiting until she had his address. She wrote on notebook paper anyway, so her notebook was as good a place as any to keep them, far from Emily's prying eyes. For several days after Bobby left, she went straight from school to the barbershop.

"Did you pick up the mail?"

"I always pick up the mail," Howard said calmly.

Amy looked around, searching near the cash register. Bills. She turned to Howard, who picked up an airmail envelope from the counter behind him and held it up while his customer waited. Amy lunged for it, pausing only a moment to look at the envelope. She ripped it open as she backed up and sat in a chair, thankfully empty as she hadn't bothered to look first. She read rapidly, oblivious to all around.

A farmer, wearing overalls and a cap that said PRESTON CO-OP GIN was seated right beside her. He watched her, but didn't try to read the letter, which he couldn't have anyway without his reading glasses.

"That from Bobby?"

Amy nodded but didn't look up.

The farmer turned to Howard. "Remember when we were young and at war and writing to our sweethearts?"

"I remember it well," Howard said.

Sandra stepped into the shop. Heads turned. They were accustomed to Amy and her sisters coming in occasionally, along with their mother, but the barbershop, any barbershop, was a place rarely visited by females of any age.

"Are you coming?" Sandra asked.

"Leave her alone," the farmer said gruffly. "She's reading a letter from her beau."

Sandra waited patiently while Amy finished her letter and then followed her as she ran to the car.

———————

AMY BURST INTO the grocery store, jubilantly waving her letter above her head. She rushed up to Kevin, who was sacking groceries, and almost knocked him over.

"Look!" Amy said. "APO 96490, same as yours."

"Yeah," Kevin said. "He's in the First Cav."

"Did you get a letter?"

"No, but his mom did."

Amy pointed at the return address and read, "Two-two-nine A-H-B. What's that?"

"Two hundred twenty-ninth Assault Helicopter Battalion," he said.

"What does that mean?"

"They fly grunts on combat assaults. I flew with them a lot."

"I thought Bobby was a supply clerk."

"He is. But everybody needs supplies. He'll probably be on a base camp, Phuoc Vinh, maybe Tay Ninh."

"So that's good, right?"

"That's good. It's not as good as Long Binh, but the First Cav is a good outfit with choppers out the ass. Plenty of firepower. Nobody messes with the Cav and lives to tell about it."

"I have to run to the post office and mail Bobby's letters. Sandra's waiting in the car. Do you need to write down his address?"

"I already got it from his mom."

"Okay, good."

"I should have the last roll of pictures back tomorrow, the ones I shot the day Bobby left. I'll pick you up tomorrow after school."

She nodded vigorously.

WHILE KEVIN HAD rarely slept under a roof, or even a tent, during his time in Viet Nam, Bobby was somewhat relieved to find he would be sleeping on an olive drab air mattress atop an olive drab canvas and wood cot in a hooch made of wood and screen wire topped by the same corrugated tin so familiar on farms across west Texas. The hooch was built on a bare concrete floor and surrounded by sandbags stacked about four feet high. To someone lying on a cot this offered some degree of protection from a mortar burst just outside the hooch. It was an entirely different story if a round came through the tin roof.

Bobby's few square feet included a dresser made of ammo boxes, left over when the previous occupant decamped. Turnover was constant. One item that had not been left behind was an electric fan. That had been sold and if Bobby wanted one, he would have to buy it, preferably from someone leaving, as the PX rarely had them in stock. A generator provided electricity for lights, radios, etc., but the Army did not want to encourage any extra usage. He stowed his few things into the dresser, opened a folder with a photo of Amy, and positioned it where he could see it from his cot. His AO, or area of operations, was like every other one in the hooch or in-country for that matter. It was not as neat, sterile, or uniform as what he had in basic or advanced training, but this was war.

AMY FOLLOWED KEVIN into his bedroom. He switched on the light, and she looked around. Without taking his eyes off her he backed up to the dresser and closed the folder with her picture. There had been some changes since she had last visited. She stepped up to a small poster on the wall. It was a black-and-white photo of an attractive young woman, wearing apparently nothing more than a T-shirt, singing into a microphone.

Amy pointed at the thumbtacks and smiled. "Are these your figure studies?"

"Yeah," Kevin said, smiling.

Amy leaned in for a closer look. "Is that Ann-Margret?"

"Yes."

"I really liked her in *Viva Las Vegas*."

"I really liked her in Long Binh."

"Long Binh?"

"She was on a USO tour with Bob Hope. We had just come in out of the bush and had a couple of days off, so we hopped a chopper to Long Binh."

Amy turned her attention to a larger poster, with the big yellow and black insignia of the First Cavalry Division and the inscription: "Yea though I walk through the valley of the shadow of death I will fear no evil, for I am the evilest son-of-a-bitch in the valley."

Next to the poster was a photo of an infantryman in jungle fatigues. Printed by hand on the band of his helmet was: IF YOU AIN'T CAV, YOU AIN'T SHIT.

"Interesting," Amy said, and then spun around, tripping over the duffel bag on the floor, spilling its contents. She bent over and picked up a *Playboy* magazine. "Research for your figure studies?" she asked coyly.

He smiled. "Yeah."

She flipped through the pages, gasping and covering her mouth, but continuing to look. She rotated the magazine and flipped open the gatefold, eyes widening.

"Doesn't leave much to the imagination, does it?" She closed the magazine.

He grinned and shook his head.

She bent over and placed the magazine on the duffel bag. "Okay, where are the pictures?"

He picked up an envelope from the dresser and handed it to her. She grabbed it, sat on the bed, and pulled out the pictures. He sat beside her on the bed as she looked at a photo of her and Bobby taken the day he left. They clung tightly together and were both in tears.

"I wasn't sure whether I should have even shot that one," Kevin said. "I felt like an intruder in a very private moment."

"I love it." She hugged him and then kissed him on the cheek. "I'm so glad you took it."

She looked through the photos again and then put them on the dresser. She picked up a small box. "What's this?"

"It's nothing."

She opened the box. "Oh, look. You got a gold star."

"Bronze, actually."

"What does the little 'V' mean?"

"Peace, brother." He made a peace sign with his fingers.

"Sister." She put down the box, picked up another and opened it. "Ooh, this one's pretty." She held it up. "It's a little heart."

Kevin laughed. "That's the easiest one to get."

"How do you get it?"

"All you have to do is get shot."

"You got shot?" She was shocked.

"Shot, blown up."

"You never said anything in your letters."

"Dear Amy, glad you had a good time at the party. It's been really hot over here. Oh, by the way, I got shot. Love, Kevin."

"Does your mom know?"

"No."

"Doesn't the Army send a telegram or something?"

"If you get killed or badly wounded, yeah, but there's a form you fill out and you can tell them to not notify your parents, or wife or whoever if you're only lightly wounded. That way your mom won't freak out. If you're shot up really bad, they notify them anyway, as long as they're on your list."

"What list?"

"You give the Army a list of who gets notified if you get killed or wounded or go missing. There's a form for that, and everything else, like what kind of work you want to do. I put photographer. And where you want to be stationed. Hawaii, of course."

"Of course. So you can take pictures of beach bunnies in bikinis."

"There it is."

Her attention turned to a bundle of letters on the dresser. She stood and picked up a bundle. "You kept my letters?"

"I'm sentimental."

"That's so sweet."

While she was distracted by the letters, he opened a dresser drawer and scraped a picture folder into it.

"What's that?" she asked.

"Nothing," he said, reaching for an envelope. "Here's some pictures from Viet Nam. Some of them are from the two-two-nine."

He handed her the envelope and she started looking through the pictures, mostly helicopters, but some soldiers. She held up one of Kevin, in jungle fatigues and a steel helmet, holding an M-60 machine gun.

"Is that you?"

"That's me."

"You look mean."

"I was mean."

She handed him the photos and leaned forward. "I want to see what you're hiding."

He reached out to stop her, but she quickly opened the dresser drawer and picked up the folder.

"It's dirty," she said.

"I carried it in my pocket. It got kind of beat up, and wet."

She opened the folder and smiled. "You carried a picture of me the whole time you were there?"

Kevin nodded. "Most guys carry a picture of their wife or girlfriend. Kathy and I had already broken up, so I just used yours."

"I was your fake girlfriend?"

"Yeah. Sorry I cheated on you in Bangkok."

Amy laughed and looked at the photo again. "You took this. Freshman year. I was fourteen."

Kevin nodded.

"Your buddies probably thought you were a cradle robber," she said.

"It's a really nice picture of you."

"I sent you a school picture from junior year."

"This one's better."

"Do you think Bobby will carry my picture with him?"

"Of course. A lot of guys had short-timer calendars."

"What's that?"

"It's a calendar where you mark off the days until you come home. There's a different picture of their girlfriend for each month. Or wife. Some of them were pretty risqué."

"Did you have one?"

"No girlfriend, remember?"

"And you sure didn't have any dirty pictures of your fake girl-friend."

He smiled and nodded. She put down the picture and they sat in silence for a moment.

"Do you want to go to a movie?" he asked.

"Right now?"

"No, later, when we can find time, with school and cheerleading and work and everything."

"You mean like a date?"

"No, just a movie."

"Okay, as long as it's not a war movie, or dirty."

He smiled. "You pick."

18

AMY HAD QUICKLY fallen into a routine. She rode to school most days with Sandra, stopping off at the post office to mail a letter to Bobby. She worked on the next letter whenever she could during the day in case she had a basketball game or something else to do at night. Kevin picked her up on his days off from the store, otherwise she rode with Sandra. Amy's first stop after school was the barbershop, where she would dash in to check the mail. Howard rather enjoyed that part of his day, especially when Amy had a letter, which wasn't every day, although some days there were two. She tried to concentrate on school, but it was becoming more difficult, not being able to look forward to Bobby picking her up. She flipped to the back of her notebook often, even when she should have been paying attention in class, to write another paragraph or two to Bobby.

An open date was finally selected, and Amy went to the movies with Kevin. He had offered to drive to Lubbock so she could have a larger selection, but with time constraints for them both, she picked one playing at the Llano Theater on the square. It was a school night, so they went to the early screening of *The Sterile Cuckoo*.

She had always held hands with Bobby during movies, along with occasional light smooching, or serious making out at the drive-in, especially if the movie was boring, but Kevin made no move to hold her hand and certainly didn't put his hand on her leg, which jibed with his insistence that this was not really a date.

He noticed that she leaned just enough toward him so that their arms made contact, but not so much that it was obvious. She would occasionally gasp and instinctively place her hand on his, which he enjoyed very much, or on his leg, which he enjoyed even more, but caused him to immediately begin debating in his head over the meaning of the gesture. He finally decided that she was merely surprised, even shocked at the movie, which was unusually mature for this theater. He knew from Bobby that she had seen even more explicit fare at the Fine Arts Drive-In in Lubbock. Unfortunately for Bobby, she would break away from making out and push him away so she could concentrate on the movie, fascinated by the sex or nude scenes, heady stuff in those days for a teenage girl from a small town in west Texas.

"Wow," Kevin said as they left the theater. "I thought it was going to be a comedy."

"Me too," Amy said, as she took Kevin's hand out of habit, before remembering it was not Bobby's. She thought of letting it go, but no excuse came to mind, and she didn't want to seem rude. It seemed quite natural, even comfortable. She had often seen teenagers holding hands in similar situations, even if they weren't going steady.

"I'm kind of surprised it was playing in Preston," he said.

"I guess they thought it was a comedy too."

"Did you like it?"

"Yes, I did."

Neither of them noticed that Logan had followed them out of the theater as they walked to Kevin's car, hand in hand. He watched as Kevin opened the passenger door for her.

Amy didn't want to stay out too late—she had a letter to finish—

but she wasn't ready to go home just yet, so they made a stop at the Panther. There were only a few people there, and even fewer teenagers, which Kevin appreciated—he didn't want people to think he was trying to steal Bobby's girl.

There was no one at the icehouse, nor were there many cars on the drag, so they just made a couple of rounds, and he took her home. Kevin had been on enough dates to recognize an uncomfortable silence, but he sensed there was something more as they sat in front of Amy's house. The silence between them was never uncomfortable. Neither of them felt any urge to jabber just to replace the silence, and he liked that about her. Tonight was different though. She seemed distant.

"Are you okay?" he asked.

"Oh, sorry. I guess I'm not a very good date."

"You're a great date. You just seem—"

"Stuck up?" she said with a slight grin. She was back.

He laughed. "No, that's not it at all. Distracted maybe."

She nodded. "Sorry. I was just thinking about Bobby."

"That's okay."

"And other things," she said. He waited for her to elaborate, but she didn't, so he let it go.

"Did Bobby ask you to look after me while he's gone?"

"Yeah."

"I don't want to take up all your time."

"I don't mind. Really. And I have plenty of time."

"Did he ask you to take me out?"

"He said you like movies."

"You don't have to do that."

"That's okay. I like movies too."

"It's kind of weird."

"What is?"

"I've never been on a date with anyone besides Bobby."

"You haven't?"

"No. In seventh grade Billy Rodman tried to feel me up at a party and then asked me if I wanted to be his girlfriend, but nobody ever asked me out on a date before Bobby."

"When you were in eighth grade."

"You remember?"

"I told him to ask you."

"You did?" She was surprised.

"Yeah. He had his eye on you for a long time."

"He did? He never said anything."

"He watched you cheering at the junior-high games."

"I remember him coming to some of the games."

"He was there to watch you, not the game."

"You were there too."

"We both thought you were hot, a lot hotter than the other junior high cheerleaders."

"I barely had any boobs in eighth grade."

"But you had great legs. Still do."

She tugged at her skirt. "You should go out with other girls, on actual dates."

He whipped his head back and forth. "What other girls? This town's not exactly a target-rich environment."

She laughed. "True, except for the teenyboppers, and we both know how that went."

"Joe Spalding said Sharon will be home for Christmas, so I'll add her to my list, but she never seemed to like me very much."

"She didn't?"

"Not that I could tell. We went out once, when we were juniors, but it didn't go very well. We just sat there at the Panther not knowing what to say. When I took her home she seemed relieved. I didn't know whether to try to kiss her goodnight or just cut and run."

"Well, her daddy seems to like you."

"Yeah."

"So does Nikki."

"If some of Nikki would just rub off on Sharon, I'd be in like Flynn."

"Maybe you should go to Lubbock," she said. "I hear Tech girls are easy."

"Who do you hear that from?"

"High school boys who struck out with Tech girls."

"I never had much luck with the ladies anyway. I guess I'm not a very good catch."

"You know if I wasn't with Bobby, I'd be all over you."

"Yeah, right."

"Well, if you meet someone, don't pass it up to babysit me."

"I'll keep that in mind."

"After all that time in Viet Nam aren't you just a little bit—"

"Horny?"

"Yeah, that. Bobby thought about sex all the time. All boys do, don't they?"

He nodded and smiled. "Pretty much. We're wired that way. Don't girls think about it?"

"Not all the time." She grinned. "But we do think about it." She looked at her house. "I'd better go in before Daddy starts flashing the porch light."

Kevin checked his watch. "It's still early."

"We've been out here a long time."

"It's not like we're making out."

"Yeah. And even if we were, we would be doing it someplace else, not in front of my house." She shrugged. "Daddies are just like that, I guess. But I do need to go in. I want to finish a letter to Bobby. Should I tell him we went to the movies?"

"Of course. If he finds out from somebody else, he might think we're sneaking around."

She nodded.

"You don't have to walk me to the door," she said as Kevin walked her to the door.

"Sure I do."

At the door she put her arms around his neck and hugged him. "I had a nice time."

"Me too."

She backed away and their eyes locked. She leaned forward and kissed him briefly on the lips. "Good night," she said as she turned and opened the door.

"Good night," he said, and then waited until she was in the house before stepping off the porch.

19

THERE WERE ONLY a few cars parked on the square and most of those were near the Llano Theater. The late show had let out and a handful of people filed out of the theater as Kevin sat at the stop sign after taking Amy home. He spotted Maggie walking. She wore tight jeans and a leather jacket. He turned the corner, pulled up alongside, and rolled down the window.

"You found the picture show."

"Yeah. Big fun."

"You want to get a cup of coffee?"

She stepped over to his car, put her hands on the door and leaned in.

"I'd rather have a beer."

"Good luck with that in this town."

"Not a problem. I have beer at my place."

"Where's your car?"

"At the hotel."

"The hotel?"

"That's where I live."

The hotel on the corner of the square had once been a bustling place, located within walking distance of both the depot and the courthouse. There was a restaurant, now closed, and a ballroom of sorts, which was still available for rental, but potential customers were put off by the shabbiness, not to mention the musty smell. As travelers took to their cars after the war the tourist court on the highway began taking away business from the downtown hotel. When a modern new motel opened across the highway from the Spalding Texaco not long after the war, the hotel never recovered. The hotel was owned by an old man in Houston, who had built a string of them near the depot in several towns across west Texas and eastern New Mexico in the heyday of passenger rail. As he aged so did his hotels, but he held onto them over the objections of his heirs who feared they would be worthless by the time the old man croaked and they could sell off his properties and blow the money.

The railroad hotel magnate's eldest son had convinced him to convert some of the rooms into apartments, which offered a much steadier revenue stream than overnight rentals. This had attracted several residents, including a few widow ladies who didn't want to maintain a house, especially those who had sold or rented out the farm and wanted to move into town; a bachelor lawyer who had an office on the square and could walk to work; and the spinster who ran the five-and-dime bequeathed to her by her father.

The hotel was also popular with young teachers who might only be in Preston a year or two before moving on, especially the assistant coaches whose employment was determined by the whims of the football boosters. The floor occupied by the younger people had the ambience of a co-ed dorm and offered the advantage of allowing them to sleep around without a nosy neighbor spotting someone else's car parked in front of their house late at night or early the next morning. This had happened on more than one occasion, followed by a meeting with the principal, informing the teacher that her contract would not be renewed at the end of the school year. All teacher contracts included a morality clause, which if invoked, could spell the end of a teaching career, so no one ever pushed it. When caught, or even suspected, the promiscuous teacher often started looking for another teaching position, closer to home, a bigger school, anything that would justify making a move.

Maggie tossed her jacket onto the bed as she and Kevin entered her room. She had on a T-shirt under the jacket and he quickly noted that she was not wearing a bra. Kevin shed his own jacket and dropped it onto the bed, never taking his eyes off Maggie, waiting for her to turn around.

Her room would have been called a junior suite when it was still rented by the day. There was a sitting area on one side of the door and behind that a kitchenette with a small refrigerator. On the other side was the bed, a bathroom, and a closet. Beads hung over the doorway to the bathroom. There were several posters on the wall, mostly psychedelic, counterculture, bands, concerts, along with a few photographs.

"How old are you?" Maggie asked as she pulled two cans of beer from the refrigerator.

Kevin smiled as she turned toward him. The T-shirt said MAKE LOVE NOT WAR.

"I'll be twenty-one in March. Why?"

"I don't want to get busted for contributing to the delinquency of a minor."

"I'll tell the cops the beer was mine."

She punctured the top of a beer can and set it on the table in front of him.

"Although Chief Harding would know I was lying," he said.

"How would he know?" she asked as she sat down and opened another beer.

"He knows I wouldn't buy piss like this even from a bootlegger."

She reached for his beer. "Then I'll drink it."

He pulled it away and took a sip. "That's okay. It's beer. I've had worse. A lot worse. At least it's cold."

"I had to drive a hundred miles to get it, so you'll damned sure drink it and say you liked it."

"I like it already. And you didn't drive a hundred miles to get it."

"I didn't?"

"You drive to Lubbock for school what, three nights a week?"

"Two."

"It's only a few more miles out to The Strip."

She shrugged and sipped her beer.

"You look like a teenager, so I guess you get carded at the beer joint," he said.

"I get carded everywhere."

"But at least you were with a big, mean-looking black guy so nobody gave you any crap."

"Oh, they still gave me crap. We've actually had cops pull us over to see if I was being kidnapped."

Kevin laughed and then looked around. "Interesting room."

"I pretend it's a room in a boarding house in San Francisco. Haight-Ashbury."

"I spent a day in San Francisco on my way to Viet Nam. I checked out Haight-Ashbury. Lots of hippies and freaks."

"You were in Viet Nam?"

"Just got back a few weeks ago."

"Kill any babies?"

"Thanks for the beer," he said, pushing back his chair.

"Just kidding."

"Nice shirt."

"I may be against the war, but I don't take it out on the guys who were sent to fight it."

He scooted his chair back up to the table and took a sip of beer.

"Thanks. But a lot of people do, so I guess I'm a little defensive.

I saw hippies protesting in Oakland on my way back home. I think one of them was wearing that same shirt."

She pulled her shoulders back and tugged at the bottom of the shirt, more clearly revealing the slogan, along with the outline of her breasts.

"Your tits are nicer than his though."

She laughed out loud, leaning forward, ruining his view.

He glanced up at the posters on the wall. "You seem to be kind of caught up in the whole hippie thing."

"It started off as a way to piss off my daddy."

"Why did you want to piss off your daddy?"

"It's a long story. But I kind of liked the hippie thing, and hip huggers and a T-shirt are a lot more comfortable than girdles and bras." She cupped her breasts. "No bra, see."

"Burn it?"

She smiled. "No. I still need it for school."

"You don't see a lot of the no-bra look in Preston, so you might want to keep them holstered around town, except when you run into me, of course."

She laughed again. "I don't want to piss my daddy off too much, though. I may go back to school and get my master's."

"And you want him to pay?"

"Of course."

"I heard you were at Woodstock."

"Where did you hear that?"

"The barbershop."

"Good grief. Worse than a bunch of old biddies at the beauty shop."

"How was it?"

"I'm glad I went, but it was a mess. Everything was covered in mud. The roads were jammed with cars stuck in the mud. They had to bring in the musicians by helicopter."

"Poor baby, mud and helicopters."

She shrugged.

"I had those every day for months, with people shooting at me, but without Joan Baez and Janis Joplin. How was CCR?"

"They were great, but Jimi Hendrix, oh, man." She turned and looked over her shoulder. "I have some pictures over there."

He followed her and she pointed at a small snapshot pinned to the wall. "That's a helicopter coming in, but I don't remember who was on it, or even what day it was."

Kevin leaned forward and studied another snapshot of several young men and women, all naked. "Is that you?"

"Yep, that's me."

He looked up and smiled.

"Never seen boobs before?" she asked.

"Not nearly enough."

She lifted her T-shirt and showed him her breasts, and not just a quick flash. He smiled and enjoyed the display.

"I'm glad Old Lady Westmoreland never did that."

"Who's Old Lady Westmoreland?" She casually lowered her T-shirt.

"My English teacher in high school. I guess you're her replacement."

"Ah yes, her. You want another beer?"

"Sure."

He watched her hips in those tight jeans as she strode over to the refrigerator and fetched two more beers. If she wasn't coming on to him this was the next best thing. He picked up the church key from the table and did his part by opening the beers as she sat down across the table.

"Did you ever mess around in high school?" she asked.

"Sure, who didn't?"

"With Old Lady Westmoreland?"

He recoiled. "Huh?"

"Book reports."

"Oh, that." He smiled.

"I thought the kids were pulling my dick, so I asked another teacher. I wasn't about to ask Colonel Klink. What's that dude's problem?"

"There's a reason he's called Colonel Klink."

"Anyway, she confirmed that there was no way that students, teenagers who were already having sex, would be allowed to write 'they had sex,' in a book report, so the code phrase was 'they messed around.' Seriously?"

"Seriously," he said. "Romeo and Juliet messed around."

"Don't they have sex ed in junior high?"

"Sex ed? Are you kidding me? Where did you go to school?"

"I went to Catholic school in Dallas."

"So, no sex."

"No sex ed," she said, grinning. "But I thought public schools would have finally come into the twentieth century."

"No way. Every member of the school board is a God-fearing Christian. There's no law that says it, but it's pretty much a requirement to get elected. Teenagers are expected to learn about sex the old-fashioned way, in the back seat of a car."

"What about birth control?"

"There's a vending machine in the men's room at the Texaco."

"That's not a problem for me, by the way."

"It's not?"

"That's what I was doing at the drugstore the day we met, trying to fill a prescription for birth-control pills."

"And the pharmacist wouldn't fill it?"

"Uh, no," she said.

"He's a deacon at the Baptist Church, and on the school board."

She laughed. "That explains a lot."

"Did you get the prescription filled in Lubbock?"

A sly smile crossed her face. "I did. You won't need to make a trip to the Texaco. I assume you have one in your wallet, but you won't need that either, unless you picked up some dread disease at a whore-house in Viet Nam."

"No, I'm good."

"What about Amy Evans?"

That caught him off guard. "What about her?"

"I saw you coming out of the movie tonight."

"Oh, that. We were just hanging out."

"You were holding hands."

"We were? I didn't really notice, but if we were it was no big deal. She's a very affectionate girl, and she's going steady with Bobby, the other guy in the drugstore. He's in Viet Nam."

"She's going steady with a guy in Viet Nam but going to the movies with you?"

"It's not what you think. We're just friends."

"So, if I jump your bones, I won't be a home wrecker?"

"Jump my bones?"

"Mess around."

Kevin swallowed hard. This was a brave new world. He stared at her for a moment, waiting for her to say, "just kidding." She didn't. He chugged his beer.

20

SEX ED WASN'T ONLY taught in the back seat of a car. It was also taught on the school bus, while cruising the drag, at the Panther, the icehouse, locker rooms, summer camp, the drive-in movie, wherever teenagers congregated. The curriculum was often sketchy, but the lab work was thorough. Textbooks and visual aids were few and far between. Most of the teenagers in Preston had been to the drive-in in Lubbock and had seen a little, maybe a lot. There was even a bit of nudity in mainstream movies playing at the Lindsey, long the premiere theater in Lubbock until the Winchester opened and took the crown. Bobby complained that he had seen Mia Farrow naked more than he had his own girlfriend. The drugstore in Preston didn't carry *Playboy*, not even under the counter. True-crime magazines often had pictures of attractive, scantily clad women, but never actual nudes. The Sears and Roebuck catalog could always be counted on for underwear pictures, even of teenage girls, but the photographers somehow made them look completely nonsexual. Encouraged by the models she met at market in Dallas, Sandra was rumored to have posed in panties and bra for a lingerie manufacturer, but no amount of searching by the boys at Preston High had ever produced any evidence. Amy had seen the photos, but her lips were zipped.

Despite all the obstacles, somehow teenagers learned about the birds and the bees. Although unwritten and unofficial, the unending mantra was "no sex before marriage." It rarely worked. Even the Baptist preacher's daughter was rumored to have gone all the way— at church camp in New Mexico no less. The most scandalous part of the rumor was that the boy was from a mixed marriage—his father was Church of Christ.

It's not that the girls were sluts, far from it. Reputation was everything. Nor was it that the boys were adept at getting the girls to put out. It was "going steady" that both facilitated and encouraged having sex before marriage. By junior year there were few unattached teenagers, certainly not among the most popular kids. After going steady for a certain amount of time it was naturally assumed that the lovebirds were doing a lot more than just making out. Some of the going-steady girls admitted to it, at least to their closest girlfriends, some denied it, and some just shrugged it off. The boys on the other hand, while not necessarily bragging about it, rarely denied it.

It had always bothered Amy that people thought she was having sex with Bobby, and it bothered her even more that he didn't set them straight, although, as far as she knew, he never actually claimed they were doing it. She had called him on it, and he had apologized and promised to do better in the future, but it wasn't worth breaking up over, and her reputation didn't seem to suffer, so she let it slide. Now it didn't matter.

To unmarried teenage girls the most serious consequence of sex before marriage was pregnancy, although venereal disease was not unheard of in Preston, especially when the local horndogs ventured afield in search of willing partners. Juarez was only six hours away and most of the local boys had made at least one trip by senior year. VD could be cured with a trip to the free clinic in Lubbock, but an unplanned pregnancy was another matter entirely. Amy and Bobby had taken proper precautions, although she had to remind him at the last possible moment, but there was always, at least for the next few weeks, that nagging possibility.

"Sometimes you miss for other reasons," Sandra said as she and Amy left the girls' restroom at school.

"What other reasons?" Amy asked. She had missed before, but not often, and certainly not for the reason she feared most.

"I don't know, nerves, stress. Your boyfriend's in Viet Nam. I'd think that would be kind of stressful."

"Maybe you're right."

Amy knew all about Sandra's sex life—indeed it accounted for most of what she knew about sex. Sandra also knew everything about Amy's lack-of-sex life. She had quizzed Amy when Bobby left for basic, amazed that her best friend hadn't finally had sex with her steady boyfriend of *three years* and was therefore convinced that Amy would be a virgin on her wedding night. She hadn't even asked if Amy and Bobby had sealed the deal before he left for Viet Nam, and Amy hadn't offered, fully intending to keep it to herself. Kevin's much-appreciated doting had occupied her in the ensuing days, leaving less time with Sandra, and Amy had never gotten around to telling her, until now. Sandra took it in stride. It was about time. She didn't ask how it was. Girl talk could come later. Her best friend was in crisis.

"Maybe you're just late. Give it a couple more days. Then if you want, we can go to Lubbock and get it checked out," Sandra said, like they were discussing a noisy transmission. There was no way they were going to get something like that checked out at the small community hospital in Preston. They needed complete anonymity.

"How was it?" Logan asked.

Amy gasped and turned. "What did you say?"

"How was the movie?"

Amy glared at him, turned, ducked her head, and walked away quickly, Sandra rushing to keep up.

"What was that about?" Sandra asked.

"Just Logan being a jerk."

"As usual."

The girls managed to put some distance between themselves and the jerk before reaching the cafeteria.

"What movie?" Sandra asked as they lined up.

"Huh?"

"Logan asked how the movie was."

"I saw a movie with Kevin. Logan must have seen us there."

"When?"

"Last night."

"You mean like a date?"

"No," Amy said emphatically. "It wasn't a date. It was just a movie. We saw the early show. Sheesh."

"Okay," Sandra said slowly. "What movie did you see?"

"Oh," Amy said, realizing that maybe she had overreacted. "*The Sterile Cuckoo.*"

"Is that the one with Judy Garland's daughter in it?"

"Yeah. She was really good."

"I wanted to see it, but Doug thought it looked stupid."

"I think yesterday was the last day."

Sandra shrugged. "I guess we can wait for it to play at the drive-in."

Amy grinned. "So you can make out?"

"Yeah, that's it," Sandra said sarcastically. She and Doug were far beyond making out at the drive-in, not that they didn't still avail themselves of the opportunity.

As she worked her way down the cafeteria line Amy looked up from her tray to see a big smile on Clara Washington's face, as usual. Clara had run the cafeteria at the colored school, south of the highway, for years. When Preston finally integrated their schools, more as a result of the cost of running two separate schools than from any sense of fairness, or respect for the law, she went to work in the cafeteria at Preston High School, starting at the bottom, where she remained, but it was a steady paycheck, except for summer, and she never complained. In addition to cooking for the VFW on Monday nights, Miss Clara was also available to cook for parties, weddings, reunions, and other special events, especially at the VFW Hall. She was also a fixture on the town square for the Fourth of July festivities, serving up barbecue cooked by her husband Benjamin, who was also the school janitor.

Despite growing up in a segregated world, Clara was a jovial woman and never met a stranger. She sang in the choir at the colored church and the local teenagers were accustomed to hearing her sing in the cafeteria when they passed by on the way to the gym. The other lunch ladies liked to listen to her sing, but she always stopped as soon as the first students started filing in for lunch, feeling it somehow improper.

Terrell Washington took after his mother and tried to be friendly to everyone, even though being in the first small group of black students in an otherwise white high school was difficult.

"Did you get Bobby's Christmas cookies in the mail, Miss Amy?" Clara asked.

"Yesterday. I hope they get there in time." She held out her tray while Clara slopped on green beans. "Have you heard from Terrell?"

"That boy writes his mama every day."

"Is he doing okay?"

"He says he is, but they don't tell their mamas everything."

"Or their girlfriends."

AMY FINISHED HER daily letter to Bobby in history class. She told him about her "date" with Kevin, certain he would understand. She also told him about the sex scene in the movie. Talking to Bobby about sex was a lot easier when his hands were nine thousand miles away. She had to copy most of the letter to a new sheet of paper, more than once, as she wrote and rewrote the bit about missing her period.

She finally decided to leave it out altogether—no reason to worry him until she knew for sure. Maybe it was nothing, as Sandra had said, just stress over him being in Viet Nam. Surely he was also under stress, although his letters mentioned nothing of the sort, just loneliness and missing her. The last thing he needed was to hear his girlfriend was pregnant or might be. That was the important part—might be. She ripped up the letter and started over.

"Miss Mills was in a really good mood today," Amy said as she and Sandra left English class.

"Maybe she got lucky last night," Sandra said.

"Got lucky?"

"Got laid."

Amy was taken aback. "With who?" She scrunched her nose. "Or by who?"

"Coach Damron."

Jeff Damron had been a basketball star in college. He was drafted by an NBA team willing to wait two years while he fulfilled his obligation to the Army after being commissioned as a second lieutenant through ROTC. An injury, not from enemy fire but while playing a pickup basketball game in South Korea, ended his hopes of playing professional ball, so he set his sights on being head coach at a major university, and used the GI Bill to get his master's degree. Like most other would-be head coaches, he had to start somewhere. Offers were few, especially from larger schools with strong basketball programs, and he had reluctantly accepted an offer from Preston to be an assistant coach, resolved to do his best and try to hire on at a bigger school at the first opportunity. On arrival, however, he was informed he would be head coach for the girls, their previous coach having resigned suddenly under suspicious circumstances. The school board was willing to let him out of his contract, but it was too late to find another job for the current school year and he needed the money.

With a shortage of females to coach in any sport, it was uncommon, but not unheard of, for a man to coach girls' basketball. It wasn't simply a matter of gender—girls played six-on-six half-court basketball, a much different game than the one played by boys, so Coach Damron had a lot to learn. He also faced an additional problem—at six-four, with hair and sideburns as long as the school board would allow, a neatly trimmed moustache, movie-star good looks, outgoing personality, and muscles everywhere, Coach Damron was a certified hunk. High school girls swooned.

Amy shrugged it off. Miss Mills was an adult, and it was none of Amy's business.

"Are you ladies riding with me?" Doug asked, slipping a hand around both their waists as Amy and Sandra walked down the hall, headed for the front door.

"That's the plan," Sandra said. "Otherwise, we're walking."

"Where's your car?" Amy asked.

"Daddy picked it up and took it in to get the points plugged or something."

Doug laughed. "This will just take a minute." He peeled off and darted into the office.

"What's he in for this time?" Amy asked.

Doug was no stranger to the principal's office.

"He just turned eighteen," Sandra said. "He has to register for the draft."

KEVIN HADN'T PROMISED Amy that he would come to the basketball game Friday night, but he had indicated that he might stop by when he got off work, after halftime, when they stopped selling tickets and let people in for free. Amy knew that, like Bobby, he cared nothing for basketball and had rarely attended games even when he was in high school unless he was shooting photos for the newspaper or yearbook. Still, she was disappointed when he didn't show up. She had no intention of telling him that she feared she might be pregnant, but he had a way of making her laugh and taking her mind off things, so she was hoping they could go riding around after the game and then park in her driveway and talk, like they had last night.

"Can I get a ride home?" Amy said as the cheerleaders gathered their things after the game.

"Sure," Sandra said.

"Thanks."

"I thought Kevin was picking you up."

"He said he might stop by when he got off work. It wasn't definite. Maybe he had to work late."

They pushed through the steel door into the chill of the night.

"Did you see Kevin?" Amy asked Doug as she and Sandra approached his pickup in the parking lot outside the gym.

"I saw him at the store when I drove by a couple of hours ago," Doug said.

"Did you even go to the game?" Sandra asked.

"Babe, you know I hate basketball."

In smaller towns most of the boys played most of the sports, but Preston High had a large enough student body to allow specialization, and few football players went out for basketball. The coaches expected them to all run track, whether they were any good at it or not, to stay in shape.

"I just stopped by to see if I could pick up some girls," Doug continued.

"Well, you're picking up two," Sandra said.

"The more the merrier," Doug said as they climbed into the pickup. "Riding around with two hot chicks will make me look like a stud."

"I don't really want to go riding around," Amy said. "You can just drop me off."

Rock and roll blasted from the radio in Doug's pickup, which was fine with Amy. She wasn't in the mood to talk and was having second thoughts about having shared her secret with Sandra. It was unlikely

Sandra would intentionally out her, but a slip of the tongue was always a possibility.

"Is that Kevin's car?" Sandra asked as Doug stopped at the corner by the hotel.

"Where?" Amy asked.

Sandra pointed. "Right there, at the hotel."

Amy leaned forward and looked. "I think so."

"That's definitely Kev's Impala," Doug said as he turned the corner.

"What's he doing at the hotel?" Amy asked.

Sandra laughed. "Hanky-panky."

"Looks to me like the boy scored," Doug said.

"Maybe he's just hanging out with Mr. Billingsley," Amy said. "They were both in Viet Nam."

"Billingsley doesn't live there," Doug said.

"How do you know?" Amy asked.

"He's black," Doug said.

The hotel was restricted, as was all other residential property in Preston north of the highway. Cliff Billingsley rented a room from an elderly widow lady, south of the highway.

"Coach Damron lives there," Sandra said. "Wasn't he in the Army?"

"Yeah," Doug said. "Maybe they're drinking beer and telling war stories."

EMPTY BEER BOTTLES cluttered the table in Maggie's room. Clothes were scattered across the floor. Kevin and Maggie lay in bed, naked, exhausted, skin still glistening with perspiration. She ran her finger over a scar on his chest.

"What's this one?" she asked.

"Chinese shrapnel."

She pointed to another, gently caressing it.

"Russian bullet," he said. "Probably SKS."

After a detour across her breast, he slid his finger under a necklace with a peace symbol.

"Woodstock," she said.

She rolled over and kissed his scars, her hand roaming across his body. She moved up and kissed him on the lips, but it was not as passionate as she expected.

"What's wrong?" she asked.

"Nothing. I'm having a great time."

"There's someone else, isn't there?"

"No, of course not."

"It's okay if there is. I'm a thoroughly modern woman. I'm just in it for the sex."

He was a bit puzzled. "Okay."

"No offense," she said.

"I wasn't planning on proposing any time soon."

"Really? I thought sure you were going to give me your letter jacket and ask me to go steady."

"Hey, no strings works out great for me."

"So you can still chase your cheerleader."

"I told you. We're just friends."

"I won't be here next school year anyway," she said, pulling the sheet up to her neck.

"Why not?"

"As if going to Lubbock two nights a week with a big black guy wasn't scandalous enough, there's Jeff."

"Who's Jeff?"

"Coach Damron, the girls' basketball coach."

"I don't understand how a guy can coach girls' basketball," he said. "When I was in school the coaches were always in the locker room. Shit, they were in the shower with us."

She laughed. "He doesn't shower with them. He doesn't even go in the locker room without knocking first."

"Oh. Okay. I guess that would work."

"He did say the girls sometimes prank him."

"How?"

She rapped her knuckles on the headboard, pulled the sheet down over her breasts, and said coyly, "Come in, Coach Damron."

Kevin laughed.

"The teenyboppers go all googly-eyed over him," she said. "I even caught your cheerleader checking out his ass."

"What does all that have to do with you?"

"He lives next door." She pointed. "There's a rumor going around that we're making it."

"Are you?"

She shrugged. "It's not like we weren't up for it but there's no reason for both of us to take the fall."

"Take the fall?"

"It seems I'm a bit too much of a modern woman for the prudes on the school board, so I'm going back for my master's next fall and save them the trouble of not renewing my contract."

"Well, I'll miss you."

"Thanks," she said.

"And I hope the new English teacher puts out."

She howled with laughter.

21

IT WAS NO LONGER a question of Amy being late—she had missed and was starting to worry. She was anxious to talk to Kevin but had not seen him anywhere in the store as she completed her grocery shopping. She pushed the cart into Patty's checkout stand and went over her shopping list one more time. Eddie stepped up and quickly begin filling paper sacks.

"Where's your car?" Eddie asked as he completed sacking Amy's groceries.

"I need them delivered."

Eddie smiled. Sack boys vied for deliveries, allowing them a few minutes away from the store, and sacking groceries.

"And I need a ride."

Eddie was now thrilled. Not only would he be getting away from the store, but in the company of the hottest girl in high school. He would have been even happier had she been wearing a short skirt, but it was Saturday, and she was wearing Levi's.

"I'll take her," Kevin said, appearing out of nowhere and scooping up grocery sacks.

"I've got it."

"I unloaded the truck, so I get the delivery."

Eddie shrugged. They had flipped a coin to see who unloaded the truck and Eddie won. Unloading a grocery delivery truck was quite a chore. The driver stood in the truck, releasing boxes of groceries onto rollers, which the store employee, Kevin in this case, had to catch before they crashed onto the concrete. He had to quickly stack the box and race back in time to catch the next one. Sacking groceries, by comparison, was easy work.

"So that's where you were," Amy said as she walked with Kevin, who was loaded with grocery sacks.

"Yeah."

"I thought you were avoiding me."

"Why would I be avoiding you? I'm always happy to see you."

She smiled. "I looked for you at the game last night."

"Oh, that. It was busy and we got out kind of late."

She nodded, wanting to trap him in a lie, but remained silent.

"Sorry," he said. "I should have at least tried to get there by the time the game was over so I could take you home."

"That's okay. I rode with Sandra and Doug."

The delivery car was a black 1949 Mercury Coupe, affectionately known to the sack boys as the Black Bomb. Very much in line with postwar industrial design, it was sleek and sinister, and looked like a bomb on wheels. It had been Robert's car when he married Patty and they hung onto it even after opening the store and buying newer cars. Bobby had driven it for a few months before getting his GTO. Robert intended to replace it when it broke down, but it was still running, and the sack boys liked driving it. Kevin and Bobby had done some tinkering with the flathead V8 and according to Hank, "it ran like a spotted-ass ape."

Kevin's hands were occupied, so Amy opened the passenger door, pulled the seatback forward, and Kevin deposited the groceries in the back seat and on the floorboard. He stepped back and held the door.

"I guess it worked," he said, looking at her hips.

"What worked?"

"Shrinking your Levi's to fit your bottom."

She grinned, covering her bottom as she sat down.

"Did you walk?" Kevin asked as they pulled out of the parking lot.

"My mom dropped me off. She took the girls to Lubbock to do some shopping. I guess I could have called in the grocery list, but I wanted to get out of the house."

"I'm glad you did. And I'm glad Eddie didn't get the delivery."

"Me too."

As Kevin drove her home, Amy struggled to come up with the words to tell him but couldn't. She hadn't even told Bobby. There was really no reason to say anything to Kevin until she knew for sure, so she just looked at him and smiled.

Kevin deposited the grocery sacks on the counter and backed away. "I'd better get back to the store. We're pretty busy."

"Sorry I came at a bad time."

"That's okay. There's no good time on Saturday. It's always busy."

"Do you have a minute?"

"Uh, yeah." He didn't have a minute, but he wasn't going to say no.

"I gathered up a few things," she said, headed down the hallway.

He followed her into her room. She put her hand on one of two paper sacks on her bed. "Can you take these with you, so it won't look so suspicious when you pick me up tomorrow?"

"Sure. What did you tell your parents?"

"I told them we were taking pictures to send to Bobby, so we'll have to be sure and do some that I can show them."

"Good idea."

She dug through one of the sacks. "I don't want my parents, or

Emily, to see everything I'm taking to wear." She pulled out a teeny bikini. "Like this. It's Sandra's. She gets a lot of free stuff when she goes to market in Dallas with her parents."

A sly smile crossed Kevin's face as he looked at the bikini. "Bobby likes that one."

She laughed and picked up the bottoms. "I've never worn a bikini this tiny." She held the bottoms up to her hips.

"I'm not completely sure I'm going to wear it." She held up both pieces. "Do you think it shows too much skin?"

"You're asking the wrong person. I think it will look great. But it's up to you. It's your skin."

She shrugged. "I have two others that you've already seen. I may just wear those." She took another look at the bikini and dropped it in the sack. "I don't know. I might wear it. We'll see, but I don't want my daddy to see me carrying it out of the house tomorrow."

Kevin nodded.

She pulled a nightie out of the sack. "Or this."

"Wow," he said.

"These are the panties."

"Double wow."

"They don't really show anything, but they're really sexy," she said. "I know Bobby will like it."

Kevin nodded and smiled. "Bobby will definitely like it."

She pulled out another nightie. "Sandra kind of borrowed this one from the store, so we'll have to be careful to not show the price tag." She held up the panties, pointing out the price tag.

"I'll watch that price tag like a hawk."

She swung the panties at his face, but he pulled away in time to avoid being hit.

"Is Sandra coming with us?"

She shook her head. "Uh-uh."

"She could help with hair and makeup and clothes and stuff."

"Oh, she wanted to come, but I didn't even tell her when we're doing it."

"Why not?"

"Because she would try to get me to wear things like this." She pulled another nightie out of the sack and handed it to him.

"Okay, now this is see-through," he said. "Do they sell this in her daddy's store?"

"No. She got it from one of the models in Dallas. She said they get to keep a lot of the stuff they model."

"The hell with college. I'm going to move to Dallas and shoot models in lingerie."

"You can practice on me," she said, taking the nightie from him. "But not wearing this one." She stuffed the nightie back in the sack. "This is more my speed," she said, holding up a pair of cutoffs.

"I like it."

She spread a checkered shirt over her chest and held it with her chin, while pulling the tails over her stomach. "I'll tie it up like this."

"That's pretty sexy, but not too much, so you can probably show your parents."

"Exactly. Do you think Bobby will like it?"

"Of course." He tugged at the collar with his finger. "Especially if you show some cleavage."

"How much cleavage?" she asked, warily.

"We can always shoot two versions. One for Bobby and one for your parents."

"Good idea." She dropped the shirt and pulled a T-shirt from the sack. "Here's a plain white T-shirt like you wanted." She scrunched her nose. "But it's not very sexy."

"It will be the way I'm going to shoot it."

She raised her eyebrows. "Can I show my parents?"

"Probably not."

She laughed. "What have I gotten myself into?"

"We won't shoot anything you're not comfortable with."

"Good."

"But I have lots of ideas and you definitely don't want to show most of them to your parents."

She blushed. "We'll look through the rest of it tomorrow. I don't want you to get in trouble at work."

"Don't worry about it. Eddie can handle it."

"This is Bobby's football T-shirt." She held up the cropped T-shirt against her chest. "I never wear it outside the house. My daddy would probably kill me."

"I have one just like it."

"Did you get the football stuff?"

"Yeah. I got it. I also got a jersey, Bobby's old number, so we can shoot one for your parents."

"Oh, yeah. Why didn't I think of that?"

He pointed at the cropped T-shirt. "That one's just for Bobby, and the photographer."

She laughed and tossed the shirt in a sack. He gathered up the sacks. She hugged him, mashing the sacks between them, and then kissed him on the cheek. "See you tomorrow."

"I'm looking forward to it."

"You're looking forward to seeing me in Sandra's bikini."

He smiled and nodded. "And the nighties."

22

KEVIN WANTED TO shoot all day Sunday, but Amy knew her parents would never agree to let her miss Sunday school and church to take pictures, which they could not imagine requiring more than an hour anyway, so Kevin spent the morning "prepping the AO," as they said in the Army, or preparing the area of operations. He had made a trip to Lubbock on a day off from the store and laid in a supply of film, both Tri-X and Plus-X. He had picked up two sheets of white poster board at the local five-and-dime to use as reflectors, along with a few other makeshift supplies.

He had used his light meter to check the sunlight both inside and outside at various times during a previous afternoon. Outside he would have a choice of direct sun, which would work well for swimsuits, or open shade for most other outfits and closeups of Amy's lovely face. According to the books and magazine articles he had read, indirect north light through a window would be ideal for shooting indoors, especially for beautiful young women. But at this time of year darkness fell quickly, so his bedroom, with windows facing both south and west, would provide extended shooting time, along with creative lighting opportunities.

The kitchen was spotless, as usual, when his mother left at dawn. He cleaned his room, made the bed, hid photos of Amy, along with anything else he did not want her to see. He debated over whether to lay out Amy's outfits on the bed but feared she might think it creepy that he had handled her underwear, so he left everything in the grocery sacks and placed those on the bed. Every item she had deposited in the sacks yesterday was etched in his mind and he had previsualized dozens of shots. They only needed twelve for the calendar and Amy would be bringing even more outfits today. He started to worry he had not bought enough film.

He checked the shot list he had written down on a notepad. It was not a matter of simply going down the list shooting and checking off. He had to weigh what he wanted to shoot against what Amy was willing to shoot. He could only guess what her boundaries were. She had put nighties in the sacks and indicated she would shoot in at least some of them. She had also put in panties and bras—did that mean she wanted to shoot them or wear them under other clothing?

What Bobby would like to see was almost certainly what Kevin wanted to shoot, but that added yet another dimension to the dilemma. Would it piss off Bobby to know that Kevin had seen Amy in her underwear or flimsy nighties, or would he just be glad to have the photos for himself? How sexy, or naughty, could the shots be? Kevin had seen nudes on short-timer calendars, but those were almost certainly out of the question on this one—Amy had already nixed the see-through nightie. Nevertheless, Kevin had previsualized a few.

He dropped the notepad on the dresser. In the end it didn't matter what they shot. Both he and Amy would pore over contact sheets and select twelve to go on the calendar. Even after printing the selected shots there would be ample opportunity to kill any that might be problematic.

———

"ARE WE SHOOTING THE DRESS?" Kevin asked as he and Amy stepped off her front porch. They carried two grocery sacks, a makeup case, a small suitcase, and several hangers of clothes.

"No. I was going to change, but Emily was snooping, so I wanted to get out of there as fast as I could. It's a good thing you took some of the stuff yesterday."

"I brought the GTO. I thought it would be a nice touch."

"I didn't even notice." She waited while he opened the door and hung the hangers on the hook in the back seat. "What did you tell Big Bob?"

"Same thing you told your daddy. We'll just shoot a couple of really tame ones with you in Bobby's car to show his parents, and yours." He looked at her, head to toe. "Maybe in that dress, on your way to church."

She laughed. They loaded up and drove out to Kevin's house.

"What time is your mom coming home?" Amy asked as they entered the kitchen through the back door.

"Late, I'm sure," he said. "She wants to spend as much time as she can with her new grandbaby."

"I don't want her to walk in on us."

"Don't worry. She'll call person-to-person and ask for herself before she leaves Snyder."

"My mom does that."

They stepped into his bedroom. "We'll have at least two hours to finish up and clear out. I can run you home and be back by the time she gets in."

Amy put her things on the bed next to the sacks Kevin had taken yesterday. He opened the closet door, shoved his clothes aside, and hung her hangers of clothes on the rod.

"We'll start with the GTO and some outside stuff, then move in here." He stepped over to the window, pulled back the curtain, and looked out. "The light will be better in here late in the afternoon."

She took a deep breath. "I hope you know what you're doing."

"I do."

"What are we doing first?"

"We really should start with the swimsuits while it's still kind of warm outside."

"It's not very warm outside."

"There's supposed to be a norther blowing in later."

"Then we'd better get started."

"Or we could start with something else, more covered, and work our way up to the swimsuits."

"No, that's okay. You've seen me in swimsuits before." She dug into one of the bags, pulled out swimsuits and spread them out on the bed. "This is my one-piece. I know you've seen it. And my two-piece. Have you seen me in this?"

He smiled and nodded. "Oh yes."

"Which one do you want to start with?"

"If you're nervous, and it looks like you are, we can start with the one-piece and work our way down to Bobby's favorite."

"Okay," she said apprehensively.

"I'll go out and get set up while you change. I'll shoot whatever you put on."

"Wait," she said, following him to the door. "Unzip me." She turned, lowered her head, and pulled her hair over her shoulder.

He unzipped her dress, debating whether to just get it started and let her finish, or go all the way. Easy decision. He went all the way, admiring the view on the way down.

"Thanks," she said.

He went outside to position the GTO near the barn. He grinned as he noticed Amy adjusting the curtains on the bedroom window to make sure he couldn't see in.

He glanced up at the sky. It was sunny, which was not a good thing—one of his first lessons in photographing people was to avoid direct sunlight, especially at high noon. He parked the GTO in the shade near the barn and checked the light.

After a few minutes he returned to the house and tapped on the bedroom door. "Are you naked?"

"Yes, but you can come in anyway."

He pushed open the door and peeked in. She wore the one-piece swimsuit.

"Uh! I said I was naked."

"You told me to come in anyway."

She laughed.

"I need my light meter," he said, reaching for the camera bag on the dresser. When he looked up, she was rubbing her arms.

"Are you cold?" he asked.

"Yes."

He stepped over to the closet and pulled out his army overcoat. "You can wear this until we're ready to shoot. It's pretty chilly out there." He handed her the overcoat. "Come out whenever you're ready."

"I'll just be a minute. I want to check my hair and makeup."

Kevin was busy focusing on the GTO, metering the light, and didn't even notice as Amy came out, wearing the overcoat.

"If you're just going to take pictures of Bobby's car you don't need me."

"I wanted to get everything adjusted before you take off the coat."

"Are you ready?"

"I'm ready when you are."

She slipped off the overcoat and handed it to him. He hung it on a fence post.

"This feels weird," she said. "I'm wearing a swimsuit and there's no pool, or lake, and it's cold."

"Bobby won't know it's cold."

They worked quickly, with Amy leaning against the GTO, sitting on the fender, and with her in the driver's seat.

"That's half a roll, and some we can show your parents. Go change." He handed her the overcoat.

They made short work of the two-piece swimsuit, in much the same poses and then she dashed into the house to change outfits while he changed film.

They quickly worked through all the swimsuits, with Kevin shooting extra of the tiny bikini, while rock and roll blared from the radio. She wore cutoffs with her shirt tied up, exposing a bare midriff and plenty of cleavage as she leaned over the fender and under the hood of the GTO, pretending to work on the car.

"Bobby will really like this one," he said.

"Yeah, because his car is in the picture."

They shot various outfits in and around the GTO, the barn, the fence, trying to remember to get some tame ones for the parents. She had just taken off her sweater and was wearing a blouse and short skirt as the norther rolled in. The radio played a slow and romantic song.

"Mood music," she said.

Kevin smiled and watched as she unbuttoned her blouse, exposing not only more cleavage, but also her white bra. He raised his camera and framed the shot as she tried her best to look sexy.

"Let's move inside," he said as he finished a roll. "It's getting cold out here."

"Bring my sweater," she said as she held her blouse closed and dashed into the house. She paused momentarily by the furnace in the hallway to warm herself while undressing. Singing along with the radio, she unzipped her skirt and held it with one hand while she unbuttoned the remaining buttons on her blouse and peeled it off.

"Oh, shit. Sorry," Kevin said as he stepped into the hallway from the kitchen and saw Amy in her underwear.

Amy's singing turned to a shriek, which was Kevin's signal to turn and look away, with an enormous smile on his face. She covered herself with the skirt and blouse.

"You can turn around," she said.

"I thought you'd be in the bedroom," he said as he turned back around, trying to look at her face and not other, more interesting parts. "I was going to knock."

She shrugged and backed up to the furnace, still covering her front with the skirt and blouse, although he still had a nice view from the side. "I was cold," she said, making no move toward the bedroom.

He smiled and nodded. "I'll go make some coffee while you warm your bottom. I think we've earned a little break." He held out her sweater.

"Don't look at my bottom," she said, pulling the skirt around to cover same. She extended one finger of the hand holding the blouse. He hung the sweater on her finger.

"Or I can make cocoa."

"Coffee's fine. I'll go throw something on."

He didn't move.

"You go first," she said.

He laughed, turned and headed to the kitchen.

A short time later, Amy, wearing a T-shirt, stepped into the kitchen and sat at the table. Kevin poured coffee and took a seat across from her. They each took a sip of coffee.

"You know what's weird?" she said.

"What's weird?"

"I freaked out when you saw me in my underwear, but Sandra's bikini shows more skin."

"I'd have to have another look, or maybe shoot some pictures, to study, for comparison."

She chuckled. "That's okay." She sipped her coffee.

"Swimsuits, no matter how much skin they show, are meant to be seen," he said. "You might be a little nervous at first, just like you were today, but you get over it quickly."

She nodded.

"Underwear, on the other hand, isn't meant to be seen," he said, "so being seen in your underwear is different than a bikini."

She leaned back and looked at him. "Where did that come from?"

"Photography magazines."

"You got that from a magazine?"

"They have articles about shooting all kinds of stuff. Shooting swimsuits and underwear might seem like it would be the same, but it's not. There's a big difference."

"Like what?"

"With swimsuits the models tend to look directly at the lens, smiling and making eye contact with the observer, in this case, the swimsuit buyer."

"Okay. That makes sense."

"But with underwear the models tend to look away from the lens, no eye contact, like the camera is an interloper."

She thought about it for a minute, recalling catalogs and magazine advertisements. "Oh, yeah, that's right."

"Lingerie, or sexy underwear, *is* meant to be seen, but only by your lover, so the models do look at the lens, with a come-hither look."

She thought about it and nodded.

He smiled. "That article was a lot more interesting than the one about shooting landscapes."

She laughed. "I can imagine."

"So were the pictures."

Time flew by as they moved into the bedroom and worked through her selection of outfits, improvising, coming up with new ideas, laughing and shooting. He noticed, quite happily, that she had not only become more relaxed, but more willing to do increasingly sexy and more risqué poses.

"Can you see anything?" Amy's hands covered her breasts as she looked down at the baby doll nightie.

"Maybe if you moved your hands."

She turned and looked over her shoulder.

"Down there."

"Not really."

She immediately covered her bottom. "Can you see anything or not?"

"No. There's two layers of fabric."

She lifted the top, exposing the panties. "What about now?"

"Just a hint."

She turned to face him, again covering her breasts. "I feel like I'm naked."

"You're not."

"Are you sure you can't see anything?"

"I'm sure."

She closed her eyes, grimaced, and lowered her hands to her side. "Now I can see your boobs."

She grabbed her breasts, a look of horror on her face.

"I'm kidding," he said as she rushed over to the dresser, lowered her hands, leaned in and looked. She adjusted and tugged at the nightie.

"See, it's fine," he said.

"You're mean."

He laughed. She turned toward him.

"You look really hot, and sexy. Bobby's going to love these."

She relaxed and took a step toward him.

"Maybe too much," he said.

"What do you mean?"

"He might want to kick my ass as soon as he steps off the plane."

"Why would he do that?"

"He just gets to see the pictures. I get to see the real thing."

She shrugged. "I can't very well take the pictures myself, so he'll just have to deal with it."

They continued shooting. He watched his supply of film dwindle, finally rationing it, hoping the day would never end. The sun had the final say, dipping lower until he could barely get an adequate exposure. Amy was oblivious to all the technical details—she was just taking pictures and having fun. Most importantly, she would be making Bobby happy.

Kevin placed an exposed roll of film in line with the others on the dresser. "I have one roll left and we're losing the light. Let's make it count."

"We've done nearly every outfit I brought."

He grinned.

"I am not taking naked pictures," she said.

"I'm sure we can find something."

"Well, I do have an idea."

"What is it?"

"Turn around."

He turned around and waited impatiently. He could hear her moving around, clothes rustling.

"Okay, I'm ready."

He turned and looked. She was in bed, the sheet pulled up over her chest, shoulders bare. He glanced over and saw the T-shirt on a chair, and then looked at her.

"Are you naked?"

"Does it look like I am?"

He nodded vigorously.

"Good," she said.

He continued to stare.

"Are you going to take pictures or just look?"

"Oh yeah, pictures." He lifted the camera to chest level. "I'll start off wide and then move in close for the last half roll."

"Okay."

He knelt beside the bed and focused. "Roll over this way."

She rolled over toward him.

"Move the sheet and show some leg."

She hesitated.

"It will make a better composition than a big blob of white sheet," he said.

She tugged at the sheet. "You do it. You know what you want."

He put down the camera and reached for the sheet. "You aren't really naked, are you?"

"Of course not, silly. I'm wearing underwear." She pulled the sheet from her chest, flashing a bit of bra with the straps tucked under her arms, and then quickly covered up.

"Good. I don't want a knee in the face," he said as he tugged at the sheet.

She laughed. "Then be careful with your hands. Bobby still has bruises."

He adjusted the sheet, leaving most of her leg bare, but maintaining the illusion. He picked up the camera and framed the shot. "Perfect."

He mentally counted each click, knowing that his dream-come-true was about to come to an end. Amy fully cooperated, eagerly responding to his direction.

He lowered the camera and looked at it. "Half a roll left. I'm moving in closer." He adjusted his position. "I'm shooting waist up, if you want to cover up."

She didn't move the sheet. He continued shooting. She smiled.

"Don't smile. Look seductive."

"How do I do that?"

"Relax your jaw, just a little, so that your lips separate."

"Did you learn that from a photography magazine?"

"Yes, and *Playboy*."

She relaxed her jaw.

He carefully framed his shot and began shooting. She had learned to move her head just slightly between shots. He looked up when the lever under his thumb refused to advance one more frame.

"That's it. Last frame. These are going to look great. I wish I had more film."

"Me too. This is fun."

He watched her for a moment as he rewound the film, stood, and put down the camera. He picked up her T-shirt and held it out. The phone rang as she reached for the shirt.

"Saved by the bell," he said. "That will be my mom."

"Good timing."

He headed toward the hallway to answer the phone. When he returned, she was in her underwear, laying out clothes on the bed.

"Sorry," he said. "I thought you'd be dressed."

"Stop apologizing. You've seen nearly everything anyway."

He shrugged and smiled.

She stepped over and put her arms around him. She hugged him tightly and kissed him briefly on the lips.

"Thank you," she said.

"For what? I had a lot more fun than you did." His hands were on her bare back, and she made no effort to back away.

"For not being a creep. I'm nearly naked and you've been a perfect gentleman."

"I was busy trying to get good shots," he said. "It's not as easy as it looks."

"Do you think we got enough to make a calendar?"

"More than enough. You can send him the leftovers for months."

She smiled. He released his grip as she backed away. He watched as she slipped on her blouse and buttoned it.

23

KEVIN HAD HOPED to take Amy out to eat, and to extend the glow that he was experiencing and hoped she was as well. Her daddy wanted her home for supper and church, so Kevin dropped her off, had a chicken-fried steak at the Hi-Way Café and was home in plenty of time to straighten up before his mother arrived. She was tired from the trip, and after filling him in on the new grandbaby, and showing pictures, went to bed. Kevin went back to town.

The newspaper office was eerily silent as Kevin unlocked the front door and stepped in. A bare light bulb hung over the Linotype machine, the only illumination, but sufficient for Kevin to make his way to the darkroom. There was no reason to waste electricity lighting an empty building when he would be working in the dark anyway.

He unpacked his supplies, chemicals, and yellow boxes of photographic paper. He went to work, accompanied by rock and roll music, along with mournful love songs, blasting from the old radio, the volume cranked up so he could hear it in the darkroom. He smiled as he agitated the developing tank, knowing what was inside but unable to see. As the developed rolls of film came out, he rinsed them and hung them on a line, waiting impatiently for them to dry so he could make contact prints. Only then could he see the images he shot, however tiny.

It was late, or early the next morning, when he finally got home. He had seen enough to satisfy himself that he had plenty of good shots to choose from, so he put the contact sheets aside, stripped off his clothes, and went to bed. He pulled a pillow into his face and inhaled Amy's scent.

He slept in on Monday morning, but not for long—he was anxious to get to work on the contact sheets. He showered quickly and then set up shop in the kitchen, almost burning his eggs while darting back to the table to examine a few more frames. After wolfing down breakfast he decided to get organized. He set up a desk lamp on the table, along with a notebook to log his picks, and went to work. He broke long enough for a sandwich when hunger started gnawing at his stomach, surprised at how late it was, and then set the alarm clock so he wouldn't forget to pick up Amy from school.

Each new look brought memories flooding back, replaying the shoot, reliving the rush. He paid particular attention to the nightie, and not entirely out of prurient interest—he would catch hell if Amy had exposed something, and he let it slip by. He thought the shots in the bedroom were the best, with the soft window light falling on her body, creating the "modeling effect" that he had learned about in his magazines and books. He couldn't wait to print them.

He was on the third pass when the alarm went off and he stuffed the sheets in a large manila envelope and headed out.

"IT'S A GOOD THING it's your day to pick me up," Amy said as Kevin held open the door of his car in front of the school.

"Why?"

"Sandra's mad at me."

"Why is Sandra mad at you?" he asked as he backed out of the parking spot.

"Because I didn't tell her we were taking pictures yesterday."

"Ah, yes. She would have pushed you to do things you didn't want to do."

"And then I ended up doing them anyway."

"You did?"

"Well, some of them."

"I didn't push you, did I?"

"No, and it's a good thing you didn't, because I would have probably done it. I was really into it."

"So I noticed."

"I've been thinking about it all day," she said.

"Me too."

"I'll bet you have."

"I think we got some good shots."

"You think so?"

"I know so."

She looked at him, somewhat confused. He tapped the manila envelope on the seat between them. She shrieked and grabbed the envelope, yanking out the contact sheets.

"They're tiny."

"They're contact sheets." He handed her a loupe. "Here, use this."

"Why didn't you get big ones, like the last time?"

"I'd have to send them out. Do you really want the people at the drugstore snooping through these?" He pointed at the contact sheets.

"Oh, yeah. I know they do that."

"And it would have cost a fortune. I shot fifteen rolls, over five hundred shots."

"Five hundred?" She was shocked, but never looked up from the contact sheets. "I haven't taken five hundred pictures in my entire life."

"That's how the pros do it, shoot a lot and edit brutally."

She smiled and nodded and continued to sort through the contact sheets. She gasped. "Oh, wow."

"What?"

She showed him one of the contact sheets of her "nudes."

"Yeah, those came out pretty good," he said.

"I can't believe I did that."

"I'm glad you did."

She rifled through the sheets and carefully inspected shots wearing the nightie. "Did anything—you know—show?" She cleared her throat and pulled her fingers across her breasts.

He laughed. "No, and believe me, I checked very closely."

She swatted at him, but he pulled away to avoid being hit.

Amy had been through the entire stack by the time they reached Kevin's house. She followed him into the house, still looking at the contacts.

"We can use the kitchen table," he said, "but the window light's better in the bedroom."

She continued to follow him into the bedroom and sat on the bed as he opened the curtains. She stretched out, facing the window, as light spilled in. He crawled onto the bed beside her.

"I marked the ones I liked," he said.

"Oh, that's what the little 'K' is for."

He handed her a ballpoint pen. "Put an 'A' on the ones you like and then we'll get to work."

Amy went through the sheets again, adding her mark. As she finished a sheet Kevin went over it and updated his list.

All three swimsuits made the list, Sandra's teeny bikini more than once. There were two nighties, but the see-through one didn't even get photographed. Amy agreeing that showing cleavage bending over the fender was sexy, not slutty, and Bobby would love it, especially because it was his car. A normal shot in the full cheerleader uniform would be set aside for parents while much sexier ones made the calendar. A shot of Amy wearing football pants and Bobby's cut-off T-shirt and holding a football made the calendar, with a similar shot wearing a jersey for the parents. And finally, Kevin's favorites, the ones in bed under the sheet.

"This one is definitely Miss November," he said, pointing.

"Why?" she asked, suddenly concerned.

"Because this is what he's coming home to."

She grinned. "Oh yeah, that. He's really going to be hard to handle, isn't he?"

"I would think so, after looking at this every day for a month, or a year. I know I would."

She looked at him and smiled.

He gathered up the contact sheets. "Okay. I'll make prints tomorrow night when I get off work and we can put the calendar together Wednesday after school."

"Can't you do them tonight?"

"I could, but do you really want me printing these with Teddy Parker looking over my shoulder?"

"Why would he be looking over your shoulder?"

"I use their darkroom. The paper comes out tomorrow. They'll all be working late tonight."

"I don't want anybody looking over your shoulder when you do them. I don't even want you looking."

"I kind of have to look."

She covered her face. "You already looked plenty."

AMY WASN'T VERY talkative on the ride home and Kevin wasn't sure why. Had he done something to offend her? Did she regret taking pictures in skimpy attire? Was she embarrassed?

"Are you having an affair with my English teacher?" she asked as he parked at her house.

It was like a bolt of lightning to Kevin.

"What makes you say that?"

"It's a small town. People talk."

"A gentleman never tells."

"So, you are."

"We hang out sometimes. Not a lot of people our age in town."

"Are you sleeping with her?"

"I'm arguing with her."

"About what?"

"The war. Why would people think we're doing it?"

"The windows of her apartment face the town square."

"So?"

"Maybe you should argue with the lights on."

He grimaced.

"I knew it," she said, nodding her head.

"Is that a problem?"

"I don't know. It's not like we're dating or you're cheating on me. It's just weird."

"Weird how?"

"She's a teacher."

"So? I'm not her student, although she has taught me a couple of things."

Amy rolled her eyes. "It's still weird."

"She's just a few months older than I am."

"Are you in love with her?"

"No, it's just sex."

"So you admit it."

He shrugged. "She feels the same way. She's leaving at the end of the school year anyway. It's not like we're going to get married and make babies."

"She's leaving?"

"Well, first people thought she was doing it with Cliff Billingsley. Then it was Coach Damron, which was somewhat less scandalous, and now, apparently me, so she's going to quit before she gets fired, and then go back to get her master's degree. Why do you care? You're graduating."

"She's a good teacher, a lot better than Mrs. Westmoreland. Emily likes her too. I hate to see her go. That's all."

"Don't tell anybody she's leaving. I don't know if she already turned in her resignation."

"I won't, and I won't tell anybody you're banging her."

"It's not like I seduced her or got her drunk and forced myself on her. She came on to me."

"Like Nikki?" Amy said, grinning.

"Yeah, but with a happy ending."

Amy laughed out loud.

"So you're okay with it?" he asked.

"I guess so. It's really none of my business. It's just going to take some getting used to. I kind of feel like I'm dating a married man."

"We're not dating."

"You know what I mean."

"If it's a problem just tell me, and I'll break it off."

"That wouldn't be a very nice thing to do to Miss Mills."

"I think we both know it's not going to last, and if you've heard about it, I'm sure plenty of other people have too."

"They have."

"I promised Bobby I'd take care of you, and I intend to. If Maggie is in the way, I need to know."

"She's not in the way. I told you to find a girl and go out on real dates and you did. I just didn't think the girl would be my English teacher or that you would jump right in bed with her."

"I didn't either. I wasn't really looking. It just happened, and not always in the bed."

Amy shrieked and covered her face. After a moment she regained her composure. "If you're happy then I'm happy. Now walk me to the door. If you're going to cheat on me then you'd better treat me nice and keep up appearances."

24

AMY RODE AN EMOTIONAL rollercoaster every day. Mornings were easy—routine ruled. Not only was it a new day but a day closer to Bobby's eventual homecoming. It was thoughts of that very event that launched the daily ride. She had held out far longer than most of her friends in high school, certainly those who were going steady, and was proud of herself for making the decision on her own to have sex with Bobby, and informing him thusly, rather than just giving in to his relentless advances in a moment of passion. In addition to the myriad other reasons for abstaining she had been concerned about what came next.

Kissing was a given and like most of her friends, Amy enjoyed it, quite willing to do it for hours with no harm to her reputation. No girl at Preston High was ever labeled a slut for kissing too much. Once a boy's hand found a girl's breast and it wasn't immediately pushed away, however, the climb to a series of plateaus began. A sense of entitlement set in, and it was difficult to retreat. In moments of weakness Amy had allowed Bobby to go much further than she would have liked. Achieving each plateau only encouraged him to strive for the next, while Amy wanted desperately to climb back down to where things were simpler, more comfortable, and less dangerous.

Sex changed everything. Bobby would now expect it, feel entitled to it, and for Amy it would not be as easy as pushing away his hand. He had received the short-timer calendar, and Miss November was his favorite—appearing to him to be an engraved invitation. One of the primary factors in her decision to delay having sex until just before he left was that it gave her a year to not have to make the decision to do it again, and again. As a practical matter, when he returned from Viet Nam, she would likely be living in a dorm at Tech, or in her grandparents' garage apartment in Lubbock. Boys weren't allowed in girl's dorm rooms, and Bobby certainly couldn't spend the night in the garage apartment with her grandparents just yards away, but it wouldn't be difficult to find a place.

Then there was the possibility, even probability, of marriage. After three years of going steady it was to be expected. There had been no proposal and little talk of marriage, but it seemed preordained. That would certainly solve everything. She and Bobby could have sex whenever they wanted, even in her old room when visiting her parents.

According to Kevin, on his return from Viet Nam, Bobby would be stationed somewhere in the continental United States. As a low-ranking enlisted man, he would not be entitled to post housing, but surely they could find a small apartment, and it would only be for eighteen months. Hopefully, the Army post would be near a college so she could take a few classes while waiting for his ETS, Army talk for Expiration Term of Service. Between Bobby and Kevin, Amy was becoming fluent in Army.

Thoughts of wedded bliss with Bobby in a small apartment near a large Army post was the apogee of Amy's rollercoaster ride. What came next was reality. Missing a period was one thing, but morning sickness was another matter entirely. It could just be nerves or maybe a stomach bug, but Amy was becoming increasingly convinced her worst nightmare was coming true. She weighed herself twice a day. She checked her calendar and counted days. The free clinic in Lubbock was looking like her only option, but it wasn't a matter of just hopping in the car and driving over. She was seventeen and in high school. Her daddy would want to know where she was going, with whom, and when she would be home. Plans had to be made, cover stories created and rehearsed.

She had tried to stay busy, especially with Bobby's short-timer calendar, which had helped keep her mind off it, but she increasingly feared a pregnancy test would only confirm what she already knew to be true—she was carrying Bobby's baby. She had written nothing to him about it, not wanting to worry him if it was a false alarm, but she now struggled with telling him. Again, her mind raced with possibilities. He would certainly find it a joyous thing and immediately propose marriage. The logistics would be a problem, with him in Viet Nam and her in high school. Or maybe he would think she was just trying to trap him into marriage. After all, he had not yet proposed, not even close. Maybe she was just his high school girlfriend. Graduation from high school was a watershed moment for many reasons, relationships not the least among them. Bobby's parents wanted him to go to college, and so did hers. Maybe he would meet someone new at college, or maybe she would.

Like sex, a baby changed everything.

KEVIN'S OLDER SISTER alternated Christmas with her family and her husband's, and it was his year, so Irene accepted an invitation to Christmas dinner at the Dalton house, and Patty eagerly accepted Irene's offer to bring pecan pies.

Patty worked the same hours as her husband and never had much aptitude for being a housewife, so she offered no resistance when Robert's mother moved in with them after her husband died and insisted on doing all the cooking. Patty wouldn't allow Grandmother to do any housework, other than perhaps the dishes, and had hired a maid to come in twice a week. It had worked out well. Grandmother especially enjoyed cooking for the holidays, and piano lessons were never scheduled for a few days before Thanksgiving and Christmas.

Kevin had been dispatched to pick up Grandmother and bring her to the store to do her grocery shopping. She filled a shopping cart, and the groceries were then placed in sacks without ringing anything up on the cash register.

For as long as Kevin had known him, Bobby had decorated the house with Christmas lights and sometimes Santa and reindeer on the roof, and always a manger scene in the yard. Kevin often helped him, and this year had been no exception, with most of the work completed before Bobby left. Kevin and Robert had finished the job over Thanksgiving and turned on the lights. He looked forward to doing it again next year, just after Bobby returned home.

Nearly every house on Silk Stocking Street was lit up for Christmas and Amy always loved driving through, or strolling if the weather permitted, and looking at the lights. This year was rather more somber at the Dalton house—there was no Santa, no reindeer, but the lights were still there, as was the manger in the front yard. Grandmother was a traditionalist and there was a candle, now electric for fear of fire, in each window facing the street.

Kevin wore a tie for the first time since arriving home from Viet Nam. Everyone was nicely dressed, much like for church. Kevin thought Amy looked especially ravishing in a tight dress well above the knee. Ever since Amy had been dating Bobby the Evans family had often been dinner guests at the Dalton house, and vice versa. It was good to get to know one's future in-laws.

There were already four women in the kitchen, so Amy decided to remain a girl for a bit longer, sitting in the living room with Emily and the men, who were talking politics and the war. This was not what Amy wanted to hear on Christmas Eve, so she stepped over to the window and peeked through the sheers.

"Here they come," Amy said, as she opened the door.

The women came immediately from the kitchen as a covey of carolers, including Lily, with rosy cheeks and fluffy Christmas sweaters filed through the door. They were of an age when boys began to rebel against such things, so the carolers were mostly girls.

They immediately launched into a Christmas carol, and then after enthusiastic applause, another. As the applause died down the girls rushed to warm themselves in front of the fireplace as Grandmother and Patty served cookies and hot chocolate. This was the last house on the caroling course by design, and Lily would be staying for dinner. It was not the only house serving refreshments, however, so no hosts were offended when the carolers only took a few sips of hot chocolate and ate one cookie. The rest of the loot, cookies, candy and a small gift, went into decorated bags tied with colorful ribbons. Here they gulped down the hot chocolate and happily accepted refills, saving the cookies and candy for later, while the chaperones sipped more potent beverages.

AMY AVOIDED THE stuffing and potatoes at dinner, but her little calorie counter book said the turkey was acceptable, without the gravy. It was so moist it didn't need gravy, and also delicious—Bobby's grandmother was a good cook.

"Will Bobby have turkey and dressing for Christmas dinner?" Amy asked.

"Yes," Kevin said. "With all the trimmings. Not as nice as this, of course, and his fellow diners will be a lot less beautiful." He nudged Lily, who smiled and nudged back. "It's already Christmas over there," Kevin added.

"Save room for dessert," Patty said as Amy finished her turkey. "Irene brought pecan pies."

"That's okay," Amy said. "I'm on a diet."

Howard had noticed that his eldest daughter had become a picky eater lately, but dismissed it as just being a teenager.

"When did you go on a diet?" Vivian asked.

"She's not burning as many calories with Bobby gone," Emily said nonchalantly, "and she doesn't want to get fat."

Kevin choked back a laugh.

Amy glared at her sister. "What's that supposed to mean?"

"Kissing burns three calories per minute," Emily said. "It says so in your little book."

"You must have burned a lot of calories over the years," Kevin said.

Emily laughed out loud. The adults seemed amused. Lily was un-interested. Amy would have slugged Kevin, but Lily sat between them. The seating arrangement was just fine with Kevin—under no circumstances did he want to take Bobby's seat next to Amy at the Dalton table. Not that he minded sitting beside her, occasionally feel-ing her arm on his, and having her touch his hand, but not in front of the families. There was nothing going on between them, but he was taking no chances.

"We could start jogging," Kevin said. "That burns a few hundred calories an hour. Then you could have a piece of pie."

"You're already getting enough exercise," Amy said sarcastically.

Kevin shot her a look. After a long enough pause for him to feel the jab she added, "How's work on the house coming along?"

"It's coming," Kevin said. "I wish Bobby was here to help."

After dinner everyone gathered in the living room where Lily played piano. While goodbyes were being said at the front door Emily planted herself directly in front of Kevin. He hugged and re-leased her, but she refused to budge. She lifted her head and looked up. Kevin glanced up at the mistletoe over the doorway and leaned down to kiss her. He aimed for the cheek, but she had other ideas, and kissed him on the lips. Lily was right behind her and got a hug and a kiss on the cheek.

Amy hugged Irene and then kissed Kevin full on the lips. No one said anything, but it was an awkward moment for Kevin. Amy just breezed through the door, unconcerned.

———

LILY AND EMILY got up early on Christmas morning to see what Santa had left during the night. Lily still wanted to believe in Santa Claus. Emily didn't, but fully expected him to bring her something. Amy slept in. Santa couldn't bring what she wanted for Christmas.

Amy could smell bacon as she finally crawled out of bed, which only made it worse. She dashed across the hall to the bathroom where Emily was brushing her teeth. Amy dropped to her knees in front of the toilet.

"Did Kevin spike your eggnog last night?" Emily asked.

Amy looked up from the toilet. "No, of course not."

Emily didn't look convinced. "Then what's wrong?"

Amy shoved her aside and washed her face. "Haven't you ever had a tummy ache?"

Having survived breakfast, Amy still faced an hour-long drive to her grandparents' house in Lubbock, something she was not looking forward to. There would be more turkey and dressing and more dessert, along with eggnog and apple cider, then the obligatory trip to see the Carol of Lights on the Texas Tech campus. It was going to be a long, tough day. Hopefully Daddy wouldn't want to stop off for a movie at the drive-in on the way home, as he often did.

25

AS IT HAD FOR as long as anyone could remember, school started the day after Labor Day and let out the day before Memorial Day. There was no spring break, only a day off at Easter. There was no week off at Christmas, and certainly not two. School let out at noon on Christmas Eve and students were back in school on the morning of the twenty-sixth. This year Christmas fell on a Thursday, so kids also got off Friday, making a four-day holiday.

Most stores maintained a regular schedule on December 26, and it was a busy day at Bob's Food Store as shoppers restocked after Christmas. Howard opened the barbershop as usual and men filed in to talk politics, cotton prices, and weather, while waiting for a haircut. The dry goods store was closed for the long weekend. If people wanted to return Christmas presents, they would have to wait until Monday. Sandra's older brother Mark was home—college students did get off a week or more for the holidays—and the Brewsters drove up to their cabin in Ruidoso. Sandra had invited Amy, but she declined, not only due to morning sickness but also an aversion to Sandra's brother, who tended to be a bit too friendly with Amy.

Sandra never noticed and Amy never said anything, but she had spent more nights at the Brewster house since Mark went away to college.

Vivian had errands to run so Amy bundled up and walked to the post office and was glad she did. It was cold but still. She would have been less likely to go out with freezing wind whipping through town as it often did this time of year. The biting air seemed to clear her head but did nothing to resolve her worries.

Amy mailed her letter to Bobby at the post office and picked up the mail. She stood in the lobby and read Bobby's letter before walking briskly the short distance to the barbershop where she delivered the rest of the mail. She sat down to warm herself and read Bobby's letter again.

"Did you walk?" Howard asked after stepping over to the window and looking out.

"Yes," Amy said.

"Well, it's a nice day for a walk. But the wind's getting up."

Amy zipped up Bobby's letter jacket and pushed on to the grocery store. She found Kevin working produce.

"Did you call her?" Amy asked.

"Who?"

"Sharon."

"Yeah, I called her."

"And?"

"We're going to Lubbock tonight to see a movie."

"What are you going to see?"

"I don't know. I'll pick up a Lubbock paper."

"Well, have fun."

"What about you? I promised I would be all yours while Maggie is in Dallas."

"I'm okay. Sandra is in Ruidoso. She asked me to go with her, but I didn't want to."

"Why didn't you tell me? I didn't have to call Sharon, didn't even want to, really."

"No, it's good you're going out with her. It might help with that other thing."

"What other thing?"

She looked around to see if anyone was listening. "That teacher thing."

"Oh, that. My car's been parked at the hotel a lot lately, hasn't it?"

She nodded.

"Do you want to do something tomorrow night?" he asked. "It'll be late when I get off, but we can get a Coke and ride around or something."

"Sounds good." She watched as he bagged lettuce. "Have you heard from Bobby?"

"Yeah, why? Doesn't he write to you?"

"Of course he does, but he probably tells you stuff he won't tell me."

"Guy stuff?" Kevin asked.

"And war stuff."

"He absolutely loves Miss November, but like I suspected, he's going to kick my ass when he gets back."

She laughed. "I told him I wasn't really—" She looked around and then whispered, "—naked."

"Thanks. Maybe he'll let me live."

"What about the war stuff? He doesn't write much about the war and sometimes that worries me."

"He's doing okay. He's at the division base camp at Phuoc Vinh."

"So that's good?"

"That's good. Better than a firebase, or the bush."

Kevin looked around the store. "Are you here with your mom?"

"No, I walked."

"You walked? It's freezing out there."

"It's not bad. I went to the post office, and then the barbershop, but then the wind started blowing."

"We're kind of busy, but if you want to wait maybe I'll have a delivery and I can give you a ride."

"That's okay. I like to walk. It gives me time to think."

"Think about what?"

"Things. I'll tell you later."

"Tell me what?"

She kissed him on the cheek. "And I need the exercise. I'm getting fat."

"You are not fat," he called after her.

Kevin followed her to the front of the store and watched as she darted across Main Street. He picked up a small package of peanuts, pulled an RC Cola from the Coke box, and made a notation in Patty's little book beside her register. At the end of the week, she would add up what he had purchased, and deduct it from his pay. He gulped some of the RC Cola, and then cupped his thumb and fingers over the neck of the bottle and dumped in the peanuts.

"What's a log bird?" Robert asked, sitting on a stool, reading a letter from Bobby.

"A helicopter that resupplies troops in the bush."

"Bobby's not flying, is he?"

"He's in the air cavalry. Everybody flies."

"Don't say anything to his mother," Robert said, handing the letter to Kevin.

KEVIN'S DATE WITH Sharon Spalding went no better than it had in high school, but she was being a good sport about it to please her daddy, although it set off a war between her and her sister.

She picked a movie that he also wanted to see, albeit with Amy, so the date was off to a good start. Unfortunately, it was only playing at a drive-in, which was always awkward with someone other than a steady girlfriend. Kevin wasn't even offended when Sharon went to sleep on the way home. At least it saved him from making conversation. It did make it harder to stay awake, but he managed. He felt obligated to at least attempt a goodnight kiss and was surprised when she shoved her tongue in his mouth.

"I can't let my kid sister have all the fun," she said as she pulled away.

"That was a mistake."

"So I heard. But it sure was funny. Here you are just back from Viet Nam, horny as hell, and think you've hit the jackpot with this oversexed little teenybopper with big tits only to find out she's jailbait."

"Did Joe think it was funny?"

"Oh, hell yes."

She started to open the door and then turned. "Look, I know you just called me because my daddy told you to. We didn't exactly hit it off in high school, so I wasn't really up for this, but what the hell. It was a good movie, and I didn't have to keep pulling your hand off my boobs, so it wasn't all that bad, was it?"

"No, it wasn't. Well, except you went to sleep on the way back."

"Sorry about that. I've been staying up late studying for weeks and I'm exhausted."

"That's okay. It saved us both a lot of chitchat."

"It did, didn't it?"

"Do I need to call you again or was once enough?"

"Once was enough. Daddy will be happy and Nicole's already furious. Besides, you don't really have time or the stamina to handle three women at the same time."

"Three women?"

"Well, two women and a high school cheerleader."

"Amy and I are just friends. I told Bobby I'd look out for her while he's gone."

"That's kind of what I thought, although Nicole's convinced you're doing her."

"Good grief."

"You can do the English teacher all you want. You might want to park somewhere else, though, and walk to the hotel."

"Does everybody know about that?"

"It's a small town."

"Maybe I could fix you up with the girls' basketball coach."

"Could you? Nicole says he's a hunk."

"I'll see what I can do. He lives at the hotel and hangs out with Maggie and me. Maybe we can have an orgy."

Sharon cackled. "Or just a double date."

KEVIN WAS OFFICIALLY worried on the way home from his date with Sharon. Clearly his relationship with Maggie was an open secret. Amy seemed to be okay with it, but he was beginning to think maybe it was time to put an end to it. It weighed on his mind all day Saturday, although it was so busy at the store, and he had little time to think about it. From a practical standpoint, having sex with no strings was a wonderful thing, the kind of thing written about frequently in *Playboy*. But he did feel like he was cheating on Amy, which made him even more confused. Amy was Bobby's girlfriend and would never be his. He had to come to terms with that and making it with Maggie certainly helped. Even better it deflected attention from being seen around town with Amy. He truly had the best of both worlds, much like a married man cheating on his wife, just like Amy had said.

"How was the big date?" Amy asked as soon as Kevin picked her up Saturday night when he got off work.

"Not as bad as I expected. We went to the drive-in in Lubbock."

"The drive-in?"

"Yeah. It was weird."

"I can imagine. Did you hold hands and make out?"

"Uh, no."

"Did you kiss her goodnight?"

"Do you want a play-by-play?"

"Yes."

"I picked her up. We drove to Lubbock. We went to the drive-in."

"Which drive-in?"

"The Circle."

"What movie did you see?"

"*Cactus Flower.*"

"I wanted to see that," she said.

"I can take you."

"You've already seen it."

"I can see it again."

"Was it any good?"

"It was okay. The girl was really cute."

"She's on *Laugh-In.*"

"What's that?"

"A TV show. My daddy loves it."

"I haven't seen much TV for the last couple of years."

"But you didn't make out at the drive-in?"

"No. Then she went to sleep on the way home. I kissed her goodnight, and she stuck her tongue down my throat."

"Whoa. Tongue?"

"She was just messing with me. She said Nikki still had a thing for me."

"She does."

"She also said Nikki thinks we're doing it."

"You and Sharon?"

"You and me."

Amy nodded. "She does."

"And that's okay with you?"

"Not really, but what am I going to do?"

"Tell her she's wrong."

"I did, but people will believe what they want, the dirtier the better. I've also been sleeping with Logan."

"You have?" Kevin was stunned.

"No, silly, but that's the rumor, and I'm sure Logan's spreading it."

"Oh, good. For a minute there I thought you were three-timing Bobby."

Amy laughed out loud. "No, just two-timing."

"Sharon also knows about Maggie," Kevin said somberly.

"Who doesn't?"

"Hopefully my mom. She wants me to fix her up with the girls' basketball coach."

"Your mom?"

"Sharon."

"Oh," Amy said. "Ew."

"It's like *Peyton Place*."

Amy laughed.

It had been late when Kevin picked up Amy, so they only made a couple of rounds. Amy had already eaten dinner, and just had a Dr Pepper while Kevin ate a cheeseburger at the Hi-Way Café. She occasionally snatched one of his fries and then wished she hadn't. As she dipped the fry in ketchup it reminded her of the reason she was on a diet, and that she needed to tell Kevin, but she couldn't get up the courage. What would he think of her? Did he even know she and Bobby were having sex? They had been going steady for three years, so surely he assumed it. He had teased her about sex, sometimes mercilessly, but that was how they were together. Without Bobby in the mix, it would have been flirting. In the end it didn't matter. She needed to tell him, but not tonight.

While Amy agonized over the calorie count of one french fry, plus ketchup, which added a few more, Kevin just watched her as she ate. Her mouth was beautiful, wide, and sexy as hell. Even her chewing was sexy. He had read in a magazine that eating off another's plate was a sign of genuine affection.

KEVIN HADN'T SEEN Maggie since Tuesday night. She had ridden to the airport with Cliff Billingsley on Wednesday after school, but her flight came in two hours earlier than his on Sunday, so she asked Kevin to pick her up at the Lubbock airport. He had made up his mind to break up with her, or at least cool it, and had rehearsed his monologue over and over.

"The principal called me into the office," Maggie said as they drove out of the airport.

"Did he spank you?"

"He knows about us."

"So what?"

"He said if we break it off, I can finish out the school year."

"Can he do that? We're not doing anything illegal. We're both adults, or close enough. I'm not a student. What's the problem, other than a bunch of gossip?"

"There's a morality clause in my contract."

Kevin started to protest, and then realized his break-up speech was no longer needed. Colonel Klink had done the dirty work for him, so he just said, "Oh yeah, right."

"I guess we could sneak off to Lubbock or Clovis and check into a motel."

"We could do that." Kevin started to weigh his options. Amy seemed to be okay with his affair, and an out-of-town rendezvous might silence the gossip while still allowing him to get laid.

"Or we could just break up. Well, not really break up, since we're not dating, just end it. It's been fun while it lasted, but we both knew it would have to end. It was just sex, right?"

"Pretty great sex," he said, grinning, "but yeah, just sex. I never really saw us getting married and living happily ever after."

"That's good, because I met someone while I was home."

"Wow. That was fast."

"Reconnected, actually," she said. "We went to school together when we were kids. Then he moved to Houston. My daddy thinks it's the perfect match. So does my mom. His daddy's rich and getting richer, in the oil business."

"Does he have a name?"

"Bradley."

"Is it serious?"

"Could be. I think so. Yeah. It actually kind of pisses me off."

"Why is that?"

"Because my daddy thinks he hung the moon. They even agree on politics."

"So you're giving up on the hippie chick thing?"

"Who doesn't? You don't see that many old hippies."

Kevin laughed. "You'll fit right in at the country club, but you might want to burn those pictures from Woodstock."

"No way. When I'm old and gray and my boobs are down around my waist, I'll pull out the pictures and reminisce about the good old hippie days."

"Good. Then you won't have to burn these either." He picked up a manila envelope from the seat and handed it to her.

"You got the pictures back?"

"They never left. I did all the processing and printing myself."

"Impressive."

She quickly opened the flap, removed several eight-by-ten black-and-white photos and began flipping through them. All the photos were of her, in her apartment, in various stages of undress, most of them nudes.

"Wow. These are great."

"I had a good model."

"No, you're really good at this. I just agreed to do it for fun. I was expecting snapshots, but these are really professional."

"Glad you like them."

"Bradley will love them."

"Story of my life."

"Huh?"

"Never mind. Do I get to meet Bradley?"

"Probably not. If he comes here, it would just be a different man in my apartment as far as the school board is concerned. He lives in Midland. He's working a big play in the Permian for his daddy, learning the business."

"Midland's not that far."

"We'll probably just get a motel in Brownfield. He said it's halfway."

"Not much to do in Brownfield."

"Sure there is." She grinned.

"Well, I'm happy for you."

"You aren't going to go all caveman on me, are you?"

Kevin laughed. "No. I'm a big boy. I'll get over it."

"At least you still have Amy Evans, but I'm guessing she doesn't put out like a hippie chick."

"It's not like that." He chuckled. "It's not like that at all."

"Are you still going to Tech?"

"Next fall."

"You'll make out just fine with the co-eds, but don't expect it to be the same as what you've had."

"Brad's a lucky guy."

26

THERE WAS NO city ordinance banning public dances in Preston, but it was impossible to rent a venue for one and the VFW Hall was no exception. Like the prom, there was a work-around. Sandra's daddy rented the hall. A hat was placed by the door and boys were expected to kick in a couple of bucks to cover the rental and the band. There were no tickets sold and certainly no advertising. Sandra invited pretty much everyone in her social group at school, and word spread. Other than local college students home for Christmas break, few older boys were admitted stag. Kevin came as Amy's date but would have been allowed in anyway.

Kevin dropped money into the hat by the door. Sandra's mother, one of the chaperones, would occasionally collect the cash and stash it in her purse lest someone snatch the hat and run. She knew all the local kids, but sometimes teenagers from the surrounding towns showed up and Sandra let them in.

The hall was packed with teenagers. Kevin felt old, but he spotted Sharon, Sandra's brother Mark, and a couple of others close to his own age. There was a band on the small stage, wearing matching blazers and skinny black ties. A large banner hung over the stage: HAPPY

NEW YEARS 1970! Kevin smiled and wondered if Maggie would have corrected the banner had she been there. Mrs. Westmoreland certainly would have.

The band was serviceable and lots of kids were on the dance floor, with many more milling around the periphery, much like any other high school dance. Boys staked out their targets and girls either maneuvered into position, or suddenly felt the urge to go to the restroom, depending on the approaching boy. Logan, dancing with Nikki, glared at Kevin and Amy as they found an empty table.

Amy sat down and Kevin went for punch. When the song was over Sandra approached Amy's table. "I thought you weren't coming."

"I changed my mind," Amy said. "It's better than sitting at home worrying."

"Worrying about what?" Doug asked.

Sandra quickly cut him off. "Did you come with Emily?"

"I'm not going out with a bunch of freshmen."

Amy was already upset that Emily had been allowed to go to the dance when she herself had not been allowed to stay out after midnight on New Year's Eve until she was sixteen. Showing up at the dance with her little sister and her freshmen friends would have added insult to injury.

"I came with Kevin."

Sandra leaned forward. "Amy, people are starting to talk."

"Who, Logan?"

"Among others."

Kevin set a cup of punch on the table in front of Amy. "Nice party."

"Thanks," Sandra said.

"Pretty good band." He took a sip of punch. "Do they have anything else to drink?"

"Sure," Doug said. "In the parking lot."

Alcohol was not allowed in the VFW Hall so everyone, including teenagers, kept their booze in cars and went outside to imbibe. It wasn't an ideal solution, but it technically didn't violate any rules. Teenagers still frequently managed to sneak in a bottle or flask and spike the punch bowl. It was difficult for any Preston teenager, even Amy, to say with conviction they were a teetotaler—the sweetness of the punch often overpowered the taste of the alcohol.

Amy looked up and saw Logan headed her way. "Dance with me," Amy suddenly blurted out.

"You know I can't dance," Kevin replied.

Amy was already on her feet and grabbed Kevin by the hand. "It's a slow song," she said. "Anybody can slow dance."

The lead singer was no Bobby Vinton, but he did a reasonable rendition of "My Heart Belongs to Only You," and most of the boys were suddenly overcome with the urge to dance, the closer the better. Targets were acquired. Countermeasures were launched, or positions revealed. Contact was made. Couples danced.

Amy led Kevin onto the dance floor, brushing past Logan.

Doug laughed and took Sandra's hand. "Come on, babe. It's a slow song."

Logan fumed as Amy slow danced with Kevin. It would have been impossible to dance any closer. It was the first time they had danced together since high school, and he certainly didn't remember her dancing this close. Maybe she did, but he felt sure he would have remembered, especially during those long nights in Viet Nam reading her letters and looking at her pictures. He would certainly remember tonight.

He came crashing back to reality when he realized she was crying softly. "What's wrong?"

"I was just thinking about Bobby."

"Oh."

She looked up at him and smiled. "Sorry. It's kind of rude to talk about a boy while you're dancing with someone else."

"That's okay."

"This is one of his favorite songs. He called it a panty-dropper song."

Kevin chuckled. "A panty-dropper song?"

"I think you can figure it out."

"Does it work?"

"Not on me."

She put her head back on his shoulder so he couldn't see the lie on her face, and they danced silently for a moment.

"At least you weren't thinking about Logan," he said.

Amy laughed, shaking, further enhancing the close contact, which he very much enjoyed. He thought his hand might be a bit too far below her waist, but she hadn't complained. She was wearing a rather slinky dress and he could feel the waistband of her panties.

"What a jerk," Amy said suddenly.

"Sorry," Kevin said, quickly sliding his hand back up to her waist, pulling back, putting a couple of inches between them.

"Not you. Logan."

She tilted her head in Logan's direction and Kevin looked. Logan was dancing with Emily, who was clearly enjoying the attention from an older boy. While Kevin had felt guilty about the position of his own hand, Logan's hand knew no such boundaries, and Kevin watched as it slid down over Emily's bottom.

"Do you want me to cut in?"

Amy watched for a moment.

"Or kill him?" Kevin added.

"No, give her a minute. She has to learn on her own."

Whack! Emily learned quickly. Logan raised his hand to his cheek, which hurt like hell and was already starting to turn red. People stared as Emily stomped away, leaving Logan alone on the dance floor.

"Looks like you raised her right," Kevin said.

"Now you can cut in." Amy slipped her hand off Kevin's shoulder and backed away. "Go."

Kevin dodged other couples as he stepped quickly across the dance floor. "May I cut in?" Kevin asked as he extended his hand to Emily.

"Where's Amy?" Emily asked.

Kevin shrugged. Emily looked and saw Amy sitting at a table. Amy nodded and Emily quickly accepted Kevin's offer. Amy laughed quietly and shook her head as Emily plastered herself to Kevin, determined to prove she was all grown up. Kevin glanced at Amy, rolled his eyes, and did his duty, which was not at all unpleasant, even if she was the same age as Nikki. She was Amy's sister, after all. They even used the same hairspray.

Amy was enjoying herself and was glad they came, despite a few disapproving looks. She made it a point to dance with other boys, especially Doug, and Bobby's other friends, when they asked, and a few did. She also encouraged Kevin to dance with other girls, including Sharon, for the same reason. When the lead singer announced ladies' choice Nikki almost knocked people down getting to Kevin while Amy was distracted, talking to Sandra about something that seemed quite serious.

Ladies' choice was traditionally a slow song, and tradition was upheld tonight, much to Nikki's delight. Kevin attempted to maintain proper spacing, which was difficult enough considering Nikki's assets, but she was having none of it and he was soon reminded just how dangerous jailbait could be.

Sharon had little interest in the slim pickings at the dance and took the opportunity to sit with Amy and Sandra. Doug seemed to be missing, so the three of them laughed and pointed and made fun of Kevin dancing with his teenybopper. He gave them a real laugh when he danced Nikki over to their table and made a faux feel of her bottom, without touching it of course. The girls howled with laughter. Luckily no one else noticed, including Nikki.

Logan was spared the indignity of not being asked to dance during ladies' choice. He was outside in the parking lot with Doug and a few other boys, passing around a bottle. He had already had too much to drink, but it was his bottle and there was more where that came from, so nobody was going to tell him he'd had enough.

"What's up with Amy and Kevin?" Logan asked, slurring his words. "I see them together all over town."

"They're just friends," Doug said.

"Looks like more than friends to me."

"He's taking care of her while Bobby's gone."

"He's taking care of her all right. He's got his hands all over her."

Doug shrugged. Logan drank.

"It's nearly midnight," Doug said, checking his watch. "We'd better go back in."

They chugged their drinks and sauntered back into the hall.

"Last dance?" Amy said as Kevin took a seat beside her. "I'm kind of tired."

Kevin smiled, took her hand and they walked onto the dance floor as the lead singer channeled Bobby Vinton once more with "There! I've Said It Again." Kevin hoped Amy wasn't listening too closely to the lyrics.

"Is that Roxanne's little brother?" Kevin asked. He steered her so she could see Emily dancing with a handsome and very polite boy.

"Ryan. He's a sophomore. They make a cute couple, don't they?"

"Yes, they do."

Amy put her head back on Kevin's shoulder and he was in heaven, but the song ended abruptly. Everyone on the dance floor looked up. It took Amy a moment to break away from Kevin, but they soon joined the other dancers, holding hands as a drum roll began.

"Ten, nine, eight, seven, six—"

Whether by design or luck, more likely design since boys wore wristwatches, there were plenty of people already paired up on the dance floor while others rushed to find a partner.

"Five, four, three, two, one. Happy New Year!"

Kevin and Amy stayed on the dance floor, holding hands, neither sure what they should do. They were obviously there together, and everyone knew she was going steady with Bobby. Kevin and Amy had kissed before, although not really in public, so it was not an easy decision. They watched as Emily and Ryan kissed, along with Sandra and Doug and everyone else who had someone. Nikki planted one on some lucky stiff while Logan fumed.

Kevin and Amy turned to each other hesitantly. They kissed, lightly at first, and then more deeply as he pulled her close.

Paper horns blew, confetti flew, people cheered.

Kevin and Amy stopped kissing but remained clinched, eyes locked.

Logan surged forward from the crowd and shoved Kevin.

"Does Bob know you're screwing his girl while he's in Nam?"

Kevin grabbed Logan by the shirt with his left hand and pulled back to hit him. Doug tried to intervene, but only blocked Kevin's punch, allowing Logan to strike the first blow. Kevin released his grip on Logan and raised his fingers to his eye. Logan moved in, but Doug shoved him back. Logan quickly recovered and stepped forward, unsteady on his feet from the booze, ready to fight.

"Stop it!" Amy shouted.

Sandra put her arm around Amy, and they backed away, lest they become collateral damage.

Doug deferred to Kevin, who had the honor, and was Logan's intended target all along. Logan stepped forward, watching Doug out of the corner of his eye, and moved in on Kevin. It was probably not a very intelligent thing to do, since Kevin's most recent employment was killing other men, by any means necessary, including his hands.

It only took one punch. Logan staggered backward, blood gushing from his mouth, splattering on his shirt. Whether it was the booze, the bashing, or both, he collapsed onto the floor. Doug stepped between the combatants, but Logan wisely stayed down.

Scattered applause and cheers broke out. Emily wanted to kick

Logan where it would hurt the most, but stood instead, together with Nikki, laughing and pointing.

This wasn't the first fight the band had experienced, so they launched into "Wooly Bully," and teenagers swarmed onto the dance floor.

Logan went to the men's room to wash off the blood.

Amy and Kevin left quickly, and the party continued.

As THEY SAT IN Kevin's car in front of her house Amy was the first to break the silence.

"I had a nice time," Amy said.

Kevin looked at her, incredulous.

"Well, except for that," she said.

She slid over close to him and examined his eye, touching his cheek softly with her fingers.

"Does it hurt?"

"Not really." He leaned forward, looked in the mirror and touched his swollen eye.

"It's going to be black," Amy said. She didn't budge, remaining shoulder-to-shoulder, even when the inside of the car lit up from the headlights of the car pulling up behind them.

Amy turned to look. "It's Emily."

"You have confetti in your hair." He reached up and plucked a piece, flipping it away with his thumb and finger. He turned toward a banging sound. He rolled down the window. Emily leaned in and kissed him on the cheek.

"What was that for?" Kevin asked.

"You're my hero," Emily said.

"For what?"

"Punching out that jerk."

Amy leaned forward. "Don't tell Daddy."

"I'm not a snitch," Amy said.

"You landed a pretty good shot yourself, for a girl," Kevin said.

"Yeah, I did, didn't I?" Emily said, nodding with self-satisfaction. "Next boy who tries to grope my young bottom will think twice."

Kevin tried to laugh, but it hurt too much. "Then you'd better learn to punch, because that's not all the boys will try to grope."

Amy covered her face and snickered.

"I can handle 'em," Emily said.

"I'll bet you can," Kevin said.

"You'd better go in before Daddy starts flashing the porch light," Amy said.

"You're the one on a date."

"It's not a date," Amy firmly corrected.

Emily backed away.

"Emily, wait," Kevin said.

She leaned back in.

"I like Ryan," Kevin said.

"Me too," Emily said with a twinkle in her eye, and then noticed Kevin's eye. "Oh, wow. Does it hurt?"

"Not as much as Logan's jaw."

Emily leaned in and kissed him again on the cheek. She backed away and raced to the front porch.

Kevin rolled up the window. "That one's going to be a handful."

"She already is."

They sat in silence for a moment.

"I have something to tell you," Kevin said.

"Me too."

"What is it?"

"You go first."

"I love you."

She smiled. "I love you too."

He looked straight ahead. She waited. He turned and kissed her on the lips. He backed away briefly, waiting for a response, and then kissed her again, more deeply. She didn't resist for a moment, but then put her hand on his chest and pushed him away.

"Kevin, don't."

"I love you, Amy."

She didn't answer, hoping that wasn't what he meant.

"I'm in love with you," he said.

"No!"

She turned away, stunned, and then dropped her head. Tears formed in her eyes and ran down onto her cheeks.

He took her chin in his fingers, raised her head, and kissed her again, tenderly on the lips. She pulled away, crying softly.

"I trusted you," she said. She slid over a little, putting distance between them.

"I'm sorry, Amy. I'm so sorry."

"Bobby trusted you."

She burst into tears, opened the door, and ran to the porch as Kevin's world came crashing down around him.

27

WORD OF THE fight at Sandra's party spread like wildfire. Students at the high school mocked Logan. Many of them had been victims of his arrogance and insults and the girls especially relished seeing him put in his place. Even better, his jaw was wired shut so he could barely speak.

Kevin had avoided Chief Harding since the dance. Hopefully, no legal action would be taken, but Logan was a first-class jerk and his father's bank held the mortgage on much of the property in Preston, so Kevin had cause for concern. Hank finally cornered Kevin on Saturday in the stockroom of the store while he was sorting bottles for return to the bottling companies. No handcuffs were produced, but Hank was insistent that Kevin attend the Monday night dinner at the VFW. Kevin was leery, wondering if this had something to do with the fight. Amy's daddy, who Kevin had also avoided, would likely be there.

Kevin had attended a couple of the Monday night dinners at the VFW since his return home. It wasn't really his thing, but he loved

Miss Clara's cooking. The dinners gave war veterans a chance to talk with those who shared a common bond, something no civilian would ever understand. Even those who managed to come through relatively unscathed had seen things, done things, and carried secrets their families could never know. Kevin knew the feeling well. He wasn't going to talk to his mother, and he certainly wasn't going to say anything to Amy while Bobby was in Viet Nam.

After his stunt in front of her house he was unlikely to say anything to Amy ever again and hadn't spoken to her since the dance last week. He agonized over whether to call her, but decided against it, fearing it would only make things worse. Hopefully she would make the first move. She hadn't even been in the store since the dance. He had spotted her going into the movie theater with Sandra and Doug, so he just drove on by. He didn't really want to see the movie anyway; it was just something to fill the void.

He wondered if Amy had already written to Bobby about what happened. The fight would be one thing—Bobby would love hearing about that—but the passionate kiss, his profession of love, was another thing entirely. He now wished he had filled out the papers to start the spring semester at Tech. At least it would keep his mind off Amy. Maybe he should just move to Lubbock and find a full-time job. His life was miserable, and it was all his fault. He had two very good things going and he somehow managed to blow them both. The thing with Maggie was fun while it lasted, and he missed it, especially the sex, but the thing with Amy had crushed him.

He screwed up his courage and walked into the VFW Hall on Monday night, ready to face the music, but was instead greeted with a round of applause. Howard shook his hand.

"Thank you, son," Howard said.

Kevin opened his mouth to speak but wasn't sure what to say.

"For defending my daughter's honor."

Kevin wondered just how much Howard knew, not only about

the fight, but the rest. He wasn't even sure if Howard meant one daughter or two. It had only been a few days, so maybe he hadn't noticed Kevin's absence. What had Amy told him?

"That little pissant got what was coming to him," a veteran said.

"You should have beat the shit out of him," another added.

"I don't know," a third said. "That would take an awful lot of beating."

There was a round of laughter after that one.

"I hope nothing comes of it," Kevin said, looking at Hank.

"I questioned a few witnesses," Hank said. "It was clearly self-defense. There was some disagreement about the details, but all the kids said Logan threw the first punch, whether they saw it or not. Either way it wasn't like you attacked an elderly man or a little kid. Teenage boys get into fights. I'm not going to waste the court's time over it."

Kevin nodded. That was a relief.

"And don't worry about the banker filing a lawsuit," Hank said. "He'd have a hell of a time finding a jury around these parts that would find in his favor."

"Or a lawyer," added a Korean War veteran who had gone to law school on the GI Bill. That brought another round of laughter.

With that off his mind Kevin enjoyed his dinner and talk soon switched to other topics of extreme importance, like politics and next year's football team. Kevin was surprised after dinner when Clara brought out a huge chocolate cake, his favorite, and put it on the table right in front of him.

"It's not my birthday," Kevin said.

"That boy done messed with Miss Amy," Clara said. "He's lucky you got to him before I did. He might ought to start bringing his lunch to school or eat at the Panther, after they cut that wire off his jaw that is."

The veterans roared with laughter. None of them had any idea why Miss Clara had taken an interest in the matter, but they all loved her chocolate cake, so nobody asked. They just dug in.

Amy was Clara's favorite for a reason. Although strides had been made, racism was far from extinct in Preston. Children learned from their parents. There had been a grudging acceptance of black students in high school, but they were never invited to the parties, dances, and other private events. Stores had gone from barring blacks altogether to serving them out the back door to allowing them through the front door, some more willingly than others.

Clara went out of her way to be nice to everybody and slowly won students over, but Amy was the first to come around, even being nice to her son Terrell.

AMY FINALLY CAME INTO the store on Tuesday, along with Sandra. Kevin searched Amy's face for a sign, but she avoided his gaze and said nothing, sticking closely to Sandra, who did the talking.

Kevin followed the girls out to the Monza, carrying a roll of butcher paper on his shoulder, which was provided free by Robert so the cheerleaders could paint signs. Sandra opened the trunk and Kevin deposited the heavy roll of paper, wedging it in so it wouldn't roll around. Under other circumstances he would have made a joke about it throwing the Monza off balance and causing a wreck.

Amy went straight to the passenger door and got in. Sandra closed the trunk. "Thanks, Kevin. Bye."

"Bye." He looked at Amy, who turned her head away from him.

Kevin sprinted into the store.

"What was that about?" Sandra asked as she closed her door.

"What?"

"Did you two have a fight?"

"No."

"It looked like you were having sex with your clothes on at the dance."

"We most certainly were not!"

"Now you're giving him the cold shoulder."

"You didn't even want me to go to the dance with him. You said yourself people were starting to talk. We just decided to cool it. That's all."

"Logan wasn't right about you and Kevin, was he?"

"No! Good grief. Logan's a jerk and he got what was coming to him. I'm with Bobby. You of all people should know that. I'm carrying his baby for crying out loud. You really think I'm going to cheat on him with his best friend while he's in Viet Nam? Give me some credit."

"Calm down. We still don't know for sure that you're pregnant."

"I'm sorry I bit your head off. I'm just upset, about a lot of things. Kevin's just one of them."

"I forgot to thank Kevin for whacking Logan. Doug is really sorry he got in the way. He should have just let Kevin pound him."

Amy took a deep breath and grinned. "Emily whacked him pretty good too, didn't she?"

"Yes, she did. Your daddy must be proud."

KEVIN WAS ALONE in the darkroom at the newspaper office, late at night, listening to a Buddy Holley retrospective on the radio. Although most of Buddy's songs had an upbeat tempo, some of them were about lost love, which Kevin felt appropriate to his mission. He printed photos of Amy from the calendar session, only this time with far more care, dodging and burning, trying to make the eight-by-ten prints look as professional as possible.

He had promised Amy he would print additional shots from the session so that she could send them to Bobby periodically, but he didn't want to use that as an excuse to try and contact her. Difficult as it was, he was resolved to let her come to him. He would send the prints directly to Bobby and keep a few for himself.

He closed his eyes and cringed at the thought that Amy might have written to Bobby about what happened. Surely she told him about the fight with Logan—if she didn't somebody else would—but it was what happened after, in the car in front of her house, that threatened to ruin everything.

He briefly considered not sending the pictures to Bobby until he heard from him and got a better idea where he stood. If Amy had told him then surely Bobby would bring it up in a letter. Or maybe not. Maybe he would just let the anger simmer until he returned and let his fists do the talking. Either way printing more photos of Amy kept him occupied, however painful. He could decide later what to do with them, but right now, looking at them made him happy, or sad, or both.

28

AMY HAD NOT SAID a word to her daddy about what happened at the dance, certainly not after in Kevin's car in front of the house, and she was sure Emily hadn't either. He had finally caved and let Emily go to the party and stay out after midnight, so she certainly wasn't going to tell him she let a senior boy grope her bottom. She didn't know if slapping Logan's face would make up for her lack of judgment in allowing him the opportunity in the first place and she was in no hurry to find out.

There was teenage gossip and adult gossip, and rarely did the two cross over. The fight had been witnessed by the adult chaperones, so there was no denying that, only embellishing. For a few days both Amy and Emily watched their daddy like a hawk, but he never gave any indication he knew everything that happened. Amy was resigned to the fact that he knew about the fight at the dance. He was a barber—how could he not? But he had said nothing to her, and she wasn't sure what to make of it.

"Can I go to Lubbock with you after school?" Emily asked at breakfast.

"No," Amy said automatically.

"Why not?"

"Because you weren't invited, that's why."

"Who's going to Lubbock?" Howard asked.

"I'm going with Sandra," Amy said.

"I thought I told you, dear," Vivian said.

"Is Kevin going with you?" Emily asked.

Amy glared at her sister. "Why would Kevin go with us?"

Lily barely glanced up from her pancakes. She wasn't going and didn't care who was.

"That might not be a bad idea," Howard said.

"We're picking up stuff for cheerleading. We don't need a boy tagging along."

"Kevin's hardly a boy. He might be a good man to have around if you get into trouble."

"What kind of trouble?"

"Flat tire. Car breaks down. He's a pretty fair mechanic."

"We'll be fine. Besides, Kevin will probably be working." She was relieved. Her daddy suspected nothing about her and Kevin. Emily and her bottom were on their own.

"Come straight home. I don't want you girls out on the highway by yourselves after dark."

LUBBOCK HAD LONG suffered from an inferiority complex relative to its larger neighbor to the north, Amarillo, which was served by three railroads years before Lubbock was even founded. Completed in 1955, the Great Plains Life Building, towering twenty stories over downtown, served notice that Lubbock was the equal of Amarillo. The building quickly filled with doctors, dentists, lawyers, architects, accountants, and all manner of other professionals and businesses.

Parking for the new tower was woefully inadequate in the already crowded downtown area, and Amy and Sandra walked four blocks to reach the building, their boyfriends' letter jackets fending off the bitter north wind, luckily at their backs. Amy looked up before entering, marveling at the sheer height of the building.

Amy was reluctant to go to the free clinic, so Sandra had arranged an appointment at a private doctor's office and loaned her part of the money to pay for it. There was no way this visit could be reported to Blue Cross. Thanks to Bobby, Amy already had a fake ID, which she rarely used, terrified at the prospect of being caught, but this seemed like a risk worth taking. The elevator ride made her nauseated but was mercifully brief.

The receptionist didn't even ask for identification, nor did she question why Amy had no telephone number. Pregnancy posters adorned the otherwise dreary green walls. Amy fidgeted in the uncomfortable chair, glancing around at the others in the waiting area, nearly all young women, some obviously pregnant. She tossed aside a magazine and walked over to the window. Sandra followed, and they looked out over the city. The streets below bustled with cars and pedestrians. Although many stores and other businesses had already moved to the suburbs, downtown Lubbock was still a busy place, the center of everything important, the courthouse, police station, a hospital, restaurants and cafeterias, drugstores, department stores, bus station, airline ticket offices, and the recently vacated Santa Fe passenger depot.

Amy leaned against the window and looked straight down.

"Bobby said he sits on the floor of a helicopter, dangling his legs over the side. I could never do that."

"That's crazy."

"Kevin said he did the same thing," Amy said, and then wished she hadn't brought him up.

"Are you still not speaking to Kevin?"

Amy ignored the question. "Bobby took me out to eat in the

restaurant on the top floor." She pointed at the ceiling. "You could see for miles around."

"I've never been up there."

"Louise," a nurse called out.

Sandra elbowed Amy and whispered, "That's you."

Amy turned and took a deep breath. The time had come. There would be no more guessing. Just through that door, held open by the nurse, was her destiny.

When it was over, the receptionist handed Amy a business card and said, "Call this number after two on Monday for the test results."

"Why does it take so long?" Amy asked as she and Sandra walked toward the elevator.

"I don't know. It just does, and it's the weekend."

"I'm feeling sick," Amy said on the ride down.

"Are you going to throw up?"

"I don't know."

"Have you eaten anything today? You hardly touched your lunch."

"I had some dry toast and coffee for breakfast."

"You should eat something."

"I'm getting fat."

"Starving yourself won't help."

"It might."

"Do you want to wait here while I get the car?"

"No, let's just go."

The wind had picked up while they were in the doctor's office and the girls pulled their letter jackets tight around their necks as they walked into the wind, using their other hand to try and keep their skirts from blowing up around their waists. Up ahead a Santa Fe freight train rolled out of the Lubbock Yard, headed west. Several Bell UH-1 helicopters rode on flatcars, mixed with other freight. The girls paid no attention.

There were plenty of places to eat in downtown Lubbock, along with several hamburger joints on the Clovis Road, but Sandra headed west on Fourth Street, pulled into the Hi-D-Ho on College Avenue, and demanded that Amy eat something.

"I guess I'm eating for two now," Amy said before biting into her Hi-D-Burger.

"We don't know that for sure."

"I've missed twice. What else could it be?"

"Let's just wait until Monday. Stay busy until then. We have an away game tomorrow. You can spend the night with me, and we'll look at fan magazines and get all silly."

Silly was the last thing Amy ever expected to be again. She glanced around at cars full of teenagers, being exactly that, silly, flirting, laughing. She turned and looked in the direction of a scream, and then watched as a teenage girl covered her face in embarrassment, maybe at a dirty joke, maybe something more. That used to be her.

As the Monza bounced and swerved in the crosswind on the highway Amy stared out the window at the bare cotton fields, stripped clean but for a few white fluffy bolls that clung to the brown stalks, flapping in the wind. She slipped her hand under Bobby's letter jacket and felt her stomach.

THE NEXT FEW DAYS were sheer torture for Amy. She tried to be upbeat in her letters to Bobby, careful to not give even a hint of what was going on. She mentioned her trip to Lubbock with Sandra, but only for cheerleader supplies, leaving out the part about the visit to the Great Plains Life Building. She filled him in on high school gossip. She expressed her embarrassment at how much his buddies loved her pictures, especially the ones that looked like she was naked. She didn't mention Kevin, afraid that he might have already contradicted anything she made up. She still had no idea if Bobby had told Kevin they had sex. She wouldn't put it past him—boys bragged, and Bobby was a boy.

Both her parents, and Emily, noticed Kevin's absence from Amy's life, but she dismissed any concern. She was busy with school and cheerleading, and Kevin was working at the store and making repairs on his house. There was nothing to be concerned about, she insisted, but Howard was very much concerned, suspicious that the fight at the New Year's dance held more significance than Amy had admitted. Teenage drama was not uncommon in his household, so he let it go. If there was a serious problem, surely Amy would tell him, or Emily would sniff it out and snitch on her sister.

Sandra had been right about staying busy. Amy had cleaned her room, organized her closet, worked on a term paper, and tried to read a novel for English class, but her mind kept drifting. There was a lot of laughing, giggling, and talking about boys on the bus ride to and from the game Friday night, but none of it interested Amy.

Sleepovers were easier, or at least more private, at Sandra's house, especially now that her brother was away at college and Amy no longer had to worry about him suddenly bursting in, which he had a way of doing when Amy was around. The girls put on Sandra's naughtiest nighties and lay on the bed poring over fan and fashion magazines, wishing they looked more like the girl celebrities and fashion models, while ogling the boys.

Amy flipped through the pages of a cheerleader supply catalog and pointed at a particularly handsome male cheerleader. "He's cute."

Sandra looked and gasped. "That's him."

"Him who?"

"Last summer, in Dallas."

"That's him?" Amy's mouth fell open as she studied the picture. "Wow."

"I told you he was hot."

"I'll say. No wonder you cheated on Doug."

"I didn't really cheat. We didn't go all the way."

"But a long way, right?"

"Oh yeah," Sandra said with a smirk. "A very long way. Further than I've ever gone with any boy but Doug."

"You slut," Amy teased.

"He really knows how to make a girl feel like a girl, if you know what I mean."

Amy shrieked and covered her face.

"It's a big world out there," Sandra said. "You should expand your horizons."

"That's okay. I'll stick with Bobby." Amy flipped the page and pointed at another picture. "Is that him?"

"Yep."

"Those tight pants don't leave much to the imagination."

Sandra laughed. "No, they don't."

"Are you going to see him again?"

"I don't know, maybe. He's a freshman at SMU, and still modeling. I guess it depends on what happens with Doug."

"What do you mean?"

"He might join the Army, or the Marines. It was fun while we were in high school, but I don't see myself sitting around Preston waiting for him."

"Like me and Bobby."

"Sorry, no offense."

"Are you still thinking about going to SMU? With cheerleader boy?"

"Probably. Daddy can get me a part-time job at the Apparel Mart."

Amy closed the catalog and rolled over, gazing at the ceiling. "Maybe I should have gone out with other boys."

"It's not too late."

"It might be. I'll know Monday."

"We're not talking about that until Monday, remember?"

"I should have gone to Dallas with you this summer, after Bobby left for basic."

"You should have. We could have had so much fun. You'd be a real hit with the photographers there."

Amy gave her a look. "In my underwear?"

"Sure, why not? You shot with Kevin in your underwear."

"That was different. It was for Bobby, not the whole world. And it was Kevin, not some strange old guy."

"A lot of the photographers are young, and hot. Makes it even sexier."

Amy grimaced.

"You should have worn that sheer nightie I gave you."

"You could see my nipples!"

"Who could, Kevin?"

"I put it on, but I didn't let him see me in it. There was no way I was wearing that thing to take pictures."

"Bobby would have loved it."

"So would his buddies. And Kevin."

Sandra laughed. "Oh yeah."

"It was bad enough wearing that other nightie."

"It's no big deal. I was a little nervous when I shot underwear and lingerie in Dallas, but you get over it really quick."

"Yeah, I know what you mean. It was weird at first, but Kevin made me feel really comfortable."

"But he still looked."

"Of course he looked. He's a boy, plus he had to take the pictures."

"And it made you feel sexy, right?"

Amy grinned and nodded.

"Miss November looked like you were having sex with the camera," Sandra said.

"Ew."

"Well, it did. I'll bet Kevin enjoyed the shit out of that."

"He told me to ignore him and pretend the camera was Bobby."

"It would have been even better if you were naked under the sheet."

"What difference would it make? You couldn't see anything anyway."

"Yeah, but you would have felt sexier, and it would show on your face."

"I don't feel very sexy right now, just pregnant."

MONDAY FINALLY CAME and Amy finished a letter to Bobby in class, dreading the next one she had to write. Making the phone call required planning—it wasn't simply a matter of picking up the phone and calling. There was no way Amy could make the call from her house, and even Sandra's would be a problem, as the long-distance call would show up on her daddy's phone bill. Several pay phone locations were considered. The one at the Hi-Way Café was in the foyer, with way too many people coming in and out, although many of them were travelers unknown to Amy, so it remained under consideration. The most secluded was the one on the sidewalk outside the local phone company office, a small nondescript building a block off the town square. People stopped by to pay their phone bill, either inside or dropping it through the slot at night, but it was hardly a high-traffic area. Teenagers rarely visited the building, so it might look unusual for Amy and Sandra to be using the pay phone, especially when their daddies had a place of business just a block or two away. The pay phone at the high school won out. Teenagers used it often, so the girls would not be at all out of place. It offered the advantage of being the quickest to get to after school, although Amy and Sandra would have to wait a few minutes for most of the students to clear out. The phone was located behind the school, but far enough from the back door to avoid foot traffic. Even if an eavesdropper overheard something, the call would be short, and it would be difficult to ascertain what was actually being discussed.

Amy gathered a handful of quarters and took a deep breath before dialing. Sandra stood in silence, closely watching Amy's face for any hint. After stating her business, Amy turned to Sandra, waiting on a nameless, faceless employee at the doctor's office to render the verdict, oblivious to the life-and-death consequences. For all she knew,

"Louise" could be a young married woman who would be either thrilled or disappointed.

Sandra stood guard, eyes tracking everyone in the area, preparing to loudly engage them in conversation should they approach.

"Thank you." Amy hung up the phone and closed her eyes.

"Well?"

Amy finally turned to Sandra and nodded, the expression on her face delivering the news.

"Oh no. What are you going to do?"

"I don't know."

"You still have time."

"No I don't. I'm already showing. I can't hide it forever."

"You're not showing that bad. It's winter. People get fatter in the winter and wear bulky clothes. You have lots of cute sweaters. It's not like anybody is going to see you in a swimsuit anytime soon, or your underwear."

Amy stared into the distance, across the parking lot, the football field, at nothing in particular.

"I need to tell Kevin."

"You'd better tell Bobby. He's the father, isn't he?"

"Of course he's the father. Good grief. Do you think I've been screwing Kevin since the day Bobby left?"

"Well, something's been going on, and now it's not. You're not even speaking to him. It doesn't take a genius to figure out something happened between you two. That's what everybody thinks."

"What does everybody think?" Amy demanded.

"That Kevin was trying to move in on Bobby's girl. That's sure what it looked like at the dance. That was some kiss. People noticed."

"It was New Year's Eve. Everybody kisses at midnight."

"It was a lot more than that. You've been going out with Kevin since Bobby left and now you aren't even speaking to him, but he's the one you want to tell you're pregnant?"

"He might know what to do."

"Why would he know what to do? How many teenage girls has he knocked up?"

"None that I know of, but he was in the Army."

"So's Bobby."

"Bobby is in Viet Nam. Kevin is here."

"Where?" Sandra looked around, exaggerating her head movements. "I don't see him. I'm here."

AMY SHUT HERSELF in her room and prepared to write the most difficult letter she had ever written. There was no need to delay it any longer. She wished Kevin hadn't ruined everything—she desperately needed him right now. Bobby had to be told, and now. She knew it would upset him, especially with him in Viet Nam and unable to do anything to help her through it, whatever it might be, but he had a right to know. More importantly, he might have a solution.

She tried once more to put pen to paper but closed her eyes and cried. She couldn't be pregnant. She just couldn't. She couldn't get fat. She couldn't show up at school with a big belly. She couldn't be seen in a cheerleader uniform. She certainly couldn't do jumps and splits. She grabbed a calendar and started counting. How long would it be before she really started showing? How long could she hide it? How long before Emily figured it out, before her mother noticed? How could she tell her parents? She had no answers.

After crying as softly as she could for as long as she wanted, she wiped her tears and started writing the dreaded dispatch. It had to be finished tonight and go out in the morning mail. Not only did Bobby need to know as soon as possible, but there was no way she could risk carrying this unfinished letter around all day at school.

29

KEVIN HAD EXPLAINED to Amy how mail got to and from Viet Nam, something about San Francisco and the Army Post Office and the Air Force and helicopters and mail bags and company clerks and mail call, but she hadn't paid much attention. All she knew was that it took at least a week for a letter to get there and an answer to come back. Once she mailed Bobby the letter there was no taking it back, no changing her mind, no waiting and hoping it would work itself out. The fat was in the fire, as her daddy was fond of saying. If he only knew. Her calendar was getting a workout as she checked off the days until she heard from Bobby as well as how far along she was. Fortunately, her clock had started ticking just two days before Bobby left, providing good cover for counting the elapsed days should someone see her calendar. Her mind raced, wondering what Bobby's response might be. Would he be thrilled? Angry? Ambivalent? She had continued to write every day, trying to be cheerful, talking about school and sports, friends and family, but nothing about Kevin. She found herself in a time warp. She was answering his letters written before he knew.

Amy was somewhat alarmed when a letter from Bobby mentioned the new pictures that Kevin had sent, wondering why she hadn't told him they were coming. He seemed particularly enthusiastic about the mystery pictures but failed to give her enough information to identify which ones they were. She had no idea what to write in response, finally deciding all she could say was, "glad you liked them." She was going to add, "I had fun doing them," but which pictures were they? Had Kevin surreptitiously shot some far racier pictures and not shown her? Surely not, that would be mean. Kevin had confessed his love for her. Why would he want to hurt her? Because she had rejected him, crushed him, that's why. Now she was worried.

With no reliable information, and no doctor to advise her, Amy was concerned about the baby in her belly and tried to tone down her jumping and kicking while cheerleading, and even considered quitting the team, but such a drastic step would have invited unwanted attention.

She checked her calendar again. It was Friday. Bobby would know tomorrow or Sunday. Maybe he would call, if that was even possible. Kevin had said something about using MARS to call home, but it sounded strange. An amateur radio operator would call collect from somewhere and "patch the call through," whatever that meant. You had to talk loudly, and you had to say "over" after everything you said because it was really a radio call even though you were talking on the phone. Bobby probably wouldn't do that. Her daddy would want to know why some stranger from Spokane or somewhere was calling her collect. More importantly, how in the world could she talk on the phone with everyone in the house able to hear everything she said. "Yeah, I'm pregnant. Over. What are we going to do? Over." It would have been funny if it weren't so serious.

It was busy at Bob's Food Store, as it usually was on Saturday. Irene checked out Clara's groceries while Kevin sacked.

"Miss Clara, I hear Terrell's a short-timer now," Kevin said.

"Yes, he is."

"How short is he?"

"That boy is so short he has to stand on a ladder to tie his shoe-laces."

Kevin laughed. Short-timer jokes were always funny, especially when most people didn't understand them.

"When is he coming home?" Irene asked.

"Thirty-two days and a wakeup," Clara said.

"He's so short—" Kevin said and then leaned across the counter to whisper the rest, obviously dirty, into Clara's ear.

Clara feigned embarrassment.

"I'll bet he's looking forward to your cooking," Kevin said.

"I want you to come over for supper when he gets home."

"If you're cooking, I'll be there."

"Look what he sent me from Hong Kong." Clara held out her hand showing Kevin a wristwatch.

"That's nice."

"He sent me a beautiful string of pearls too, but they look really expensive, so I only wear them to church."

Kevin nodded and smiled, glancing up to see his mother also smiling. Millions of mothers had received jewelry purchased by their sons in various R&R destinations or at the PX, and she was no exception. Kevin finished sacking and headed out with Clara's groceries while she paid the bill in cash.

As Kevin returned to the store, Sandra's Monza pulled into the parking lot. She quickly stepped out and approached him.

"Do you have a minute?"

"Not really. It's Saturday." He continued walking.

"It's about Amy."

He stopped, suddenly having a minute.

"What about her?"

"What's going on between you two?"

"Nothing's going on."

"Well, ever since Bobby left you two have been practically going steady, and now suddenly you aren't speaking to each other."

"We weren't going steady. We weren't even dating."

"Call it what you like, but there was something going on."

"We're friends."

"Friends who don't speak to each other?"

"Haven't you and Amy ever been mad at each other?"

"Yes, but we get over it. That's what friends do. They don't break up."

"We didn't break up. We were never a couple. People were starting to talk, so we decided to cool it, especially after the fight."

"That's what Amy said."

"There it is." He turned to leave.

"Well, whatever it was, maybe you should apologize."

"It's really none of your business." He walked away.

EIGHT DAYS. That's how long it took for Amy's life-changing letter to cross half a continent, an ocean, a jungle, and for Bobby's response to retrace the same route. No one involved in the process had any idea about the urgency of the messages contained in the mailbags, not just Amy's and Bobby's letters, but thousands of others riding along with them. Relationships would come to an end, others would sprout. Births and deaths would be announced. Lives would be forever changed.

Amy walked out of the barbershop, ripping open Bobby's letter. She read furiously as she approached Sandra's car. She opened the door and slid into the seat, still reading.

"Well," Sandra said.

Amy held up her hand to ward off additional conversation, concentrating on the letter, her actions answering Sandra's unfinished question. This was the one. This was Bobby's response.

"He's going to get emergency leave and come home so we can get married," Amy said, unable to contain her excitement.

"Emergency leave?" Sandra asked, unconvinced.

Amy nodded while she read.

"I don't think so," Sandra said.

"Why not?"

"That's for when your mom dies or something, not so you can come home to marry your pregnant girlfriend."

"You don't know that."

"Yes, actually, I do."

"How do you know?"

"Everybody knows that. Ask Kevin. Oh, that's right. You aren't speaking to Kevin. Then ask your daddy, or my daddy, or Bobby's daddy, or anybody else who's ever been in the Army."

"Bobby's daddy was in the Navy."

"Same deal."

"What about R&R?"

"What about it? That's where guys go to get laid. How's that going to help?"

"Guys go on R&R to Hawaii and meet their wives there."

"You aren't his wife."

"We could get married in Hawaii."

"You have to be eighteen to get married, and you'll be ready to pop by then."

Amy nodded, defeated. "What am I going to do?"

"Take care of it. Nobody has to know."

"Bobby would have to know."

30

AMY WAS NOW desperate. She had been momentarily ecstatic after receiving Bobby's letter, but Sandra had quickly, and rather rudely, destroyed those hopes. Even if Bobby could get emergency leave, she would have to tell her parents that she was pregnant and had to get married. But according to Sandra, who was probably right, that option was off the table—there was no way Bobby was getting emergency leave to return home to marry his pregnant girlfriend. Amy now realized her next best option—jetting off to Hawaii to get married—was probably a fantasy as well. She had never been on a plane. She had barely been out of Texas. Plane tickets to anywhere were expensive, and Hawaii had to be even more. A sleepover at Sandra's was good for a night, maybe two, but there was no way she and Sandra could ever concoct a cover story for a week in Hawaii. There was no reasonable course of action that didn't involve confessing to her parents.

Except one. She shuddered at the thought. Her mouth went dry. She cried and cried, and then wiped her tears and picked up pen and paper. There had to be a way. She dashed off a letter to Bobby, quiz-zing him first on emergency leave, and then on R&R, desperate for any hint of a solution. Then she waited. It would be another eight days, hopefully seven. There were only so many of these slices of time left until she could no longer hide her secret and matters were out of her hands.

BOBBY'S GTO TURNED the corner on the square and drove slowly past the courthouse, stopping briefly at a stop sign before turning and proceeding through a residential area, finally stopping in front of the Evans house.

Alone in the house, Amy washed her hair in the shower, her eyes closed, letting the warm water cascade over her head and shoulders, washing away her worries. She ran her fingers over her belly and started crying again. She stepped out of the shower and dried off. She didn't hear the front door open.

She pulled Bobby's cropped football T-shirt over her head, her damp hair falling over her shoulders, soaking into the shirt. She stepped out of the bathroom, head down, toweling her hair. She flipped her hair back, looked up and shrieked.

Kevin, holding sacks of groceries, stood at the end of the hallway, staring. There was certainly something to stare at. Amy wore nothing but the cropped T-shirt and a pair of white bikini panties. She didn't notice the shirt was wet, but Kevin did.

"You scared the crap out of me," she said. And with that it was like nothing had ever come between them.

"Sorry."

"What are you doing here?" she asked as she brushed past him, toweling her hair, making no effort to cover herself.

"Delivering groceries. Your mom said the door was unlocked."

He followed her into the kitchen and put the groceries on the counter. "I didn't think anybody was here."

Amy dug through a sack and pulled out a package of meat wrapped in white butcher paper.

"Mom took Emily to the dentist in Lubbock and Lily went with them," she said. "I just got home."

Kevin watched closely as she opened the refrigerator.

"How have you been?"

"Okay, I guess," she said, closing the refrigerator door, seemingly oblivious to the fact that the T-shirt barely covered her breasts even when standing up straight.

"Have you heard from Bobby?" He was curious to know if he had been ratted out, but afraid to ask.

"Almost every day, why?"

"Just wondering."

"Have you heard from him?"

"Yeah, but not as often as you."

"Did you send him some pictures?"

He nodded. "We kind of promised him we would, and I didn't want him to not get them because of—you know."

"Thanks. I'm glad you did. Which ones were they?"

"In bed, under the sheet."

"That's what I thought."

She dug through the grocery sacks, looking for perishables.

"How long do you have to be in Viet Nam before you can get R&R?"

"Depends on where you want to go."

"What about Hawaii?"

"You have to be in-country for at least six months to go to Hawaii, maybe more, and they give preference to married guys. I doubt Bobby would want to go there anyway. The shopping would be a lot better in Bangkok or Hong Kong, if you could trust him to stay out of the massage parlors and bathhouses. He could get you some really nice jewelry and stuff." He studied her closely. "Whoa. Hold on. You don't think your daddy would let you go to Hawaii to spend a week with your boyfriend, do you?"

"A girl can dream, can't she?"

"You can dream, but there's no way Bobby's getting R&R in Hawaii unless he extends his tour for six months. But I'm guessing he's not going to do that." He glanced down and then back up, smiling. "Well, I don't know. Maybe for that."

She looked down at what she was wearing. "Oh crap," she said, trying to cover herself with both hands, and then throwing them up.

"We should have put that on the calendar."

She smiled and nodded. "Yeah, we probably should," she said wistfully, thinking back on her photo session with Kevin, where she tried to keep things covered, embarrassed to be seen by him in such skimpy attire. All that now seemed so unimportant.

"Look, I know you miss him, and he misses you, but you'll get through it. Millions of people have. Just take it one day at a time and it'll be over before you know it."

He started to go, but then stopped and turned.

"Amy, I'm sorry."

"For what?"

"Everything. I should have just kept my big mouth shut and done what Bobby asked me to do."

"And I shouldn't have led you on, with all the hugging and kissing and holding hands."

"No, it's all my fault. I never meant to hurt you, or Bobby."

"I wrote to him about the fight, but not what happened after."

"That's a relief. I've been worried sick about it. I'll own up to what I did, and he can beat the shit out of me when he gets home, but he really doesn't need to know while he's over there. Trust me."

"I'm in love with Bobby," she said softly, lowering her head.

Kevin nodded.

"We're just friends," she said. "Or at least I hope we still are."

"Of course we are."

"Good, because I really need a friend right now." She looked up at him, hoping he would pull her into his arms, hug her, kiss her on the forehead, and make it all better, but the front door opened. Emily raced in, chased by Lily, with Vivian bringing up the rear. Emily quickly hugged Kevin. "Hi, Kevin," she said, and then fought with Lily over the grocery sacks.

"Thanks, Kevin," Vivian said. She turned to Amy. "What are you wearing?"

"Bobby's T-shirt."

"Do you think that's appropriate?"

"I wasn't exactly expecting company. You're lucky I wasn't naked."

Emily and Lily snickered.

"You practically are."

"It's not like he hasn't already seen—" Amy looked at Kevin. "—girls in their underwear before."

"I'd better get back to the store," Kevin said.

Amy followed him into the living room, with Lily close behind. Lily sat at the piano and began playing Beethoven's "Piano Sonata No. 8, Op. 13," one of Grandmother's favorites.

Amy looked at Lily, wondering if the music would cover their conversation, decided it wouldn't, and then turned to Kevin. "Can we talk later?"

"Sure," he said, thrilled at the prospect of reconciliation, on whatever terms she dictated. He opened the front door.

"Why are you driving Bobby's car?" She quickly stepped behind the door to keep from exposing herself to passersby, although there was little traffic on the quiet street.

"Bobby didn't want to put it up on blocks, so Big Bob decided to use it for deliveries."

"He wants to get a new one when he gets home."

"Yeah, I know."

There was no attempt at a hug, much less a kiss, even on the cheek. Enormous progress had been made and Kevin wasn't going to risk screwing up again. He just waved and smiled. "Bye. Talk to you later."

Amy hid behind the door and watched as Kevin sprinted to the GTO.

31

KEVIN WAS OFF WORK the next day and agonized over whether to pick up Amy after school, as he had every Wednesday since Bobby left, until he made his idiotic profession of love. He finally decided it would be presumptuous and he didn't want to destroy the progress that had been made. A first step had been taken. She had said she wanted to talk, so the only sensible course was to wait for her to come to him, and hopefully soon. He hammered and sawed in the barn, worked on the fence, climbed the windmill to do an assessment, anything to pass the time. Maybe she would call when she got home from school. Maybe tonight.

Amy didn't call after school, or that night, and it required a lot of self-discipline for Kevin to not pick up the phone. He would give it one more day and then find an excuse to call.

Thursday dawned rather chilly, and a blue norther rolled in before noon, turning the sky first gray with clouds and then brown with blowing dirt. Men, and women, on the Llano Estacado had long toiled under such conditions, but there was nothing outside really that pressing, so Kevin stayed in. He listened to mournful love songs on his record player and pored over the contact sheets of Amy, selecting additional frames to be printed. Maybe a couple more eight-by-tens of Amy would help, or maybe they would just cause Bobby to wonder what else went on while Kevin had Amy in his bedroom, nearly naked, with him in Viet Nam, unable to protect his turf, defend his lady, smash Kevin's camera, and his stupid face.

Kevin finally had enough moping, drove into town and had lunch at the Hi-Way Café. He filled the tank of the Impala and drove to the grocery store.

"We're out of milk," Kevin said to his mother.

"I'll bring it when I come home, or you can take it now."

"You can bring it. I think I'll go get a haircut."

His hair had not been cut since he got home, at first because he enjoyed not being required to do so, and for the last couple of weeks he had been uneasy about walking into the barbershop, not sure of what Howard knew about his relationship with Amy.

Kevin took a step toward Patty's register. "Have you heard from Bobby?"

"Not for a couple of days," Patty said. "Hopefully we'll have a letter tomorrow."

"I haven't either."

"I'm sure Amy has heard from him," Patty said.

"Probably. I'll check at the barbershop."

A glance at the number of cars parked around the square dissuaded Kevin from driving the two blocks to the barbershop, so he pulled up the collar of his field jacket and headed out on foot.

"I thought you were MIA," Howard said, sitting in the barber chair, looking up from his newspaper as Kevin pushed open the door. "Haven't seen you around lately."

"Been busy, working on the house," Kevin said as he stepped in. "Has Amy had a letter from Bobby in the last couple of days?"

"Nothing today, or yesterday, for that matter. She'll probably have three tomorrow. You know how APO mail is."

"Yeah. Or he may be on the move. He said something about his outfit moving to Firebase Buttons."

"Where's that?"

"At Song Be, up near the Cambodian border. That could delay his mail a day or two."

"That's one thing about the Army. If you don't like the scenery just wait a few days."

Kevin stood in front of the barber chair. "You still cut hair here?"

Howard laughed and stood. "I thought you were going to let it grow out like a hippie."

Kevin sat in the chair and Howard draped a cape around his neck.

"I was, but then I'd have to buy a blow dryer. I don't know how girls do it."

Howard laughed. "Especially now that long hair is back in style. You should spend some time at my house."

"I like long hair, on girls. It kind of sucked when I was in high school, beehives and bowling balls."

"Takes longer to dry, though."

"I'd also need some—what do they call it—products."

"Yeah, there's some fancy shops in Lubbock that charge five dollars for a haircut. Then they try to sell you their overpriced hair products." Howard snipped in silence for a moment. "Is Amy doing okay?"

"I guess. Why?"

"Nothing in particular. She just seems a little, not herself lately. At her age friends know more than parents."

"Well, her boyfriend is in Viet Nam. That has to be hard on a girl."

"I guess you're right."

Howard glanced out the window. An Army sedan pulled in and parked at the courthouse. "Looks like the Army recruiters are back in town."

Kevin turned and watched as two soldiers in class A uniform got out of the car and walked into the courthouse.

"What are they doing at the courthouse?" Kevin asked.

"I don't know. They usually just go to the high school."

"Maybe they're not recruiters. Maybe they're doing background checks."

"No, those guys wear civilian clothes, and they drive GSA cars. Army Intelligence. They always come in here. If you want to know something in a small town, come to the barbershop."

"Spooks. In Viet Nam they wore jungle fatigues like the rest of us, but no rank, just a shiny brass US on their collar, and they only saluted field-grade officers. Nobody knew whether to salute them or not. Weird guys. Always wore sunglasses, and they carried snub-nosed thirty-eights, not exactly my choice of weapon in a firefight."

Howard laughed. "I'll take an M-1 any day."

"I met one of them once. My company had raided an NVA camp and recovered an American PW, young kid. He had only been missing a couple of days, but he was scared shitless. A spook came in on a chopper to escort him back to division. Apparently, nobody but spooks are allowed to talk to repatriated prisoners until they are debriefed. They sent me along to ride shotgun. That was a happy kid."

"I'll bet his mama was even happier."

"Made me pretty happy too. I got a day off and a hot shower and chow in Phuoc Vinh."

Howard laughed.

"And a hell of a poker game at our battalion rear," Kevin said. "I won twenty bucks."

Kevin stood at the cash register, paying for his haircut, watching as the soldiers returned to their car.

"Don't be a stranger," Howard said as Kevin pulled open the door.

Kevin saw the Army sedan pull into the grocery store and stop. One soldier got out and the other drove away.

"Shit," Kevin said out loud. He started running, dodging cars.

Howard stepped out onto the sidewalk and watched as Kevin sprinted across Main Street against the light, almost getting hit. Cars screeched to a stop and drivers laid down on their horns. Kevin ran into the grocery store. Howard continued to watch, a bad feeling creeping over him.

Kevin raced out of the grocery store. He sprinted to the Impala and turned the key. Nothing. He tried again. Still nothing. He climbed out of the Impala, ran past his mother's pickup, and jumped into Bobby's GTO.

Hank, waiting at the light, watched as the GTO exploded out of the parking lot, gravel flying, sliding sideways onto the brick street. Hank turned and watched for a moment, but didn't give chase, instead pulling into the parking lot of the grocery store.

AMY SAT IN Maggie's class, doodling, writing "Amy Dalton" in her notebook. She smiled, liking the way it looked.

Doug was the first to notice the Army sedan pull in and park in front of the school. Amy looked out the window and saw the car, but didn't give it a second thought, assuming it was recruiters, and they already had her future husband, so she was not at all interested. She went back to her doodling.

Benjamin Washington looked up from his dust mop as Principal Klein and a soldier walked briskly down the empty hallway.

Students in Maggie's class turned toward the sound of the GTO. Even street-legal it was loud and moving fast. Doug leaned forward and looked out the window.

All eyes turned the other way as the door opened and Principal Klein stepped in and motioned for Maggie to come over. He spoke to her quietly. Maggie turned and looked at Amy, who was still doodling.

Students were trying to look both ways at once as the GTO screeched to a halt on the street in front of the school. Amy looked up and was somewhat bemused as Kevin leapt out of the car and raced toward the school.

Doug watched Kevin for a moment and then looked back at the door and saw the soldier standing in the hallway. He immediately realized what was happening.

Amy had no idea what was going on, but apparently Kevin had lost his mind. She had told him they would talk, but why was he coming to school? She wouldn't be out for another half hour, at least. All eyes were on her as she turned away from the window.

Kevin flung open the heavy steel door at the front of the school. The crash echoed through the school, causing even more students in other classrooms to turn and look. He sprinted down the hallway and up the stairway, taking the stairs two at a time, breathing hard.

Amy stood in the hallway, just outside the classroom, with Principal Klein and the soldier. She was in a daze, the only sound a buzzing in her ears, until she heard another loud crash and the upstairs fire door slammed into the wall. Kevin hurtled toward her as fast as he could.

Amy screamed, gulped air, and screamed again. Her screams shook everyone in the classroom, even through the closed door, as Maggie stood, not knowing what to do. Sandra shrieked and then burst into tears. Other girls soon joined her.

Amy started reeling and went down. Principal Klein didn't move, but the soldier reached out. Kevin got there first, falling to his knees and sliding the rest of the way, catching Amy's head just before it hit the floor. She wailed and sobbed and clung to him as he gathered her into his arms.

Students jumped out of their desks and moved toward the doorway. Maggie tried to hold them back, but Sandra was having none of it and pushed her aside. Sandra reached for the door, but Doug grabbed it first and shoved it open. Other students crowded into the doorway. Maggie was lost in the crush.

Doors opened all up and down the hallway. Teachers stepped out to see what was going on, followed quickly by students who swarmed out and massed around Amy, in Kevin's arms. Principal Klein tried without success to keep everyone at bay.

Amy was inconsolable. Sandra felt her pain and was herself in shock. Kevin struggled to stand, but Amy was no help. It was like trying to deadlift a sack of potatoes off the floor. Doug surged forward and helped Kevin get to his feet while never letting go of Amy. She buried her face in his chest, still wailing.

Students immediately cleared a path as soon as Kevin turned and indicated his direction. The crowd parted as Kevin carried Amy, with Doug and Sandra close behind.

"Take her to the nurse's office," Principal Klein called out.

"I'm taking her home," Kevin said.

"I can't allow that. She needs to see the school nurse."

Kevin ignored him and looked over his shoulder. "Doug."

"Yo," Doug said, hustling closer.

"You drive."

"You got it."

"Douglas! You can't leave school," Principal Klein said.

"Hide and watch."

"I'm going with you," Sandra said.

All along the hallway students stood back and watched, whispering, crying, gasping, stunned.

Kevin somehow made it down the stairs, not an easy task with both hands occupied, carrying Amy, but Doug's grip on his shoulder steadied him. Students fled in front of him, spreading the word. Two of them held open the steel fire doors on the ground floor and Kevin marched through.

Benjamin Washington bowed his head. "Lord have mercy."

Emily raced down the hallway, screaming, "Amy! Amy!"

Doug caught Emily before she could crash into Kevin and Amy. He took her into his arms and hugged her as she cried. Kevin didn't slow down—he was a man on a mission. Just as Doug was about to scoop up Emily and carry her, she collected herself enough to walk and Sandra put an arm around her waist.

Hank waited near the office. "You carrying her home?"

"Yes sir," Kevin said.

"You'll follow me. Then I need to get back to the store."

"Thanks. They're coming with us." He tilted his head toward Doug.

"You can't leave school," Principal Klein insisted, rushing forward, trying to take charge.

"They're with me," Hank said, turning toward the front doors, both of which were held open by students.

"Go!" Sandra said. "I've got her."

Doug released Emily to Sandra and sprinted through the doors. He raced to the GTO and held open the passenger side door. Emily, now fully ambulatory, climbed into the back seat with Sandra. With Doug's help, Kevin somehow managed to sit in the passenger seat with Amy in his arms.

Hank was already in his car, backing up, preparing to roll, as Doug raced around the GTO and jumped into the driver's seat.

The bell had not yet rung but Colonel Klink had lost all authority over his captives. Scores of them congregated on the brown grass in front of the school and watched somberly as Doug followed Hank. Others scampered to their cars.

Shifting gears was a bit of a challenge with Amy's feet in the way, but Doug managed it. He checked the rearview mirror. Sandra cuddled Emily like a child.

Howard was already running home when he saw the police car approaching. There was no need for flashing red lights or siren and no hurry. Hank parked on the street as Doug pulled into the driveway.

Howard stopped briefly to talk to Hank. Few words were

required. Phones were already ringing across town. Howard shook hands with Hank and then rushed to his daughter's side.

The parking lot at Bob's Food Store was packed when Hank returned, but there were few customers shopping. Most had come to offer support to Patty and Robert. "Let me know if there's anything I can do," was the common refrain, although for some it was simply a given—no words were needed—their mere presence was enough. Irene was among the latter. She simply sprang into action, taking command in the store, telling Patty and Robert they could go home, and she would keep the store open until closing time, but so many people were already congregating in the store it was easier for the Daltons to just stay there.

A pall fell over Preston.

32

WHEELS WERE TURNING even before Robert called the funeral home to make the necessary arrangements. The local chapter of the VFW already had a procedure in place. They had buried many veterans over the years, mostly older men whose time had come, but not since Korea had they dealt with a KIA. They were far better informed on the Army's procedures than most in town, but even they had no idea when Bobby's remains would be returned, or how. The funeral director, a veteran himself, immediately took charge. Long-distance calls were made, connections exploited, politicians nudged. A call was made to Fort Sill, Oklahoma, the nearest major Army post, notifying them that an honor guard would be required, date and details to follow.

The *Preston Post* was on the story within minutes. Becky Parker ditched the rest of the school day and raced to the newspaper office with her brother. This was as close to breaking news as it got in Preston. Becky tearfully searched for file photos of Bobby. It was clearly the lead story of the next issue. A single shot of Bobby in uniform was preferred as the main photo on the front page, above the fold, but one of Bobby, Kevin, and Terrell, in football uniforms, arm-in-arm after the 1966 game in Sweetwater, also seemed utterly appropriate. Becky was assigned to write a sidebar with the accompanying three-shot. Sports was not her thing, but she had gone to school with all three of the boys in the photo, so she readily accepted the assignment. Old Man Parker wisely decided there would be no editorial in the next edition. This transcended politics. He would have more to say on the subject later.

"How is she?" Irene asked as Kevin came through the kitchen door.

"The doctor gave her a sedative," Kevin said. "She was asleep when I left."

Irene turned to the cook stove. "I'll make you some supper."

"I'm not hungry."

She opened the refrigerator.

"Why in the world would the Army do that? Couldn't they have just told her parents?"

She put a carton of milk on the table and then fetched a glass from the cabinet.

"There's a form you fill out," he said. "You can tell them who you want notified. I guess he put Amy's name on it too."

"I just wish she didn't have to find out that way."

"Yeah, me too."

He sat quietly, drinking milk, as Irene whipped up supper, which he ate and then went to his room.

AMY STIRRED AND looked at the alarm clock. She could read the numbers, so she knew it was daytime. She looked around the room. Sunlight spilled in around the curtains. She was late for school. She sat up with a start. Then she remembered. Tears formed. She fell back onto the bed, buried her face in the pillow and cried.

She had become accustomed to waking up worried, terrified at her pregnancy being discovered, making plans to deal with it, no matter how far-fetched, but this was different. Bobby was dead. He would not be coming back to marry her and make all her problems go away. He would never be coming back. There would be no happily ever after. She ran her fingers over her stomach. Only a few more days. If she could just make it through a few more days, then she could worry about her growing problem.

SANDRA SLAMMED HER locker shut and turned around, crying. Doug took her into his arms as Principal Klein walked by.

"Let's keep that kind of thing outside of school, Douglas," Principal Klein said.

"Asshole," Doug muttered as the principal walked away in search of his next victim.

Students murmured as they walked to class. The death of a student, or even a recent graduate was rare, especially one as popular as Bobby. Everyone knew him. Everyone knew Amy.

Emily walked with Ryan, his arm around her shoulder, daring Colonel Klink to pop off, but the commandant was distracted by a skirt that was surely too short. He stared at Nikki, who was in tears. It wasn't compassion that restrained him from ordering her to drop to her knees while he whipped out a ruler and measured her skirt, but he had better things to do and let her pass unmolested.

Students stared at Amy's empty desk all day. Most of the teachers tried to carry on as usual, but Maggie was visibly upset in English class, which seemed odd as she hardly even knew Bobby, although Amy was clearly one of her favorite students, so maybe that was it.

KEVIN CALLED BEFORE breakfast to check on Amy. He spoke to Howard, and they agreed on a time for him to come over, early afternoon before the girls got home and before the store got busy. Surely Amy would be up and around by then. Howard agreed to call the store if anything came up.

It was decided that Howard could more easily take a day off work than Vivian. There was another barber in the shop and men could wait a little longer for a haircut. They would understand, although the shop quickly filled up with men wanting to keep up with the latest news. Calling in a substitute teacher would have been a more difficult task.

Emily had insisted on staying home with her sister but was over-ruled by Howard.

"What if she needs girl stuff?" Emily pleaded.

"I can handle it," Howard said, practically shoving Emily out the door with her mother and Lily.

Amy spent part of the day cuddled with her daddy on the sofa, saying little, crying a lot. Howard made sandwiches for lunch, but Amy picked at her food. She spent the rest of the day in her room, mostly in bed, listening to records, looking at pictures of Bobby, reading his letters.

Howard knocked on Amy's door. "There's someone here to see you, honey."

"Who is it?" Amy asked, not really wanting to see anyone. She was still in her regular sleepwear, a T-shirt, wore no makeup, and her hair was a mess.

Howard opened the door and Amy rushed into Kevin's arms. Howard would have preferred she put on some clothes, but he let it slide. He backed out and closed the door. Boys in bedrooms were dis-couraged in the Evans household, especially the way she was dressed, and under no circumstances were they allowed behind closed doors, but this was an obvious exception.

Amy cried on Kevin's shoulder for a long time, with no words spoken. She finally wiped her tears, took him by the hand and they sat on her bed.

"When is the funeral?" she asked.

"We don't know yet. They have to get him back to the States first."

"How long will that take?"

"A few days at least. There's a whole procedure to follow. The guys at the VFW are working on it."

"What kind of procedure?"

"You don't need to think about that. It's all being taken care of."

"Do I have to go to school tomorrow?"

"I don't know. I guess your mom will find out."

"I don't want to go back. I'm so embarrassed."

"You don't have anything to be embarrassed about. Everybody is there for you."

"I don't remember much, just you carrying me down the hall, people staring at me."

"Have you talked to Sandra?"

"She called at lunch. She's coming over after school. She said she'll brush my hair."

"I can brush your hair."

"It's a girl thing. Except when it's a daddy thing. He brushed it this morning, but then I went back to bed and now this." Amy splayed her hair with her fingers. She picked up a photo of her and Bobby from the nightstand.

"I'm glad you took pictures of us together before he left." She looked closely at the picture. "So I can remember him just like this."

Kevin pulled her close and held her while she cried.

AMY DREADED HAVING to go to church on Sunday. Bobby was dead, and the preacher would drone on about how he had gone to live with Jesus. Maybe she would call Kevin and he could kidnap her Sunday morning and they could sneak off to a matinee in Lubbock, maybe a comedy, definitely a comedy. It would look really bad, but it would be a lot better for her fragile psyche than listening to a solemn sermon about how Bobby's death was God's will, and he was in a better place, and then the mournful hymns from the choir. Church won out—she had an obligation to Bobby and his parents to stay strong and carry on.

Howard insisted that Amy return to school on Monday. Moping around the house was only going to make it worse. Being with her friends at school would help. Amy knew he was right but wished she could just bury her face in her pillow and never get up.

"Are you ready for this?" Sandra asked as Amy climbed into the Monza Monday morning.

"Not really, but Daddy says I can't miss any more school if I want to graduate."

"He's right."

"I don't care if I graduate. They won't let me graduate anyway when they find out I'm pregnant."

"We could ditch and go to Lubbock, have lunch at the Hi-D-Ho, see a movie."

"No, let's get it over with."

Doug was waiting when the girls arrived at school. Amy immediately rushed into his arms for a hug. She was embarrassed as some students fawned over her and others avoided her, not knowing what to say or do, or maybe it was because when she and Sandra walked the hallways there always seemed to be one or two football players a step behind, ready to pound anyone who bothered her, along with a cheerleader in case Amy needed girl things.

33

TWENTY-FOUR DAYS and a wakeup. Terrell Washington had already marked off another day on his short-timer calendar and was busy cooking breakfast, if you could call it cooking, and if you could call it breakfast. For more than a decade the magnificent feast in front of him had officially been known as MEAL, COMBAT, INDIVIDUAL, but nobody ever called it anything other than C-rations. The weather had cleared during the night which raised the possibility of a morning log bird hauling cases of C-rations along with ammo and mail, so Terrell and others in his squad treated themselves to the more desirable, or least undesirable, of their hoarded C-rations.

A cardboard box of rations contained a meat unit, bread unit, and dessert unit, all canned, along with an accessory pack containing condiments, coffee, toilet paper, matches, and cigarettes. There were twelve individual boxes, all different, packed in a case. It was rare for a soldier to like the contents of each unit in a box, so trading was common, and the least desirable units were simply discarded. Many of the units had colorful, often profane, nicknames.

Terrell ended up with a meat unit consisting of "Beans with Frankfurter Chunks in Tomato Sauce," universally known as "beanie weenie," a bread unit with cookies and cocoa powder, a dessert unit with peaches. Each can had come from a different box. His accessory pack contained a four-pack of Marlboros, always good trading material for a nonsmoker, which he traded for a can of pound cake.

The meat units could be improved somewhat by heating, a task accomplished with a boonie stove. An empty C-ration can was perforated with a church key to provide ventilation. A heat tablet, or preferably a chunk of C-4 explosive if available, which burned hotter, was dropped into the can and ignited with a match from the accessory pack. The lid of the meat unit can was cut almost off and folded back, creating a handle to place and remove the can from the boonie stove.

It certainly wasn't Miss Clara's cooking, but on a wet, chilly morning in the Central Highlands, it was better than nothing. With each bite of beanie weenie Terrell pictured his mother's chicken fried steak, mashed potatoes with gravy, and fried okra. He then mixed the peaches with pound cake as he pictured Miss Clara's peach cobbler. Twenty-four days and a wakeup.

Like Kevin, Specialist Terrell Washington was a grunt, Eleven Bravo, an infantryman. Terrell was in the Fourth Infantry Division, but the job was the same. His platoon's current assignment was providing security for a firebase blasted out of the jungle a few days ago. Artillery pieces were flown in slung under helicopters. The artillery would then fire on targets in support of infantry operating in the area. Firebases could remain operational for a few days, weeks, or months, depending on the mission. No field kitchen had been established, so Terrell expected this one to shut down soon and he might find himself once again humping the boonies, not a pleasant thought for a short-timer. Other than frequent patrols outside the wire to prevent the enemy from mounting a ground attack, firebase security was mainly waiting to take your turn on the green line. The downside was that you remained in a static position, and it was only a matter of time until the enemy had your coordinates, and the rockets and mortars began raining down at night, with a few occasionally lobbed in during daylight for an added degree of terror.

Terrell and his squad buddies looked toward the sky as they heard the faint but unmistakable whap whap whap of the rotors of a UH-1 helicopter.

A soldier approached at a brisk pace. "Washington!"

"Yo."

"Grab your shit. You're going out on the log bird."

"What's up?"

"How the hell should I know? The CO wants to see you."

There wasn't much shit to grab. Nearly everything Terrell brought into the country, or had acquired since, was in his duffel bag, locked away in a CONEX at Pleiku, the Fourth Infantry Division's basecamp. Since everything had to be carried on their backs, grunts traveled as lightly as possible, wearing the same uniform for days or weeks until they could get to a laundry and bath company where they turned in their dirty uniforms, showered, and received a clean uniform on the way out—one size fits all. The only thing they kept were their boots. Nobody wanted to break in new boots, or wear someone else's.

After a short session of speculation with his buddies, including a gonorrhea diagnosis, in-country R&R at China Beach, a court martial, or a battlefield commission, Terrell made his way to the center of the firebase. A few other soldiers waited to unload the log bird, which would only be on the ground a few seconds to avoid drawing mortar fire.

The Huey swooped in, and Terrell waited while soldiers rushed forward and dragged off what wasn't kicked off by the crew chief. At an opportune moment he climbed aboard, shoving off a couple of cases of C-rations. There was a single bench seat behind the pilots, but Terrell sat on the floor, facing forward, his back against the wall, M-16 across his lap. On a combat assault his preferred position was sitting on the side with his feet hanging out, making for a faster exit, especially when under fire, but he expected this trip to be rather uneventful. Dismissing most of his buddies' speculation, he did, however, wonder and worry about what had caused him to be snatched out of the bush and summoned before his commanding officer. Since being drafted he had avoided confrontation, and the brass, seeking to quietly do his duty and go home, attracting as little attention as possible.

After landing on the flight line at Pleiku, Terrell had even more time to worry as he trudged along the dirt road toward his company headquarters. The dirt was mixed with Pentaprime, an oily black sludge, being sprayed from a truck a few yards ahead. He stepped off the road into the bar ditch, but it was impossible to avoid the rivers of goo that coated his boots and sloshed up onto his fatigue pants.

Thankfully, his wait in the orderly room was brief and Terrell was soon standing at attention in front of a makeshift desk where a captain, his company commander, glanced at a document.

"You know a guy named Robert Dalton Junior?"

Terrell hesitated. "I know Bobby Dalton. He's in the First Cav."

"He's KIA."

The normal response, in a civilian world, would be to ask "how?" But this was war. It didn't matter how. Soldiers die in war. Terrell said nothing.

"He's entitled to an escort home," the captain said. "His family asked for you."

"Yes sir." Terrell had learned to not ask questions but had many he wanted to ask. "What do I do?"

The captain handed him a stack of papers. "The company clerk will get you processed out. Looks like you're headed to Tan Son Nhut. Graves Registration will fill you in when you get there."

"Yes sir."

"You're short, so I doubt you'll be coming back."

Terrell was stunned and still processing what had just happened as he looked down at his orders. It was no longer twenty-four days and a wakeup, maybe not even a wakeup—he was going home.

EVERY MEAL HAD been rather somber at the Evans house since the notification, and Amy continued to pick at her food.

"I'm going to the airport."

"I don't think that's a good idea," Howard said.

Amy looked up and clinched her teeth. "You wouldn't let me go to the airport when he left."

Emily kept her head down, but raised her eyebrows, waiting for the fireworks.

"So I'm going now," Amy said.

There were no fireworks. Howard knew it would do no good to argue. She certainly had the resources to go with or without his permission. She would learn nothing sitting in class fuming, although she would at least be counted present.

PRINCIPAL KLEIN FULLY expected most of the high school students, including the entire senior class, to want to skip school for Bobby's funeral, so he flatly refused to allow six football players and six cheerleaders to take off a half day to go to the airport in Lubbock to pick up the remains. That was the funeral director's job. Less than ten minutes later Klein's phone rang, and the president of the school board disabused him of that notion.

There were immediate disagreements over transportation. Amy had already decided she would ride with Kevin, and they had arranged a time for him to pick her up. She would walk out of class, permission or not. Once the trip became official Sandra tried to persuade Amy to ride the school bus with the rest of the students.

"I'm riding with Kevin," Amy insisted.

"He can ride the bus," Sandra said.

Amy shook her head. While she appeared stubborn to Sandra, she simply did not want to be on a bus with twelve other students, enduring stares and strained conversation. Alone with Kevin she could speak or not, cry or not, without judgement.

Cliff Billingsley not only volunteered to drive the bus but insisted on doing so. He had watched as his own fallen soldiers were loaded onto helicopters in body bags and now saw it as his solemn duty to be there when one came home. Unable to find a substitute in time, Colonel Klink would have to take Cliff's classes.

THE CHEERLEADERS WORE school clothes, the football players white shirts, dark ties, and letter jackets. Some sat in the airport lobby, some milled around near the windows, searching the skies for the airplane bearing the body of their friend. The lobby was quiet, departing passengers and others awaiting arrivals, seeing the hearse and police car parked on the tarmac, were aware of what was unfolding. Airport and airline employees went about their business as quietly and unobtrusively as possible.

Amy sat silently between Kevin and Sandra, staring at the windows. Kevin wanted badly to hold Amy's hand or put his arm around her and pull her close but thought better of it as eyes continued to glance their way.

Patty and Robert sat nearby, stone-faced. Robert was first on his feet when he saw Hank open the door to his police car and step out, quickly followed by the undertaker in the hearse.

Amy immediately noticed the movement. Kevin stood, took her hand, and they moved toward the doors. Passengers and visitors parted to allow them through. Amy could see the Continental Airlines DC-9 touch down and zoom past. An airport employee opened the door and people streamed out into the biting cold.

The DC-9 braked, slowed, and turned around, taxiing toward the terminal. Robert led the way, his arm around his wife, followed by Kevin and Amy, and then the rest of the entourage.

It seemed like an eternity to Amy, but the DC-9 approached them head-on, turned at a right angle, and parked. The roar of the jet engines ceased. Ground crew swarmed. The airstair emerged and low-ered onto the tarmac.

"Praise God," Clara whispered as Terrell was first off the plane, bounding down the stairs. He was a man on a mission and waved at his parents before heading directly to the undertaker. He handed him a large manila envelope and then shook hands with Robert and said a few words to Patty. Amy burst into tears as Terrell and Kevin hugged. Terrell had little time for niceties, however, as the cargo door opened, and baggage handlers converged.

Both arriving and departing passengers stopped and stood silently, hands and hats over their hearts as the casket, draped in the US flag, rolled down the ramp, guided by baggage handlers, and into the waiting hands of six football players. Terrell followed as the casket was carried to the hearse. Terrell, Kevin, Robert, Hank, Cliff, and the undertaker saluted. Amy burst into tears, as did Patty and most of the cheerleaders.

As the casket was loaded into the hearse Amy asked, "Can I see him?"

"No," Kevin said. "Not here. Maybe later. Let's see what the funeral director says first."

"Why?"

"Amy, please, just trust me."

He seemed unmovable on the subject, so Amy let it go, for the time being at least.

No one had yet seen any official report, only word that Bobby had been killed in action. Both Kevin and Robert were concerned about how he had died and the condition of the remains. The funeral direc-tor was aware of the situation. Robert had asked Kevin to view the body with him at the funeral home as soon as it arrived and make the decision on whether to open the casket for the funeral, or even whether his mother would want to see him.

Bobby's death had been abstract for Amy until now. People told her he was dead, but she had no evidence, no proof, could not know that for a fact. His letters still arrived, every day. But now there he was, inside that casket. Kevin wouldn't let her see him, but Amy no longer held out much hope for a miracle. No one had told her how he died. Maybe no one knew. Was he burned beyond recognition? Was he in little pieces? She burst into tears again just thinking about it. There certainly seemed to be a lot of people, men with experience in such matters, who were taking pains to see that everything was done properly.

Patty hugged Amy and they both cried. The funeral director waited quietly. He had done this before and would be ready when the time came.

Terrell stepped forward and hugged Clara. She released him and backed away, wiping tears. She felt guilty hugging her own son while Patty stood nearby, her son's body in a casket in the back of the hearse. Clara wasn't going to come to the airport for that very reason, but Patty had insisted she be there.

"You take care of your business, and then we'll see you at the house," Clara said. "I expect you're hungry."

"Yes, ma'am," Terrell said. He shook hands with his father, and they hugged briefly.

"Welcome home, son," Benjamin said.

Terrell walked briskly to the hearse.

Clara turned to Patty. "Only a mother can know the pain, Miss Patty. If there's anything I can do, you just let me know, anything at all."

"I will, Clara," Patty said. "Thank you."

As soon as Hank crossed the county line, he turned on the flashing red lights and radioed the dispatcher. Cars and trucks pulled off the highway as the small procession passed by, a police car, a hearse, three cars, and a school bus.

Hank slowed as he entered Preston. The Hi-Way Café emptied out and employees and customers stood outside in the cold and put their hands over their hearts. A deputy sheriff held traffic at the high-way intersection and waved the procession through the turn. Joe Spalding stood on the corner of the Texaco and saluted as the hearse passed by.

By the time the procession reached the veteran's memorial on Main Street bells were tolling at the First Baptist Church. Throngs of people, hands and hats over their hearts, came out of the courthouse and stores on the square and watched solemnly as the procession drove slowly past. Howard and other veterans came to attention and saluted.

Irene and her customers were outside in the parking lot, the store unattended, as the procession turned the corner on the way to the funeral home.

Robert Dalton Jr. had come home.

34

AMY HAD ONCE AGAIN taken to bed, having sent Sandra away. She cried for a time, and then just stared at the floor, occasionally looking up at a picture of herself and Bobby, which only made her want to cry again. It was late afternoon, and she could hear Lily practicing the piano in the living room. She could tell from the sounds and smells that her mother was in the kitchen, preparing supper. Her daddy would be home soon. Emily, if she was even around, was thankfully silent. Amy reread Bobby's first letter in response to news of her pregnancy. It was hardly the most romantic of proposals, but he had said he wanted to marry her, and that was good enough for her. She felt some sense of peace, however slight.

Everyone seemed to accept that Bobby was dead, but all she had seen was a casket with a flag on it. People told her Bobby was in it, but she had not yet been allowed to see him, touch him, kiss him. Only then could she be sure. It didn't change her more immediate problem—she was pregnant. All hopes that it would work out well had been dashed. She would have to deal with it herself, and soon.

There was a knock on Amy's bedroom door.

"Who is it?" Amy asked.

"Kevin."

Amy raced to the door and opened it. He was pleased to see that she was dressed, just Levi's and T-shirt, but at least it was a sign of progress.

"What did you find out?" Amy asked, closing the door as Kevin stepped in.

"The funeral is tomorrow."

"When can I see him?"

"You can't."

"Why not?"

"Amy—" Kevin tried to choose his words carefully. "His mother hasn't even seen him and doesn't want to."

Amy was stunned. "What? Why not?"

"The funeral director opened the casket to see if anything else needed to be done, but the Army had done everything they could possibly do."

Tears formed as Amy closed her eyes.

"Your daddy was going to come over and cut Bobby's hair, but the funeral director said that wouldn't be necessary."

Amy burst into tears. Kevin put his arm around her and pulled her close. She put her head on his shoulder.

"Do you know what happened, how he was killed?" Amy asked.

"Yes. There was a report in the packet that Terrell brought."

Kevin offered no further information.

"Tell me," she said.

"Are you sure you want to know?"

"Yes. I'm sure. If they won't let me see him then I want to know how he died."

"He was on a log bird. It was a routine resupply mission into the bush. They dropped off their load, picked up a couple of guys, and headed back to Firebase Buttons."

He paused, squeezing her shoulder. She looked up, waiting for him to continue.

"The chopper was struck by ground fire at fifteen hundred feet, exploded, crashed and burned."

"How tall is the Great Plains Life Building?" she asked.

"I don't know, twenty stories, about two hundred fifty feet, maybe more."

She closed her eyes and tried to imagine the height, tears streaming down her face. After a moment she opened her eyes and wiped the tears.

"You really don't want to see him," he said. "Nobody will. They're having visitation tonight at the funeral home, but the casket won't be open. It's mainly just for people to pay their respects to Patty and Robert."

"I want to go," she said, pulling away from him.

"I'll wait in the living room while you get dressed."

She turned her back and peeled off her T-shirt. Before he could make a move toward the door, she was wiggling out of her jeans. She was wearing underwear, so there was no reason to leave now. He watched as she opened the closet door, pulled a dress off a hanger, and slipped it over her head.

"Zip me," she said, turning her back and holding her hair. He zipped her.

She sat on a stool in front of the dresser, checked her makeup, which was almost nonexistent, put on lipstick, and then ran a brush quickly through her hair. "Let's go."

Kevin followed her into the kitchen.

"We're going to the funeral home," Amy said.

"Daddy will be home soon," Vivian said. "We were going to go after supper."

"I want to go now," Amy said.

"What about supper?" Vivian asked.

"I'm not hungry," Amy said as she turned away and headed for the front door.

"I'll try to get her to eat something," Kevin said.

THE US FLAG was draped over Bobby's casket, at one end of the viewing room, although there would be no viewing. Terrell stood nearby, exhausted from a long day, but determined to do his duty to Bobby. There were several other men in the room, all veterans. More would arrive later to take shifts through the night—Bobby would not be alone before he was buried. Patty and Robert sat on a sofa in the corner of the room, receiving visitors. There was already a line, and pages in the guest book were filling up.

Several people were waiting to speak to Patty and Robert when Amy and Kevin entered, so Amy went directly to the casket. All the veterans immediately stood, prepared to block everyone else, but the other visitors stepped back while Amy reached out and touched the casket. On the drive over she had resolved to not make a scene, like something out of a movie, but couldn't hold back tears, knowing that her beloved, the father of her child, was just inches away. She couldn't see him. She couldn't touch him. She couldn't talk to him. Ever again.

Kevin stood ready to catch her should she faint, but she stayed strong, other than the tears. As Kevin led her away from the casket she stopped and turned to Terrell. "Thank you for bringing Bobby home," she said, and then hugged him, raising eyebrows in the room.

Amy hugged Robert, and then Patty as they both cried.

"I'M NOT READY to go home yet," Amy said as they got into Kevin's car.

"Do you want to get something to eat?"

"No."

He leaned forward to start the car and then hesitated.

"What's wrong?" she asked.

He reached into his hip pocket and retrieved a folded envelope.

"I've been debating over when to give you this. There's really no good time."

"What is it?"

"It's from Bobby."

She looked at him, confused.

"He told me to hold it for him, and one for his mother, just in case."

She burst into tears as he handed it to her, and she realized what it was.

"I can take you home now if you want to read it alone."

She stared at the letter, her hands shaking.

"No, let's ride around. I don't want to be alone."

She carefully opened the envelope. He started the car and switched on the dome light. He pulled out of the parking lot, and they cruised in silence, while Amy read Bobby's letter, tears flowing.

When finished she folded the letter, returned it to the envelope and put it in her purse. She pulled out a tissue and dried her tears.

"Did you write one of these to your mother before you left?" she asked.

He nodded. "Everybody does."

"Did Bobby hold it for you?"

"Yes."

Amy pointed at the unfinished memorial on the corner of the square as Kevin turned onto Main Street. "I want to stop at the memorial."

The veteran's memorial covered one corner of the square along Main Street. The foundation had been poured and the stones were in place, but the sidewalks and landscaping had not yet been completed. The original plan was for eight red granite monoliths, bearing the names of those who had served, with one or more stones per war. Placing the stones in a straight line, along with a centerpiece naming the memorial, appealed to the sense of order shared by the veterans. It also presented a problem, however. The World War II stones would be divided by the centerpiece, and the one blank stone at the end would likely be soon filled and additional stones would be needed for wars to be named later, throwing off the symmetry. Hank laughed and said, "Soldiers in a straight line get mowed down. Set them like they're on patrol, randomly spaced and oriented." Howard seconded the motion, and a new plan was drawn up and scattered across the memorial were the eight monoliths, surrounding the centerpiece. The monoliths were oriented in various directions, just like soldiers on patrol, scanning the horizon for signs of trouble, guarding the centerpiece. A granite bench was placed in front of each stone.

Kevin parked and they walked up a dirt path that had strips of wood staked along the sides. Soon workmen would begin distributing the nine yards of sand that had been dumped at the site, and red bricks would be laid for sidewalks and a plaza.

"Watch your step," Kevin said, taking Amy's hand. "They haven't finished the sidewalks yet."

They stopped at the stone for Viet Nam, which contained several names, representing veterans not only from Preston, but the entire county. There was scant moonlight, and lights at the base of the monoliths had yet to be installed, so the streetlight on the corner provided the only illumination. Amy squinted at the list for a moment and asked, "Where's your name?"

Kevin pointed to the bottom of the list. "It'll be here, at the end. They're putting them in the order they came back, and I wasn't back when they engraved the names. Terrell will be next."

"Then Bobby?"

"No. I wish it was that way."

He took her by the hand, and they stepped over wooden forms, rocks, and construction debris to get to the centerpiece, an obelisk, twenty feet tall, surrounded by three eight-foot triangular columns. Kevin found the correct column and pointed to a blank space. "Bobby's name will go here, in the center, reserved for those who gave all." He turned and waved his arm toward the other monoliths. "The rest of us will be standing guard, forever."

Amy burst into tears.

35

IT LOOKED LIKE a short school bus headed northwest on US Highway 84, but it was painted olive drab, not yellow. There were sixteen soldiers in class A uniforms aboard, one of them driving. Several of them had removed their jackets—even in February the sun warmed up the bus enough that a couple of windows had been opened slightly for ventilation. The soldiers didn't give much thought to the purpose of the trip—it was a day off from their regular job and, more importantly, it got them off KP and guard duty for as long as they were on the burial detail.

Joe Spalding wasn't really hustling business, just hoping to make the honor guard's trip to Preston as easy as possible and ensure that Bobby's services and burial went off without a hitch, so he put in a long-distance call to Fort Sill. The Army bus stopped at the Texaco for diesel fuel and the soldiers went next door to the Hi-Way Café for lunch. Joe accepted a government voucher for the fuel, but lunch was on him—he knew the soldiers could use their meal vouchers later almost anywhere. The sergeant had directions to the church and cemetery, but a VFW volunteer was standing by at the Texaco to serve as navigator.

After lunch at the café the soldiers boarded the bus. The sergeant stood at the front of the bus, looking at a clipboard. "This is a KIA from Viet Nam, eighteen years old, so it may be pretty emotional, but we don't expect any protesters or other trouble."

"Don't worry about protesters," the volunteer said. "This is west Texas, not California."

With hundreds of thousands of military personnel stationed on scores of bases across the country, the government provided honor guards for all deceased veterans whose family requested it. Most of these veterans were older men dying from natural causes. Their funerals, sometimes only graveside ceremonies, were little different than any other funeral for an elderly person whose time had come. The honor guard seemed like a historical footnote. With more than one hundred young American men being killed each week in Viet Nam, however, some funerals were far more emotional, and sometimes drew war protesters. For the honor guard it was luck of the draw.

"Who's presenting the flag?" the sergeant asked.

"I am, sergeant," a soldier said.

"The girl sitting with the family at graveside is the girlfriend, not the wife. The mother gets the flag."

"Roger that."

The sergeant checked his watch. "Let's move out." He took a seat at the front of the bus along with the volunteer.

"Hang a right," the volunteer said as the driver shifted gears and released the brake.

THE FIRST BAPTIST CHURCH was the largest in town and it was expected to be full. The Daltons were members, but the church would have made its facilities available for any other denomination under the circumstances.

Patty and Robert had insisted that Amy sit with the family. Kevin and Doug were both honorary pallbearers, so Sandra offered to sit with Amy. Patty and Robert didn't object, but Amy said she didn't need a babysitter. She would take her rightful place with the family, not because she was Bobby's girlfriend, not because she was his secret fiancée, but because of the biggest secret of all—she was carrying his child, who certainly was family, at least for the time being. She took her position beside Grandmother, directly in front of the flag-draped casket. Sandra sat across the aisle in the second row with the cheerleaders, ready to rush to her best friend's side should the need arise. Kevin, seated to the side with the honorary pallbearers, frequently craned his neck to check on Amy.

Colored people were rarely seen in white churches in Preston, but Patty had asked Clara to sing. Benjamin would have waited with her in the wings, but they were escorted to seats on the front row, to one side so that Clara could easily mount the stage at the appointed time. Terrell, in uniform, stood beside the casket, facing the congregation, keeping an eye on both the casket and Amy.

The service itself was mercifully short. Although Robert went to church every Sunday, he informed the preacher that his son's funeral would not be used as an opportunity to proselytize. There would be time enough for that on Sunday, in everyone's own church.

Delivering the eulogy was the most difficult thing Kevin had ever done in his life. It wasn't that finding something nice to say about Bobby was difficult. It was that he felt like a horse's ass saying it, having betrayed his best friend who now lay dead in a casket at his feet while the girl they both loved looked him in the eye and cried as he said it.

As MOURNERS LINED UP outside the church it was all Kevin could do to keep from breaking ranks and rushing to Amy's side, but he had to do his duty to his best friend. The military pallbearers carried the casket. Terrell walked close behind, followed by the honorary pallbearers, including Kevin, Doug, and four of Bobby's closest friends. Sandra had already taken up position next to Amy and Howard stood nearby.

Amy paused just outside the front door of the church, at the top of the steps and looked out at the assembled throng. This should have been a joyous occasion. She should have been wearing a beautiful white wedding dress. All those people should have been throwing rice as she and Bobby walked down the steps into his brand-new GTO, decorated with signs, dragging tin cans, and raced off to the fanciest motel in Lubbock for a night of wedded bliss. Instead, she wore black. There were no tears of joy, only heartbreak. And yet she soldiered on, making it down the steps into a waiting limousine.

It was the largest funeral anyone in Preston could remember. The local funeral home only had one hearse and one funeral car. The honorary pallbearers could have ridden in private cars and the Army pallbearers on their bus, but two additional funeral cars arrived from competitors in nearby towns. There would be no bill rendered nor payment expected. The favor would be returned when the time came, and it always did.

Hank Harding led the funeral procession. The county sheriff himself stood on Main Street, holding traffic, saluting as the hearse drove past. The procession was halfway to the cemetery before the last car pulled out of the church parking lot.

Kevin helped Amy to a seat directly in front of the casket at the cemetery and then rejoined the honorary pallbearers only after Howard assured him that he would be nearby, along with Sandra. Amy sat on the end, next to Grandmother, with Robert between his mother and Patty. Terrell stood at attention next to Patty.

Tears flowed as Clara sang "Amazing Grace."

The preacher was again brief, the Army pallbearers and honor guard efficient. Amy watched as they held the flag above the casket. She flinched when the firing squad, just out of sight, fired the first volley. Two more volleys followed, each one like a knife in Amy's side. She somehow endured through "Taps," played by an unseen bugler.

Finally, the flag was folded, and a soldier approached. He dropped to one knee in front of Patty and held out the flag.

"On behalf of the President of the United States and a grateful nation, I present you with the nation's flag as a token of appreciation for your son's sacrifice."

The soldier stood, took one step back, and came to attention. Terrell stepped forward and turned to face Patty. Terrell and the soldier saluted, as did Kevin and dozens of other veterans, along with the honor guard. Amy cried. She had somehow managed to get through it. Now came her real test.

36

SILK STOCKING STREET was crowded with parked cars. Men
loitered on the large front porch of the Dalton house. Mourners filed
in, some carrying covered dishes. In the kitchen and dining room,
ladies organized the food offerings, with Clara clearly in charge. The
living room and dining room were packed. Emily and Nikki served
coffee. Grandmother and Lily sat at the piano, playing "Canon in D
Major."

Kevin and Terrell leaned against a wall.

"Mr. Dalton said it was your idea for me to escort Bobby home,"
Terrell said.

Kevin nodded.

"Thanks for getting me out of there."

"I didn't know if you were going to extend to get an early out."

"No way. I was in some real shit over there."

"Yeah. A few weeks is a long time in the bush."

"There it is."

"You have orders?" Kevin asked.

"Fort Polk, pushing troops."

"Polk, shit."

"That's okay. I can do six months standing on my head."

"You going to stay in when your two years is up?"

"I don't know. It's not a bad gig for a black guy, but my mama wants me to go to college on the GI Bill."

"I hear you, brother."

"I might use it to go to trade school, maybe diesel mechanics, jet engines, something like that."

"Nah. You should go to college and be a football coach."

"Not a lot of black coaches around these parts."

"You could be the first. Preston might hire you. Hell, they hired Cliff Billingsley and the walls didn't fall. No white girls fainted."

Terrell laughed. "Is he the brother at the airport?"

"That's him. LT with the Hundred and First."

"Yeah, my mama wrote me all about him. I'm sure he'll be over for supper real soon so he can give me advice on college."

"Hey, I'll be there too. I'm looking forward to your mama's fried chicken."

"And sweet potato pie."

"Yum yum." Kevin looked around. "Have you seen Amy?"

"She was just here a minute ago."

Kevin went searching and knocked softly on Bobby's bedroom door. There was no answer, so he opened it. Amy lay on the bed, her back to the door. He stepped in and lay down beside her. He slipped his hand over her waist, and she quickly grabbed it.

"Are you okay?" Kevin asked.

She wiped a tear with a tissue. "I feel so selfish."

"Selfish?"

"I'm not crying for Bobby because he died. I'm crying because I lost him."

"That's probably normal."

They lay silently for a moment.

"He left his keys on the dresser," she said.

"You don't need keys over there."

"Will they send his things to his parents?"

"Yes."

"Will they see the calendar?"

"Maybe not. His buddies will go through his stuff looking for rubbers or dirty pictures or anything else parents or wives shouldn't see."

"The pictures weren't dirty."

"No, they weren't. They were beautiful. You're beautiful. You could be a model."

"I guess I'm a tease. I was half-naked when we did the pictures. It must have been hard on you."

"It was definitely hard."

"Sorry," she said.

"That was a little joke."

She thought about it for a moment. "Oh, okay. I get it."

"You didn't know how I felt about you at the time, so you weren't being a tease. But I certainly enjoyed it, and we did a good thing for Bobby. His buddies sure liked it."

"They did?"

"Of course. Who wouldn't?"

"You sure did." She nudged him with her elbow.

He smiled. "Yes. I did."

"I was really nervous. I'd never done anything like that. I can't believe we did it, but I'm glad we did, even if his daddy does see the pictures."

"Big Bob was in the Navy. I doubt he'd be shocked."

"I guess you're right." She snuggled up against him and stared into space for a moment. "Did it hurt?"

"What?"

"When Bobby got killed."

"No. It was quick," he lied. He had seen choppers go down, more than once, from various altitudes, some in flames, some not. It was entirely possible that Bobby had lived for several seconds in pain, agony, and terror, but there was nothing to be gained from telling her.

"What am I going to do without him?"

"I don't know."

"He was everything to me."

"I know."

"We were going to get married, have babies, grow old together."

"Boys or girls?"

"Bobby was an only child, so definitely a boy to carry on the family name, but one of each would have been nice. And maybe an extra girl."

"You two would have made beautiful babies."

"I need to tell you something," she said after a moment.

"What is it?"

"I wanted to tell you before, but then—"

"What?" He was becoming concerned.

"I'm pregnant."

She closed her eyes, held her breath, and waited for his reaction. He didn't express surprise, disappointment, or say anything at all. He just scooted closer to her as they lay there on Bobby's bed, hearing only the sound of each other's breathing. She rolled over and studied his face. He kissed her on the forehead.

"It's okay," he said. "We'll get through it, somehow, together."

After a few minutes Kevin realized she was asleep. They were in a rather awkward position and his left arm was numb, but he didn't dare move and wake her. He let her sleep, his mind racing, considering possible courses of action, things she had no doubt already thought of, but those two words, "I'm pregnant," had brought him into her private hell and made him a full participant.

The piano playing had stopped, and he could hear guests saying their goodbyes. There was a knock at the door, but before Kevin could answer, the door opened. It was Howard. Kevin looked up and then quickly checked to see where his right hand was. Fortunately, it was on Amy's waist, not her hip or leg, but he was still in an extremely compromising position.

"Is she asleep?" Howard asked.

Kevin was relieved. Nothing was going on, but he was in bed with the man's teenage daughter, face to face, her knee over his leg, her dress hiked up.

"Yes," Kevin said. "So's my left arm, but I didn't want to wake her. I'm guessing she hasn't slept well lately."

"No, she hasn't," Howard said. "I'm tempted to just leave her here, if you can get your arm out from under her."

Kevin tried to free his arm. Her sleep disturbed by the movement, Amy awoke and looked at Kevin, his face only inches away.

"What time is it?" she asked.

"Time to go home, honey," Howard said.

"Daddy?" Amy turned and rubbed her eyes. "I went to sleep."

"So I see," Howard said. "With Kevin."

Amy chuckled, lay her head back, right in Kevin's face, and put her fingers on his cheek. "Your daughter's sleeping with a boy," she said.

Kevin was a bit unnerved, but Howard seemed amused. Amy was obviously still half asleep, in pain, but her dry wit was irrepressible. Howard knew she would eventually be okay.

37

EMILY SWISHED HER fingers around in the bathtub, whipping up
bubbles. She squeezed in more bath oil and swished some more,
finally achieving the desired volume of foam. She wiped her hands on
a towel, struck a kitchen match and lit a few candles. Amy, wearing
a towel, padded into the bathroom as Emily snuffed out the match
with a flick of her wrist.

"I thought it might help," Emily said.

They hugged.

"It will," Amy said. "Thank you. For everything."

They hooked pinkie fingers. "Sisters?" Amy asked.

"Forever," Emily said.

Amy stepped into the tub. Emily flipped off the light and closed
the door behind her. Amy leaned back in the tub. She ran her fingers
over her stomach. She was certain she was showing, but no one had
said anything or seemed suspicious. Until just hours ago only Sandra
knew, and now Kevin. She took comfort in that. She lay quietly in
the tub until the water turned cold.

There was a knock on her bedroom door as Amy got ready for bed.

Howard came in to kiss her goodnight, but instead took her hand and they sat on the bed. He picked up a framed picture of Amy and Bobby, taken by Kevin just before Bobby left.

"You look good together," he said.

Amy smiled.

"Your mother and I expected to hear wedding bells when Bobby got home."

"We talked about it."

He put the picture on the nightstand. She waited nervously, wondering why he hadn't just kissed her goodnight and gone to his room.

"Sometimes it looks like war will take every mother's son," he said. "Your mother and I only had girls, so I foolishly thought it wouldn't affect us."

"It didn't work out that way though, did it?"

He shook his head. "No. It didn't." He looked away for a moment and then back at her. "Your mother was pregnant with you when I shipped out to Korea."

"She was?"

Howard nodded. "She wasn't much older than you are now. My unit was called up just before Christmas and we went straight to the courthouse and got a marriage license. I left Lubbock on a train in January."

"Whoa," Amy said. "Hold on."

Howard grimaced as Amy counted on her fingers.

"Your anniversary is September fifteenth," she said.

Howard smiled. "That's when we celebrate our anniversary, exactly nine months before your birthday."

"Mom was pregnant when you got married?"

"Yes."

"Wow."

"Don't tell your sister."

"Don't worry," she said. "I'm saving this juicy little tidbit. I might need it later."

"The truth always has a way of coming out."

Amy nodded. "And you've been harping on me to save myself for marriage all these years."

"Just like you'll be doing twenty years from now, with your own daughter."

"Twenty years?"

"Four years of college, meet someone, get married. In twenty years, your daughter will be about fifteen, sixteen maybe."

Amy savored her new knowledge. Howard could see the wheels turning. Then her smug look disappeared. She was going to tell him. Now was the time. He had just admitted that he and her mother had sex before marriage. How could he hold the same thing against her? How could he possibly be angry or even disappointed in her? But it was not the same. Her baby's father was dead. There could be no quick marriage and then looking the other way on the timeline. She would be sent to a home for unwed mothers and her baby given up for adoption. That was the fact of the matter. There was only one other option, like Sandra had said, "take care of it." Amy held her tongue. She knew what had to be done.

"Where did you and mom meet?"

"At the Hi-D-Ho."

"On College Avenue?"

He nodded. "The Hi-D-Ho was mostly a high school hangout, so she had been going there for years. It was August, just before her freshman year at Tech. We hit it off right away, obviously."

Amy laughed. "Obviously."

"When I got back from Korea, we lived in the garage apartment at her parents' house. They had built it just after World War II, when all the boys were coming home and going to Tech on the GI Bill and needed places to live. I got a job in a barbershop downtown. I walked to work, or sometimes rode with your granddaddy if he was going to the depot. Your mother walked to Tech. It was just a one-room apartment, so it was kind of cozy. Saturday night was date night."

"Date night?"

"You'd sleep in the main house, in your mother's old room."

"Oh, okay. I get it." She grinned. She couldn't believe she was having this conversation with her daddy.

"We didn't have much, but looking back, those were good times."

"Did we still live there when Emily was born?"

He nodded. "That little apartment got even cozier then. We had hoped your mother would graduate in the spring, but she took a semester off with Emily, so we stayed there another six months."

He smiled, reminiscing. "Emily was just a baby and your grandmother kept both of you while your mother and I went to Austin to watch Tech play Texas. There was a platform alongside the Brownfield Highway, across from Tech, and the Santa Fe used to pull special trains up there for football games and holidays and when school started and let out. Everybody traveled by train back then. Your granddaddy was a special agent for the Santa Fe, and always rode the special trains to football games, so he got us on for free."

"Kind of like when we went to Sweetwater?"

"Yes, exactly like that, only rowdier."

"Did Tech win?"

"Oh, yes," he said, smiling. "It was the first time we beat Texas, and we did it in Austin, which made it even better. That train was rocking all the way back to Lubbock. Your granddaddy had his hands full."

Amy put her head on his shoulder. "We should talk more often."

"When I was in Korea my biggest fear wasn't of being killed, but of leaving your mother alone with a baby, with you." He hugged her. "When a soldier is killed in action it's usually over quickly, sometimes it's even painless. But for those left behind the pain can last for years, a lifetime."

"I don't know how I can go on without him."

"I can't pretend to know the pain you are in. No one can who hasn't been there. I know it's hard right now, and you think your own life is over, but you're young, and single. Someday the pain won't be as bad as it was the day before. You'll go to college. You'll meet new people. You'll marry and have children of your own."

"I don't want to forget Bobby."

"And you never will. He was a very important part of your life. He always will be. When you find the right young man, he will understand, and accept it."

He hugged her tightly and then held her head with his hands and stared at her face.

"You were sixteen months old when we first met. It was love at first sight, for me anyway. It took you a little longer to warm up to me, but you eventually came around."

Amy smiled. She had no memory of it, but she could imagine herself being held and kissed by this stranger.

He kissed her on the forehead. "You smell good."

"Emily made me a bubble bath. She said it might make me feel better."

"Did it?"

"Yes."

"Then I guess we should keep her."

Amy grinned and nodded. Her opinion had changed somewhat over the years since that squalling brat had so rudely inserted herself into Amy's happy little family.

38

MAGGIE HAD ONLY been back from her rendezvous in Brownfield for a few minutes on Sunday evening when she answered a knock at the door. She expected it to be another teacher who lived in the hotel, or maybe the manager. She was surprised to see Kevin.

"Are you stalking me?"

Kevin smiled and shook his head. "No. I was just waiting for you to get back."

"Come in," Maggie said.

Kevin stepped in.

"I'm sorry about your friend," she said. "It must be hard on you."

"It is."

"You want a beer?"

"Sure."

He wandered over to her bed and picked up a framed photo from the nightstand. "Is this him?"

"That's him," she said, fetching two beers from the refrigerator.

"He looks like the Marlboro Man."

"Yeah, he kinda does, doesn't he?"

"Is he good in bed?"

"Does a bear shit in the woods?"

"Are you two officially going steady?"

"Going steady is so high school."

"Are you engaged?"

"Not really, but it's probably headed that way. Why, do you miss me? Or just miss the sex? You're not getting laid, if that's why you're here."

"It's not," he said. "And don't worry. I parked at the pool hall and walked over."

Maggie opened the beers and they sat at the table.

"Why are you here?"

"Where would a girl go if she was pregnant?"

"There's a home for unwed mothers in Fort Worth."

"I think you know what I mean."

"Did you knock up some teenybopper?"

He shrugged.

"Were you cheating on me?"

"I thought you were just in it for the sex," he said.

"I'm just pulling your dick, but I did expect you to be more careful. I guess banging a hippie chick on the pill spoiled you."

"Accidents happen."

"How far along?"

"Ten, twelve weeks."

"Ten or twelve?"

"Does it matter?"

"Yes, actually, it does."

"Ten weeks, I think."

"Is she one of my students?"

"I'd rather not say."

"Local girl?"

"What difference does it make?"

"Well, if she's in Dallas, she can catch a nonstop to New York."

"She's not in Dallas."

"College girl? Texas Tech? You know what they say, 'If you're going to hell from Texas you have to change planes in Dallas.'"

"She's not in Lubbock."

"If she's a local girl, then Albuquerque is probably your best bet."

"Albuquerque?"

"New Mexico. Right over there." She pointed west.

"I know where it is."

"I know girls who have gone to Albuquerque, even some from Dallas. It just depends."

"Depends on what?"

"A lot of things. Airline schedules. Money. Do they have someone to drive them? Do they have a reason to go to New York, or Albuquerque? I mean who has a reason to go to Albuquerque?"

"A lot of people, apparently."

"How old is she?"

He didn't answer.

"Well, if she's a minor, then she might have to lie about her age, unless her parents are there to sign for her, but I'm guessing that's not the case, or you wouldn't be asking me."

He nodded.

"I don't really know the details, just what I've heard. I've never done it, knock wood." She rapped her knuckles on the table. "I just know girls go there and come back not pregnant. A couple of days later they're good as new. Personally, I'd go to New York. Nicer hotels and restaurants and you can catch a couple of Broadway shows."

"We're not up for any shows."

"I can call someone if you're serious."

"I'm serious."

"Okay."

"Is it legal?"

"Depends on how she answers the questions."

―――――

KEVIN HAD ONLY been cruising for a few minutes when he spotted Amy and Sandra in the Monza. He made a U-turn, quickly pulled up alongside and nodded. Sandra followed him to the icehouse, where she parked, and the girls climbed into Kevin's car.

"What did she say?" Amy asked as she slid over beside Kevin.

"Albuquerque."

"What about New York?" Sandra said, closing the door. "I know somebody who went there."

"Who?" Amy asked.

"Nobody you know."

"I know the same people you do."

"It was a model I met at market in Dallas. Models go to New York to work all the time, so it was an easy cover story."

"Yeah," Kevin said. "She mentioned New York, but there's no way we could make it there and back in time."

"How far is it to Albuquerque?" Amy asked.

"About four hours. Less if you drive like hell."

"How much will it cost?"

"Don't worry about it," Kevin said.

"How much?"

"Around three hundred."

"Where am I going to get three hundred dollars?"

"I can cover it," Kevin said.

"How?"

"Savings. There's not much to spend your money on in Viet Nam, plus you get combat pay and overseas pay, and ten percent interest on your savings account, tax free."

"That's your college money," Amy said.

"The clock's not ticking on my college education."

"I'll pay you back. I don't know how, but I will."

"We'll worry about that later."

"When are we going to do it?"

"She said you have to call and make an appointment. I have the number. Do you want to call, or do you want me to?"

"I'll call," Sandra said.

"No, I'll do it," Amy said. "It's my problem."

"Do you have fake ID?" Kevin asked.

Amy nodded. "Bobby got it for me, but I've never used it."

"She said you'll probably need it, so your parents won't have to sign," Kevin said.

"You told her it was me?" Amy was alarmed.

"No, of course not. I just said the girl in question was under eighteen."

"Oh, sorry. I'm just a little jumpy right now."

"That's okay."

"We can call tomorrow at lunch," Sandra said.

"I'm going in to work tomorrow to see if they need me," Kevin said. "Swing by the store after school and let me know what you find out."

Amy nodded. "When should I make the appointment for?"

"Saturday," Sandra said. "You can tell your parents you're spending the night with me Friday and we're going to Lubbock on Saturday to see a movie and do some shopping."

"Kevin has to work on Saturday," Amy said.

"So?" Sandra said.

"He's going with us," Amy said.

"Why?" Sandra asked.

"It's not like going to Lubbock," Amy said. "Two high school girls driving across New Mexico isn't very smart."

"I'll take off work," Kevin said. "I'm not sure what I'll tell Patty, but I'll think of something. Don't worry about me. Make the appointment for whenever you can. Maggie said you need to do it really soon, something about trimesters."

"Oh, yeah," Sandra said. "We'd better take the first appointment they have. We'll just have to ditch school and worry about it later."

39

PATTY AND ROBERT both came in to work on Monday morning, but there was plenty to do so Kevin stayed and worked. He had just finished helping Robert load bags of ice into a pickup when Amy and Sandra pulled up after school and parked nearby. The pickup drove away, and Robert headed back into the store. Kevin waited for the girls to get out of the Monza.

"Wednesday morning at nine o'clock," Amy said.

"This Wednesday?" Kevin asked.

Amy nodded.

"They had a cancellation," Sandra said. "Otherwise, it would be at least a week."

"We'll have to go tomorrow night," Kevin said. "We can't risk trying to drive up on Wednesday morning and miss the appointment."

"We have a game tomorrow night," Amy said.

"Where?"

"Here."

"Can you skip it?"

"Not really," Amy said. "Sometimes my daddy goes to home games."

"And we can't both skip it," Sandra said.

"Are you still planning on going?" Kevin asked.

"Of course I'm going," Sandra said forcefully.

Kevin mulled it over for a moment. "We can leave right after the game. We'll get in around midnight New Mexico time, so you should be able to get some rest."

"Okay," Amy said.

Kevin watched the girls for a moment. "So that's it. We'll just take off after the game. You won't go home tomorrow night, won't go to school on Wednesday, and you think nobody will even notice?"

Sandra shrugged. "We still have to work out the details."

"Are you going to leave your car at school after the game?"

"Doug can take us to the game, and you can pick us up."

"Does he know?"

"Know what?"

"About Amy."

"No," Sandra said. "I haven't told him and don't intend to."

"He'll want to know why you're both leaving the game with me," Kevin said.

"Let me worry about Doug," Sandra said.

"Does anybody else know?" Kevin asked.

"Nobody but us," Amy said.

"What about Emily?" Kevin asked.

"She suspects something, but she doesn't know, or at least she hasn't said anything."

Kevin stared into the distance, thinking it over. "Okay, here's what we're going to do. You tell your parents you're sleeping over at Sandra's tomorrow night."

Amy nodded.

"You'll both ride to the game with Doug, like usual, right?"

"We can do that," Sandra said.

"I'll pick up Amy at the game, and you'll leave with Doug."

"And then you'll pick me up at my house?" Sandra asked. "What's the point in that?"

"You're not going," Kevin said.

"Not going? What the hell?"

"We need you here to cover for us."

"Cover for you how?"

"Amy's parents will think she's with you tomorrow night. You can't both be gone." He turned to Amy. "Forge a note from your mother, saying you're sick. Have Emily turn it in at school Wednesday morning. Can you trust her?"

"I don't know. She can be a real brat sometimes, but I don't think she would rat me out for something this serious."

"You don't actually have to tell her what's going on," Kevin said. "Just tell her you want to ditch Wednesday. Tell her you're going to Lubbock with me to see a movie or something, just to get away from everything."

"Okay. That might work."

"And if anything goes wrong," Kevin said, turning to Sandra, "you can cover for us."

It was clear Sandra was not happy with the plan.

"Kevin's right," Amy said. "We can't both tell our parents we're spending the night at each other's house and then both ditch school. They'll call the cops."

"I still think I should go. You need me there with you."

"I'll be okay with Kevin."

"What if you need, you know—"

"What? It's not like I'm going to have my period or need a sponge bath or something."

Kevin grimaced.

Sandra sulked.

"I'll come over tonight to check on you and we can go over the details, but it might be late," Kevin said. "Big Bob wants me to go with him to the VFW tonight."

"Do you have to go?"

"He just buried his son. I can't blow him off."

Amy nodded. "Come by when you can. Sandra's spending the night, so we'll be up."

CLIFF WAS GRADING papers at his desk after school when Hank walked in and extended his hand.

"Hank Harding, Chief of Police."

Cliff shook his hand. "Cliff Billingsley. What can I do for you, Chief?"

"We put on a feed up at the VFW every Monday night. We haven't seen you there."

"I wasn't invited."

"I'm inviting you."

"Isn't that a restricted club?"

"Yes, it's restricted all right. Restricted to veterans of foreign wars. I believe that includes you, does it not?"

"It does."

"I'll pick you up around a quarter to seven."

"Do you know where I live?"

"I know where everybody lives."

KEVIN DISCOVERED THE purpose of the load of ice as soon as he walked into the VFW Hall just before seven and saw a considerable amount of beer iced down in number three washtubs. There was one exception to the no-alcohol policy at the VFW—when a member died. Bobby wasn't a member but certainly would have been when he returned, so no one even questioned it and the turnout was larger than usual. Veterans milled around, sitting, standing, visiting, waiting for everyone to arrive. Clara was busy in the kitchen and whatever she was cooking certainly smelled good.

Shortly after seven Hank pushed through the door, followed by Cliff and Terrell. Conversations suddenly stopped. Clara peeked out of the kitchen to see what was going on. She gasped and covered her mouth.

"This is Cliff Billingsley," Hank said with authority. "He teaches up at the high school. He served with the 101st Airborne in Viet Nam. He tells me he'll likely be leaving us at the end of the school year. I expect he'll join his local chapter at home or wherever he alights, but while he's in Preston I hope he'll join us from time to time, whenever he can."

There were a few murmured "welcomes" and other greetings.

"And you all know Terrell, Clara's boy," Hank continued. The door to the kitchen swung open and Clara stepped out, wiping her hands on her apron. "Terrell is our newest member," Hank said.

There was a moment of silence while Clara expected the worst, but Robert started it, Kevin joined in, and enthusiastic applause erupted. Veterans lined up to shake hands with Terrell and Cliff. Clara shrieked and nearly knocked people over getting to her son to hug him.

"Terrell still owes Uncle Sam a few months," Hank said, "but he'll be here every Monday night to eat his mama's cooking while he's home on leave, and then when he gets out."

"He'll be going to college on the GI Bill when he gets out," Clara said. "But this will always be home." Clara Washington was the proudest mama in Preston at that moment.

The veterans ate Clara's world-famous, or at least locally famous chicken-fried steak, mashed potatoes with gravy, black-eyed peas, fried okra, and biscuits so flaky they melted in your mouth. Dessert was apricot cobbler with ice cream, or chocolate cake, or both. They washed it all down with cold beer and lots of it.

Kevin and Terrell, the only minors present, didn't dare reach for a beer, until Hank put one in front of each of them and pried off the caps with a church key.

"I'm not the damned bartender," Hank said. "Help yourself after this, but don't let me catch you driving drunk."

Terrell looked at Kevin, who shrugged. They quickly reached for bottles and clinked them. "Here's to Bobby," Kevin said, standing.

"Hear, hear," came rolling off tongues as everyone stood and raised their bottles of beer.

There were several other toasts, but Terrell brought down the house. "To Bobby Dalton, best passer I ever had." The veterans roared.

Pictures of Bobby were pinned to the wall, including many shot by Kevin. He lingered over the ones that included Amy.

Those who knew Bobby the best told stories, some funny, some sad, some ribald, eliciting cackling from the kitchen. It wasn't Clara's first rodeo.

"HAVE YOU BEEN DRINKING?" Amy asked when Kevin stumbled into her bedroom.

Sandra quickly closed the door behind him.

"Wait till you see your daddy," he said.

Amy was indignant. They had important plans to discuss, and he had been out drinking. "You're drunk."

"We had a wake for Bobby," he said. "I guess that's what you'd call it."

"Why wasn't I invited?"

"No women allowed. It was at the VFW."

"I guess my daddy's drunk too," Sandra said.

Kevin nodded. "Terrell was there. He's drunk too."

The girls had no way of knowing that Terrell was the first black man to be a member of the local chapter.

"Chief Harding brought him," Kevin said, but the girls still seemed unconcerned as it had no bearing on the discussion at hand.

Sandra reloaded the record player and turned up the volume. They got down to business, the music covering their voices, although they still spoke in hushed tones.

"Did you talk to Emily?" Kevin asked as soon as the music started playing.

Amy nodded. "She'll do it, but I'll have to cover for her later when she wants to sneak out with a boy."

"What did you tell her?"

"I told her I just wanted to get away from everything for a few hours, so I was ditching school and going to Lubbock with you."

"Good." Kevin said.

"I don't know if she believed me, but she said she would do it."

"Can we trust her?"

"We don't really have a choice, but if anything goes wrong, she may figure it out."

"What do you mean?"

"We share a bathroom. She's already suspicious."

Sandra nodded. Kevin was confused.

"Let's hope nothing goes wrong," Kevin said. He turned to Sandra. "What about your parents?"

"What about them?"

"Will they notice Amy's not spending the night?"

"We spend the night with each other all the time," Sandra said. "They don't care. They never call to check, which is why I should be going with her."

Kevin ignored her. "I'll be working at the store tomorrow, but I'll bug out at lunch and go to the bank to pick up the cash. I'll come to the game after I get off work."

"I'll leave with Doug after the game," Sandra said, "and tell him Amy is going riding around with you."

"As long as nobody misses Amy tomorrow night, and Emily hands in the note Wednesday morning, it might work," Kevin said. "When we get back, I'll drop her off at your house and you can take her home, maybe spend the night at her house. She might need you."

"I might."

"I'll go straight home from school and wait for you to call," Sandra said.

"Good," Kevin said. "I don't know how long we'll have to wait at the hospital, but we'll leave as soon as Amy can travel." He turned to Amy. "You can lie down in the back seat if you need to."

Amy nodded. Kevin looked at Sandra.

"I'll stop and call when I can after you get home from school, but it's a long way between towns."

"Be sure and take a bunch of quarters," Amy said, smiling weakly. "Bobby used to go through a lot of them went he called me."

"I will." He reached out and took her hand. "Are you okay?"

Amy nodded.

"You haven't said much," Kevin said. "We've been doing all the talking, making plans like it's already been decided, but it's still up to you. Is this what you want?"

"It's not what I want, but I don't really have any other choice."

"Okay. Then this is what we'll do."

40

IT WAS THE first time in two weeks that Amy had worn her cheer-leader uniform and it felt a bit surreal. Basketball was nowhere near as big as football in Preston, or anywhere else in the state, but there was still a bit of game-day excitement in the air at the high school. Amy tried to smile occasionally and exhibit some degree of school spirit, but it was hopeless. She grew more withdrawn as the day dragged on. In English class she surreptitiously studied Maggie's face and body language, looking for any sign that Kevin had, however unintentionally, revealed that she was the pregnant girl in question. If Maggie suspected anything it wasn't obvious.

Throughout the day Amy struggled with her decision and ran through alternatives in her mind. She didn't like lying to her parents, but after agonizing over her decision, she felt she had no other choice.

Sandra was well aware of the extreme pressure her best friend was under and did whatever she could to make her day easier. Doug also sensed something was going on with Amy, something other than just grief, but he kept his mouth shut and carried their books while shadowing them through the hallways like a hulking bodyguard.

———

KEVIN HAD FABRICATED a story about needing cash to make a deposit on a car he had his eye on in Lubbock, but the teller at the bank just smiled, made an entry in his savings passbook, counted out the cash, put it in an envelope, and slid it across the counter without asking any questions.

He drove to the Texaco, where he checked the oil and tires while Joe Spalding filled the tank.

"It was good seeing Terrell at the VFW last night," Joe said, making small talk.

"Yeah, I'm glad Chief Harding brought him," Kevin said.

Country music blared from the radio as Kevin followed Joe into the office. Hank leaned back against the wall in a rickety wooden chair, sipping coffee while Joe rang up Kevin's gasoline purchase. Kevin pulled a New Mexico map from a rack next to the cash register.

"And this," Kevin said.

"You taking a trip?" Joe asked, ringing up the map.

"Albuquerque." A bit of truth always made a lie more believable. "I'm seeing a buddy from Viet Nam."

"You don't need a map to get to Albuquerque," Hank said, pointing west with his coffee cup. "Just head out the Clovis Highway and turn left on Route 66 at Santa Rosa. You can't hardly miss it."

"That's okay. I like maps. I like to know what's out there."

"I had my fill of maps in the Marines. And there wasn't nothing out there but jungle."

Kevin laughed. "I know the feeling." He glanced at Joe. "I guess there wasn't nothing out there but water for you."

"As far as the eye could see," Joe said.

"They got some good Mexican food in Albuquerque," Hank said. "It helps if you speak a little Spanish."

"I speak enough to order chow. Besides, my buddy's Mexican, so I'm covered." He was pleased with himself for that bit of extemporaneous detail.

————

HOWARD SAT IN the barber chair, reading the newspaper. Amy came in, grabbed the mail and rifled through it.

"How was school?" Howard asked.

"Still weird," Amy said.

"It'll get better."

Amy put the mail back on the counter. Howard folded the newspaper, stood, and turned. She watched as he opened a drawer, picked up some airmail envelopes and handed them to her.

"These came today," he said. "I thought about holding onto them for a few days, but you may as well have them now."

Amy looked at the envelopes. They were her letters, addressed to Bobby. They were rubber-stamped: DECEASED—RETURN TO SENDER.

She closed her eyes and took a deep breath. "I'm not going to cry."

Howard hugged her and kissed her on the head.

"I have to go," she said. "Sandra's waiting in the car."

"Hold on. There's one more thing."

"What is it?"

"Big Bob came by the shop this morning."

Amy froze.

"They got a letter from Bobby," Howard said.

Amy's heart sank. He knew. Bobby had written to his parents and told them about the baby.

"He said you two were getting married," Howard said.

She had to say something, but what? She chose silence, still unsure of what else Robert had told him.

"Why didn't you tell us?" Howard asked.

"It wasn't really definite, so I didn't say anything, and now—"

"Well, Bobby must have been pretty definite about it. He made you the beneficiary on his GI insurance just a few days before he died."

"What's that?"

"Life insurance, paid for by the government. Unless it's gone up, we think it's probably still ten thousand dollars."

Ten thousand dollars? Amy was shocked, but the money meant nothing to her—she'd much rather have Bobby.

"I can't take it. It wouldn't be right. It should go to his parents."

"Of course you can take it. Bobby wanted you to have it. You can go to college, wherever you want. That's what Bobby would have wanted."

He was right, of course. She nodded. "We'll talk about it later, but I really have to go."

She turned to go, and then turned back. "Don't forget, I'm sleeping over at Sandra's tonight."

"It's a school night, honey. Y'all were up late last night."

"She wants to help, and it's good to have someone there."

She put her hand on his shoulder and kissed him on the lips. "I love you, Daddy. I love you so much."

She wiped tears as she raced out the door.

AFTER WATCHING PART of the basketball game, and making sure Amy and Sandra had seen him, Kevin went out to the parking lot to wait.

"Yo, Kev," Doug called out as Kevin walked to his car.

Kevin turned and saw Doug sitting on the tailgate of his pickup with a paper cup in his hand.

"Are you leaving?" Doug asked.

"No, not yet."

"You want a drink?"

"No thanks. I'm good." Kevin sat on the tailgate beside Doug. There was a six-pack of Coca Cola, a stack of paper cups, a cooler, and a brown paper bag. "Aren't you pushing your luck, drinking in the parking lot?"

"Can't drink in the gym."

Kevin laughed and pulled his field jacket up around his ears. "Shit, it's cold out here."

"I'll stash it before Colonel Klink comes out," Doug said. "He'll probably be right behind the cheerleaders, measuring their skirts."

"You got that right."

"Is Amy riding with you?"

"Uh, yeah."

"I just wanted to make sure," Doug said. "They both came with me."

Doug chugged his drink and tossed the paper cup over his shoulder into the bed of the pickup. "Is Amy okay?"

"I guess so, under the circumstances."

"It's not just about Bobby," Doug said. "They seem to whisper a lot and get real jumpy, and it's not like being on the rag, it's like they have some kind of secret between them."

"Chicks."

Doug stared at him for a moment. "What's going on, man?"

"What do you mean?"

"Sandra said Amy's spending the night with her."

"Yeah, that's what Amy said."

"So Amy's going to ride around with you and then you'll drop her off at Sandra's house?"

"Yeah," Kevin said.

"What if we decide to go park and make out? What are y'all going to do, just keep riding around?"

"We have a lot to talk about."

"Don't shit a shitter," Doug said. "What's going on?"

"Nothing's going on. Amy just needs company right now. She doesn't want to be alone, and she doesn't want to be a third wheel with you and Sandra. That's all."

They watched as people began streaming out of the gym.

"I think I figured out what it is," Doug said.

"Well, if you did, then keep it to yourself. And if the shit hits the fan tomorrow just follow Sandra's lead."

"You got it, brother."

Doug reached for the six-pack of Coca Cola. He picked up a bottle, turned it over and said, "Lubbock."

Kevin picked up the six-pack, looked at the bottles on one side, then the other, finally selecting one. He turned it over. "Waco." He showed it to Doug.

"Shit. How do you do that?"

Kevin smiled. "Sack-boy secret."

AMY WAS CURLED UP on the floorboard of the Impala as Kevin headed west on the highway.

"All clear," he said. "We're out of town."

Amy scrambled up into the seat, peeled off her cheerleader sweater and tossed it over the seat. He watched with interest as she slipped her hands under her skirt and pulled off her gold-colored briefs. He stared.

"What are you doing?" he asked.

"Changing clothes. What does it look like?"

"It looks like you just took off your panties."

She held up the briefs.

"These are briefs, not panties," she said.

Kevin took another look.

"Did you really think you can see a cheerleader's panties when you look up her skirt?" she asked.

Kevin nodded.

"Well, you can't," she said. "You see these. Briefs. School colors."

"You just destroyed years of fond memories."

She got up on her knees and bent over the seat, reaching for her bag. The skirt hiked up and he couldn't help but look at her white panties. The car swerved off the pavement.

"Eyes on the road, big boy."

"Sorry. I couldn't help myself."

She stuffed the briefs in her bag and pulled out a pair of Levi's and a flannel shirt. She dropped back into the seat and pulled off her blouse. It was nothing he hadn't already seen, but the car swerved again.

He continued to divide his attention between her and the road. She pulled off her skirt and tossed it over the seat. She arched her back and raised her hips, wiggling into the tight Levi's, but also putting herself on full display to oncoming traffic.

"Get down!" Kevin said.

Amy ducked onto the floor, not an easy task with her Levi's around her knees. Kevin waved at the driver of a large truck as it whizzed by.

"Who was it?" she asked.

"Old Man Frankford."

"Did he see me?"

Kevin looked in the rearview mirror. "I don't know, maybe."

She finally got the Levi's over her hips.

"Do you think he recognized me?" she asked.

"He was definitely not looking at your face."

Neither was Kevin as she zipped up her Levi's.

"You don't have to watch."

"Sure I do. I'm a guy."

She shrugged. He had a point, and she enjoyed all the little sexual innuendos that had been part of their relationship since he came home. This exchange was harmless enough and brightened her mood. If he got a little thrill out of seeing her in her underwear, it was okay with her.

"You could have changed in the back seat," he said. "It would have been harder for me to look."

"You could use the rearview mirror," she said as she buttoned her shirt.

"You could sit over there," he said, pointing to the right back seat.

"You could still sneak a peek."

They both started laughing at the same time. She was glad he was laughing about it because she was starting to feel a twinge of guilt, hoping she wasn't being a tease. He was in love with her, after all, having declared so himself.

She slid over next to him, grabbed the rearview mirror and yanked it. He turned his attention back to the road—she was fully dressed now—nothing else to see, except her face, which he liked looking at. She looked in the mirror, fluffed her hair and checked her makeup, what little there was—she certainly didn't need any, in his opinion anyway.

She poked at the mirror. "You'll have to fix it, unless you want me to climb in your lap." She couldn't resist one last jab.

"Okay. Go ahead."

"You wish." She slid over and settled back on the passenger side.

He adjusted the mirror. "Yeah, you'd probably cause me to wreck out."

"And you'd have to explain to my daddy why we were out on the highway headed toward New Mexico when I was supposed to be at Sandra's."

"I'd just tell him we were running off to get married," Kevin said, before wishing he hadn't.

"He'd probably be okay with it," she said nonchalantly.

"He would?"

"Daddy likes you. He always has."

"He never said anything."

"What's he supposed to say? I was going steady with Bobby. It's not like he was going to try to fix me up with another boy."

Kevin shrugged. She dug through her purse, pulled out a compact, flipped it open and used the little mirror to apply lipstick.

"How do I look?"

"You look great. You didn't have to change just for me."

"Did you really want to check into a motel, late at night, in another state, with a high school cheerleader?"

"You could stay in the car while I check in."

"Oh, yeah. Well, this is better for a road trip anyway. It's more comfortable, and warmer, and safer."

"Safer?"

"You won't keep trying to look up my skirt and run off the road."

"Why are you being so feisty all of a sudden?"

"Because I don't want to think about where we're going and what I'm going to do when we get there."

He couldn't argue with that. She turned on the radio and they drove west into the night.

"Are you hungry?" he asked as they entered Clovis.

"Not really but we can stop if you want to get something."

"I'm starved."

"I might have a hamburger," she said, "as long as we're stopping."

It was unlikely they would encounter anyone they knew, but Clovis wasn't that far from Preston, so Amy kept her head down while Kevin walked up to the window at a hamburger joint and ordered.

"Oh, that smells good," Amy said as he put the food on the seat, carefully balancing the box holding the drinks. She dug out the burgers as he pulled onto the highway.

"I thought you said you weren't hungry," Kevin said, watching her chomp down on her hamburger.

She nodded. When she finally swallowed enough to speak, she said, "I've been on a diet ever since I first suspected I was pregnant, but I guess it doesn't matter now, so I might as well pig out."

They kept up a spirited conversation to keep Kevin from nodding off at the wheel, but after stopping in Santa Rosa for gas and a bathroom break, Amy stretched out on the seat with her head in his lap, leaving only the radio to keep him awake.

Kevin couldn't tell if Amy was awake as the run-up to the KOMA Kissing Tone played, not that it mattered—he had no expectation of kissing her under the circumstances. As he turned his attention back to the highway she suddenly sat up and kissed him on the lips. Without a word, she lay back down, head in his lap, as he drove on.

He slowed down on the outskirts of Albuquerque and pulled over at a motel that appeared to fit his budget. Amy waited in the car while he went in to register. After a few minutes he approached the passenger side of the car. She could hear the neon on the motel sign buzzing when she rolled down the window and he leaned in.

"They only have one room left."

"We only need one room. It's not like my reputation will be ruined."

"It only has one bed."

She laughed. "I saw this in a movie."

"We can go on down the road and try to find something else."

"No, it's okay."

"I'll sleep on the floor, or in a chair."

"We can both sleep in the bed. I promise I won't try to take advantage of you."

"Okay, but the guy says you have to come in and sign the register."

"Ha!" she said, opening the door.

"What?"

"Cheerleader."

"Try to look older."

It was a single-story motel, not unlike hundreds of others that dotted Route 66, their glory days behind them now that Interstate 40 was rapidly replacing The Mother Road. Most were built decades before cookie-cutter chain motels began polluting the highways, and this one was no exception. It had something of a mission theme, brown stucco mimicking adobe, with rough-hewn cedar logs supporting a portico.

The room was not at all inviting as Kevin unlocked the door and pushed in, flipping on the light. The aroma of cleaning products tried in vain to overcome the stale odor of cigarette smoke. There was indeed one double bed, along with two straight-back chairs parked at a small table.

"Well, this is depressing," Amy said as she dumped her bag and sat on the foot of the bed.

"Yeah, it is kind of a dump." He hooked the chain latch on the door.

"But it was cheap, right? And we'll only be here a few hours." She leaned forward and opened a dresser drawer. "Do people really stay here long enough to use all these drawers?" She looked up at the large mirror, spanning the entire length of the dresser. "Oh, look. You can watch yourself doing it."

"I'm sure people do that."

"Ew," she said, falling back onto the bed. "I hope they changed the sheets." She looked to her left, where there was a little nook with a place to hang clothes, along with a door to the bathroom, and then to her right, at the heavy curtains on the windows. She giggled and sat up. "I'm not even supposed to have boys in my room with the door closed, and here I am in a motel with a boy, with the door locked. My daddy would crap his pants."

"Probably." He pulled his shaving kit out of his AWOL bag. "Do you want the bathroom first?"

"No, you go."

Kevin could hear the TV for a few minutes while he was in the bathroom, and then it went off. Amy was digging through her bag when he came out.

"Crap," Amy said.

"What's wrong?"

"Do you have an extra T-shirt?"

"Why do you need a T-shirt?"

"Because I don't wear pajamas."

"Neither do I." He opened his AWOL bag.

"You are *not* sleeping naked tonight," she said.

He smiled as he handed her a T-shirt. She raised her eyebrows as she took it, and then disappeared into the bathroom.

Kevin undressed and climbed into bed.

Amy stared into the bathroom mirror. Tomorrow it would all be over. Hardly anyone would know. She would go back to her life, or what was left of it, and graduate from high school. She'd go to college and meet new people, like her daddy said. But she had to get through this first. She had made her decision. The time had come.

Kevin lay in bed, studying his New Mexico map, the Albuquerque inset. He looked up as Amy came out, wearing his T-shirt, which was huge on her, the way she liked it, serving as a nightgown.

She stepped over to the bed and lifted the covers.

"Am I on your side of the bed?" he asked.

She looked under the covers. "No, just checking," she said, grinning.

She went around to the other side of the bed, climbed in, and pulled up the covers. She lay on her back and looked at the map.

"Are you trying to figure out where we are?" she asked.

"Trying to find the best way to get to the hospital."

"Did you find it?"

"I think so."

She fidgeted and looked around the room.

"Is this what they call a fleabag motel?"

"Probably, only I hope there's no fleas."

"Ew!" She lifted the covers and looked. She raised up on her elbow and checked underneath her body. Finding nothing, she lay back down.

"I'm glad you came with me instead of Sandra."

"Me too. I'll bet she can't read a map."

"You make me laugh. She doesn't, most of the time anyway."

"Come to think of it, she doesn't have much of a sense of humor."

"I've never slept with a boy before."

"Evidence to the contrary."

"You know what I mean. I wish I'd had a brother to horse around with and see him naked, play doctor, practice kissing, normal stuff."

"Is that why you freaked out when you saw me naked?"

"Yes. It is. See, I should have done that years ago."

"You should have asked. I was available."

She laughed. "I've led a very sheltered life."

"Says the teenage girl in bed with an older man in a motel in Albuquerque."

"Well, if you put it like that."

"You never spent the night with Bobby?"

"No, never. He always had me home by midnight. Of course he always tried to get in a full night's work before then."

Kevin laughed. "I can imagine."

"All those times I pushed his hand away from my boobs or pulled it out from between my legs. I'd give anything to have that fool feeling me up right now."

She looked at him.

"What?" he asked.

"You're supposed to say, 'I'd be happy to feel you up if that's what you want.'"

"I know when you're playing and when you're being serious."

"You do, don't you? You can put your arm around me if you want."

He put his arm under her neck, and she snuggled up.

"As long as you don't try to cop a feel," she said.

"That was playing, right?"

"Try it and find out."

"No thanks."

"Okay, enough playing. My daddy's not here, so you can kiss me goodnight." She turned to face him.

He looked at her for a moment.

"It's not a trick," she said.

"Goodnight." He kissed her on the forehead.

"Goodnight." She rolled over away from him.

He studied the map for a moment.

"Kevin."

"Yes?"

"We did it in your bed."

"I know."

She rolled back over. "He told you?"

"No."

"Then how did you know?"

"I smelled your hairspray on my pillow."

"Oh, sorry."

"That's okay. It smelled good."

"No. I'm sorry we did it in your bed. We wouldn't have if I'd known how you felt. That would have been mean."

He folded the map and put it on the nightstand.

"We only did it once," she said.

"In my bed?"

"Ever."

"How was it?"

"It was good, I guess. I don't really have anything to compare it to. Bobby certainly seemed to enjoy himself."

"Do you regret it?"

"No."

41

ON WEDNESDAY MORNING Patty and Robert went to the cemetery before opening the store. They had purchased two grave spaces several years ago, assuming Bobby would marry and be buried beside his wife. Like most parents, they never imagined he would be buried beside them. He was eligible for burial in Arlington National Cemetery, and Patty and Robert briefly considered it. He would not have been the only Preston man buried there. But Patty wanted him close by so she could visit whenever she wanted, so Robert purchased three new spaces together. They would decide later what to do with the original pair.

Patty would be in the middle, flanked by her men, under one headstone. Bobby and his father would have veteran's footstones. A tin marker would stand over Bobby's grave until the stones were placed.

AMY WOKE UP on her side, her back to Kevin. He was still asleep, pressing against her, his hand on her waist. Her T-shirt was hiked up well above her waist and she could feel the warmth of his bare skin against hers and his breath on her neck. She tugged at the front of her T-shirt, covering herself. She was glad she had her back to him but concerned that they may have tossed and turned during the night and been in an even more compromising position. She glanced over her shoulder.

She imagined being in bed like this with Bobby. She had been for a few brief moments, in Kevin's bed, before the alarm went off and they had to vacate. She wished she had been able to spend an entire night with him. Sex was one thing but waking up in bed with your lover seemed so grown-up. There was morning breath and bodily functions to attend to. She assumed there was stubble on Kevin's face, probably more than Bobby would have had. When they first started dating, she had teased him about the peach fuzz on his face.

She listened to Kevin breathe and could feel his every breath against her back. She liked it, even if they weren't lovers. She assumed Kevin had spent the night with girls before—he certainly seemed comfortable doing it. She gingerly took his wrist with her fingers and moved his hand off her waist. He moved it back, higher up this time. She looked at his hand, and then looked over her shoulder. He was asleep. It was an unconscious action, or so she hoped. Surely he wasn't trying to grope her breast. She smiled, took his wrist and moved it again, pushing it all the way over his back, where she dropped it. She checked him again. Still asleep. She wriggled free and slipped out of bed. She watched him sleep for a moment and then stepped silently into the bathroom.

Warm water trickled down her body as she stood in the shower. Her fingers lingered over her stomach.

She finished her shower, dried off, brushed her teeth, wrapped herself in a towel and flushed the toilet. She looked at Kevin as she stepped out of the bathroom. He was dead to the world. She leaned over the bed and looked closer. Sound asleep. She waved her hand in front of his face. Nothing. Certain he was asleep, she peeled off the towel and dropped it on the foot of the bed. She dug in her bag and pulled out underwear.

The phone rang. Amy turned, startled. It rang again, and it was loud. Kevin rolled over and reached for it but stopped to look at an unexpected but welcome sight. Her hands went instinctively to her vital parts. Otherwise, she stood frozen, like a deer in the headlights, eyes wide. The phone rang again. Finally, she had the presence of mind to turn around and cover her bottom with her hands.

Kevin answered the phone. "Hello," he said, never taking his eyes off Amy, thoroughly enjoying the view.

Amy could hear the clank as he hung up the phone. She quickly reviewed her options. She could wrap the towel around herself, pick up her underwear and rush into the bathroom, but the towel was on the bed, and she would have to turn around to pick it up. Or she could just get dressed where she stood. No matter what she did she would have to move her hands, giving him at least a good look at something. She decided to act all nonchalant, like a grown-up, and not a squealing teenager.

"Who was that?" She stepped into her panties. She still had her back turned to him, but suddenly realized he was getting a fantastic look compliments of the huge mirror on the dresser.

"Wakeup call."

She slipped on her bra and turned to face him while she fastened it. He continued to watch, and smile.

"Now we're even," she said.

"Even?"

"We've seen each other naked."

"No. I'm pretty sure I'm way ahead on that deal."

She picked up her towel and threw it at him. He caught it, pulled back the covers, and started to get out of bed.

"Wait," she said.

He lay back.

"Scoot over."

He scooted over. She lay down beside him.

"What are you doing?" he asked.

She took his hand and placed it on her stomach. "Can you feel it?"

He felt her stomach. "Feel what?"

"The baby."

"No. Not really."

"See if you can hear it."

He hesitated, but then moved down and put his ear on her stomach. He listened, and then raised his head.

"I can hear your stomach growling."

"I'm starved."

"We have time for breakfast."

"I can't eat before they do it."

"Sorry, I forgot."

"You can eat."

"That's okay. I can wait."

"You can get something while I'm in there."

"I'm not leaving you."

"I don't think they'll let you watch."

"I mean I'm not leaving the hospital."

"They probably have a cafeteria."

"Yeah, probably."

"Try again."

She put her fingers on his head and pulled it down onto her stomach. He listened. Nothing. He raised up.

"Is there a problem?" he asked.

"If it's kicking, they won't do it."

"They won't?"

"That's what Sandra said."

"Do you want them to do it?"

"We came all this way."

He pulled the covers up over her and stretched out beside her.

"We can go back if you want."

"No. I can't have this baby. My daddy will kill me."

"He might not be happy about it, but I doubt he'd go that far. Doesn't that church you go to preach forgiveness?"

"I know what the preacher would say."

"What?"

"Well, after he looks at me like I'm a whore, he'll tell Daddy to send me to a home for unwed mothers in Lubbock or Fort Worth or somewhere."

"Maybe not."

"I'm too young to have a baby, especially with Bobby gone. A baby needs a daddy."

"I could be its daddy."

She looked him in the eye for what seemed an eternity. "I'm not going to marry you just so people won't talk." She stared at the ceiling. "People would talk anyway. They'd say I cheated on Bobby."

"Then I'll be an uncle. Bobby was like a brother to me."

"So you're saying I should have it?"

"It's not up to me."

Amy pondered for a moment. "I know. It's up to me." She whipped back the covers and sat up on the side of the bed. "Let's get this over with."

THE SCHOOL SECRETARY walked through the deserted hallway of the elementary school, her heels clicking on the hard floor. She opened the door to a classroom. Thirty young heads immediately turned toward her. Vivian stepped over to the door.

"Do we need to send Amy's work home with Emily?" the secretary asked. "We don't want her to fall behind. She's already missed a lot of school."

"Why would you need to do that?" Vivian asked.

"Amy's not in school."

"She should be."

"Emily brought in a note. It said Amy is sick and won't be in today."

"Could you call the barbershop? Maybe Howard knows something I don't."

"The note had your signature on it."

Vivian was now concerned. "I didn't write a note. Is Sandra Brewster in school?"

"Yes."

"Amy spent the night with her last night."

"I'll see what Sandra has to say and let you know."

KEVIN AND AMY gathered their things from the motel room. He opened the door.

"Wait," she said.

He closed the door and turned.

"Would you really raise another man's child?"

"Like it was my own."

"Okay, assuming that we could get together, after a few weeks or months, and assuming that I could come to feel about you the way you feel about me, and there's no guarantee I could—"

"I understand."

"Wouldn't it be a lot easier if there was no baby?"

"Of course it would."

She paused while choosing her words carefully. "If it doesn't work out between us, like you want it to, and it might not, then you could be hurt."

"I've been hurt before."

"Badly."

"I can't possibly be hurt as badly as you're hurting right now."

She didn't respond.

"Look, Amy. I'm in a difficult position here. You know I'm hopelessly in love with you. It's very tempting for me to try to influence you one way or the other to get what I want, which is you. But I can't do that. I love you too much to do that. You have to do what's best for you, and for the people you care about."

"I care about you."

"Except me."

She put her arms around him, and he held her tightly.

SANDRA SAT IN the principal's office, trying hard to not appear nervous as Principal Klein looked at a piece of paper on the desk.

"We received a note this morning saying Amy Evans was ill and would not be at school today," he said.

Sandra shrugged. "Yeah, I noticed she wasn't here."

"Neither of her parents wrote the note."

"I sure didn't write it."

"Amy told her parents she was going to spend the night with you last night."

"She didn't."

"Do you know where she is?"

"I haven't seen her. I wondered why she wasn't at school. I even tried to call her house on the pay phone, but nobody answered."

"She rides to school with you, doesn't she?"

"Not every day," Sandra said, quickly adjusting her story. "Sometimes she rides with her mom."

The principal was unconvinced.

"Oh, I know," Sandra said. "There's an away game Friday, so we talked about spending the night then, and maybe going to Lubbock on Saturday, see a movie, go shopping, to kind of take her mind off things. She's having a hard time since her boyfriend got killed in Viet Nam." Sandra knew how to work it. "Maybe she just decided to ditch today. I know I would if my boyfriend got killed."

KEVIN TURNED THE ignition key in his car outside the motel room, but the car wouldn't start.

"Shit," he said.

"What's wrong with it?" Amy asked.

"I don't know." He tried it again.

"Is the battery dead?"

"No, it's turning over. It just won't start."

He got out of the car and looked under the hood.

"Try it," Kevin said.

Amy slid over into the driver's seat and tried it.

Kevin closed the hood. "It's not going to start."

"What are we going to do?" she asked.

PRINCIPAL KLEIN SAT at his desk. Emily was in the hot seat. Hank stood menacingly nearby. Howard paced, and then put his hands on the desk and leaned toward Emily.

"Honey, please. If you know where she is, you have to tell us. This is serious."

Emily fought back tears, trying to stay strong.

"Did she go somewhere with Kevin?" Howard asked.

"Why would she go somewhere with Kevin?" Emily said, taking a shot, although clearly, they were on the right track.

"She rode to the game last night with Sandra and Doug, but Doug said she left with Kevin," Howard said.

"Maybe they went riding around," Emily said. "I did. Lots of kids do after the game."

"She didn't spend the night with Sandra, she didn't come home, and she's not in school. Where is she?"

Emily stalled for a moment, her mind racing. "She said she wanted to skip school and go to Lubbock with Kevin. I thought she spent the night at Sandra's."

"I saw Kevin at Spalding's yesterday. He said he was going to Albuquerque to visit a buddy from Viet Nam," Hank said.

"Did Amy go with him?" Howard asked.

Emily's eyes darted back and forth between her daddy and Hank. They knew Kevin had left town, probably with Amy. The jig was up.

"Your mother is worried out of her mind," Howard said. "So am I. If Amy's in trouble you need to tell me, now."

Emily burst into tears.

AMY LEANED AGAINST the Impala as Kevin closed the hood. A taxi pulled up, driven by Miguel, a young man in his twenties, wearing an Army field jacket with the First Infantry Division patch on the left shoulder. He rolled down the window.

"You call a cab?"

"Yeah." Kevin stepped forward and gave him their destination. "You know where it is?"

Miguel glanced at Amy, then back at Kevin. "I go there a lot."

Kevin transferred their bags to the trunk of the taxi. Amy slid into the middle of the back seat. Kevin sat beside her and closed the door.

"The last time I was in a taxi was from Oakland Army Base to the San Francisco Airport," Kevin said as the taxi pulled out of the motel parking lot. "There were four of us and the driver tried to charge us all separate fares."

He looked up to see Miguel looking in the rearview mirror.

"Sorry," Kevin said. "No offense."

"None taken. I took the same ride."

"Viet Nam?"

"First Infantry. Been back about a year."

"Well, if you're going to be one," Kevin said.

"Be a big red one," the boys said in unison and then laughed.

Amy had no idea what they were talking about, but she was used to Army talk.

"What's wrong with your car?" Miguel asked.

"Probably the fuel pump. I could fix it if I had my tools."

"I have tools."

"I couldn't ask you to do that."

"You didn't ask. I offered."

"We're in kind of a hurry to get back. We'll probably take the bus, depending on what time we get out. I'll come back later to get my car."

"I'll keep an eye on it for you."

"People will see us get off the bus together," Amy said quietly.

"We'll call Sharon and have her meet the bus in Clovis."

"I'll give you my number," Miguel said. "Bring your tools when you come back, or we can use mine. I know where to get a good deal on parts."

"Thanks, man."

Amy stared out the window as the taxi entered the downtown area, but it was all a blur, ordinary people going about their ordinary lives, oblivious to the Texas teenager in the taxi whose life was crashing down around her.

Miguel pulled up and parked in front of the hospital. He handed a business card over the seat. "Call the number on the front when you're done and ask for me. If I'm nearby, I'll swing by and pick you up. My home number is on the back in case I miss you and you need to come back for your car."

"Roger that," Kevin said.

ANOTHER BARBER CUT hair while Howard was on the phone. Several men waited, all eyes on Howard. Hank stood nearby.

"I'm her father," Howard said. "She's seventeen years old."

"I'm sorry, sir," the switchboard operator said. "I can't give out information on patients."

"So she is a patient there."

"I'm sorry, sir. I can't give out that information."

Howard slammed down the phone and turned to Hank.

"Is there anything you can do?"

"Not unless you have reason to believe she was kidnapped."

"We both know she wasn't kidnapped."

"I can put in a call to the Albuquerque PD. They might could check the hospitals, looking for Kevin's car, but that's a long shot. Even if they find them there's not much they can do."

KEVIN OPENED THE door of the taxi. "Are you ready?"

"No," Amy said.

"Can you give us a minute?" Kevin said.

Miguel nodded. "Sure," he said.

Kevin closed the door. Amy sat silently for a moment, collecting her thoughts. Kevin waited patiently.

"Bobby is the last thing I think about before I go to sleep at night and the first thing I think about when I wake up in the morning," she said. "Daddy said that someday it won't hurt as much as it did the day before. He's right, of course. I'm not the first pregnant girl whose boyfriend got killed in Viet Nam, or some other war."

Miguel shut off the engine. This was not at all what he expected.

"I'll just run in and get some coffee," Miguel said. "You want some?"

"Uh, yeah," Kevin said. "Black."

Miguel dashed into the hospital.

They sat silently for a moment. "I can't imagine ever loving you, or anyone else, as much as I love Bobby. Maybe that will change in time, but I don't have time. You said you were in a difficult position, and I realize that, every time you look at me, every time you touch me." She looked at him and smiled. "Every time you kiss me, whether we're playing or not."

"Amy—"

She held up her hand to stop him. "I can't give you what you want, what you need. Not right now. Maybe never. I just don't know."

He nodded.

"But I need you," she said. "You have no idea how much I need you."

"I'm here for you, no matter what."

She started trembling.

"Are you cold?" he asked, pulling her close.

"I'm scared."

He pulled her closer.

"I'm terrified," she said.

"Tell me what to do."

"Hold me."

He held her tightly while she cried softly.

HOWARD RELUCTANTLY WENT back to cutting hair. The line was getting long and standing by the phone wasn't doing him any good. Robert, Patty, and Hank stood on the sidewalk outside the shop, debating strategy. They all turned when they heard the phone ring.

"Barbershop," Howard said.

"I have a collect call for anyone from Amy Evans. Will you accept the charges?"

"Yes! Yes!" Howard signaled Robert.

"Go ahead, ma'am."

"Daddy." Amy was sobbing.

"Oh, honey, where are you? Your mother and I are worried sick."

"Albuquerque," Amy said.

"What are you doing in Albuquerque?" Howard said as Robert stepped through the door, followed by Patty and Hank.

"I'm pregnant."

"Are you okay?" Howard asked, avoiding asking her outright whether she had gone through with it, but her statement seemed to indicate that she had not, at least not yet.

"I'm okay, just scared."

"Scared?"

He waited while she cried.

"I didn't want to disappoint you and mom."

"You could never disappoint us, honey."

"You're going to be a granddaddy."

Howard covered the mouthpiece and looked upward. "Thank you, Jesus." He removed his hand. "That's great, honey. That's just great."

"I'm so sorry I didn't tell you. I wanted to. I really did. I didn't know what to do. I was so scared."

"That's okay, honey. That's okay. Hold on, Robert and Patty are here. I'm sure they'll want to talk to you."

Howard handed the receiver to Patty. "You're going to be a grandmother."

Men flocked forth from chairs, slapping Howard on the back and shaking his hand while Patty talked to Amy, tilting the receiver so Robert could hear.

"I'll go next door and call the school so they can tell Vivian," Hank said.

KEVIN AND MIGUEL leaned against the hood of the taxi, sipping coffee, watching Amy, a few feet away on a pay phone near the door to the hospital. They watched as Amy talked on the phone, laughing and crying at the same time.

"You think my car will be okay at the motel for a couple of days?"

"I'll talk to the manager," Miguel said. "If he gives me any shit, I'll call my cousin and we'll tow it to my house."

"Thanks. I'll try to get back this weekend, maybe Sunday, with a trailer."

Amy turned toward Kevin and held out the receiver. "Daddy wants to talk to you."

Kevin, with his arm around Amy and her face buried in his chest, talked not only to Howard, but also Robert. He checked his watch. Plans were made. Miguel watched as Kevin hung up the phone. He quickly got in the taxi and started the engine.

Kevin held the taxi door open for Amy and they slid into the back seat, sitting close together, holding hands.

"Is there a restaurant at the bus station?" Amy asked. "I'm starving."

"Yes, there is," Miguel said. "Pretty good one too."

Amy cuddled contentedly under Kevin's arm for the ride to the bus station. After saying goodbye to their new friend from New Mexico, they went inside to purchase tickets, check their bags and, most importantly, chow down.

"I hope he likes cheeseburgers," Amy said as she attacked her cheeseburger and fries and washed it down with a milkshake. "His daddy sure did."

THE HEADSIGN ON the bus said LUBBOCK as it headed east, the sun low in the sky behind, turning everything orange. Amy sat by the window, staring out at the landscape, the diesel engine rumbling soothingly. Kevin stared at her. He felt her hand on his and looked down as their fingers intertwined. She turned to him and smiled contentedly.

Kevin still had his pocketful of quarters, and even though word had quickly spread, Sandra still raced home from school and sat by the phone. Amy called during a brief stop in Fort Sumner and she and Sandra cried and laughed and made big plans.

As the bus approached Preston, Amy was curled up asleep with her head on Kevin's lap, his hand on her waist, occasionally sliding down onto her belly, comforting his stepson or nephew, depending on what the future might hold, hoping to feel him kick. Or her.

Kevin could see the red lights on top of the grain elevator in Preston as the bus negotiated a jog in the road necessitated by a draw that cut through at an inconvenient place on the otherwise straight highway.

"We're almost there," Kevin said.

Amy sat up and looked out. All she could see was night. A few lights from farmhouses twinkled in the distance.

As the bus neared the highway intersection the driver noticed an unusual amount of activity at the Texaco. Dozens of cars were parked at the filling station, café, and across the street at the Panther. A police car was parked on the corner, red lights flashing. A few teenagers stood in the highway, waving their arms as the bus approached.

"Something's going on at the Texaco," Kevin said, leaning out into the aisle so he could see through the windshield.

"What is it?" Amy asked, trying to see over the seatback.

"I don't know," Kevin said. "Maybe it's a wreck."

The bus driver stopped at the highway intersection and evaluated the situation. Westbound buses simply pulled over and stopped between the filling station and the café, but eastbound buses had to make a left at the light, circle the building, and come up on the east side of the café so that passengers wouldn't have to cross the highway. The bus driver was hesitant to circle the building and end up trapped by all the cars parked around it. He glanced around, reviewing his options. Up ahead, people flooded out of the café and filling station. He looked left and saw dozens of teenagers swarming out of cars at the Panther and headed across the state highway.

Chief Harding stepped off the curb and signaled the driver to turn left, as Terrell sprinted into the street to hold back the crowd of teenagers.

Amy spotted Sandra and Doug in the crowd, waving and screaming. She waved back, and then turned to look out the other window as the bus turned behind the Texaco, waved in authoritatively by Cliff. Some of the teenagers chased the bus while others headed toward the café.

The bus driver made his final turn behind the café on faith and discovered that ample room had been left for the bus. People surrounded the bus as he stopped and set the brake.

Kevin took Amy's hand. "Are you ready?"

She smiled and nodded.

The bus driver was still unsure what was going on, but he had a schedule to keep, so he opened the door.

Amy was crying before her feet hit the pavement. She rushed into her daddy's arms, and then her mother's, until her sisters demanded their turn. There were hugs and kisses by the score, along with plenty of tears. Hank stood in the highway in front of the bus, one eye on the crowd and the other on traffic. Terrell helped with crowd control.

Amy hugged Sandra and they cried and cried while Doug shook hands with Kevin, who saw Maggie out of the corner of his eye, standing next to Cliff. Kevin looked at her and smiled. She nodded. It appeared Kevin was a much better man than she had given him credit for. She intended to tell him so, and apologize, but not tonight. Cliff raised his right hand and saluted. Kevin smiled and returned the salute.

Howard and Robert cornered Kevin, shaking his hand and slapping him on the back, and immediately began dispensing advice.

Kevin turned to see Amy looking at him, beaming, her mother on one side, Bobby's mother on the other, flanked by Irene, Grandmother, and Clara. He wished he had his camera, but it was an image burned indelibly into his mind.

A few blocks away bells began ringing at the First Baptist Church.

Robert Dalton III had come home.

ABOUT THE AUTHOR

C. David Stephens is a screenwriter whose best-known work is *Cabin by the Lake*, USA Network's highest-rated original movie. He has several screenplays in various stages of development, including *Granny*, a horror film co-written with the late Blake Snyder; *An Affair of Honor*, a tragic love story set in France and North Africa in 1940, and *Every Mother's Son*, the original screenplay on which this novel is based. His teen comedy screenplay *Wish List* was featured in *Written By*, the Writers' Guild magazine, as one of the best unproduced comedies in Hollywood. He is the author of *The Angel of Music* series of novels. After graduating from high school in a small town in west Texas, he served as a counterintelligence agent with the First Cavalry Division (Airmobile) in Viet Nam from 1969–1970. He lives in Lubbock, Texas, on the Llano Estacado.

ABOUT THE TYPE

The text of this book is set in Garamond #3. It is a machine-set version of the foundry type ATF Garamond from American Type Founders, which was designed in 1917 by the prolific type designer Morris Fuller Benton. ATF Garamond was one of the first revivals of centuries-old types from Europe. It was based on punches at the Imprimerie Royale (Royal Printing Office) in Paris, which were long believed to be the work of Claude Garamont (1510–1561), a French punchcutter. In 1927, research proved the punches were the work of Jean Jannon (d. 1658), although clearly influenced by Garamont. ATF's popular type retained the name Garamond and in 1936 it was adapted for machine composition by the Mergenthaler Linotype Company. Linotype's two existing versions of Garamond were discontinued, and Garamond #3 survives today in digital form.